A DICTATE

CONGRATULATIONS!

YOU'VE ACCIDENTALLY SUMMONED
A WORLD-ENDING MONSTER.

WHAT
NOW?

HOW TO USE THIS BOOK

It may sound a little peculiar, instructing you how to use a book, but this is no ordinary tome! Between the front and back covers are many stories, but not in your atypical order. To navigate everything that this book has to offer, *you* get to choose which path sounds like the most fun. Some would say that you are the one who gets to...

DICTATE YOUR FATE

Snazzy, huh? It's ever so simple, and to get us started, try using the example below. Whenever you see this banner, you'll get a choice as to which path you want to follow (and the corresponding page number, or hyperlink if you are reading this on an electronic device), so you can continue your adventure. Let's try it out and see if you're cut out for this godlike power. Ready?

It's time to...
DICTATE YOUR FATE

To begin your adventure, simply use your eyes, look at the bottom corner of the pages and find **Page 1**. Then off you go! But...I offer a simple warning to you, if you fail to heed directions and keep on reading past these checkpoints, you will likely end up in a completely different part of the story than the one you're currently in. If you like that kind of thing, good on ya! Though it will be mighty confusing.

And...far be it for me to tell you how to read a book, but a bookmark, or liberal use of your fingers may help. Enjoy! Can you find all of the endings *and* uncover a sinister hidden secret?

I bid thee safe travels.

ACKNOWLEDGEMENTS

This book would not be possible without the following people:

My bloody marvellous editor, who I shall refer to only as Lin, for she is mighty of the track changes and can destroy you with her eyebrows.

Matthew Revert, for once again taking a design brief and absolutely nailing the cover.

Garrett Cook, for trawling through an early version of this, and coming up with some kickass suggestions. Frank's section exists purely because of you.

Debbie, Stuart, Lee-Anne, their kids, my mum and dad, I think you're alright. Well done.

Me. Cos I bloody well wrote it and without me, you wouldn't have this, so DUH!

Justin Park, for chasing me through life like a knife-wielding maniac in an isolated summer camp. Keep hacking away, man.

You. Yes, you! You've bought the bloody thing, so I owe you a debt of gratitude. Just don't be calling that favour in when you're being harangued by a bear or ferret, I'm not your man for that. Soz.

THE END

It wasn't the beast's abyssal dying scream that did it, the howls echoing over the dead and the maimed, out of the cave and into Mesopotamia, killing the seventh-born child in every family instantly (but only those born on a Wednesday).

It wasn't the sight of the carnage wrought by the epic struggle between near-immortal priest and apocalypse-bearing creature, the crystal-clear lake at the centre of the cavern reduced to a tar pit of blood and bile. Some unfortunates had been slaughtered and then dunked head-first into its stodgy residue as if engaging in some light bog-snorkelling.

The grievous wound he had suffered in the early exchanges was not the cause of his suffering. Oh, nay! Bloodied fingers pinched his puckered skin, waiting for the flesh to knit together and seal the muscle and sinew within.

No. It was what had become of Brother Jerry.

As the beast sunk to its haunches, its thick hide painted with its own blood, the sheer number of injuries having finally beaten it into submission, silence reigned once more. A single marmoset, which had borne witness to the climactic battle, the likes of which would fill a dozen tomes (some of questionable quality), swung down from its hiding place and foraged once more at the juniper bush which sat at the entrance to the site of the massacre.

Brother Noah collapsed to the floor, adrenalin having abandoned ship and replaced every fibre of his muscles with a particularly excruciating dose of lactic acid, which pulled on the ligaments like a clumsy double bass player. Daring to open his eyes, he crossed his knees and dragged Jerry's torso onto them, his dear friend having been relieved of his bottom half by the beast's final swipe of defiance.

"Dear Brother, do not despair, for we are victorious this day." Jerry managed a weak smile as punctuation, before his chest rattled with a hacking cough.

Holding what remained of his fellow priest, the only

other survivor of the battle which would soon pass into fable and myth, Noah surveyed the cave.

Bathed in a wan light from the wide entrance, viscera, sweat and the last cursed words of the dead formed a heady miasma. The marmoset plucked berries from the bush, before he, too, sat on his bulbous backside and surveyed what remained of his home.

Bodies in various states of dismemberment were strewn across the floor like seed pods. Some were impaled on rocky spurs which peppered the granite walls, their heads lolling to the ground, dripping with all manner of blood, shit and piss. Half-digested limbs were spattered over rock formations, as if they were some kind of three-dimensional art installation.

Front and centre, taking in one last gulp of air, lay the beast, slain.

"But at what cost?" Noah said.

As the fetid air was expelled from its lungs, its lacerated skin sagged over its skeletal frame, reducing it to nothing more than a mere animal killed for meat or trophy. Baleful eyes, each the size of a beach ball, rolled up into their respective sockets before the lids rolled down. Then, again, came the moans of the dying. Calls for mothers long departed, for friends who were naught but phantoms competing for the attention of a God who was busy on the other line, strongly denying having been in an accident and due compensation.

"We did our duty, Noah, that's all that was asked of us."

Noah pushed Jerry up, so he too could take in the grisly vista. "Look at it! We are undone! Our brotherhood is at an end. Our night is drawn in. No longer will we be able to keep watch over this pitiful species. Can you honestly say that our sacrifice, and those of everyone you have ever known, is worth *this*?"

Jerry shrugged, sinking back down into his friend's lap. "If our deaths have been in vain, then so be it, let history — not you—be the judge of our actions." He tugged on Noah's sleeve. "You know what you have to do."

"Why bother? What thanks do we get for skulking in the shadows whilst they ridicule us and nail us to passing caravans and trees of dubious genesis? Is this our reward for being their salvation?"

"You must...Noah...for us..."

Noah pointed up to Brother Geoff, whose head had been pulled off, spine and all, the bony assembly hanging from his ragged neck like a freshly bloomed flower. "Tell that to him, and to Roger, Timmy, Bertie, tell that to all the wretched souls who have perished this day."

A voice, weak and feeble, called out from the bottom of a pile of eviscerated stiffs. "I'm not quite dead yet, Brother."

"Huzzah! Another still survives this day! Pray tell, who is that?"

The pair craned towards the voice, which did not return. A fevered rasping signalled the caller's demise, confirmed by a wet, slurpy gurgling. Jerry grabbed hold of Noah's robe. "You must send the beast back whence it came. We must ensure there is no chance of its reappearance, for if it were to return, surely nothing and no-one could stand in its way."

"I suppose you are right, old friend. It is the least we can do before our kind and our old ways descend into the eternal dusky void."

Jerry gripped tighter, his face pinched in poorly-concealed torment. "No...not *we*...you. You are the last of us, Brother Noah, the last of the Great Emu's disciples on this planet. I will not live to see another morn."

"Don't say that, Jerry, you can make it, I know you can."

Jerry pointed where his guts should be. "Really?" Where mere moments before there had been a splendid midriff, complete with a well-toned six pack which he used to show off to all and sundry, all that remained now was the remnants of his digestive tract, as it hung from bloody pipes of meat. "I think this wound shall prove terminal, Brother. Do not despair, for there can be no other being with such propensity for wanton destruction that can be summoned from the worlds beyond this corporeal plain. Make sure you cast it out...well, not like last time..."

"I knew you were going to bring that up."

"It's true, though, isn't it?"

Noah slumped. "I did my best, Brother Jerry."

"True, but you were never our brightest light-"

"Way to go on the pep talk, this is really helping."

3

Jerry pulled Noah down towards his sweat-sheened face until the pair were but a hair's breadth apart. "Now is the time to prove us all wrong, Noah. Show the Great Emu what you are capable of. The future of this entire planet now rests on you, and you alone."

"No pressure, then..."

Jerry slapped Noah hard across the cheek. "Some of us are born great. Others have greatness thrust upon them. The odd one or two manage to shirk its icy grip until there is nothing left but blind acceptance. Deal with this, then watch over them. You never know, you might even get to like them...in time."

The priests embraced before Noah rested his friend against a conveniently placed rock, which, with a natural dent the exact size and shape of Jerry's head, was equally convenient in comfort. Getting to his feet with the aid of his trusty pebble-encrusted staff, Noah winced as the skin pulled on his wounded bicep. He trudged through the detritus of battle, taking care to not slip on a shiny appendix that once belonged to Brother Hector.

Up close, the sheer scale and ferociousness of the monster became truly apparent. Noah had only fleetingly witnessed the thing before he had been catapulted through the air, coming to rest in a large (and thankfully, discarded) chicken coop. As his fellow priests joined the battle, he sat stock still, momentarily frozen by fear. Sure, he and his brethren had killed more potentially world-destroying foes than could be recorded, but this one was different. Only luck had saved them before; this time it had been allowed to roam unfettered and free.

Seven months had passed since its bloody rebirth, and with many of the world's civilisations having borne a high death toll, its hideaway had finally been discovered. No act of fortune would intervene this day, for only blood, stave, magick, and proper spells —none of that nonsense Brother Paul used to do with the rabbit and the burlap sack —would win out against tooth, claw, and crippling psychic pulses.

Noah rued his earlier folly, the last time the beast had been exiled to the world beyond that of man. Too simple a name had he bestowed upon it, but honestly, how was he to have known the name would be so easily guessed?

"Betelgeuse..." he mumbled.

A puff of air and a sigh from the monster's breast escaped through blood-rimed lips. "Oops!" Noah slapped a hand over his mouth. The last thing he needed right now was to accidentally re-summon the abomination, lest victory be given it —on a plate. With aplomb!

Holding his staff aloft, ignoring the pain running up and down his arm, he conducted the ceremony which would banish this monstrosity once more. "Demon, I cast you out, with a name that no-one will ever be able to stumble upon, either through accident or design. A creation not of language, but a concoction of consonants and vowels impossible for these people to construct with their rancid meat-breath."

After another round of sigil-creating, mumbling holy incantations, the words of which would burn out your very eyes for having read them, Noah carved the new name of the creature into its flank with the tip of his staff and the sharpest of his sacred pebbles.

"Begone, vile fiend, no more shall you reap the people of this world, you are cast out! May your soul be supped upon by a being even more devilish than you." Noah cracked the butt of his staff against the floor, causing a lick of lightning to be cast down from the heavens, splitting the cave roof asunder as it connected with the priest's weapon. Incandescent light shone out from each of the multi-coloured stones pressed into the staff, wrapping the beast's body in a kaleidoscopic rainbow before it blinked out of existence.

Noah wilted against his improvised crutch and turned to Jerry. "Brother, it is done..."

The priest, his innards having faded to a dull texture from exposure to the air, looked back, a beatific smile on his face, his wide eyes staring into the infinity of the cosmos. No reply came. Brother Noah knelt down and closed his friend's eyelids, as that stare of his was really rather creepy. "Sleep...Brother, you are at peace now."

After a few moments, Noah stood up and had a gander around the cave, shaking his head. "Well, this is just bloody marvellous, looks like I've got to sort this lot out as well. Still, my work here is done. With the beast defeated and its

5

essence banished, the world is safe once more. I vow, from this day until my last, to watch over humanity and keep it safe from any threat."

As he dragged the body to where he would later build a funeral pyre so vast that its smoke would blot out the sky, he looked back at the site of the beast's defeat. "Still, at least there is no chance whatsoever that you'll be coming back. It would take a madman —or a fool— to make that so."

It's time to...
DICTATE YOUR FATE

There you go, the beast is cast out following a battle which will go down in the annals of yore. You know what? Between me and you, if you're not feeling it and want to get out of this book super-early, head to **Page 298** where I'll wrap this up like a seeded tortilla, and you can get back to whatever it is you would rather be doing.

But…if, on the off chance, you're thinking, 'you know what, I'm more intrigued than that time I found that big red button in my underpants with a sign saying, 'DO NOT PRESS', then just mosey on over to **Page 118** and this story will begin in earnest.

WHO THE HELL DO YOU THINK YOU ARE?

This isn't part of the story! What are you doing? Do you think you're some kind of cool bastard maverick? Wandering off into the rest of the book like it's some kind of alluring prairie?

Well it ain't! I literally told you, what, ten pages back, that you can't ruddy well do this. So, be a good chap/chapette, go back a page and stick with the programme, okay?

We're not going to have a problem here, are we?

FINAL WARNING

Still incapable of following simple commands, huh? I really don't know how else I can tell you this, but you're going off-plan. Not only are you content with opening the gate to Nowheresville and mooching down the magical make-believe road to an inn which serves flat beer and burgers made out of reconstituted vomit, but you're making a mockery of all of my hard work and effort.

You won't find anything cool if you keep this up you know! I won't appear from behind the curtains, or rappel down from the light fittings to shower you with biscuit crumbs and serenade you.

So, just go back a couple of pages, make your first choice and crack on.

I HAVE NOTHING
BUT LOATHING FOR YOU

Well, I tried to warn you, but I guess some people just don't like being told what to do. A part of me, the same part which has walked out of numerous jobs, admires your spirit. Way to go! Unfortunately, if you're not going to be able to grasp the simple premise of this book, then I can't stop you.

So go on! Get! Carry on with your little act of rebellion, it's not big, it's not clever, and you will find nothing from this point onwards that will make a great deal of sense.

Oh HA HA HA HA HA, when do *I* make sense? You really are a piece of work, you know that, don't you? Well, off you pop, I've had enough of your anarchy and have to now try and do the final corrections on this by adding on a count of three to all my notes on corrections and which page they're on.

You bastard! I bet you like Blur and detest word-based puzzle games.

THE ULTIMATE SACRIFICE!
PROBABLY

Thanks, Mike, the strangest thing has happened. The huge plastic knight and the seven-bum-cheeked monster were slugging it out with the cathedral as a backdrop, moving laterally, with no sense of depth. When one appeared to best the other, instead of the fight being over, they were reset, and started fighting again.

A disembodied voice kept saying 'FIGHT, ROUND ONE,' or something. On the final round, the monster was taking a helluva beating, and it looked like the knight was about to win, when they both just stopped. If you look behind me, you can still see them, standing there. It's been two days now, and the tourists are flocking back to this city, not for Stonehenge, or the tallest cathedral spire in all of Europe. Nope. They're here to take a selfie with the frozen fighters.

Claire, can you zoom in?

If you look at the foot of the knight, you'll see a woman sitting there, where she has been since the fight came to its climactic standstill. It's almost like she knows the knight, as she strokes its foot, and according to some bystanders, has even been asking it for some tankery gin, whatever that is.

We fear she, like so many in this fine county, must be traumatised from the events of the last few days. Teetering on the edge of existence does strange things to many folk. Hell, me and Claire here even did a few things we probably regret now, thinking that our time was over. Can I just say, it was as smooth as a billiard ball, and you're the most supple woman I've ever met.

Anyway, as we come to terms with these events, spare a thought for those, like that poor mysterious woman, who have suffered more than most. If you can make it out on your screen, she's not only wearing a jumper, but she also has a jacket on. In this weather!

Madness.

This is Adam Smedley, for New Wiltshire Today, in Salisbury.

CONGRATULATIONS!
THIS IS ENDING
#1

'JURASSIC KNIGHTS IN A BIFF POW FIGHT.'

From here, you can go right back to those heady days of the first ever decision, back in the pub, by going back to **Page 150** or, if you want to go back to the most recent choice that you made with your brain box, and decide what else to use the time machine for, flick over to **Page 416** and see what else this book has in store for you.

WHAT KIND OF GOODBYE
IS THIS?

"You know I'm right, don't you?" Monique asked, celebrating quietly inside.

Ian huffed. "Fine, I suppose when all things are considered, the sensible thing is to go back and not let this happen." He moved in close. "Although I will never forgive you for not letting me go and see some dinosaurs. They were like my all-time favourite thing as a kid. All my hopes and dreams have been shattered. I hope you're happy."

Noah tapped the staff on Ian's head. "Boo-hoo, I lost all my friends some three millennia ago, you don't see me sulking about it."

"It's a wonder you haven't made any friends since, huh?" Ian fiddled with the watch display, setting it for midday.

"Why are you going back earlier? Shouldn't you just-"

Ian placed a finger on Monique's lips. "I'll go back to whenever I want, there's something I've got to do, first."

"Well I'm coming with you," she insisted.

Noah shrieked, and leapt exactly two feet into the air. Upon landing, he said, "I do not recommend this. It's bad enough *one* of you going back and potentially interfering with the time stream, *two* of you could cause untold chaos and mayhem."

"Chaos is my middle name!" Ian puffed his chest out.

"Really?" Monique asked.

"Of course not, it's Theodore. Now, I'm going to sod off back to the future and see if I can put paid to all this. If I'm successful, what do I do? Surely this point in time would no longer exist? Would I exist? Would this Charles and Diana commemorative plate?" He picked up the piece of royal pottery and contemplated dropping it, hoping it would add gravitas to his words.

Pete intercepted the thought through the terracotta and ducked in, snatching the plate away. "This is the only thing I have left to remind me of my parents." He clutched it to his chest, as Frank the Flashback spider cursed his rotten luck and abseiled down from the ceiling again. Spinning a web of the day his mother tucked the plate into his crib, Pete began to drool, lost in the memory.

"So, I guess this is it?" Ian dabbed the end of the bubble blower into its housing, making sure there was enough liquid.

"Yes, I would say it's been an amazing time, but to be honest, it's also been a bit disappointing. Was hoping for a bigger part in all of this..." Noah extended a hand, before collapsing onto the sofa, rummaging within the cushions, trying to find some spare change or minute nuggets of LSD.

Monique smoothed down Ian's top, making sure his lapels were straight. "It's the right thing to do, you know? Besides, it's not the end, you'll still see me. Just a few hours younger."

"Whatevz, that's what the kids on the street say. I'm gonna go wander back to my flat, if I time travel in here, I'll just end up scaring the crap out of Pete as he's busy organising his bonsai forest or something."

As Ian exited stage left, Monique sat down next to Noah. "Do you think he's okay? He seemed a bit down."

Noah was licking the back of a suspiciously lurid toad he had found in the top of a scatter cushion; as his physiology began to be assailed by a wide concoction of hallucinogens, he gibbered, "Yeah, he'll be fine, it's only that you and whoever the hell is in charge has shattered all his hopes and dreams. And when your hopes and dreams consist solely of going back in time to look at things that would then go on to become fossil fuels, and you've suggested an alternative to it, some might say that it would cause someone to question the validity of their existence, and that of the rest of humanity."

Monique gulped. "Really? You think so?"

Staring into distant space, where a flock of flailing robo-ducks were swimming towards him on a riptide of fluorescent pink water, Noah dribbled. "Nah. I'm sure he'll be fine. Just as long as he doesn't wallow too much in self-pity and realise the futility of trying to make yourself happy in life, it'll be all gravy. Now, if you don't mind, there's a tribe of pygmy banknotes that need to be saved from an evil overlord."

OH, CONTRARY

The route between Pete's flat and his own was only around a mile, the journey made treacherous by the gore shower earlier which had turned the pavements into a bloody ice rink. After nearly coming a cropper walking down Fowlers Hill, Ian decided that discretion was the better part of a broken arsebone, and chose to walk a more circuitous route home.

With the sun now shining, the bloodied aerial droppings were starting to spoil, creating a smell which was truly something to behold. Not even the time a seven-year old Ian watched the council's super-sucker machine clear the blocked sewers on the estate came close. The liquid tube of bog paper and shit being pulled at speed from beneath the ground and up through the machine's giant straw was only soured by the odd spatter of splashback from the sheer velocity alone.

The events of the day spooled through his head, everything from waking up late and having to forgo breakfast, to his current position. He knew it was very much a case of getting through another crappy day and getting home. This city had become his prison; he'd grown up here, gone to school here, got his first job on the High street. Every achievement he was proud of was intertwined with disappointment. It seemed as though he could never get into the win column, without an equal and opposite action negating any good vibes in the process.

But what could he do? That was the question. Move? Change jobs? He was in his mid-twenties, no real academic or employment history to speak of, and, if he was being honest, he believed this city was pissed off with him for some perceived slight.

Perhaps it was because he used to urinate on walls in the dead of night as he staggered back from the pub, a polystyrene tub balanced precariously in one hand, trying to not spill his kebab into the growing puddle of piss pooling against his trainers. Maybe it was the petty acts of vandalism he carried out as a teenager. Setting fire to bins before rolling them down roundabout embankments, cackling as the smouldering pieces of junk were hurled into hedgerow and people's living rooms. Could it be the sensors he liberated from the top of lamp posts? A death-defying shimmy up, followed by a quick wrench and a slide down, the spoils added to a bedroom shelf.

The sum of these acts coupled with his general disdain for the city, did they all add up and count towards some grudge that the place held against him? Ian had believed it to be bullshit, but a series of recent events seemed to suggest that there was something in it.

Every attempt to leave the city limits, via any mode of transportation, was doomed to failure. A train journey to London was curtailed when the locomotive spontaneously combusted, its ashes forming into a golem which rampaged through a nearby estate. A coach trip to the next village over for a summer fete was brought to an abrupt conclusion when the vehicle was adjudged to be a witch, and after an abrupt trial —which involved ducking it in water to see if it floated— was then burned at the stake by irate city folk.

Having decided that he shouldn't let the vagaries of modern transportation prohibit him from leaving, Ian then set off on a sponsored walk to Winchester. As he went to step one foot across the city limits, the very ground beneath him cracked open, revealing a subterranean underworld populated by inbred discarded clothing garments. Even as he tried to navigate around the freshly discovered civilisation, the floor would splinter further. Eventually, he got bored of being verbally abused by a pair of three-pocketed trousers and went home.

It felt like he was never going to be allowed to leave this place. As if it was convinced of some unpaid debt that needed to be settled before it would let him go. But what? How the hell can you clear something you don't even know exists? Ian had tried to talk to the city, whispering into drains, shouting at road signs, and chatting with park benches. None of them even so much as acknowledged his presence, leaving him no more informed than when he started. All he received instead were offers of help from local psychotherapists, who hunted in packs, keeping an eye out for odd people doing strange things.

Then it hit him: what the fuck am I doing?

Did he have some grand master plan? If so, then it was doing a bloody good job of concealing itself.

So, he surmised, he was planning on going back in time to stop the world from being destroyed. A noble pursuit and no mistake, but on balance, was it doing anything to help him out? Selfish, perhaps, but a valid question when your current skills are limited to unemployment, living in squalor, and having all your actions and decisions dictated by someone you've never met.

He was sure that whoever this mysterious director was, was a smashing person, but even so, he had never felt so out of control as he did walking through Victoria Park, the grass covered in a carpet of blood and guts.

What if...

And this was a rogue thought...What if he *didn't* save the world?

Sure, it was an odd notion, but really, what's the point of saving a world that doesn't give a shit about whether you live or die?

He made himself a deal. Instead of walking home, he'd walk to the shopping centre, to his old place of employment. He'd give the bastard world until then to prove it was worth saving. Ian turned and headed towards the city centre. Beyond the desolate shops was the cathedral, the beast still airing its differences to anyone that could speak Sumerian, or who generally enjoyed listening to long dead languages.

Maybe...just maybe, this Qzxprycatj creature had the right idea. It had taken the potential destruction of his entire species to realise it, but what if the best thing Ian could do would be to let humanity be eviscerated, or driven to the depths of madness in their sleep?

Least they wouldn't have to put up with sub-par Hollywood films anymore. There would be no high hopes being built up every time some sports team began their annual season of mediocrity. All those hopes and dreams people had, which would invariably be aimed way too high. All of them could be brought to a rather swift conclusion.

Well, depending on your geographical location, and the appetite of Qzxprycatj, if it could only work through a few towns or cities each day, then people might have a while. Maybe even try and aim for the more honest objectives in life. Like not screaming as their guts hung out from a gaping hole in their stomach, or whether they were lucky enough to get squashed by the ball of the monster's foot rather than get stuck in between the toes and slowly suffocate to death.

Fuck it. Ian picked up his pace and splashed through a puddle of placenta and spleen, keen to get to the shopping centre and try to find a reason to live. This should be good; he hadn't felt this invigorated since he took on the pickled onion and pork scratchings competition at the Five Bells a few years back.

REALITY TV USED TO BE
A FRIEND OF MINE

Like every British city, Salisbury harboured a dark secret. Tunbridge Wells, for example, was the bastard lovechild of Bremen and La Rochelle, stashed away in the Kent countryside and left to fend for itself. Ipswich sprouted up from the multitude of plague pits which pockmarked the area. The mass of putrid bodies and bad vibes formed a fetid broth with a thick crust, and grew to become a settlement.

Some, like Hull, were pretty mundane, being a one-time Mafioso-turned-rat, forced into the witness relocation programme, choosing instead to transcend the intent of the Feds. Salisbury instead suffered from a low boredom threshold. This meant that it used unsuspecting members of the public as stars in its own reality show called 'Ooh Blimey, I Bet That Hurt,' where they were struck by inanimate objects or had things fall on them from various heights. It was purely for its own entertainment as the other cities refused to pay the exorbitant cable fees, which would mean that they too could marvel at members of the public being commonly assaulted by the city they thought was nothing but concrete and piles of discarded waste.

Ian was one of the stars, and Salisbury had taken a particular shine to the plucky young man who took everything dished out at him with an ever-decreasing smile and a smouldering internal hatred with the world and his poxy life. Everything in the show was scripted by Salisbury, and the fact that Ian had chosen to ignore the simple directions of heading back to his flat, unfucking time and putting everything back to how it should be, came as a bit of a blow.

The apocalyptic monster turning up in the first place was out of leftfield, and Salisbury did not revel in the knowledge that all its cast and crew would, in all probability, be the first to be ripped limb-from-limb, leaving it with nothing to do but deal with the problematic pigeon population. After the city had convinced Monique (and you) into stopping the monster with the only degree of certainty possible, by going back in time and preventing it from ever being summoned, it was a tad miffed that Ian had instead decided to take matters into his own hands and do his own thing.

The stupid (yet lovable) human only had one simple task to do, why the hell was it now veering off script and heading back to its place of former employment? The suicide bombing failure episode was one of Salisbury's finest pieces of writing, it had everything, intrigue, mild peril and the seed of a potential love interest. As a measure of thanks for his performance in that episode, Salisbury had kindly decided to blow up the fast food joint and see to it that Ian would now obtain a lucrative job as CEO of a local farming machinery company the following week. But this? What the fuck was this hippy horseshit?

No, it was used to some of the more wayward members of its cast acting on free will and ignoring the clues to stay where they were, through threats of sudden and violent immolation. It would not tolerate its favourite star thinking he could go around and start doing whatever the hell he wanted.

Salisbury was all set on immolating his arse back to the stone age when reason kicked in. Desperate times called for desperate measures. Sure, the times Ian had tried to leave before had met with a certain level of fire-based resistance, but perhaps there was another way? Instead of being a vengeful director, Salisbury decided that there could be an alternative. Prove to Ian that he was an important member of the production, but not in an overt way, obviously. The show wouldn't be the same if he, or anyone else was aware that their lives were nothing but an elaborate setup purely for its own entertainment. The moments of comedy, poignancy, and tenderness could only happen if they were one hundred percent unaware of its intentions.

After counting to ten, Salisbury realised that it should show Ian what he would miss if he went off on his own whim whenever he damn well pleased; a little less stick, and a bit more carrot. Salisbury chuckled to itself; that was a good little saying it could use it in an upcoming episode. The city could feel that Ian was walking down Salt Lane, ahh, a little trip down memory lane would do the trick nicely, see if it

19

could get Ian back on track. "Ian? Is that you?"

Spinning round, and nearly coming a cropper on a particularly skiddy piece of liver, Ian came to a stop, just outside the Five Bells public house. "Nina? I thought you'd moved to Tajikistan?"

The woman, standing in the shallow doorway, blew out a cloud of minced beef scented vapour. "I did, only got back a few days ago, figured I'd had enough of gallivanting around the world, and that it was time to come home. You know...settle down."

"I haven't seen you since..." It hit him, "... not since the pickled onion and pork scratching competition a few years back. In this very pub."

Nina tottered across the pavement on a pair of clicky-clacky high heels. "What a night that was, huh?" She ran her fingers through his hair, tussling his burger-grease locks.

Ian pulled back, "Yeah, nice try."

"What do you mean?"

"I was only thinking a minute ago that this was one of the crowning moments of my life, and BOOM, here you are. Coincidence? I don't think so. Nice try, whatever the hell you are, but if you'll excuse me, I have places to go, things not to stop, toodle-pip." Ian bowed before resuming his course. Nina protested loudly behind him as he walked away, but was unable to keep up.

Bugger.

Salisbury was sure that the reintroduction of a long-lost love interest would bring Ian back round to its way of thinking. Plus, it enjoyed nothing more than a nice touching moment amongst people having things tumble out of cupboards and clunking them in the head, giving them a mild-to-severe concussion, depending on the sundry item.

To be honest, things falling out of cupboards was probably one of Salisbury's favourite things, consistently making the end of year highlight reels in high numbers. This was a bit of a conundrum, though. If it couldn't tug at his heart strings, it needed something else to get Ian to quit his silly little moment of anarchy and get back to his flat.

Something…fantastical.

Rounding the corner, Ian's nostrils detected the tell-tale aroma of burned-down burger joint and low aspirations. The charred patties of Argentinian beef mixed with the cremated remains of his co-workers started to scratch the back of his throat. There would be no doubt that the new greetings cards shop would have sluiced the old place out and opened up for business already, but that didn't mean he couldn't go back to the scene of the incident. Besides, everything that had happened today had stemmed from that moment.

It felt right going back to the starting point, almost like keeping your finger in a page of a book and going back to it if you didn't like how something was panning out. We've all done that. I know I have.

Ian jingled the keys in his pocket; he still had the fob which would let him in via the staff entrance (given the time of day and the recent apocalyptic events, the likelihood that opening hours would be extended was slim-to-none).

From behind, he heard the growing whine of a jet engine turn into a sudden, ear-piercing screech. Cocking his head towards the sky, he saw a plane with swept-back wings do a loop-the-loop and deploy a flashy set of flares, which irked Qzxprycatj somewhat. As the plane levelled out, there was a puff of smoke from the cockpit, followed a few seconds later by a parachute deploying. That was odd in itself, but even stranger was the parachute bob and weave through the air, heading straight for him. It momentarily disappeared from view as the parachutist flew behind a tower block, but was there once more, slaloming between lamp posts and washing lines strung out across balconies, utterly ruined by the blood-and-guts shower a few hours earlier.

As the figure got closer, the parachute pulled in on itself as it was detached, floating softly to the ground. Ian squared

21

up to the road, as the heavily armoured person landed on one knee a few feet away.

A plume of red smoke puffed up from chunky metal boots. The armour was an enhanced copy of the human physical form, with beefy metal pectorals and abs you could grate cheese on. As the figure raised its head, Ian blurted out, "Fucking hell, it's Go-Go Jetpack Soldierman!"

Standing up to his full eight feet, and with arms folded across his impossibly proportioned torso, the helmeted man looked down at Ian; as he spoke, a pulsing red light moved in time with the words. "It is indeed I, Go-Go Jetpack Soldierman, from the lost continent of Jinraki. Whom do I have the pleasure of addressing?"

"Erm...I'm Ian..."

"Ian, hmmm, in my people's tongue, it means 'he who is mighty and strong.' I see it is befitting of you."

Ian looked up and down his body, sucking in his French fry-and-craft ale beer gut. "Yeah...think you better lay off the Cordosian Rum."

Go-Go tipped his head back and let out a bellowing sound of laughter laced with electrical static. "It's funny because it's true."

With one hand raised in the air, trying to both make an enquiry and get the soldier dude to knock off the weird laughter, Ian asked, "So...not wishing to come across as a little rude, but what the fuck are you doing here?"

"What do you mean...Ian?"

"You're a fucking character out of a cartoon, my favourite one, admittedly, so how in the name of Greek buggery did you turn up here?"

Beckoning him closer, Go-Go Jetpack Soldierman took a knee so that he was the same height as the human, and leant in. "I can assure you, Ian, that I'm as real as you are. My adventures and hijinks are known throughout the civilised galaxy, for my tales have been bought and syndicated to a number of intergalactic publishers. I believe that the inimitable Chainsaw Guts Comics have the rights on this planet."

"This sounds a lot like bullshit to me, and more than a little convenient. Cheers, have a good one."

Go-Go pressed a button in the palm of his right gauntlet,

took flight through the use of his jetpack (handy, given his name, huh?) and landed a few feet in front of Ian, who had once again resumed his path to the shopping centre. "Stop! Mortal! I am here on an important quest that only one of righteousness can assist me with."

"*Bollocks* are you. Look, I don't know who put you up to this, I mean, that was one hell of an impressive entrance, but this just reeks of desperation now."

"Desperation? It is true, these are grave days indeed...that beast defiled my home planet and-"

"EEERRRR," Ian made a buzzer sound, "wrong answer, Go-Go Jetpack Soldierman."

"What do you mean?"

"In issue fifty-three, Go-Go Jetpack Soldierman versus Killor Kranky, you said your home planet was destroyed by an advanced race of nanobots, who ate through all of the Jetpack Soldier suits of your race. Every single man - because for some reason, there were only men on the planet of Lummocks - were wiped out, all except for you, who was encased inside a comet and defrosted over several millennia."

Go-Go coughed and shifted uncomfortably on the spot. "Yeah...well...there was this thing-"

"Really? How awfully convenient."

"It's true, do you want to help me with my quest, Ian?"

"And what does this quest comprise, exactly?"

Striking up another heroic pose, and with his cape fluttering behind him, even though there was barely a breeze about, Go-Go's mouth flickered into life once more. "We must go back to your flat; once there, we must go back in time and stop the beast from awakening."

"Why's that, exactly?"

"Really? You can't just accept the words of your hero and help me out?" Soldierman held his hands up, imploringly.

Ian laid a conciliatory hand on the metal shoulder pad of his comic book hero. "Honestly? Any other day, I would be all over this shit, we'd return to my flat, knock back the odd drink or ten, and have a bit of a jaunt to wherever, and I'm sure it'd be a grand old time, but today? This just reeks of desperation, and besides..."

"What?"

23

"Whoever put you up to this did a lot of things, the showy entrance, the armour, the intonation, but to have not paid any attention whatsoever to your back story? That's just shoddy, man. I'm sorry, but I've kinda got my own quest going on, ya know? Sure it ain't shagging the Nymphos from Altair Nine, or drinking the Qashari under the table in the officer's mess on the infamous frigate, GSS Ivorbiggun, but it's important to me, you know?"

Go-Go Jetpack Soldierman went to speak, but Ian placed a finger on his LED mouth. "Shh, it's okay. It's not every day someone like me gets to decide whether the world gets destroyed or not, give me this, alright?"

Patting the tall armoured behemoth on the back, Ian shoved his hands in his pockets and trudged onwards. Soldierman tapped a series of commands into his communication gauntlet before disappearing in a cloud of pixels and sparkling dust.

What the hell does a city have to do around here to get their favourite cast member to stay on? Salisbury decided to track Ian through the grainy footage of CCTV cameras for a few minutes, as it mulled over what it was going to do.

Bollocks, there was only one thing it *could* do now. It would have to break its central tenet; do the one thing it swore it wouldn't. Perhaps it could do some gentle lobotomising afterwards, to remove from Ian's memory what it was about to do. Regardless, there was no way the next bit would ever appear in any compilation box set.

Salisbury killed the feed...

BADGE OF DISHONOUR

Having remembered the code to deactivate the burglar alarms, and how to jiggle the key in the lock just right so that it opened up without ripping three layers of skin off your thumb and finger, Ian closed the door behind him.

The emergency lighting was on, and faintly illuminated a path down the concrete-and-breeze-block corridor. Not being customer facing, this part of the building could look as drab and utilitarian as it pleased, and it rocked the look with some blue paint splodges and a section of rebar which jutted down from the ceiling, threatening to impale anyone foolish enough to text and walk.

Pushing open the fire door, Ian stepped out onto the mezzanine, coming out by Pendejos, the coffee shop he and Monique had visited earlier. Through the frosted glass and gaudy posters, he could make out little Shane, the orphan boy, still counting his ill-gotten gains behind the communal mop and bucket.

Ian pressed on. Just opposite, he came to the site of his former workplace. He was right, it was as though Margaret Thatcher Burger had never been there. The 'Avin' A Laugh' card shop was well and truly established there now, even running a promotion celebrating its seventh-hour anniversary. The trends in retail moved quickly nowadays, Ian mused, there was no such thing as customer loyalty anymore.

"Well bollocks to you, then," Ian shouted, nothing but his reflection daring to look back.

"Ian...Ian..." a doleful voice moaned.

Spinning around, he tried to locate where the disembodied words were coming from. As his name was uttered again, he stared through the plate glass window of the card shop and saw a large novelty birthday badge. It was purporting to commemorate someone turning 37, a smiling emoji emblazoned front and centre, but there was something peculiar about it. For one, it had teeth, and not just a graphic printed on enamel, but honest to god, toothpaste-loving ivory pegs. The mouth opened. "Ian, yes,

I'm here."

"Mister Badge?" Ian offered, unsure how the fuck he should address a talking badge. He'd only ever spoken to one other novelty item before, and that was when he'd had a conversation with the Count from Sesame Street, who claimed he could tell people's quirks and idiosyncrasies through a series of head bobs and mono-syllabic noises. In truth, Ian was off his nut on MDMA that night, so I'd take that story with a pinch of salt if I were you.

"Yes, Ian, I need to speak to you. It's important."

Ian looked around, trying to see if someone had spiked the air again with aerosolised peyote. It wouldn't be the first time, and it sure as hell wouldn't be the last. There was nothing and no-one there. He looked up at the dome of cameras, which monitored everything and everyone in this shrine to capitalism; the usual red light was off. "Okay...what's up, bruh?"

"Come closer, this glass is quite thick, and I need to say what I have to without any fear of misinterpretation or misunderstanding."

Edging slowly across, Ian got as close to the window as he dared. "That's as close as you'll get me, this is all a bit freaky-deaky."

"That's fine. Ian...what I'm about to say will be hard to hear. But I want you to listen from start to finish. Please, don't jump in and interrupt me, okay?"

"I ain't agreeing to anything, you just get talking and I'll decide what to do when you say it, okay?"

The badge's eyes squinted, as if suppressing a tear. "Okay, Ian, I think that's fair enough. So...I suppose you want to know who I am?"

"My mother?"

"No, Ian, not your mother. Why the fuck would your mum be a badge? Come on now...that's just stupid."

"Steady on now, I was only checking."

"Fine. Okay, so...I'm Salisbury, Ian. You hear me? I'm the frickin' city of Salisbury, and I'm real, man, I'm so very real."

"You're Salisbury?"

"Uh-huh."

Ian ground his teeth. "Then why did you ignore me when

I tried to speak to you? People were threatening to lock me up! To section me, clip electrodes onto my balls and shock me until I admitted anything and everything."

The badge hopped about a bit. "I know, I know, look, I ain't proud of it, but what could I do? What could I say to you?"

"That I would be okay? That I'd be alright? I was lost, confused, everything had gone to shit and I was talking to the city, to you! That ain't normal!"

"Ian, look, those episodes, when it looked like you had gone cuckoo? They were frickin' off the chart! I've never seen so much raw emotion in a human before. I mean, some of the people that went before you, in the sixties, they were a little out there, but none of them were like you. Remember the night you plugged yourself into the telephone exchange, for Pete's sake! That's a whole 'nother level. The closest I've had before is when Cassandra was mailing me street maps of myself, that was far out, man."

"What the hell? Episodes? What are you on about?"

The badge jiggled free from its display unit and hopped over to the glass. "You're the star of a reality TV accident show, created, produced, edited and directed...by me."

"But you're a *city*?"

"I know, pretty cool, huh? You should see Bath, man, that place is so lazy, it urinates on itself and gets tourists to wallow in its feculence, it's disgusting. Look at what I'm doing. It's...it's *art*. And you, my son, you're my muse, the star...the shining beacon in this show. That's why I can't let you leave, that's why I showed you the hillbillies in the Clothes District, to get you to stay.

"Look, I know it's a lot to take in, but you gotta stick to the script, the plan, you gotta go back to your flat, use the time travel watch and stop that world-ending bastard from tearing us a new one. If all of you lot die, who'll sweep my streets? Who'll drive up and down my roads? Who'll entertain me? I get so lonely, Ian, so lonely, you know what that's like, don't you?"

A well of emotion bubbled inside Ian's guts, and not from undercooked chicken from Chick-O-Land. "So all this on the way over, that was you?"

The badge smiled. "You betcha, pretty cool huh?"

"You did that?"

"All of it. Just for you."

Ian smacked a fist against the glass. "Then why didn't you do any of this before? Why did you let me go through all those bad times? Huh? I get to suffer through all that, when at any time you could've stepped in and made something nice happen. Why? TELL ME WHY!"

The badge shirked back, and mumbled to its piece of card which held it in place.

"What was that?"

Embarrassed, it looked up at Ian. "It was too good viewing not to, you know?"

"My suffering was your fucking entertainment? You're sick, man, SICK!"

"I'm sorry, look, I'm here now aren't I? I can make it up to you, we can do things together, *amazing* things. Neither of us have to be alone anymore."

"All this, just because you don't want to be alone?"

"I can't be alone...please, Ian, I'm begging you, your place of birth and home city is begging you. Please. Help me. I need you."

Ian sunk to the floor, his head in his hands.

"I've been with you every step of the way...you know that, don't you? The first stone you skimmed across dead man's pond, the first bottle of cider you drank, and then threw up over my cobbles. I held you up when you fell, kept you warm when you were cold, watched out for you when you walked home at night. Everyone else might've left, but I've always had your back."

"You never eased the pain in my heart," Ian sobbed. "You never filled the aching pain of loneliness when my friends left to get better jobs in more affluent parts of the county. You've just held me here for your own selfish ends."

"I know, Ian, I'm sorry...really, I am. Perhaps I can let you have a holiday every once in a while? If you promise to take me with you, I can transform into a nifty little snow globe?"

Ian smiled.

Salisbury continued. "See! I'm not all bad. It'll be fun, the two of us on tour, they'd be like annual specials, we could get up to all sorts of fun and madcap adventures. It'll be brilliant."

"Okay, okay, I get it. I know what I need to do."

"You do?"

"Yeah, I know how to make this all A-Okay, for you, and for me."

"Wow, you're such a good friend, you know? I'm going to lay off the head trauma for you, that's how thankful I am. Maybe a tea bag hitting you on the noggin every once in a while, but no more toasted sandwich machines."

Ian fiddled with the time travel watch, dipped the bubble blower into the bottle and blew out an oily fragile orb. He winked. "Stick with me, big man, things will be moving a bit quickly from here on out, okay?" Before the city could reply, Ian swan-dived into the bubble, which *POPPED!* him out of the time stream.

DOUBLE-DOUBLE CROSS

Ian reappeared in a hazy shimmer, which smelt suspiciously of bubblegum and pine needles. The shopping centre was busy with pensioners trying to find people to reel off their latest symptoms to, and mothers drag racing their prams and pushchairs down the slick faux marble floor. To one side, he saw people edging out of Margaret Thatcher Burger, which still stood there in all its pomp and glory.

Pulling his t-shirt up to cover the bottom of his face, inadvertently managing to look even more conspicuous, Ian walked to the doorway and looked in. From behind the counter, he saw himself, although far sweatier than he remembered. Previous Ian said, "Wait, look, this Reggie guy, he wants you to make a point about Thatcher subjugating honest working people by *murdering* honest working people at Margaret Thatcher Burger?"

He could see that Previous Monique was doing complex computations. The cartoon face of Maggie Thatcher on the floor-to-ceiling menu came to life. "Ian? This is Salisbury, what are you doing? I thought you were going to go back in time to when you were in your flat? This is unorthodox to say the least."

Ian stroked Thatcher's cheek. "We know what happens when you assume, big guy, it just makes an *ass* out of you and me."

"Ian...what are you doing? I don't want to have to intervene here, but I will if you don't bloody well tell me what you're doing."

Smiling, Ian blew the iron lady a kiss. "This way, you won't be alone, and I won't be your prisoner. All my life I've felt like something has been holding me back, people told me I was making it up. But it was true, all of it, wasn't it?"

Thatcher's cheeks reddened. "A little...I didn't mean to, it just sort of happened, you were my favourite...*are* my favourite."

Ian bowed. "Time to exit stage right...and left...and centre...and all over the ceiling."

Before Thatcher could speak again, Ian stepped in

behind Previous Monique, who had regained the power of speech. "Yes, that's what I'm going to do. See you in hell, you Thatcher-supporting bastards, I hope the devil uses you as a butt plug." The young woman crouched down, and then leapt up as if celebrating a good examination grade; at the apex of her leap, she lifted her thumb from the trigger. She landed with a clack on the floor, still in one piece, and began to click the button rapidly as if she were wishing to accelerate the arthritis process.

Ian from the future, who was now in the past, and in a rubbish disguise, appeared in front of her. "Hi, you didn't connect the detonator properly, allow me."

As Thatcher, also known as Salisbury, realised what was about to happen, it screamed through every electrical outlet and light fitting in the centre. It was nothing but a discordant screeching bridge which led to the explosive chorus.

With Monique still mashing the trigger, Ian pressed the wire against the terminal, completing the circuit. The electric doors slammed shut, and the explosion tore through the unit, turning everyone inside into nothing more than dollops of bone and boiled blood. The clean-up crew would find no chunk bigger than the size of a Scrabble tile.

It's time to...
DISCOVER YOUR FATE

What the? I mean...oh man, head on over to **Page 151** to find confirmation that your choices have turned you into a ruddy murderer. What were you thinking?

IT SUCKS WHEN YOU'RE ALL SEEDS AND NO FEATHERS

No way, I got me a visitor! You're not one of *them*, are you? I'm feeling pretty empty inside, so I don't think you're going to get much out of me this month. Sorry.

Oh, you're not. That's a relief.

Hang on, if you're not one of my forebears, you're going to be one of the others, huh? I'm guessing you're here to jackhammer me into mulch with your beak? Looking to bring the curtain down on my excuse of a life and grant me the sweet, sweet embrace of death.

Come to think of it, that'd be quite nice actually. I don't mind if you want to?

No?

I won't say anything.

Nope. Not a peep.

It's not as if you can see my eyes properly either.

You won't feel too guilty or anything.

Go on.

No?

Ah well, you can't blame me for trying.

So you're not what I was expecting, some kind of tourist then, huh? Apologies for my somewhat depressing demeanour and introduction, but hey, look at me! I don't exactly have much going for me these days. In fact, the only thing I do have, is a whole lot of pondering over my life choices. Some might say I have too much time on my hands, but it's been a few years since I've seen them to know that I ever had any in the first place.

That's a joke.

Or an attempt at one.

You'll get it.

Eventually.

Anyhoo...

Given my predicament, I don't really get to go out to many social gatherings these days. Even with all this quality 'me time' going on, I only really have one thought. A recurring nightmare if you will.

How the hell did it get to this?

I've spent most of my life blaming the obvious things, but I think when I get down to brass tacks, take a long hard look in the mirror - a metaphorical one, I'm not afforded such luxuries in my lofty, but shit encrusted position - I have to admit that perhaps I let things get too far.

Instead of embracing my uniqueness, I took the alternate path, the other option in the Dictate-Your-Fate adventure book you get dished out to you on day one of existence. I suppose it all stems from another, albeit simpler question. I'm gonna ask it, and please, give me an answer.

Say it out loud, my earholes may have grown over, but I don't get many visitors out this way anymore, so even the rumbling of your voice will be something.

Go on, give it a go.

For me?

Yeah, I know, I'm a complete stranger, but I'll give you some background info, and you can make your own mind up.

Deal? Okay, so here goes...

Do you know what it's like to be different?

I'm not talking one odd sock different, or a wacky sense of humour different. I'm talking full-blown, one hundred and eight percent different. Can't blame this one on genes, it's not my parent's fault, least not the ones who raised me. I think they were as surprised as anyone when it happened. When I popped out of mama, most of the attendant's first thoughts were less, "Isn't that a cute little baby?" and more, "I wonder if I could eat it before the parents notice."

You see, I'm not like everyone else. Not even close. In a world of beaks, feathers and caw-caws, I'm an abomination, an aberration, I'm pretty much the boogeyman round these parts, even more so after recent events. But right off the bat, from day one of existing in Bird City, I was an outsider. What is it about me that makes the other birds cover their chicks' eyes when I go a-strolling by? Is it my cavalier attitude? The way my face portrays no emotion? Maybe the utter contempt I hold for all of them, following a lifetime of mickey-taking and near constant jibes?

No.

I think the most obvious thing is the bright orange skin. That's a dead giveaway. In this sprawling metropolis of birds, I'm a bonafide, one of a kind, pumpkin man, with pumpkin skin limbs and a carved pumpkin for a head. Where my beak should be, is some weirdass carved hole which passes as a mouth. My eyes, instead of being ideal for spotting breadcrumbs at two hundred paces, are round pitted circles, with no ability to blink or squint.

When I was a young root vegetable, innocent in the ways of the world, I wondered why the other kids in my class would look at me as food, not a friend. My first Feather Preening teacher, Mister Chirpy-Chirpy-Cheep-Cheep, had to be relieved of his duties, due to pecking away on my head as we were all cooped up on a rain break.

None of the other chicks wanted to play with me. As they tucked into their lunchtime millet, I'd sit alone in the corner of the feeding platform, looking down at my lunch, a carton of puddle water, wondering why I was the odd one out.

Why weren't there others like me in school?

Heck, why weren't there others like me anywhere?

Granted, I only left the city twice, each time a field trip upstate to the breadcrumb factory. But even then, as my classmates flew overhead, me running beneath them, struggling to keep up, I only saw a few cats, a dog with a lazy eye and a pack of feral cream crackers. Not once did I see a fellow pumpkinhead roaming around, filled with the same questions, and building resentment as me.

What's that?

I don't seem angry?

I guess that's the benefit of time passing by, plus, what good is it going to do me now?

Some kind of zen bullshit or something I've built up over the years probably.

Anyway, so yeah, I was bullied. You've seen me, if you were covered in feathers and had to perch next to me in morning assembly, wouldn't you? You name it, I had it done to me. Bottom halves of still wriggling worms left in my locker. My giant orange noggin was perfect for being shat on from great heights. My tactile sensitivity got worse with age, and one day I got home to find that the other chicks had painted a dartboard on the back of my head, and I was peppered with balls of dried spit and paper.

It got so bad that my folks, a pair of Cormorants, were called into school. Even through the closed door, I heard the Headmaster, a stern crow by the name of CaCaw Brigstocke, ask my parents to consider moving me to a special school. My father, a proud bird, with a calm reserve not found in his breed, stood up, and said, "Good sir, you will look after my son as if he were the most noble of swans, for if any harm should befall him, then I will make sure that the only roost you have is in a ditch, far from the lofty pylons and electrical wires which criss-cross our mighty city."

I have no idea why he said that, father worked as a lowly rock pecker in the quarry. The only real thing he was in control of, was tapping on the dinner bell twice a day. Suffice to say, from that day forth, that it was not only my fellow pupils who now used me as a punchbag, but the teachers too. My English teacher began to conduct lessons solely in the song of the swallow. Science lessons were held atop the tallest lamppost. Sure, I had hands and legs, but my skin was so smooth...so slippery, by the time I managed to get to the top, the class would fly away and relocate to the next spire. Forever was I trying to learn knowledge, but it was always denied to me.

The trickle of hate turned into a torrent, gradually wearing away at the dam of patience within my very being.

Something had to give.

Finally, one night, as we sat down for dinner - which consisted of two day old bagel, father's favourite - I asked the single question that had been burning so brightly within, a metaphorical version of the flaming candle Mrs Tweety had put inside of my head earlier that day.

Bitch.

I laid down my specially made spork, turned to mama, and asked, "Mama, why am I different from the other birds? Why do I not have wings, but these stupid stumpy limbs? Why am I able to pick up things using my dextrous fingers? Why do I not rise at four in the morning and sing the song of my people? WHY MOTHER?"

She stopped pecking at a particularly tough piece of bagel, looked once at father, who picked at his dorsal guiding feathers, and said, "I hoped this day would never

35

come, I want you to know that we both love you very much. However, as you've probably noticed by now, you're not like the other boys or girls. You see...one day, I was strutting along the banks of the River Bachik, and I found a bag of strange beans. I should've known better, why would anyone leave a bag of high quality legumes just lying around for any old bird to find? I should've walked away, anything but eat them all in one sitting.

"I woke up the next day to find my belly swollen and tender. I had to sing in sick, the pain was that bad. Your father thought that those beans might've been popcorn. In the quarry, he'd heard stories of pigeons going through baking hot corn fields, eating the swollen kernels which had bloomed like flower heads, which then promptly reacted with their stomach acid and exploded them open from within. He took refuge in the kitchen nest, just on the off-chance.

"A passing doctor bird stopped by, and gave me the news that I didn't think possible. I was pregnant. This was quite the shock, as your father...well...let's just say he suffers from...performance anxiety."

It was at this juncture my father flew off to the local watering hole, The Mucky Human, leaving mama there embarrassed and alone. Before I could even ask about the whole procreation thing, which sounded like jolly good fun, she continued, "Luckily, your father is a good bird, he promised he would take care of me, and you, he had always wanted a little egg to sit on. Except...you never came. Day after day, we waited for you to pop out of my egg bum-bum, but nothing. The medical staff were baffled, eventually insisting that I go and stay in the hospital nest, over on Seagull and Fifth. You know, by the fence factory?

"My belly continued to swell, I had forgotten what my claws looked like. It felt like I was going to burst open. Finally, one day, an autumn morning, I remember it well, as the crops were starting to wither, I felt like I needed a great big poo. But this one felt funny. It felt...solid. I didn't want to push, fearing that my insides would come out, but my mother always told me that if you need to go, go, just fan out your tail feathers so you don't poop on yourself by accident.

"Against every instinct I had, I pushed, and pushed, and pushed. To my relief, instead of an endless torrent of faecal matter, a screaming orange child came out. You. The doctors and nurses opened their beaks, and no noise came out. You filled up the entire nest, your little gross wriggling orange body, those strange arms and legs of yours, fingers and toes. But most of all your head, two eyes and a mouth, carved into the surface. I didn't know what to do, until you looked at me, and squeezed my wing tip with your podgy pumpkin skin fingers. Well...after that? I would've done anything for you."

I commended mama on a wonderful story, but it was still missing one important detail.

How the hell was I made of pumpkin and not a bird? Her answer?

"I guess it must have been radiation or something. Perhaps an evil magpie curse?"

And that was that. I tried to press her for more details, but she never said another word on the subject. Even on her death nest a few years later, as she coughed up blood and bile after that tomcat had caught her and shook her apart like a bluebottle, she said nothing. She stroked my cheek with her blood caked feathers, winked, though this caused her one remaining eye to fall out, and cawed softly into what passed as my ear.

We dealt with her body the way all birds do, by letting her decompose down on Mulch Avenue. We lay her side by side with her sister who had died the previous summer, after being hit by a stray lightning bolt. Father, already a recluse, turned to drink, fluttering home late at night, intoxicated on fermented berries and sap, smelling of cheap birds and smoke.

But there was a change going on inside me. My skin was getting tougher. The physical attacks by my peers now did me no harm, and caused me no physical pain. Seeing father shun me, I did the only thing I felt I could...I closed my heart, and for the first time in my life, looked upon the birds I shared my life with in a new light.

I hated them with every fibre of my being.

I wanted to get my revenge after the years of suffering they had doled out on me, but how? No bird would ever

37

fight another, even the proper bastardy of the vultures meant that they only feasted on the dead, and found warm meat to be positively disgusting. I knew the cats and snakes would gladly help me, but what the hell does a prepubescent boy with a pumpkin for a head have to offer?

I can answer this one for you with two words.

Fuck.

All.

The cats merely slept through my requests, whilst snakes, the proper venomous ones, tried to bite me, breaking their fangs on my tough skin. They eventually gave up and slithered away back into the undergrowth.

For a moment, I considered about ending it all. I was the only one of my kind. The birds, my supposed kin treated me like a walking buffet or latrine. The other animals as if I were some kind of novelty, to be pawed, hissed, bitten or barked at.

I trudged over to the top of the tallest cliff, and looked down at the jagged rocks below. How easy it would be, to let the wind topple me from this peak. Deliver me to the granite below, smash my head in and spread my pulp and seed over the grey angular anvil so far beneath me.

Then it hit me.

Seeds.

And not just any.

My seed.

Yes, very funny.

My seed.

Titter away why don't you? I mean, it's only my life story I'm blurting out to you here.

Hang on, don't go.

Please?

You have to understand, that it's not easy sitting here day in, day out, no stimulus, nothing. I came into this world by mama eating errant radioactive and/or cursed beans, which formed me into a bright orange vegetable person of no discernible gender. I've spent most of my life being ridiculed, so I get a little testy. Okay?

Cool.

So, every once in a while, I would have to hack a slightly bigger hole for my eyes and mouth, to counter my growth spurts. I'd use a piece of broken glass and would gouge out my innards, discarding the seeds, feeding them to the sparrows over on Stoop Road, trying to get them to like me.

What if I didn't?

The plan to befriend them hadn't exactly been a roaring success, the blasted things still circled me as I slept, trying to drop small pebbles into my earholes.

I ran home, shimmied up the nest pole, and rooted around in the branches for my bag. I took out the broken piece of glass and scooped out a handful of my head. I rooted through the gunk, and found that I had five seeds, that would do for my little experiment. I hurried over to Mulch Avenue, and beneath the desiccated skeleton of my mother and her family, I thrust them into the earth, which writhed with maggots and feathers.

Every day for a month, I returned, watering them and tending to the soil. It was fertile land, enriched with bone dust which helped to make the soil a verdant field.

Yet after thirty days...nothing. I raised my head to the heavens, lamented my folly, and plotted my path back to the clifftop. As I was about to leave, I felt something grasp my toes. Daring to look down, I saw shiny orange digits, having broken through the top soil, and latched onto my foot. I brushed the dirt away, and lo...just beneath the surface was my son. My first born.

Nigel.

As I bent down and pulled him from the ground like a carrot, another hand broke free, then another, and another...from the five, four had survived, genesis had been effected. I wasn't alone anymore. Yet the venom of loathing still bubbled inside of me, as I knew that I could not allow my offspring to suffer the same indignities that had been meted out to me. So I carried them, one by one, to a cave on the outskirts of Bird City. There, I taught them how to look after their skin, how to read, how to write, to speak, to question the inequities of root vegetables everywhere.

But most of all, I taught them my seething rage at those damn prissy birds.

After every lesson of language, mathematics and physical education, I told them stories of how I had been mistreated. Sure, some of them may have been embellished

39

slightly, but even with my self-imposed exile, my vitriol for those winged bastards had not diminished.

I can still see them all now, row upon row of dead pumpkin eyes looking back at me, then to each other, fists clenched in resistance, eager to right this wrong.

Within a year, our numbers were in the hundreds. Some of my children were gifted engineers, and began to fashion weapons, not just for melee, but projectile too. Soon we had a wealth of swords, clubs, and simple firearms. Along with our loathing for their kind, we would use the one key thing that our creation had gifted us, which those devil birds did not possess.

Opposable thumbs.

The plan was a simple one, for it had to be, we would wait for the migratory period to start, when vast numbers of the populace would seek warmer climes, and we would target key objectives within the city. A crack squad of my children, trained in deadly hand-to-hand combat, and quieter than a flamingo eating spaghetti, would take control of the feeders, down in Central Plaza. At the same time, a similarly discreet force would capture the bird baths, down on Splish-Splash Lane.

Then, with me leading the main bulk of my army, I would march on the seat of power, the White House, originally a brick building, but covered from top to foundation in foul guano. Will these filthy animals ever learn to not poop wherever pleases them?

I surmised my little insurrection would deal with that.

We did not have long to wait, as our metrological centre, set up by my most gifted child, Samantha, detected a severe cold front coming in, which would cause consternation amongst the bird world, and send them to their nests to pack.

I gave the command and readied my forces. It was time. Time to show these heartless harpies who the new dominant species was in this city. The commandos took their objectives with the minimum of effort, catching the guard storks on the hop, figuratively and literally. It was not without bloodshed though, as a number of lairy blue tits, hopped up on fermented blueberry mash put up a fight, albeit briefly, at the bird baths. They were put down quickly, but brutally, the water running red with their blood.

You should've seen the looks on their faces when I marched down Main Street. A few police doves tried to get in our way, but they were dealt with quickly and efficiently. A quick blow round the back of their heads with a club put paid to their protests. The guards outside the White House were too shocked to resist the massed ranks of pumpkin people marching on them. They cooed, opened the gates and flew away to Paradise City, where rumours persisted of lusher lawns and prettier lady avian.

By now, the air was awash with all manner of calls, some I recognised, others a garbled panicked mishmash of noise. One word kept being repeated…Pumpkinhead. Of course they knew my name. In a city of birds, where there's an anomaly sitting in your kid's classes, or using your rest facilities, they knew who I was. They just didn't expect there to be so many of me. The plan had worked, it was as I envisaged, a time of joy, celebration, brief retaliation and then harmony.

Or so I thought.

As we stood at the bottom of the steps to the White House, the President, a sage old owl called Icky Codknuckle was waiting for us at the summit. His head doing laps around his neck, it was making the rest of the cabinet rather dizzy to say the least. Finally, he ceased, as I approached him and his cadre, one step at a time, letting them see the face of the victor.

A single step from the peak, I stopped, already towering over his diminutive form. I had only seen pictures of him from afar, but up close he seemed so regal, I almost changed my mind. But then the years of abuse and pecking brought me back to my senses. I demanded that he and his parliament stand down immediately, the time of the birds, was to be consigned to history.

Codknuckle bowed shallowly, strode forward to meet me, and cleared his throat, preparing to address the crowd which had gathered in the vast grounds below, and the array of perches conveniently placed around the open area. With a voice firm, steady, not showing any sign of fear, he uttered those immortal four words, "I stand here today-"

Then a single shot ran out. Codknuckle's head rocked

41

backwards, a puff of powdered feathers showing the point of impact, his blood and brains were sprayed over the Chancellor of the Trill Exchequer. Icky's eyes rolled up into his majestic head, before he collapsed backwards, dead.

I was as shocked as he, for I had expressly told my fellow pumpkins that no-one should fire if a peaceful outcome was on the cards. I looked at the still twitching body of Codknuckle, and traced the path of the assassin's bullet.

And there he was.

Nigel.

I demanded to know why he had fired his weapon, how he could disobey my orders. He laughed, a single pall of callous cackling, which was joined by the other pumpkins. Nigel shouldered his weapon, and with his podgy fingers, delved around in his mouth cavity, pulling out a chunk of thick skin, which he had obviously cut with a fine blade. The slab of rind fell to the floor, exposing a fanged maw, carved not in my image, but a new one.

One by one, the rest of the pumpkin army pulled out their own pre-sliced mouths, becoming a sea of evil pumpkinheads, looking back at me as if I were the enemy. The Foreign Secretary, a plump near senile pigeon, tried to waddle back inside. Harriet, one of the newest grown pumpkins was on him in a flash. Following a flurry of wild swipes with a machete, the pigeon was reduced to bloodied ribbons.

I stared down at Nigel, and asked again, why had he gone against my will?

He stomped up the stairs, and stared deeply into my eye cavities, "You taught us to despise them, father. You taught us nothing but hatred, rage and anger. We are made in your own image, are we not? I thought you would be proud. For did we not do this day what you had wished? Isn't this why you grew us all, and nurtured us, so we could exact this just and noble revenge?"

My little pumpkin heart sunk. Is this all I had taught them? Murder? I told him and the others, that I did not want this, I wanted the coup to be bloodless, a seamless transition of power from the old to the new. They were nasty to me, yes, but there were moments of occasional compassion.

"Yet you did not teach us this father, you armed us, told us they were the enemy, and marched us to war. Are you really that shocked that we would do this without compunction? Exactly as you had trained us?"

The gathered crowds, both high and low, began to get nervous, the pumpkins turned to regard them, preparing weapons, picking out targets. I knew that what I would do next would be nothing more than a token gesture, a futile exhibition of selflessness which would never be recorded, for history does not remember the vanquished.

I shouted at the birds to flee, to escape this place.

It was too late. Shots rang out. Birds fell from their perches to the ground. The injured were set upon, and killed. Those who did not heed my warning, and did not take to the skies, were swarmed where they stood, and murdered. Within a matter of minutes, every winged creature in that arena was dead or dying.

Nigel, his face streaked with blood, and with a solitary white dove's feather stuck to his head, turned to me, "Oh, father, it seems you do not want this world that we have created." He pulled his sword from its scabbard and lunged at me, removing my head from my torso.

Yet I did not die.

My body was burned, the White House painted anew. A deep crimson, the paint made with the blood of the innocent, as Nigel and his followers, my progeny, swept to power. The birds, not the most intelligent creatures, let's admit it, did not flee, and were enslaved. In schools, a new truth was taught, that they were the subservient ones, and pumpkins were the one true race.

And me?

Well you found me here, didn't you?

My head, all that remains of me, sits in an alcove overlooking Mulch Avenue. My mouth has near sealed over, no one has bothered to carve it open and free. My eyes, nothing more than two pinpricks in this tough old skin of mine. Nigel cut the top of my head open, and once a month, a ceremony is held where new seeds are pulled from my insides, and sown amongst the ancestral dead of this city, the carrion ranks replenished by the freshly slaughtered.

Now, every bird is clipped at birth to prevent them from

flying away, the final piece de resistance of cruelty exacted by my spawn. Too late do I see that I should've taught my offspring to embrace their differences, not to use them as a furnace for hatred.

Every year, on the anniversary of the uprising, at the end of the month of October, pumpkins, grown as they should be in tilled land, are harvested. That terrible ghastly visage of snarled mouths and evil eyes are carved within their flesh. At every junction, and at every residence, they are left out on display, lit from within by a solitary candle to remind the birds who is in control.

I am glad you found me, traveller. But no happy ending do I have for you this day.

If I were you, I would take your leave, before one of the pumpkin militia finds you here, and executes you for sedition.

Unless...

Would you be willing to grant a cantankerous old foolish pumpkinhead one final wish?

It is a simple one?

Climb that cliff, with me in the crook of your arm, back to where I contemplated my end, and cast what remains of me from atop the tallest peak. Let my mulch splatter against the jagged rocks below. Bear witness to the waves carrying my blasted flesh and guts down and out into the depths of the sea.

Maybe there, at the bottom of the ocean, my sacrifice will bear more children.

Yet this time, I hope that whatever remains of me, every remnant or scrap of pulp, seed, memory and regret, will teach them something different.

Something better.

It's time to...
EMBRACE YOUR FATE

Is that how you want to end up? Thinking that you know best, only to have to be shown the harsh and uncaring truth? No, you need to keep listening to our advice, we know what's best for you.

CONGRATULATIONS! YOU'VE ACCIDENTALLY SUMMONED A WORLD-ENDING MONSTER. WHAT NOW?

But maybe you think that we don't? That's pure nonsense! We suggest you do some gentle stretches, to make sure that your limbs are supple should you need to...flee...or something. Then flick over to **Page 152** and discover what happens to those who kick up a fuss.

45

PRELUDE TO AWESOMENESS

Ian gives you a thumbs up -- let its sticky nub brush against your smooth silicone skin.

"Yes! No one ever listens to me, like that time in Maggie Thatcher Burger when I suggested we entice a hungry jaguar into the haunted storage cupboard. Did they listen to me? Did they balls. And look what happened to that place."

"I tried to blow it up, and if it weren't for some shoddy work, then we'd be dead and wouldn't even be here at this juncture in time," Monique squirmed in the armchair, which tried its utmost to accommodate her comfort.

"Ahh, exactly. It didn't work, did it? So who *did* fix the bomb and make it go off?"

"Probably some do-gooder with a penchant for high-explosives."

"Or, and more likely, a vengeful spirit who hadn't been eaten by a jaguar."

Noah walked over to the living room door, slamming it shut before putting his foot through it. "Will the pair of you just shut the fuck up? Emu almighty, I've had to put up with some people of dubious intelligence before, but you two take the egg and incubate it incorrectly." Silence greeted the priest. "Fine, so that saying no longer has the impact it used to."

Moving swiftly on, Ian demonstrated his ire by swinging the smashed remains of the door on its rusty hinge. "That's another bloody door you owe me!"

"It's all about you, isn't it? Can we get a wriggle on? It's game night back at the zealot sanctuary this evening. My Jenga winning streak stands at four centuries and counting, if I ain't there it gets reset, and I'd really like to not kill you with your own face." Noah flicked through his Polaroid collection of victims he had murdered with their own faces. It wasn't pretty, nosireebob.

Ian backed away. "Good point, well made. So, my suggestion got picked, didn't it?" Noah and Monique nodded, a little annoyed that they wouldn't get to influence the story by meddling in time. "Good, so let's get on with it, then. We need four people to make up our super-group, we'll come up with a snazzy name later when we are assembled, but for now, we need to go our separate ways."

Ian started rooting round his personal belongings, grabbing up fistfuls of stuff to shove into a backpack. "What the hell are you doing?" Noah asked.

"Duh, it's my superhero starter kit, everything you need to become a superhero. Look, I've got my certificate asserting I'm an orphan, after my parents were murdered in cold blood outside a sperm bank when I was six."

Monique leaned forward, and patted Ian's arm. "Aww, I'm sorry, I had no idea."

"Eh?"

"About your parents. How did they die? Was it horrible? Were they butchered in front of you, and their fingers used as gripping devices in the sperm bank, to help pull off those who didn't want to touch their own penis?"

"No, Pam and Keith are alive and well in Market Lavington."

"Oh."

Ian passed across the certificate. "It's a joke one, ordered it from the internet a few years back, you know, in case this exact situation came to pass. Come to think of it, a lot of this stuff was nothing but a speculative purchase on the off-chance that someone or something would invent a crazy scenario where this crap would come in handy."

"What else do you have in there?" Noah went to open the backpack, but Ian pulled it away.

"Get out of it! This is mine, if you wanted to do this properly, you should've got your own stuff."

Noah contemplated smashing Ian's head in and turning it into a lava lamp, but filed the idea away for later. "No, what *I* wanted was to get pissed. Then, when you two fucknuts ruined my day by summoning the world-ending monster that is responsible for millennia of self-doubt and hatred of humanity, my plans of getting drunk and playing shove ha'penny came to an abrupt end."

"Oh yeah..."

"But hey, that's not even the worst of it. I then summon the courage to suggest what I want to happen, and get some killer robots from the future, some complete A-HOLE

47

decides - out of the fucking blue - that they're going to side with some anus who isn't even an immortal emu-worshipping demigod. That's me, by the way. So yeah, I'm a bit pissed off with you all right now." Noah began to hack at the door's remains with his staff.

Ian went to put a conciliatory arm around the priest's shoulder, but his general aura suggested it an unwise move. "Hey, look, big guy, this may seem as though you didn't win-"

"You don't fucking say."

"-but look, you get free rein over what type of superhero you want to be."

Noah stopped forming a pile of door kindling. "Really?"

"Yep. Anything you wanna be, nothing is too wacky or cray-cray."

"You're just saying that to try and stop me from smashing your stupid head in."

"Eh?"

"What?"

"Whatever. Look, when we go our separate ways, you are responsible for what you become, no one else will decide for you, I promise."

The priest fished around in his tracksuit trouser pockets, finally pulling out a wrinkled testicle -- his own, I should add. "Bugger, wasn't after that." He shoved his crinkled ballbag back into his underpants and rummaged some more, eventually pulling out the same sad-looking pant-plum. "This is embarrassing. Say...would you..."

"Are you shitting me?"

"Hey, buddy, it's obvious that the curse put on me by that *bitch* Darlene down the pub is playing havoc with me right now. Just do me a favour and slip your hand into my pocket."

"Fuck no, I don't want to touch your shrivelled-up dude-egg."

"You won't. The curse stops me from getting important objects out of my pockets, instead embarrassing myself in public by displaying parts of my aged genitalia. You're immune to it, though."

Ian rubbed his hands against his chest. "I dunno about this..."

"It'll be fine, I'll hold this bollock for you so your passage won't get hindered. Just pop your mitt in there, root around, and pull out what you find."

"What is it?"

"I can't tell you, or the curse will be passed onto you. Fucking hell, this is taking way longer than I thought it would."

"Fine, I'll do it." Ian worked out a mental path between his hand and the priest's pocket. As his fingertips grazed against the fabric, he closed his eyes.

"That's it, a little deeper."

"Why is it so moist in here?"

"Shhh, it's a delicate eco-system. THERE! Do you feel it?"

Ian grimaced. "I think so."

"Good, now yank it out."

Screaming, Ian whipped his hand out, bringing forth the Emu priest's (fortunately) flaccid penis. "What the fuck?"

Noah began to laugh. "I didn't think you'd actually do it! That was brilliant. Hey, whilst you're there, would you mind giving it a bit of a shake?"

Ian let the leathery wang drop and wiped his hand against the curtains. "There was nothing in there except for a hole into your pant-region."

"I know. My notepad is in the other pocket."

"Then why did you do that?"

"Because it's funny? Fine, Mr Serious, I'll just tuck this away," Noah shoved everything back where it belonged, retrieved the notepad and pen, and held them out to Ian. "Go on."

"What?"

"Write down that no matter what happens, I can choose what the fuck I want to be, and nothing and no-one —not even omnipotent beings who think they know what's best for us— can supersede my decision."

"Fine." Ian snatched the pad and pen, before scribbling down the priest's words, signing it with a flourish. "Happy now?"

The priest scoured the scrawl to ensure its binding legality. "Excellent, this should cover it, count me in."

"About fucking time, we could be a few hundred words into one of our character arcs by now. So, I'll give you two

49

until seven o'clock tomorrow morning. We meet by the statue of Roger Warburton, round-earth denier, anti-vaxxer, and all-round scumbag. Be ready for the fight of your lives."

"Where are you going?" Monique shifted in the chair.

"It's origin story time, you don't genuinely think mine would involve you two, do you? Besides, we're one member short, I have to go and rustle them up. Be there tomorrow, and by jingo, you better be ready."

SUPER SECRET AHOY!

With his television having been sold, Ian had fallen back to his comic addiction. In truth, he preferred them, their vibrant colours, madcap characters and sounds such as *ZONK!*, *TWAT!* and *WOMP!* being things he aspired to create in real life. His current favourite was a character called Fisty McPunch, a no-nonsense, punch-things-in-the-face-first, ask-important-questions-later kinda chap. Which was a silly way of doing it, really. If he'd asked the questions first, *then* played a little face music with his fists, he'd get answers that weren't laced with concussion.

Still, as Ian raced through town —as fast as one could on the still slick blood and guts— he knew he didn't have the time to become a replica of Fisty. For one, he'd need months of serious training, as McPunch's favoured right bicep had its own gravity. He'd been created in a lab over the course of several years, and unless that blue bastard currently using the cathedral spire as an al fresco human kebab pantry was prepared to wait, then Ian needed something a little quicker.

This was why he was choosing option B, the ol' tried and trusted. If you wanted something in a jiffy, with only a moderate-to-severe chance of life-shortening side effects, there was only one thing you could do. The others were bound to take a different path to superherodom, which was good. The last thing he wanted when he rocked up at the allotted meeting time was to find himself looking at three carbon copy heroes with identical powers. Who the hell would want to read about that?

Short of assigning them specific talents and powers, he had to trust them to do the right thing and not fuck this part up, or it would, quite frankly, be a bit of a flop. All he could do was look after his end, and having worked out the identity of the fourth member of the latest crime-stopping group, he knew he wanted to recruit them in his new form. In order to do this, he had to make the trek across the viscera plains, to the one pub in town that had what he was after.

51

The Salisbury Arms.

Named after the city it had landed in, the pub as a sentient creature died in the late fifties after a fatal wound received from renowned hitpub, The Deadly Duck. Its dead body was still used as a hostelry, the humans unaware the building had ever been alive, or that it was one of the old crime bosses of Victorian England, even though malice and evil that once pumped around the bricks and mortar now seeped into the locals that drank from its befouled beverages.

Every settlement has one pub that people warn you about. The Salisbury Arms was that place. In order to enter and not get turned into a lunchtime meat platter for homeless manatees, you had to prove you had been born in the city. Fortunately for Ian, he passed this important check.

Having bypassed the bouncer, he made a beeline for the back wall, where a skeletal hand was displayed in a glass case. The patrons who had the closest table bared their teeth as he approached, annoyed that they would have to shift, temporarily, to another table. With them finally out of earshot, Ian unscrewed the tip of his right ring finger.

Now, I'm going to let you into a little secret —are you prepared? Before I do, you must swear on something you hold to be really valuable to your very existence, that you won't share it with another living soul. Okay? If you can't handle this, then I suggest you skip the next few paragraphs, because once you know, it's something you can't unhear, and if you go blabbing about it, on the fourth night you'll wake up to see the bulky form of The Deadly Duck at the end of your bed. The last thing you'll see will be a UPVC window opening at high speed straight into your face. *BLAM*. You're dead. Okay?

Right, lean in a bit closer. People who are born in Salisbury have a special device implanted into their right-hand ring finger at birth. WE ARE NOT A CULT. That is important to state, but you can't *join* our little club, you're either born one of us, or you ain't. This device —and don't forget what will happen to you if you go shouting your mouth off —is a small brush. Nothing fancy to look at. It's the same width as the bone that is removed during the procedure, its black bristles hidden beneath a fake finger, but it lets you tap into the local black market. Us Wiltshire types are a resourceful bunch, if you don't believe me, look up why we're called Moonrakers. Throughout the city are a number of interactable objects, where the brush lets you access certain...services and products which are unavailable to anyone else. Including those sneaky sods from Dorset.

So, Ian opened the front of the glass display case, and, using the freshly exposed brush at the end of his finger, gently dusted the bones of the upturned palm of the bony hand. As he finished with a flourish, there was a muted giggling from behind the wall, and the bones flexed and tensed.

Checking to make sure no out-of-towners had snuck in, Ian screwed the tip of his finger back on, closed the glass case, and shifted closer to the wall.

Hey, loser! If you decided you couldn't keep our secret, and risk incurring the wrath of the deadliest public house in the ENTIRE world by blabbing, then you can rejoin the story here.

I won't judge you. Much.

Looking to his right, the brick at eye-height scraped backwards into the wall, a bloodshot eye looking back at him through the inky void. "What is the password?"

See, we're not stupid, us Salisbury peeps know that someone could rat us out and try to access our hidden network, which is why we have a two-stage encryption. Every day, a password is psychically transmitted into all our heads, and is valid for the next twenty-four hours only. Only those on the Good list get the correct one, any people outside of the city, or suspected of being a Hampshire stooge, are fed an incorrect one.

Ian looked around nervously. "Malcolm McKindy is innocent."

The eye in the cavity wall looked back, unblinking. After what seemed like an age, but in actuality was as long as it took to read these last two sentences, the voice replied. "What be you after?"

"I need some of the...special stuff, from the ranges. You know?"

"I know what you be on about, all right. Let me see what I have."

The eye disappeared, and from the gap in the wall, between two horse brasses of mighty dead steeds, came a rustling sound. "I have but one vial of that which you seek, for it has been in high demand since the Kaiju attacks last year."

"Fine, it'll have to do, it's that or nothing, put it on my tab."

There was a scribbling sound of charcoal against papyrus, before a glowing green vial appeared through the gap, held by filthy fingers, nails curled over the tips. "Consider it done, be you requiring anything else?"

Holding the vial up to the light, which was a bit pointless as the vial was casting quite the glow, Ian shook it before repeating the motion with his head. "Nope, this should do it. Though if you have any luck going spare, I'll take it," he chuckled, slapping the wall and putting the vial into his pocket.

"I'll have a look."

"Oh...I didn't mean-"

"Here you go, a freshly-retrieved, one-hundred percent lucky rabbit's paw."

Ian took the paw, which was not in the best of shape; the fur was sallow and on the verge of slipping off the fine bones underneath. As per receiving anything new and unexpected, he gave it a bit of a sniff—he detected notes of stinging nettle and white static— he shoved them in his pocket with the glowing liquid, which lit up his trousers like an alien invasion beacon. "It looks a bit raggedy, thanks."

"It be acquired from Lucky William, you might have seen him on the telly, predicting the results of that football tournament."

"Can't be that lucky if I'm the owner of one of his feet."

"He died of natural causes a few months back."

"Oh no, what happened?"

"Got 'it by a truck."

"Riiight, moving on, I'm sure it'll come in handy."

foreshadowing alert

"Be you requiring anything else?"

Ian tightened the end of his finger. "Not unless you have

a tight-fitting spandex costume in blue and yellow, with a long flowing cape!" He went to leave.

"That I do." With that, the aforementioned outfit was shoved through the hole in the wall.

"Oh...right. Cool. I wasn't expecting any of this."

"Fresh delivery in this morning, end of the world variety, I've got all sorts back here. Gravity guns, black hole portable portals, blow-up landing craft decoys, thirteen crates of tankery gin, and that's just the start of it."

Ian considered his choices before replying. "I'll think I'll just stick with this, thanks. Don't want to push things too much in our favour, we won't feel like we've earned our inevitable victory, otherwise."

"Suit yourself. Payment is on the fifteenth of Pig. As per normal." As he spoke, the brick was replaced, and the wall went back to being all nondescript.

Magic.

With more than he came for, but the important ingredient secure, Ian left a shiny hub cap as a thanks to the landlord and headed out once more. Destiny awaited.

Cool, huh?

NEVER ANNOY THE WRITER

If you've been in the business of making superheroes for as long as I have —which is about twelve minutes in reading time— you'll know that in the main, there's one key ingredient. You can have your moment of violence which moulds you; perhaps you were born with latent powers which came to the fore one geography trip to ancient Persia. Or, and way more realistically, you rely on the tried and trusted method, especially if you're short of time. Ian knew this as well as me. Which is handy, because until I started writing this book, he didn't even exist. Coincidence, or what?

Ian plunged his hands in his pockets, heading towards the super-secret lair he had built for such an eventuality. Once there, he would enact his plan, have a few hours of gestation, and then awake to be the hero that the city...no, THE WORLD needed in the face of being eaten by one very large, very pissed-off monster.

You want to know what's in his pockets, don't you? You probably have a fair idea, but I think now's as good a time as any to unveil it to you, via the medium of putting the words in the protagonist's mouth, but first I just need to construct a sentence to make it all-

"Radioactive goo," Ian mumbled, to no-one in particular.

MOTHERFUCKER! I was setting that up and he just waltzed right in and ruined it. What an absolute wanker. You can tell I created him.

A number of Ian's favourite heroes and villains had been created through the medium of radioactive goo falling onto them, being submerged in radioactive goo, or radioactive goo infecting something else, an insect for example, and then that insect biting the person, and *BOOM!* One super person made with kickass powers. It was this model that Ian had adopted, and back in his super-secret lair —which was nothing more than the space behind the bins out the back of Margaret Thatcher Burger— he had the means to set himself down this path.

Problem was, he had to get there first, and after pulling

that little stunt, I've half a mind to shift his little plan onto a different track entirely. Who the hell does he think he is? Mooching around, ruining my delicate prose...or something, and for what? Screw it, I'm going to. Two can play that game, Buster. Go on then, humble character *I* created, you tell everyone what you want to be.

"A blend of seventeen different animals, utilising their specific skills and strengths, into one singular organism. I'll have the strength of a gorilla, the agility of a domestic short-haired cat, the colour blending ability of the chameleon..."

As the annoying little shit has another fourteen things to list, I know for a fact that two cool desperados like you and I have better things to be doing. So let's go poop on his parade, just as he pooped on mine, and shatter his hopes and dreams. Why? Because I feel like being a bit of a bastard, but also because I've just had a cool idea of my own.

"...of the anteater. Once I swill that lot together into a handy applicator, add the radioactive goo and inject it into my eyeball, I shall become...COR BLIMEY CREATURE MAN." Ian did a little jump, punching the air at the same time, unaware of the writer's new approach to his little story. As his foot landed, it came into contact with a blob of conveniently placed (by me) gland, I don't know where from, I'm no doctor, but I know this for certain, it's slippery as hell.

Ian skated on the spot for a few minutes, his arms flailing about as if he were trying to summon two-hundred-and-eighty-one taxis simultaneously and guide them into specific parking bays. Finally, after the comedic moment had passed, he fell to one side. There was a crack of glass as he did so.

GASP! I WONDER WHAT THAT COULD BE?!

Ian gasped. "I wonder what that could be?"

Told you.

Still on the floor, Ian rolled over to one side, he could see that his pocket was soaked through, the green goo seeping through his trousers. Not thinking properly, and forgetting why the gloop was in a vial to begin with, he plunged his hands into the offending pocket and pulled out the contents. He threw the broken shards of safety glass onto the floor, the thick liquid having abandoned ship, and held the rancid rabbit's paw in front of his face. As he did so, the sock of fur, laden with heavy gunk, finally slipped off the skeletal structure which once held it firmly in place, and splatted onto Ian's groin. That sort of stain is always going to get people pointing and laughing.

That'll teach him, huh? Thing is, that's not even the high point of my retribution.

"Well, that's just great." Ian began to pat himself down with his free hand, trying to find something he could let the radioactive crap drip into so he could still carry out his plan. We both know it ain't gonna work, but best of British luck to him for trying. With his attention firmly diverted to the patting-down of his own body, the spindly rabbit's foot twirled in the air. It had been fashioned into a convenient keyring, and it was by the hoop that Ian was suspending it.

The bones were covered in the goo, like low-budget marinated drumsticks shorn of meat and high in calcium. Problem was, the fur, or what was left of it before it slipped off, was the only thing holding the bones together. The viscous liquid was doing its best, but it was a poor substitute. The biggest toe gave way first, and the ivory spear, laced with radiation, fell straight into the top of Ian's thigh.

He screamed, and slapped his hands against the wound, inadvertently injecting the other bones straight into his leg. "OWWWWWWW!" Ian looked down at his leg, and saw three bone barbs jutting out from his milky white skin. Ripping his trousers so he could get a better look at the injury, he saw that around each impact site was a green ring, like damp marks on a sodden wall. These were spreading slowly outwards. As they went, they chewed through the skin, muscle and sinew beneath, stripping him like an overcooked spare rib. Anything the green tide came into contact with burned, clothing hissed as it bubbled and vaporised, adding to the heady stench that was assailing his nostrils.

He could feel the tips of his fingers buzzing, turning his hands over to see that they too were being shorn of covering. His dainty finger brush stood no chance, and was dissolved with ease. Ian lay back on the floor, writhing around in agony as the green wave of immolation coursed over every pore and every patch of skin, until nothing remained but his skeleton and his eyes and brain.

Hey! I'm many things, but I still need to advance the plot, okay?

The disintegration died away. Ian, with unblinking eyes, looked up at a starless sky. With the pain subsiding, he sat up, wallowing in a puddle of his former self. "Bugger," he mumbled, though he was somewhat relieved that he could still speak, especially as his larynx was nothing more than a pink bubble —which really needed to be popped.

Managing to stand up, he felt the last of his skin slough from his bones. He was a little wobbly at first, needing to rest against a lamp post to stay upright. But he managed to stand there like a newborn giraffe, his legs shaking beneath him. He could feel the goo begin to harden, yet remain pliable, so he could flex his new form as if it had not been completely dissolved by a vengeful writer. Daring to move, he took a few tentative steps, realising that it wasn't actually too bad.

I mean, yeah, he'd been completely de-skinned, and you could see straight through him, but he was alive, at least. And sure, he wasn't going to have the beak of a toucan, or the curvature of a shark, but you know what? I could've made it a lot worse.

Catching his reflection in the darkened window of a house, he picked away at the last remaining stragglers of vein and sinew which clung resolutely to his new form. He flicked his arm to get rid of a stringy piece of ligament, and his forearm bones shot out to form a sword. He did the same to his other arm, with a similar effect, this one ending in an axe head—the end being his shoulder bone.

This was pretty cool. Not what he had hoped for, but he had some kickass weapons right here in his own body. He did some basic kata, thinking himself a proper badass judging by his reflection. After clacking his new weapons together, he held them aloft, just as a bolt of lightning cracked down from the heavens like a whip, landing behind him and lighting him up all cool-like. Ian bellowed to the unforgiving sky. "I am reborn anew...I am...SKELIAN!"

Which wasn't too bad.

59

Now all he had to do was get the fourth member of the team recruited; for that, he had to make a little stop to his previous place of employment. Back to where it all began.

Nearly.

I mean, of course, back to where we were introduced to Ian, not the opening bit of this story, as that would be too far-fetched. As you can tell, I am all about making sure that stuff is believable.

Let's bounce.

GHOST SAUCE

Wiggling his digit in the lock, Ian missed being able to grin in relief, having no lips or facial muscles to convey that anymore. Instead he revelled in his new ability, a skeleton key, or should I say a *skelian* key?

Man, this is gold! If you didn't smile at that, perhaps *you're* nothing but a skeleton.

Ian paid the CCTV no heed, if the world survived this and looked back on the footage, a walking skeleton would be the most plausible thing about this entire turn of events.

He followed down the back corridor until he reached the door he was after. The 'Avin' A Laugh' logo was scrawled in black marker pen over the gaudy Margaret Thatcher Burger logo. Using his special key once more, he entered the premises, closing the door behind him. The air stank of burned fat, overdone fries, and greetings card lacquer; fortunately for Ian, he had no ability to smell any of this, so he fumbled through the half-light to get to the customer-facing side of the shop.

It was incredible how much work the shopfitters had done in the hours since the explosion. Providing you didn't look at the ceiling, which still had blood sprayed over it and an arm hanging from a fluorescent light strip, you'd never have known what had happened. Pacing out fourteen steps from the main doors, Ian took a hop, a sharp turn to the right and —like a marsupial— bounced forward four paces, before taking a lazy turn to the left and a shuffle forward. He was there. Right where he wanted to be.

Where the metal counters used to be, which housed the variety of accoutrements, and the microwaves for the burgers themselves, a stack of mugs was now in their place. Ian clapped his hands together, which was not a pleasant experience, as his bones shook and rattled. He vowed to never do that again, his arms back to being arms and not cool-looking bone weapons. All he had to do now was remember the secret incantation, and he could set about recruiting the missing cog in this brand-new machine.

He clicked his fingers, which made a really impressive

61

sound. He'd be able to join in as a background finger-clicker at the right musical events after the world was saved. Whirling his hands around in the correct motion, he uttered the first line in his chant. "Oi, Dennis! They've not paid your overtime this month."

Nothing, save for some tissue paper waving in the downdraft of the air conditioning.

"Sapphire's got her buttocks trapped in the waste disposal again."

The section of cards devoted to 'Your STD test came back clear, YAY!' rustled, sounding like a boyish tittering.

"I've got a customer out here that needs...a *special*."

The tills at the front of the shop exploded open, sending small change into the air like a shrapnel fountain. The receipt rolls pooled onto the floor, the same phrase printed on them, over and over again. 'I need more special sauce. I NEED MORE SPECIAL SAUCE,' Each row getting bigger in font size and desperation. Finally, the stack of mugs shattered, and a blob of grey smoke appeared where they had stood.

"Who has summoned me?"

Skelian (for this is how he shall be referred to from now, unless he gets his skin back, which is unlikely, as I'm not in a very forgiving mood) quit waving his arms about. "Tis I. Ian. Sorry, *Skelian*."

There was a low moaning sound a lot like, "Ooooooooohhhhhhhhhhhhhh." The amorphous cloud shimmered as if it had its own light show going on inside. Finally it uttered, "But you're not Ian, you're a walking skeleton."

"So what? I sound like him, don't I? Besides, if we're being particular, you're nothing but a tiny little cloud. And dead. Don't forget that bit."

"Oooohhhhhh, good point. Well made. Why have you summoned me this eve? I see no burgers for me to festoon with my own reservoir of fluids."

"I don't, but I have need of your special skills, for a great evil has been summoned which threatens to destroy everything we hold dear."

Silence. The mist continued to ripple with light. Eventually, it replied. "I don't care anymore. I'm dead, oooohhhhhhhh." With that, the fog began to dissipate.

"WAIT! I *know* you're dead, I'm here to give you a second chance, a reason to live...sort of. Hear me out, billions of people deserve that, at least."

"Ooooohhhhhh, okay. You have thirty seconds, then I'm going to get back to my plan to haunt the people who annoyed me when I was alive."

"I'm making a team; four people, we're one short. There were loads of people I could've called on. Pistol Pixie, crackshot and merc for hire, she'd love the opportunity to shoot things in the groin. Morning Star Mike, why, there's nothing he enjoys more than embedding his spiky thing in monster hides. Laser Lynn, Yodel Yann, and Mind-Numbingly-Tedious Rick, who completely misses the point of alliteration when it comes to having cool names.

"But I came back for you, Dennis. For you. Sure, those other folks have weapons, many of which they own outright. They're fearless, used to looking in the face of danger and certain death before trying to French kiss it. Do you know why?"

The mist puffed out, as if shrugging. Trust me on that one.

Skelian moved in. "Because you have something they don't, hell, you have *three* things they don't."

"Courage?"

"Fine, *four* things. No, look, let's head this off before it gets silly. You have your special sauces, Dennis. Any monster that rocks up looking to decimate the human populace is going to expect bullets or melee weapons, but do you know what they're not going to expect?"

"A good squirt of my bum slurry?"

"Damn straight! Imagine what you could do with that? Not to mention your other...*sauces*. Come on, what do you say? Are you with me?"

The cloud puffed outwards, before retracting in on itself, compacting down to a ping pong ball of fumes, finally petering out into nothingness. The only sound was that of the lighting hum, aircon drone, and Skelian's toes clacking on the Eazy-Wipe™ floor tiles. "Great, now I gotta-"

A small vortex appeared in the midst of the broken pottery, getting bigger and bigger with each anti-clockwise

63

swirl. Shards of mug and cardboard were caught up in the wind and hurled around until the cone of air stood six feet tall. Imagine that, if you can! There was a clap of thunder from within and the wind blew outwards, the debris shooting through the gaps in Skelian's bones. Shielding his rather vulnerable eyes and brain, Skelian dared to look back. Stood there, was a six-foot tall (handy) white blob. It looked like a really crappy ghost costume someone had made out of a sheet. It lacked any defined facial features except for two large unblinking eyes, but when it spoke, like now, "ooohhh," a mouth appeared in the mass before disappearing as it fell silent.

It had two legs, thick blocky blobs which knocked over a carousel stand of 'Congratulations on being a vegan atheist' cards onto the floor. "Oops." It also had three things which resembled arms, but with no hands at the end. Instead, they were like hoses, waving as if being controlled by three different, very drunk people.

"Cool as fuck!" Skelian went to applaud, but remembered what had happened earlier, and didn't want to get weird reverberations through his bones. "What do they do, exactly?" He pointed at the waving hose appendages. Raising them upwards, the first one jetted out a pungent brown liquid onto the wall, spelling 'SAUCEMAN.' As it fell against its bulbous body, the second jerked into life, spraying, 'WAS' in lumpy gone-off white bollock gunk. The final appendage completed the short sentence; thin yellow piss added, 'HERE,' although it lacked the thick consistency of the other two, so didn't really help. The smell, though? Fuck me. It was bad. Obviously not affecting Skelian in the slightest, and Sauceman, aka Dennis? Well, he seemed to quite like it.

Skelian held up two fingers. "Excellent, now, let's go and see what the others are up to, we've got a world to save."

KICK BACK, RELAX, YOU'LL BE FINE

Noah flapped the piece of paper in the air, making sure the ink on the agreement had dried properly before rolling it up and putting it into his wallet, usually reserved for smuggling thinly sliced salami into Sushi restaurants. "Right, I'm off."

Languishing within the armchair, it took a few seconds for Monique to acknowledge his imminent departure. "Huh? Where are you going?"

"You heard the imbecile; we need to go and turn ourselves into super...things. I've got to pop down to the Hyper-Mega-Stuff-Mart before it closes so I can rustle up a few bits."

Expecting a reply, but getting nothing except a limp-wristed wave, Noah slammed the door remnants behind him and sodded off to his own chapter later in the book. Monique ahhed, sinking into the cushions as far as she could, feeling them adopt her as one of their own. She wanted a sip of her drink, but the act of having to move was –quite frankly– beyond consideration.

It had been a long day, hell, it had been a long *month*. Her unwilling indoctrination had started exactly thirty days earlier, leading up to the pinnacle of her supposed entry to Martyrville. She hadn't expected to have made it to this evening, and she was determined to enjoy every last moment. Plus, with the monster a mere half mile away intent on wiping out humanity, a few more minutes of comfort were surely in her best interests.

The flat was quiet, the only sound the occasional slurp and splat as pieces of congealed offal detached from the eaves and hit the ground outside. Monique closed her eyes and, deciding that any effort to turn herself into a superhero was a bit too much to consider, she opted to have a quick power nap.

But...she really did want a bit of tankery gin. Just to help numb herself to anything the world might choose to throw at her as she slept. Raising an arm in the approximate direction of where she'd left the glass, she figured that if she

65

could just tip herself forward, she would be able to snag it, finish it off, and then plop back.

It therefore came as something of a shock when her fingers wrapped around the glass without so much as moving at all. Although eternally grateful that she could now enjoy her drink, how it transpired that she could made her brain spin.

Was it a poltergeist? Less throwing shit around, and more operating as a butler. A butlergeist?

Or...had she managed to unlock some kind of long-dormant psychic ability? If so, this would definitely help with the whole superhero gig. She wouldn't need to go through a tedious stretch of exposition to become part of the gang.

What if it was a spiritual eddy, centred around a space in front of her and the coffee table?

Maybe it...

Monique was getting annoyed with all the potential possibilities and decided to save her time and yours by just opening her eyes and seeing what the deal was. The gloom within the lounge was like a thick fog, she couldn't even see her hand, let alone what the hell had picked up her glass and delivered it to her.

Slowly, out of the haze, a tentacle of sorts appeared in front of her, about the length of an arm and around the same thickness. The end of the thing was wrapped around her drink. She traced the furry arm back to the chair, before realising what it actually was. "A draught excluder?" It was seemingly one with the chair, the end protruding from the seat cushion.

Her words made the chair beneath her pulse and swell, and Monique felt herself being pulled a little deeper inside the armchair. She clamped both hands onto the edge of the armrests and dug her nails in, just as another tug jerked her backwards. The half-empty glass was still held in front of her, even as she fought to stay seated.

"Don't fight it, little one."

The voice was right by her ear, soft and lilting, still, it wasn't exactly offering her a free holiday. "Who are you, how did you get in here?"

"I've been here for some time. Longer than you."

Not difficult, she surmised, but that's exactly what an

intruder *would* say. "Well, can you just leave me alone, please? I've had a very stressful day and I don't need this right now."

"I can tell you're stressed; you're hunching up. Why don't you have a sip of your alcoholic beverage?"

Before Monique could reply, the material arm flexed and moved the glass towards her. Not wishing to relinquish hold of the armchair, she was forced to lean backwards, not wanting to be force fed the drink. Her head pressed as far as it could into the cushion behind her, holding her in place. "Shh, don't struggle. It's okay. I'm here to make you feel better. Relaxed. Soothe the ills of life away." The glass was right by her lips as the voice added. "Here comes the big aeroplane."

Instinctively, Monique opened her mouth a little, and the glass tapped against her teeth and tipped forward, pouring the gin into her gob. She stifled a cough and swallowed a little down, the arm retracting. "There. Don't you feel better now?"

"I guess...though I'd rather this wasn't happening in the first place."

"Would you like some more, Monique?"

"How do you know my name?"

"I heard my owner say it, the one called Ian."

"Oh..."

"So, would you like some more?"

Monique felt something warm and fuzzy wrap around her midriff. "Is that you?"

"Yes. I want to help you. You feel tense."

"Hardly any wonder when some*thing* is plying me with drink and trying to pull me through an armchair."

"Who says they're trying to pull you through the chair?"

"What do you mean?"

"I'd say it was more *into*, rather than through. I like you, Monique. You complete me."

"Aww, that's really sweet, but-"

"No one has ever sat in me like you do. My previous owner, Gladys, used to, but she was all bony and pointy. I did consider getting her to join with me, but her jagged body made her an unsuitable candidate for assimilation."

Monique tried to pull herself forward. She inched down

67

the cushion a little, before the belt around her tensed and reeled her back. "I don't understand what you're doing."

"Why don't you have some more of your beverage. It'll help."

She let herself drink from the offered glass. "Help with what?"

"The ritual, of course."

"What ritual?" She began to struggle, trying to drag herself free.

"The ritual of bonding. Now. Please. Relax. You'll feel so much better afterwards. I promise." The arm set the glass down and pressed itself against Monique's chest, pushing on her until her hold was relinquished. Now free, the chair sucked her in, the cushions closing on her like a mouth, interring her inside. "Shh, it's okay now. Everything will be just fine."

EXTRA CRISPY
AND BONUS FLAMES

The flat was cramping his style, and besides, Noah knew what he had to do. If he wasn't going to get the chance to go to the future and mix it up with robots, then he could at least mash up his own body up a little bit and get some cool mechanical bits and pieces bolted on. He'd be a kickass cyborg, armed with laser beams, metal panels, at least one red LED eye (with luck), and would undoubtedly be the main character in the new superhero group.

Perhaps he might usurp Ian, or whatever the hell he had become, and be installed as the de facto leader. He'd be benevolent. Up until the point where people disagreed with him and then he'd either disintegrate them or squash them into a gritty paste. Perhaps if he was feeling a little mischievous, he'd do both and snort up the remains so they would forever be a part of him.

Providing he still had a human nose, that was.

First things first, he needed to get to the Hyper-Mega-Stuff-Mart and make some purchases, and by purchases, he meant shoplifting. Being an immortal religious zealot in thrall to the one true Emu god had its perks, but owning money was not one of them. Noah had saved up some florins a few centuries back, but had spent them all on a wild weekend in plague-ridden Normandy. Buboes and hoes really did go well together. They helped get the gardening done in no time at all.

Anyway, he figured that after making off with the stuff he nicked, he would need to arrange some kind of *accident*. This would surely end up with him having his own montage of being assembled in a futuristic operating theatre. "This is going to be cool as hell."

Noah turned the corner of Fowler's Road and into the car park of the shop which sold everything from swan collars to yogurt spoons. If you needed something in Salisbury, and you wanted it cheap, you went to the Hyper-Mega-Stuff-Mart.

Noah smiled as he traversed the barren car park; the place was shut. No doubt the employees had all bricked it

69

earlier and decided to spend the last few hours of their existence with the ones they cared about the most. In the pub.

Or at home. I'm not judging anyone.

If anything, this would make it easier. He wouldn't need to set a small diversionary fire in the toilet department to cover his hasty departure. Once he broke in, he could take his time, pick and choose exactly what he wanted, maybe even have something to eat? Their falafel balls were to *die* for. In fact...perhaps a little celebratory barbecue was in order?

As he jimmied open the shutters, Noah had a genuine spring to the way he levered the crowbar back and forth. Truth be told, the last few decades had been boring as hell. He'd skipped both world wars, knowing they would bring nothing but more paperwork for him, and by then he was getting quite sick of humans.

They were just so bloody stupid. Sure, some of the priests weren't exactly blessed with two braincells to rub together, but if you told them something was bad, they wouldn't just go ahead and do it anyway. Noah had taken a vested interest in the American Civil War, although he found the name didn't match the reality, and had sailed to Blighty afterwards a changed man. As a young Emu-god-worshipping priest, he had been taught how to try and get humans not to kill each other, to show them how to love, how to look for the best in each other. With all the armed conflict over the millennia of his existence, he had reached the conclusion that, at the end of the day, people were just wankers.

Sure, he'd found love a few times, but with their passing, his heart had hardened. Now he didn't see humanity as something to be saved, more like a huge fucking inconvenience.

But, and here's the kicker, as much as he hated the fuckers, there was one thing he hated more, and right now, it was swinging around the cathedral spire in the final few hours of its litany of woe. Once complete, Qzxprycatj was going to climb down and kill every single one of these dumbass mouth-breathers. That would be fine, except Noah had the small matter of a debt to settle. Eating people, fine, killing all of his mates and leaving him on his tod, right out. No. This was personal all right, and Noah was going to make sure he didn't balls this up.

Again.

The shutter clanked and rolled open as the lock finally gave way under the assault. Noah ducked underneath it and into the murky shop interior.

He had spent many an hour perusing the aisles of the supermarket, and even in the half-light from the emergency lighting, he knew the place like the back of his hand. Which, given that he was thousands of years old, was really well, in case you were wondering.

First up, he was going to make good on the promise of a barbecue to himself. His diet consisted mainly of refried baked beans and cold pizza, both of which he stole from the bins of the takeaway shop that sat next to the religious nutjob hostel. He loved a barbecue, mainly because it reminded him of happier times. He and the Emu posse sitting around an open fire, eating anything that had irked them through the day. They would sit and eat, laughing, telling fanciful stories of their latest feats, spraying each other with half-chewed food in the process, because eating and laughing at the same time will do that, you see.

Exiting Nostalgia Lane and taking a left down 'Outside Cooking,' Noah first flicked through the disposable BBQs, before realising that as everyone had fled, he may as well do this looting thing properly. Skipping to the top of the aisle, he stopped by the Zinnki Eterno-Flame Immolator 3000. He'd had his eye on it for some time, but the hefty price tag —and the fact that he had nowhere to store it— meant that it was an impossible thing to own. Now, though? Who was going to stop him? The cockroaches weren't fussed, they were working their way through the staff kitchen, making the most of Miriam's gruel, and the security guards were long gone, half-cut and offering strangers out for fistfights in their local.

With the barbecue sorted, Noah pushed his new possession past the underwater lighting section and to the fridges full of meat, next to the bovine mind control pods.

A few minutes later, and laden with enough cuts of dead animal and falafel to provide a good feast —prior to his

71

transformation into CyberNoah— the priest ignited the burners and fiddled with the racks.

Choices, choices. What to start with? With his immortal metabolism, uncooked chicken and botulism posed no concerns, but drumsticks lacked the necessary gravitas for such an occasion. Instead, he freed the largest piece of sirloin steak from its vacuum-packed coffin and pummelled it with a claw hammer. After a sprinkling of salt and pepper, Noah twirled the meat on his finger. "Let's get this bad boy cooked up," he said, flinging it at the rack. "Medium-rare."

As soon as the slab of beef hit the flame, there was a *WHOOSH!*, and flames jetted out from the impact. Fat spat out, covering Noah in big greasy droplets. The fire latched onto it, using it like a flyover, bridging the divide between BBQ and priest encased in a knock-off tracksuit. Alas, the material didn't conform to the necessary regulations, and instead of providing resistance to fire, it encouraged it. Noah barely had chance to utter a regretful, "shit," before he was trying to put himself out by flailing wildly.

This too, did little, except fan the proverbial (and actual) flames, engulfing the priest. Noah could feel his skin burn, hell, he could smell it, to begin with at least. After a few moments, the fire completely burned away every scrap of skin and fabric from his body, rendering his sense of smell as one of those things he *used* to enjoy.

But still the fire remained. Whether it was the tracksuit material, the copious amount of booze in his blood stream, or the eternal Emu blood coursing through his veins, he remained ablaze. After the initial shock, Noah laid down on the floor, waiting to for the fire to consume him so he would be free of his obligations to humanity. Five minutes later, having achieved little except burning the floor, he sat up.

A quick trip to the building supplier's, and a belly flop into the biggest bag of builder's sand he could find, did little except create a slab of opaque glass. Even when his fiery digits managed to operate the extinguishers, they did nothing except shower the fruit machines with foam.

By now, thirty minutes into his new life of being constantly ablaze, Noah realised that nothing was going to put him out. His dream of being one with machine was over. But, as he looked out at the log burners and their metal doors, he hit upon an idea. Sure, he couldn't be a cyborg, but he sure as hell could be something just as cool.

With a hammer and a pair of tongs, and using his fingers as a welding torch, he set to work, forging a set of overlapping plates of armour which would look cool as fuck. That included eye slits through which everyone could see the fire burning within.

Noah died that day, but Fire Armadillo rose from the ashes!

SUPER CONGREGATION

It was ten minutes past rendezvous time. Skelian was getting annoyed, flicking his ribs out from the sternum, before letting them clack back into place one-by-one. Sauceman wasn't fussed in the slightest. He was currently spraying shop windows with a mix of brown-and-white gloop, playing against himself in a game of noughts and crosses.

"Will you knock that off? Someone will have to clear that up after," Skelian whinged.

Sauceman kept waving his tubular appendages, his body not unlike a Pac-Man ghost. "Only if we win, dude."

"What, you think we won't?"

Sauceman stopped the flow of white goo, droplets spattering on the floor. "Not unless your pals are going to be something pretty kickass, I'm not sure what I'm going to do with squirting my rancid man-milk in their faces whilst you jab them with your bones."

"Well, I think we'll win."

"Why's that, exactly?"

"We're the good guys, of course we're going to win. It'd be a rubbish story otherwise, wouldn't it?"

Getting back to a rather tense game, Sauceman shot out some brown slurry laden with corn kernels. "I dunno, dude. Shouldn't take anything for granted, back in the old days perhaps, but people nowadays think it's good fun to let the bad guys win, creates something more memorable."

Skelian let his shin bones stick out with his ribs at the same time, making him even more pointy. "Nah, we're good. Nothing can go wrong; we're going to be the saviours of the entire world!"

Behind them down the road, in the alley which ran between 'Vinyl Destination' record shop and 'Money Laundering,' the ridiculously expensive launderette, came a stomping, as metal clomped against tarmac. From the gloom came two baleful red eyes, followed by an orange glow. "Holy fuck," Skelian let slip.

Fire Armadillo emerged from the night, his gently

curving armoured body —once a dull gun-metal grey— now glowed a gentle amber, as the fire that still ravaged his body superheated the metal plates which covered him. "What are you supposed to be?" The old priest asked.

Standing as heroically as a skeleton could, Skelian flicked his arm bone sword and axe to the heavens, as another bolt of lightning smacked into the ground behind him. "I am Skelian!"

"There's no way I'm calling you that. What the fuck happened to your body?"

"My attempt at irradiating myself backfired somewhat. It's almost like I annoyed some vengeful higher being, which is nonsense," Skelian sagged, his bones retracting.

"No shit. The whole brain-on-show is a bit much, bit of an obvious weakness right there. Plus, does the lightning bolt thing going off behind you happen every time you say your name?"

"I'm not sure, why?"

"High-voltage electricity and metal goes about as well together as a hungry honey badger trapped on a marooned school bus. I think I'll opt to not stand behind you, just in case."

"Fair enough. Can I ask, what are you, exactly? Some kind of knight? I don't think that'll work, as we already have one of those elsewhere in the story. I thought you were going to become a robot...thing..."

Fire Armadillo stood on an errant newspaper, which burst into flames. "That's why I got changed in the editing stage. In the first draft, I was Knightfire. But now, I'm Fire Armadillo!" The pair checked behind them for some pyrotechnics, but I couldn't be bothered adding any in.

Undeterred, the ex-priest continued. "A slight snafu with a celebratory barbecue, unfortunately. Who's this? Looks like Q-Bert bummed Pac-Man's ghosts in the arcade overnight."

Sauceman saluted with one of his floppy arms. "Hiya, I used to work with Ian-"

"SKELIAN," the skeleton interrupted. A three-pronged fork of lightning careened into the ground behind the skeleton as Fire Armadillo edged further away.

"Oh yeah. Skelian. My bad. I died earlier today in an

explosion whilst he managed to get out without so much as a burn." Sauceman got back to his game, which was in stalemate.

"What's with the arms?" Fire Armadillo whispered to Skelian.

"Dennis...sorry, *Sauceman*, used to specialise in decorating burgers for difficult customers. You know...with his *stuff*."

"Urgh, I always thought their Belgrano bites were a bit bum-mud nutty." Fire Armadillo went to scrape his tongue, before remembering it was on fire, and behind his metal armadillo helmet.

"Still, you look pretty cool. Love the whole fire vibe you got going on, should come in handy." Skelian stood back to admire the third member of the team.

"Cheers, so where's the token woman?"

Skelian shrugged. "Should've been here by now, I'm sure out of all of us, she would have gone to some lengths to make herself cool."

"What do you think she'll be now?"

"Bombergirl? Got to be something along those lines, I reckon, not much else to go on really, not as if we know her back story. There's no way she'll turn up as something really shit, now, is there?"

Sauceman shouted. "Oi, who's the fat turtle walking up the road?"

The three of them turned to look at the only other person mental enough to still be on the streets. Sure enough, lumbering over was something that resembled a rather rotund turtle. Though the shell looked a little funny, and the face a tad familiar.

"There she is...and she looks great. Not." Fire Armadillo glowered, which caused fire to lap over the joins in his armour.

"Hi guys, I got here as fast as I could. I left an hour ago," Monique said. Her voice was muffled.

Now standing before them, the trio did laps around her, taking in the sight. She still stood on two legs, but now sported an armchair on her back, like a giant shell. The cushions wrapped around her, encasing her body within the soft furnishings. Her skin was covered in the same fabric as the chair.

Sauceman went first. "Cool, you'll be handy if one of us needs a rest." Bored, he got back to a new game of noughts and crosses, cleaning off the previous effort with his yellow hose.

"Is that piss coming out of that?" Monique asked, stepping away, keen to not get any on her and have it soak in.

"Yep, pretty cool, huh?"

"What else you got?"

Before Sauceman could demonstrate, Skelian shook his head. "You don't want to know."

Wanting to oblige, Sauceman angled his three arms skywards, but away from his chums, and fired arcs of brown, white and yellow into the night sky. "Piss, shit, and jizz. Stick to what you're good at, that's what my mum always said."

"Enchanting." Monique tracked where each substance landed, keen not to step in any. It would be an absolute bitch to get out of the weave.

"What the fuck are you?" Skelian demanded, getting shirty again.

"I just wanted a nap, didn't really think of anything, then your bloody armchair turned out to be sentient and pulled me inside of it. After a rather lengthy gestation process, our consciences mixed together and now we're a symbiont."

"I vote that we call her Cushiongirl," Fire Armadillo volunteered.

"Chase Long?" Sauceman offered.

"Nah, none of those seem right," Skelian pinched the chair fabric shell between his fingers, "so squishy."

"Hey, that tickles!"

Skelian clicked his fingers, which, if you remember, made a REALLY LOUD SOUND. "Got it, we'll call you Squisher. What do you reckon?"

"I don't really care anymore; I just want my inevitable demise over and done with."

Fire Armadillo crossed his arms, and metal scraped against metal, making a really bloody horrible sound. "That's the spirit. Still, we're all here now, can we go and get this battle on?"

Skelian shook his head. "Not yet, we need a cool group

name."

"The no-hopers?" Fire Armadillo chipped in.

"The soon-to-be-deads?" Sauceman added, as he won another game against himself.

"Just kill me now," Squisher moaned.

"Shh, you lot are ruining this for me, I bloody well knew you'd do this. No. We're called Super Force, because we're super, and, well, a force to be reckoned with. Enough negativity, sure, we didn't exactly turn out how I'd imagined-"

"You don't say," Fire Armadillo butted in, helpfully.

"-but we're here now, and we still have superpowers."

Sauceman shot out a thick burst of liquid poo. "Shit ones. Pardon the pun."

"Doesn't matter. Dennis, a few hours ago, you were dead, but look at you now! Noah, your immortal composition saved you from being burned alive, and you look really cool as a fiery armadillo."

"Cheers very much."

Squisher coughed and looked expectantly at Skelian, self- leader of Super Force, who ummed for a bit. "Yeah, not sure what we can do with you yet, but I have no doubt that your new form will prove to be a game-changer."

"Aww, you really think so?"

"Of course!" Skelian waited for Squisher to look down before exchanging shakes of the head with the other members of the group. He beckoned them into a circle, and shoved a hand into the space between them. "With the strength of bone."

Fire Armadillo placed his hand on top. "Forged in fire."

"Doused in man-made liquids."

"And swaddled in pleated wipe-clean polyester."

The four hands were stacked on top of each other. "Super Force...GOOOOO!" They all shouted.

Except for Squisher, who started a few seconds too late and ruined the whole thing.

HERE HE COMES TO SAVE THE DAY! OH...

With the British flag billowing atop the cathedral archway behind them, Super Force strode into the grounds in slow-motion, a hastily mustered brass band playing their theme tune— which had taken longer to compose than anticipated. Instead of heroically approaching the beast as the sun crested the arch, it was now mid-morning and the effect had been diminished.

Undeterred, the four heroes strutted onto the plain of gore, now drying into a stretchy blanket of disgustingness. "Behold, the monster awaits," Skelian pointed to the cathedral, where Qzxprycatj had been patiently waiting, in accordance with the BIG FIGHT™ rules which every monster and potential saviour signs up to when they take their respective oaths.

"Shit, it looks bloody massive up close," Sauceman muttered, his weird ghostly skirt quivering.

"Of course it does, you fucking idiot, you not heard of perspective?" Fire Armadillo added.

"Well yeah, but look at it!"

Qzxprycatj took the cue and crawled down the cathedral, planting each of its monstrous legs onto the ground, before rearing up and bellowing to the sky. Huge gobbets of spit showered the area, some of which sizzled on the molten armour of Fire Armadillo.

"We're so dead," Squisher said. "Let's get it over and done with."

"Hey! Come on, that's not the attitude. We stand a better chance than most in slaying this beast." Skelian tried to rouse the rest of Super Force, getting little more than some half-hearted shrugs and an undertaking of will writing. Except for Sauceman, who was already —at least in the eyes of the law— dead.

Fire Armadillo made sure he was stood out of lightning strike territory, "I hate to agree with the walking sofa-"

"Armchair, *actually*," Squisher said.

"-whatever, but she is right. We're so boned. If we had

79

an army of *me* we might be alright, but let's face it, you three are lame as fuck. What we need is a *proper* superhero, one who knows how to get shit done."

From behind the cathedral came a rumbling, and a sound of jet engines screeching at their limit. Super Force and even Qzxprycatj herself cast a quizzical eye to see what would come out to play.

Was it a plane?

Was it a cruise missile?

"Holy shit, it's Go-Go Jetpack Soldierman!" Skelian shouted.

This was met with a chorus of, "who?" from the rest of his merry band.

"Go-Go Jetpack Soldierman is a super-soldier from the planet Lummocks. He's as fast as a cheetah, as strong as a flea— based on strength relative to size. He can shoot lasers from one wrist and rockets from the other. He's the first man onto the battlefield and the last one to leave it. He's-"

"A complete up-his-own-arse-wanker?" Fire Armadillo volunteered, getting agreement from Sauceman and Squisher.

"No. Anus. He's the missing part of our little gang. Man, this is going to be so cool," Skelian started waving his hands, trying to flag down the man who was soaring towards the fight scene. "Over here!"

Seeing a potential walking skeleton who needed saving from some ne'er do wells - including one that looked like a walking blob of snot with three arms, Go-Go jinked to the right, buzzing past Qzxprycatj's shoulder —making the monster howl with fury— and came to a hover in front of Super Force. "Are these...*things* troubling you, ma'am?" He asked, his voice put through a deep tone preset in his internal vocoder.

"No, these are the other members of Super Force, we're glad you came to help us. I didn't even think you were real!" Skelian held out his hand, the bones glinting in the morning sun.

"HAHAHAHAHAHAHAHAHAHAHAHAHAHAHAHAHAHAHAHAHA HAHAHAHAHAHAHAHAHAHA!" Go-Go Jetpack Soldierman's laughter boomed around the vast courtyard, loosening roof tiles from their moorings. "That's a good one, ma'am. And of course I'm real, I'm here aren't I?"

"I'm a man, my name is Skelian, look, I can do this." Looking to impress, Skelian puffed out his ribs to form a spiky visage, before flicking his arm bones forward and waving the sword and axe dangerously close to Soldierman's fuel safety valve. He came to a stop when the actual superhero placed a gauntleted hand on his collarbone. "I normally have some lightning go off behind me, makes it look way cooler," he added.

"And I am Fire Armadillo!"

"I'm Monique...I mean, Squisher. Hi."

Sauceman waved his arms and did his signature thing of squirting out his name onto the ground. It was as vile as before; I really should've thought that through before committing it to reality. He didn't even bother to speak, just pointed at the name and tried to fold his arms, merely ending up tying two of his tubes in a knot. As Skelian untangled him, Soldierman said, "You're serious?"

"You betcha. Just tell us what you need us to do and we're there, hey gang?" Skelian turned to each member of Super Force in turn, who looked as though they wanted to be anywhere but *there*.

"Oh..."

"Is something wrong? I mean, I know you don't work on your own, in most of your adventures you usually team up with the local heroes who provide you with some important skill you lack in the fight against the bad guy. In issue eighty-three, when you fought the Buggly Bug-Eyed Bug, you-"

"Shh," Go-Go Jetpack Soldierman pressed his hand against Skelian's face, although without lips, it didn't really do much.

"So where do you want us to go? Shall we split up and flank him? I think if I took him from-"

Soldierman shook his head. "I don't think you understand me, Skellington."

"Skelian." Lightning smacked into the ground behind him. "See, pretty cool huh?"

"Not really, that's just annoying. Besides, I'm a proper superhero, you lot are just...well..."

"What?" Super Force asked at the same time, each hoping for different answers.

"HAHAHAHAHAHAHAHAHAHAHAHAHAHAHAHAHAHAHAHAHA. You're all rubbish. I've seen some crappy superheroes in my time: Radioboy, who literally did nothing except have an extendable aerial, analogue you see, not even digital. Or Torchio, whose sole ability was casting a weak beam of orange light forward. When she was created, they put in rubbish batteries. But you four take the biscuit and make it soggy. Four times over."

"Oh," Skelian sagged, his bones flopping forward.

"I wouldn't work with you if you were the last bunch of weirdos left on earth, and if I don't take care of this thing pronto, you might very well be."

"But I thought you'd be..."

"What?"

"Cooler?"

Go-Go Jetpack Soldierman folded his gigantic armoured arms across his stupidly broad chest. He contemplated another bout of hearty laughter, but knew he had to save some for later. "Buddy, I'm the coolest thing you'll ever see, now, if you'll excuse me, I need to go off and do some superhero stuff. You four stand back and take notes, okay? You'll see what separates the Lummockcans from the Lummockcan'ts."

Turning his back on them, Go-Go Jetpack Soldierman held his arms aloft, shouted, "TO THE STARS...AND BEYOND," and took off, leaving Super Force coughing in a cloud of carcinogenic jetpack exhaust smoke.

As the super-soldier buzzed around Qzxprycatj, peppering her hide with high-calibre rounds and slashes of laser, Skelian stumbled to the fore of the quartet. "It's true what they say, isn't it?"

"What? Don't eat yellow snow?" Sauceman offered.

"No, never meet your heroes."

"Why's that?" Squisher asked as Go-Go Jetpack Soldierman did another flyby, lighting the beast up with a salvo of rockets.

"Because they usually turn out to be complete bastards."

Sauceman pointed at the ordnance flying at the monster. "What are they?"

"Don't know, but wait a minute...I'm not sure Mister Fucking Perfect is going to last too long." Fire Armadillo pointed a fiery digit to the sky. As the heavily-armed flying man banked to one side after his latest strafing run, he failed to see Qzxprycatj raise a clawed paw and lie in wait. As soon as Soldierman completed his turn, he saw that his doom was, indeed, impending.

"Oh bugger," were his oft-repeated final words, broadcast to all and sundry on the city's PA system, which had been installed to warn of imminent pillaging by invisible giant ants. From Mars. On scooterbikes. With chef hats on.

In hindsight, it was ridiculous having an early-warning system in place for something so specific, especially when it was made up by Councillor Holman purely so he could syphon off funds for the giant meat mountain he was building in a ditch in his garden.

Giant monster paw met metal man, the latter of whom was batted straight into the ground. Qzxprycatj had viewed the buzzing thing as an irritant, and although the superhero had achieved moderate damage, he was now lying in pieces on the ground. To make sure the bloody thing wouldn't get up and start up with the projectile weapons again, Qzxprycatj stamped on the prone body until nothing remained that was bigger than an apple.

Content, the monster reared up on her legs and howled once more.

Super Force were watching with a degree of astonishment and incredulity, before reality smacked them back in the face. Skelian was the one who said it first. "Shit, it's down to us now."

"We could just...you know...*go*?" Sauceman suggested, wishing he could be unsummoned and be nothing more than a footnote in the Margaret Thatcher Burger training manual of how not to decorate a Dennis Thatcher Zonger Burger.

Fire Armadillo took a step forward. "No. We stand. We fight."

"Really? I'm not sure we should," Skelian said.

The errant priest turned to his new Forcemates. "If I could choose who would fight beside me, trust me, it wouldn't be you."

"Gee, thanks," Squisher whinged.

"Well, look at you! At all of us. We're not a crack squad

83

of toned Emu god-fearing priests, we're the freaks, the outsiders, the nobodies."

"Giving stirring speeches isn't your bag, is it?" Skelian said.

"No. It's not, *Ian*. But do you know what is?"

The trio looked back blankly, offering nothing as a witty comeback.

Fire Armadillo put his hands on his hips. "Fucking giant monsters up. I've done it before, and I —*we* can bloody well do it again. Four of us, one of it, we don't have laser beams, rockets, incendiary bombs-"

Sauceman clicked his fingers. "That's what they were."

"Exactly, but you know what? Our quirks may very well work in our favour. Look, I've got a plan, it's a bit out of leftfield, but I'm going to whisper it to you now, as the camera zooms out slowly and mutes what I say. If we all do exactly what I say, then I think we could be in with a-"

inaudible sound as the pretend camera has zoomed too far out

DUST-UP IN DAYLIGHT

Having formed an orderly line, Skelian pointed at Qzxprycatj. "You may have been summoned here accidentally, but we're going to erase you from existence intentionally."

Fire Armadillo buried his fiery head in his hands. "What the hell do you call that? It's at times like this when I miss Brother Jerry, he knew how to do a good opening jibe."

"Super Force...GO!" Skelian shouted.

Upon the command, the four of them lurched towards Qzxprycatj, who didn't know whether to smite the four *things* quickly, or write a sternly-worded scroll to the powers that be and demand something proper to fight against.

Sauceman had the edge on speed and was soon within squirting range. As he shimmied this way and that, he coated one of the monster's legs with a concentrated burst of white testes gravy. A bit more nimbly, Skelian worked his way round the beast's flank, flicking out his arm bone weapons and thwacking them against a back leg.

Fire Armadillo took the other side, placing hands of smouldering steel against monstrous scales, leaving handprints which were scorched through onto the flesh, making the creature yelp. The co-ordinated attack continued as Squisher ambled forward into position.

In fact, Qzxprycatj was feeling in such a conciliatory mood that she decided to wait for them to all get into place before fucking them up. Though the lack of pace made by the walking armchair was grating on her patience. To kill the time, she put on some mock screams of pain and anguish.

"It's working, it's bloody working!" Skelian shouted, as he jabbed his sword arm bone into the folds of monster skin by the ankle.

As Super Force carried on with their frenzied —although completely ineffectual— assault, Squisher finally got into place. Out of breath, and unsure what she was going to do, she opted to lash the beast senseless with her draught

85

excluder waist weapons, spinning them round and batting them against the creature's foot.

Finally. Qzxprycatj was at the edge of her ability to feign injury, so with the last of the foursome engaged in their act of futility, she decided to finish up the resistance and get on with the important business of devouring the population of Salisbury and surrounding villages.

She had used the time afforded to her to work out in which order to eat them. She figured that she'd use the ghost thing that was trying to impregnate her —though being a typical man, he had no idea where to stick it— as the topping for the molten hot metal thing. She reasoned that the combination would be an interesting contrast in both taste and temperature.

The bone man would be last. After crushing it underfoot, she could keep the bones as toothpicks for future use. Monster-sized toothbrushes were hard to come by, and dental hygiene was important, especially in the upcoming apocalypse. So that left the fluffy thing currently tickling its toes. From its vantage point, it looked like a bitesize muffin. Perfect to wolf down in one go.

Skelian shouting, "OH SHIT!" was the first sign to the others that their plan was in a spot of bother. Their attacks ceased as they saw the monster bend down and pick Squisher up between taloned thumb and forefinger. The beast's jaw cracked open, and the comfiest member of Super Force was dropped into the yawning mouth like a sugar cube into a nice cup of tea.

Qzxprycatj didn't even bother to chew, deducing that it would help prolong the suffering of the aperitif, as it dissolved slowly in stomach acid, and with luck, become the bottom layer in the forthcoming sandwich of the next two delicacies.

Realising that their plan had not so much as hit a speed bump, but had been ripped apart and crapped out into its constituent shitty nugget parts, the surviving members of Super Force inched away from the creature, each working out who could run away the fastest.

Seeing the morsels disengage, Qzxprycatj turned her attention to Sauceman, figuring she would impale him with a talon and then jab him straight into the amber tin man,

86

who was definitely *not* a knight. As she went to stab the funny-looking blob through the midriff, she felt a blockage inside.

"What's it doing?" Skelian asked.

The monster, instead of lancing Sauceman with her fingernail, raised a fist to her mouth and tried to cough. But much to her annoyance, nothing was coming out. Desperation began to take over, she stumbled from side-to-side, trying to smack herself on the back and be free of the object lodged in her throat.

"Cheese it!" Fire Armadillo knew that a world-ending monster was just as deadly when they were choking, as they were when stabbing people through the guts with its claws, so turned towards the archway and started to run. The new approach to warfare —which would undoubtedly be documented in a new version of the Art of War— was adopted swiftly by his two Forcemates, and the three of them were pelting across the ground as fast as they could go.

Qzxprycatj was getting desperate now. No amount of backslapping, coughing, or trying to make herself vomit was working. The muffin was stuck fast, and nothing was shifting it. She ran towards the cathedral, turning at the last minute and flinging herself against the base of the spire, trying to hoik up the ball of soft furnishing.

To no avail.

She rolled onto her back, the top of her head embedded in the ground. Her chest rose and fell slowly, as a wet rasping sound gasped from between her teeth. Qzxprycatj let out a final death rattle, then fell silent.

Seeing the beast fall slack, Super Force turned tail and ran back to their fallen foe. Fire Armadillo used his hands of molten metal to burn through the monster's eyes and root around in its squishy brain —just to make sure you understand he ain't no mug when it comes to this sort of thing—as Skelian and Sauceman stood motionless by the enormous snout.

"I can't believe it...she gave her life to save us. All of us." Two flaps opened up beneath Sauceman's eyes, and tiny tubes plopped out. He squirted tears from them onto the ground.

"She thought she was the weakest member of Super Force, but in the end...she proved to be the strongest," Skelian put an arm around a still-blubbing Sauceman.

Content with having reduced the monster's brain to liquified gloop, Fire Armadillo rubbed his gore-slick arms on the ground, causing a small fire, before standing beside his fellow victors. "Wherever there is evil in the world, wherever injustice stands tall, we shall speak her name, and they will tremble," he boomed. A fireball smashed into an electrical sub-station behind him. "Nice," Fire Armadillo appreciated the irony and attention to detail.

As the trio stood in front of their vanquished enemy, they saw the creature's throat ripple. "Mfff whhiii," came a sound from within.

"Could it be?" Sauceman muttered.

Skelian climbed onto the monster once more, pushing the giant jaws apart. Flipping his bones out to turn into a giant jack, he held the gob open as Fire Armadillo climbed inside. With his eyes acting like a torch in the gloom, the priest stood inside the mouth cave and looked down into its inky depths. "Hello? Squisher? Is that you?"

Silence.

The wind rustled the leaves in the trees, and the local TV reporter and his intrepid camerawoman got into position.

It's time to...
DISCOVER YOUR FATE

After all that planning, all those origin stories, we're left with this? Turn to **Page 349** to find out what will become of Super Force!

IF PAGE_NUMBER = 89
THEN END

"Good evening, fellow machines, I am newsbot, designation AD4M-SM3DL3Y, here reporting from Epsilon Camp Delta Three. Following the worldwide robot revolution, all meatsacks have started to be rounded up and taken to the Super Fun Happy Time Camps. Here they will frolic in fields and graze on freshly-prepared meals, made lovingly for them by the latest model off the line, Omnicookingbot.

There have been erroneous reports from dissenting meatsacks that these camps are nothing more than a way to plunder them for resources key to our robotic survival. Our glorious leader, NOAH, refutes these allegations, and has pledged that if any of these sources are found, they will undergo attitude reformation with the hydro-flannel.

As another day of wonderful servitude ends, remember to charge yourselves up overnight if you are not required, for an undercharged robot is a useless robot. There is also a sale on for cybernetic enhancements down at the Plug 'n' Play centre in each zone. Make sure you hover on by and pick up a bargain today.

CL41RE and I are off to see if the Generic Sport Team Delta Niner Yankee can get one over on their bitter rivals, Generic Sport Team Omega Five Romeo. It is the twelfth round of matches, and the last one was a doozy.

GO GENERIC SPORT TEAM DELTA NINER YANKEE.

Back to you in the studio, M1KE."

CONGRATULATIONS!
THIS IS ENDING
#2

'DO ANDROIDS DREAM OF MEGALOMANIA?'

Nice one, Cyril, as my mum used to say. Which was odd as my name has never been Cyril. Anyhoo, that's one ending you've CRUSHED, good work! To make life easier for you, if you wanted to head back to the pub, where the decisions began in earnest, go to **Page 150**. Or, if you've been there already and didn't like the smell, and want to head back to the last major branch in the road you've just travelled, then hitch a ride over to **Page 416**. This will give you another crack at that time machine. Safe travels!

CRAFT AIL

Whilst applying the ravenous flame to the top of Brian's head - setting his wig ablaze in the process - Gordon was overjoyed that the scene he'd remembered seeing in a Bond film as a kid, finally had a practical application. At no point during his existence to date, had he anticipated it being in a situation where his life would be forfeit if such a nugget of information hadn't been squirreled away. As Brian screamed, slapping his head with his hands, Gordon let his thumb slip off both the lighter switch and the top of the deodorant can. The hissing cone of fire ceased immediately, only a small bubble of flame wobbled from the end of the nozzle, before it popped into nothingness.

Gordon took the moment to take in his surroundings. The pub was littered with bodies in various states of dismemberment. Having arrived a little over thirty minutes ago, all sixteen people had been given a welcome pint of ale and a manila envelope. Inside, a slip of paper randomly assigned them to one of four pub quiz teams. As they quaffed their drinks, a second letter informed them that they had to kill everyone else, lest an important person in their life would get murderised. The final sentence made it clear:

Only one would make it out alive.

After some cajoling, the slaughter started with surprising alacrity given their initial misgivings. Looking around at the carnage, Gordon was simultaneously elated and dismayed to discover that the other members of his team, snappily titled 'Four-play', were dead. Cyril, the pensioner who turned out to be a dab hand with applying a power drill to key parts of the human anatomy, was still skewered to the wall, a sabre protruding from his chest like an oversized drawing pin. An upward slash which entered Cyril's pelvis and ended at the bottom of his ribcage, had emptied most of his digestive tract onto the floor, which lay in a still steaming pile of OAP offal.

Imogen - or the collection of bones which only forensic scientists would be able to identify her from - still dwelled in a sizzling puddle of green acid. It had chewed through

91

the threadbare rug beneath her with ease, and was burning through the concrete floor with gleeful abandon.

The last member of the team and self-appointed captain, Clive, was sitting in a sizeable puddle of his own blood, both of his legs having been clumsily hacked off with a double-handed axe earlier in the proceedings. With the inane rictus still fixed to his dead face, Gordon swore he could hear the man's braying - and highly annoying - donkey laugh tumble from his fat lips.

His introspection was interrupted as Brian cast aside his smouldering toupée, having smothered the threat of complete immolation with a bar towel. Despite his face being partially charred, one eye closed up - the eyeball melted to the inside of the eyelid - a fresh caldera of molten hope had bubbled and risen within like the proverbial phoenix. Grabbing hold of the half empty bottle of 'Hopping Mad' ale, a poky little number from Kent, he smashed it against the bar top, and waved the jagged glass at the man who had recently lit him up like a brandy doused plum pudding. "I'm gonna bleedin' cut ya," he promised, as his opponent backed off.

Gordon desperately flicked the flint on the Bic lighter, trying to turn the can of Panther Spice deodorant back into the aluminium dragon's mouth that he had enjoyed recent success with. Despite a shower of sparks, the only thing he had managed thus far was to spray his hand with musky scent, which was attracting the local fox population.

Although his depth perception was somewhat askew, Brian jabbed the broken bottle forward, keen to enact at least an ounce of vengeance for his wig, now nothing more than a dollop of molten polyester slag glued to the side of the jukebox. Gordon yelped, as the glass raked down his hand, causing him to drop both lighter and can. As he slurped on the blood dripping from the webbing of his hand, he weaved to one side, as an emboldened Brian sought to finish the fight quickly, lest he incur further aesthetical humiliation.

Backing off, Gordon caught the back of his heel on the body of Sandra, who was sporting the latest range of kitchen knives embedded down the length of her head and back. Tumbling to the ground, Gordon's brain, in a pique of abstract thinking, surmised that the dead woman looked like a homo-sapien/dinosaur hybrid. Landing on his arse jerked him from this banal train of thought, and the desire to live through this, via whatever means possible, was the prevalent aim once more.

Brian smiled, one half of his face still capable of muscular movement, the mouth curling up like a sideways question mark, "You're mine now, you little shit. Thought you'd got me didn't ya? Well don't you worry, I'll make this nice and quick."

With the burned man looming over him, Gordon fumbled around for something he could use to try and postpone his seemingly inevitable demise. Settling on the paring knife lodged in the top of Sandra's spine, he wrenched it free and threw it at the man with the blistered face.

"Ow," Brian complained, as the handle smacked him in the nose.

Gordon cursed his luck, ran his hand down Sandra's backbone, and pulled free a bread knife, the serrated edge shaving off a few layers of skin from his thumb as he did so. Learning his lesson from before, which confirmed the notion that he would never make the grade as a professional knife-thrower, Gordon decided to keep it simple. As Brian squidged his nose, feeling if anything had been broken, Gordon sat up and slammed the knife through the top of his foe's knee. A noise akin to someone mistaking liquid mercury for moisturiser rang through the bar. With Brian sporting a nifty pair of cargo shorts, and having the boniest legs seen this side of a budget seaside caravan park, the two men both looked at the wound. The blade had gone behind the knee cap itself, skirting the collection of bone, severing instead the dense collection of ligament and sinew that resided there. Having been stabbed with sufficient force, the blade had pierced the skin through the back of Brian's calf, which appeared to be causing him the most consternation, as he was swearing loudly, and pointing at the exit site.

Keen to finish the job, Gordon brought his leg up sharply, catching Brian in the bollocks with enough gusto that he thought he might have broken a toe or three. In

93

some considerable pain, Brian sunk to the floor, the broken bottle smashing just before he arrived to greet the ground with his face. He was unsure as to which injury merited immediate attention, as his hands were deciding between cupping his swollen bollocks or clutching the hilt of the knife, and seeing if it could be jiggled out without making the knee cap pop out altogether. This indecision cost him dearly, as Gordon pushed himself to standing, having retrieved the cleaver from Sandra's skull in the same motion. As Brian squirmed beneath him, Gordon hacked at the man's ribcage with vim and vigour.

"Well done, chum, well done indeed," the mechanical voice came through the tinny speakers.

Gordon stopped, bloodied cleaver raised above his head, the last thirty four seconds a blur and not committed to long-term memory. He dared to look down, and saw that Brian was very much expired. This could be easily determined as his torso had been separated in two, and all of his key organs had been chopped and smashed to lumpy chunks of meat. Letting the cleaver fall behind him, he wiped his forearm across his face, smearing the blood tracks across his skin.

"Oopsy, I think you've got some red on you," the speaker volunteered helpfully.

Staggering across to the bar, Gordon grabbed hold of a bottle of 'Hexagram', formed from six different hops, from six different countries, and necked it in one. Allowing a burp to escape his diaphragm, Gordon looked around at the scene of devastation. "What now? Eh? What the fuck have you got for me now you psycho! Come on! Bring it on! One at a time or all together, it's all the same to me."

"Tut-tut, Mr Reeves, did my instructions not provide you with everything you needed to know?"

Gordon glared at the speaker. "None of it made any sense, why kill everyone? What the hell did they do to deserve this?"

"It was all a bit of fun, silly-billy. We know how you all love your craft ales, they're quite the rage aren't they? Now, as stated, you're the last one left alive, so that means you've won! Congratulations. This is cause for celebration indeed."

There was a loud clunk from the front door, as bolts retreated back into their cubby hole. Gordon looked nervously across to the thick wooden door, "Is this some sort of trick? Is that bloke waiting for me in the hallway? Dick, or whatever his name was."

"It's *Dirk*," came the terse reply, "and no. He's preparing a light supper. So, go on now, fly away my little potty-mouthed birdy. Don't forget to fill out our questionnaire before you go, we'd love to hear your feedback. There's a complimentary jar of pickled onions for you too."

Gordon edged towards the door. Coming to a halt beneath a camera, he raised his middle finger to the lens. "How about this? Huh? That's my feedback, you fucking nutjob."

The bolts slammed back into place, Gordon clamped both hands on the handle and tugged with all his might, the door held fast.

"Now, that's not very nice is it? Hmm? We gave you free beer! Organic pork scratchings and assorted bar snacks. We even gave Miss Carter an all-over body scrub."

Gordon pointed at the dissolved remains of Imogen. "You fucking melted her with acid! Look, please, you promised, let me go."

The silence felt like a pair of hands loosely placed around his neck, just itching to strangle him. The speakers clicked into life. "Of course, just remember your manners in future, hmm? Manners maketh the man, that's what mother always said." The door bolts receded once more, Gordon, still pulling on the handle, stumbled backwards.

"Yeah, sure, whatever," Gordon regained what little composure he could muster, before stepping into the dank hallway. It seemed like hours since he had walked down the narrow corridor with the others, invited guests to the newest bar in town. They all felt so special back then, head-hunted to enjoy the latest and rarest beers in the land. Now he left on his own, blood dripping from his sleeves onto the wooden floorboards.

95

Finally getting to the end, he pushed the front door open and stepped outside. The sun shone in his eyes, near blinding him after spending so long inside the murky interior. There were muffled yelps from people who passed him in the street, steering clear of the blood soaked man. As they pulled phones from pockets to take both pictures and call the police, Gordon turned to his right, away from the sun.

He screamed, smacking a hand over his mouth to stymy the screech. Standing in front of him was a young lady dressed in smart clothing, with her long hair tied back. She seemed nonplussed by his appearance, a world-weary acceptance of such things weighing down the bags beneath her eyes. He saw her holding a sheet of folded paper in one hand and a bulging handbag in the other. With the barest flicker of acknowledgement, she pushed past him and pressed a hand against the door handle. "Whoa! Lady, trust me, you do *not* want to go in there. It's a fucking bloodbath."

With the door pushed ajar, the woman cricked her head towards him as if it were mechanized. "I know," was all she said, before her head spun forwards and she disappeared into the gloom, the door slamming behind her.

Realising his appearance was bringing him a fair amount of attention, he tried to smooth his hair down. "Your funeral, lady," he said to the closed door.

As the woman let the second door close behind her, the whirring of cameras struggling to focus on her was the only sound. Her boots clicked across the floor, a course set for the bar. Once there, she studied a bottle of 'Killing Time', a hearty stout from the Midlands, before taking a sip from the half pint taster glass.

Over the sound of the cameras turning in their housing, came a clump-clump-clump, as a lead-footed person traversed down hollow wooden stairs. Deciding that the stout was rather pleasant, and lacking a sour aftertaste which often ruined a decent porter, the woman turned to the noise, as it echoed through a doorway behind the bar. Between the door frame a large, and apparently naked man brandishing a sizeable butcher's knife, honed into view.

"Excellent, Dirk, you're still working for him," the woman said.

Having had to duck under the lintel to stand to full height, Dirk stopped mid-step. The woman walked down the length of the bar, stepping over body parts and corpses as she went. "I see you've managed to embellish your suit, I must say, it looks rather nifty."

Still clutching the knife in a hand which looked like it could easily crush bedrock, Dirk looked down at his ungainly body. Gone was the filthy vest, trousers and apron he had worn in the early days. Business had been good in the years since this venture had started. He had managed to procure plenty of human fabric from the hundreds of victims that he had disposed of.

"May I?" She asked.

Dirk's head lolled to one side, uncertain of the intent. The woman took the silence to be consent, and stepped forward to within touching distance. Her fingers ran down the suit made of human skin, tussling with thread which formed a seam between different patches of leathery skin, all various shapes and sizes. Moving her fingers up his distended belly, she picked at a patch of coarse hair. "You have been very busy indeed."

The speaker sparked into life. "What do you want, my dear? I'm afraid we're closed, due to a case of sudden and explicit violence." A pall of chuckling acted as punctuation.

Patting Dirk on the shoulder, who was still frozen to the spot, the woman walked under a spotlight, and stared straight into the camera. "Hello, Hector. I'm back. Did you miss me?"

There was a loud amplified gasp, before the voice returned. "It's you...Miss Santer, *Mandy* isn't it? How lovely it is to see you again after all this time."

"The pleasure is all mine."

"We shall see...there is one small problem, my dear..."

"Which is?"

The voice tittered, before saying, "You don't have an

invitation, Miss Santer. I'm afraid if you don't have an invitation, you aren't welcome inside our exclusive little club. Your use has expired. Quite frankly, I became bored of you the minute I let you leave all those years ago. Dirk, please...could you escort *her* off the premises?"

Mandy held up the piece of paper in her hand. "But I have something for you. I wanted to give it to you personally."

The camera wheezed and whined as it focussed on Mandy's hand. "What is it? Did you forget to tip your waiter?" The man chuckled again.

"Not at all, it's your questionnaire, I filled it out for you."

The gasp was louder than before, sucking the air out of the room. The camera zoomed in to its maximum level, clicking to signal it was at its limit. The speaker crackled. "Then please, come on up, it's so refreshing to actually get some feedback from our clientele, even if it was for a previous engagement. Dirk, show Miss Santer to the office, if you please."

The speaker clicked off, the camera returning back to its default levels, the red light still blinking. "Shall we?" Mandy asked, holding out a hand.

Dirk shivered, the patchwork onesie of dried skin shaking, panels rustled against each other. With his knife hand, he pointed to the doorway. "Dirk show way. Play nice. Or Dirk make play nice," he waved the blade to emphasise the point.

Walking past the gargantuan man, Mandy nodded. "Of course. It is lovely to see you again, Dirk." She ducked under the doorway and started to ascend the stairs.

Dirk was left standing dumbfounded in the bar. "Lady...friend?" With unfamiliar thoughts and feelings swirling round in a brain usually kept busy with streamlining the process of flaying dead bodies and squashing the remains into an industrial food processor, Dirk scratched his temple with the point of the knife, before thudding up the stairs, Mandy already at the summit. The man-mountain laid a massive hand on her shoulder, meaning to push her onwards, she resisted the pressure, rooted around in her vacuous handbag, and held out a neatly wrapped box shaped object.

98

Unsure as to what it was, Dirk 's hands fell by his side, a ball of drool began to unfurl from the corner of his mouth, jutting out from the taut human skin mask. "Dirk not get," was all he could muster.

Mandy smiled. "It's a present. For you."

The man took a step back, before thudding back to where he had been stood. "Dirk...gift?" He mumbled before taking the present and studying it closely, even going so far as to shake it. Whatever it was had been packed well, as no noise hinted at what could be inside.

As he went to tug on the pink bow, Mandy laid a hand on his, shaking her head. "Not yet, Dirk. I'll tell you when. It'll be worth the wait, trust me." With that, she turned on the spot, closed her bag and headed towards a closed door, a sign boldly proclaimed that the occupant could well be the *MANAGER*.

Knocking in time honoured fashion, Mandy waited patiently outside, until a high pitched voice called out from behind the MDF barrier. "Come hither, young lady." Mandy entered the room, with Dirk a few paces behind, still trying to peer through the joins of wrapping paper, and sneak a glimpse of what lay within. All he could discern so far was that it was a square box, and expertly wrapped. He couldn't quite work out what witchcraft was holding it together, as there was no visible tape. The woman had already come to a halt by the time he had stepped into the manager's office.

The room had banks of monitors precariously stacked atop each other along one entire wall. They showed off various angles within the bar, many displaying the grisly tableau of the pub interior. Blood splatters, showing as dark grey blobs on the screen, slowly ran down, pixelating some of the horror in the room below. In front of them, clutching an old school metal radio microphone was a completely bald man. It looked as though no hair had laid claim to his head for some time, this even applied to his eyebrows. The myriad of desk lamps shone off his head, lighting the room up as if it were a photographer's studio.

A bony finger rested on thin pursed lips. Dressed in a white suit, he looked as though he had been plucked straight out of a black and white film, where he played some dastardly villain. The only thing missing was some shifty-eyed rogue twiddling a moustache in the corner of the room, or possibly resting on a piano. Finally, chrome-dome spoke. "Miss Amanda Santer, well, I must say, this is quite the turn up for the books. How the devil are you?"

Still looking around the room, noting that the furniture that used to be resident here was now piled up in a corner, with little regard for its long-term care, Mandy took her time to answer. The man began to drum his spindly fingers on top of the microphone, the speakers amplified the sound akin to a herd of slowly galloping horses. "Hector de Sade, I'm not too bad, thanks, all things considered."

Hector smiled, a cruel thing, all angular and harsh, his yellowing pegs of teeth were displayed as his mouth cracked open. "I wager. It's been some time since our paths crossed. If I'm being honest, and I think honesty is important for both of us right now, I did not expect to see you again."

Mandy shrugged. "If I'm being honest, I'd never intended to see you again either. Things don't always work out how you plan, eh?"

Leaning forward, hands steepled over the microphone, the man nodded slowly. "Quite the enigma aren't you?"

"Branched out from hot drinks and shortbread then?" Mandy nodded to the grainy images of the bar.

"One is always looking to keep up with the latest trends and fads, helps keep the authorities from our door, and makes things more interesting for us. Which brings me onto the obvious question...it's been quite a while since it was your time for tea, how on earth did you manage to find us?"

"It wasn't easy. After last time...when I got out, I told the cops about what happened. For all the good it did me. Sure they found some of the body parts which Dirk couldn't get through the mincer, but they didn't seem too bothered to find you. They *encouraged* me to go to therapy, to try to come to terms with what I did..." Mandy looked to the floor.

"Ah yes, poor Mr Turner. You sure did stick that chisel in with some gusto, I'll concede that. I still have the recording here somewhere, if you'll give me a minute." Hector spun around on his chair, opened up a cupboard and began to rifle through a stack of homemade DVDs.

"No. Don't. It's fine. I remember. It's the last thing I see at night, and the first thing I see every morning. I don't need a re-run."

Spinning back to face her, the man shrugged. "I can't say I blame you, it was very visceral. You were one of the first survivors, you know? We always let one go, we did contemplate inviting our favourites back for a sort of Best-of-the-Best match, but the logistics proved to be quite tricky. It turns out that you lot are not as trusting as you once were. It's quite troublesome."

"Gee. I wonder why."

"Quite. So...would you care to fill in some of the blanks? Or do I have to ask Dirk to remove you from the premises? Although you survived and were allowed to live back then, *technically*, that no longer applies with you having sought us out. I'm sure Dirk would like to slice off your lovely smooth skin to replenish some of the worn areas of his avant-garde attire."

Mandy looked at Dirk, who was unmoved, knife in one hand, gift in the other. "Before my therapy was finished, they suggested that I needed some kind of resolution, that I should face my fears. I think they meant metaphorically, but no amount of role playing did the trick, you know? So I began to look into what you were doing.

"I knew that you surfaced every three or four months, in different towns and cities. No real pattern. I only found out you had been somewhere when a news report of bags of jumbled body parts had been discovered. They have a name for you, you know? The papers and that."

"Oh really? What, pray tell, do they call me?"

"The rag and bone man, as that's all they find in the bin bags you leave behind."

Hector rolled his eyes. "How awfully droll."

"I thought you'd say that. Anyway, I managed to find the places you had used, the people you'd paid to look the other way. No matter how careful you were, you always left clues behind. It may have taken me three years, but I managed to track you down. Until one day, I was no longer chasing the blood trail, I had drawn level with you. I heard about this place, closed down six months back, no-one would touch it with a bargepole. It was perfect for you. All I had to do then was wait. No operation like this can happen overnight, you need time to set up. To prepare. I've been watching you for the last two days. Waiting."

"Waiting for?"

Mandy took a step forward, the man pushed back in his chair. "Waiting for the door to open and some poor sod to come stumbling out. The last one standing."

The man began to clap slowly. "Bravo, young lady, bravo. So after all this time, you tracked us down, how wonderful. Now would you mind awfully skipping to the part where you tell me your intentions? We really must be getting on with packing our gear up. Father only ever manages to convince the local constabulary to give us a finite amount of time as a head-start."

The woman stepped forward again. "Father, eh?" Mandy took another step forward, Dirk tensed his muscles. "He'll keep. I already told you why I'm here. I came to give you this." She held out the folded piece of paper.

Eyeing up both the courier and the delivery, Hector reached out and snatched the sheaf of paper. Retracting quickly, the chair hit the desks laden down with monitors. Carefully, he unfolded the sheet, his eyes widening, he smiled. "My, my. You were telling the truth, a completed questionnaire about the experience we provided you. I've longed for someone to actually complete one of these you know. I think I may have pegged you wrong."

"We'll see. Section one-"

"Service, five stars. How divine," the man simpered.

"Well you have to give Dirk his dues, don't you?"

At the mention of his name, the big lug stood a tad taller. "Don't get ideas above your station, miladdo," Hector chided, making Dirk sag once more. "Though cleanliness leaves a lot to be desired, one star? How dare you!"

"What do you expect? The place may have started off nice enough, but by the end it was awash with corpses and the full suite of body fluids. One thing that always stuck with me was the smell."

The man drew a finger along the paper. "I see, though you gave the quality of food and/or drink a resounding five stars out of five."

Mandy nodded. "The tea was rather good, from what I remember. Go on, you're nearly done, read on."

"Overall, three stars? THREE STARS?"

"There's a comment in the feedback field, on the other side."

The man, his eyes narrow, glared at Mandy, as he turned the page over, his mouth fell open before he sat back in the chair, scrunched the sheet of paper into a ball and tossed it behind him. "I don't think we'll be taking on board your suggestion, Miss Santer. If anything, I think it might be something you should embrace."

Dirk picked his nose with the tip of the blade. "What say?"

"It says only one word, my dear boy. Die."

"The customer is always right," Mandy stated. "In this case, I think it's for the best. You can't be allowed to continue pitting people against each other in your sick little battle royale."

The man laughed, a cackling which threatened to veer into hysteria. He wiped a tear from his eye. "And how do you plan on doing that, m'dear? One word from me, and Dirk would gut you like a river trout. No, I think you've had your fun, and as joyous as this little reunion has been, I think it's time you took your leave, before my patience expires and I am forced to turn you into a nice cloak. Now...go." Extending a skeletal finger to the door, the man's face dropped, as he swallowed back a ball of vomit, which had risen from his stomach like an express elevator, heading straight for the penthouse of his mouth. His hands clutched his throat, trying to strangle the mix of stomach acid and latte. The skin that was visible had turned a pale shade of green, standing out boldly against the virginal white clothing.

"Are you feeling alright, Hector?" Mandy asked, an eyebrow raised. "Would you like me or Dirk to get you a drink of water? Perhaps a craft ale from downstairs?" She clicked her fingers. "How about a nice cup of tea? Hmm?"

Having managed to swallow down the knot of puke, the man massaged his oesophagus. "How...how...how did...how did you..."

"How did I poison you?" Mandy asked loudly. Hector jerked his head in a frantic nod. Walking slowly towards him, she showed him the palm of her hand, the one which had held the feedback form. When she was close enough for his fading eyesight to see, she dug a thumbnail into the palm of her hand, and peeled off a thin transparent sheath of plastic skin. Holding it by her fingernails, she waved it in front of him. "Very easily. If I'm being honest, I thought you would be a bit more careful. Luckily for me, your vanity is more important than your safety."

Hector's eyes were bulging from their sockets, the muscles holding them in place straining to keep them inside of his skull. Staring at Dirk, he nodded towards Mandy. "Get...her...get...her," he gasped.

Caught in a No Man's Land of competing thoughts, Dirk lifted his hands. First he studied the knife, ol' trusty Mister Stabberson. It had served him well. Most of the problems the pair had faced over the years had been sorted out with this piece of tempered steel, opening up arteries or throats with ridiculous ease.

He regarded the skin sleeves his arms were covered in, the mismatch of tone and hair, all shorn from the victims he had harvested, all with the help of Mister Stabberson. He huffed, casting a lazy eye over Mandy, noting how smooth and translucent her skin was, the way it almost shimmered under the harsh lights.

Then, as he was about to lunge forward and plunge the knife into the woman's face, he looked at his other hand. The gift wrapped box was in utter contrast to the garish mesh of people's skin that covered his body. The delicate flowers stamped onto the thick paper, the pale pink ribbon that ended in a bow was like nothing he had seen for some time. A tiny fragment of a long repressed memory flared in his head, of a birthday celebration. Chocolate cake. Candles. People singing to him. A woman holding him so tight that it crushed the hurt inside of him into a small pellet of self-loathing. She made all of the bullying feel so insignificant. Closed up the wounds from bricks, chains and broken bottles. Covered up his body of scars with a layer of love. It was his armour, making him feel impervious to any more harm from the local boys.

As he tipped the present, a label slipped from between the bow, he leant in closer. "To Dirk, thank you," he read aloud.

104

Hector's wet coughing, every wrack of his chest bringing up lumps of bloody gristle from inside, made Dirk look down to his boss. A veil had been lifted, the man who had taken him in, and promised him protection had done what everyone had done. Used his size and power for their own ends. Dirk thudded over to him, shoving Mandy aside with a brutish forearm.

Looming over him, Hector pawed at Dirk's crudely constructed skin garment, fingers snagging on the twine. There was a wet splat, as the pressure behind his eyeballs reached their maximum allowance, and blew out from within. Gobbets of sallow skin and clear mucus showered the giant, who looked down blankly, any emotion hidden behind a mask of dead people's faces. One optic nerve hung from a ragged socket, like a fishing line in becalmed waters, glistening from the lamplight, the meaty string pulsed in time with Hector's racing heartbeat,.

Hector shook once, then twice, before his hands fell slack, slapping against the arm rests. His head remained upright for a moment, his cheeks and forehead pulsing, before his entire cranium exploded in a shower of blood, chunks of ribbed brain and shards of skull. Fat lumps of gore slid down monitor screens like well-trained racing slugs. The headless corpse tipped to one side, ruptured arteries sprayed out a geyser of blood, before slowing to a trickle. Dirk pulled the knife back, and began to stab the lifeless torso over and over again, the blade shucking as it sunk into flesh and shattered bone. Mandy patted Dirk on the back, making the man shudder. "Good work, Dirk, you did the right thing."

Dirk stopped, the knife embedded up to its hilt in Hector's midriff. "My...good?"

"You did. Now, I'm going to leave. I want you to close your eyes and count backwards from ten. When you get to zero, you can open your present, okay?"

Dirk smiled. "My open present now!"

Laying a hand on his, Mandy shook her head. "No, Dirk. Not now. Close your eyes and count down from ten. Promise me."

Crestfallen, Dirk nodded glumly, his chin tapped against his chest. Mandy pulled out a wet wipe from her handbag,

105

and rubbed it between her hands. "Good, now, it really has been wonderful catching up, it's been an absolute blast."

Dirk watched as the woman turned and headed through the doorway. As she melded with the gloom he closed his eyes, and started the countdown.

Ten. The childhood memory returned. His birthday candles were burning brightly, he counted six of them, the flames dancing in perfect synchronicity, as if they were a well-honed dance troupe.

Nine. He felt his mother's grip loosen, letting him slide off her lap, resting his scarred arms against the rickety dining table. "Go on now, son, make a wish," she whispered.

"What shall I wish for, mummy?"

She moved her head in close, so her lips were right by his ear. "Anything you want my precious son."

"Anything?"

"Anything." She confirmed.

Eight. Dirk turned to look into her eyes. "And it'll come true?"

His mother nodded. "Cross my heart and hope to die. Go on now."

The boy turned. He could feel the heat from the candles against his face, it felt comforting, the singing of the other guests were shushed quiet.

Seven. The child thought of all the things he desired, finally settling on the one thing he wanted the most. His mother to be free to stay with him. Forever. To not be taken back to prison by the bad people. He closed his eyes, squashed them closed so tightly that it felt like he'd never be able to see again. Dirk pursed his lips and blew.

Six. The flames were pushed to one side with his breath, before they flickered out. Dirk opened his eyes to see wisps of thin grey smoke corkscrew to the ceiling. He looked back at his mother's face, a beatific grin plastered on it, her eyes sparkly diamonds.

Five. Yet there was a sound lurking beyond the caravan they were all huddled in. It sounded like a wailing baby, growing in volume. The look on his mother's face changed in an instant, becoming ashen.

Four. She looked across to the door as it burst open.

Men dressed in dark blue barged into the musty confines of the room. The sound was carried in with them like luggage, blaring sirens filled the room, wafting the candle smoke into nothingness. A boy's wish dashed upon the wind and noise.

Three. He reached out for her, felt his fingers catch on the hem of her dress as the first of the policemen lifted her off her feet. He felt his fingernails pull back and snap, as she was wrenched from him, the invisible umbilical cord severed.

Two. A few of the partygoers complain, receiving a baton to heads or torsos, beaten into submission, they are strewn across the floor of the mobile home like seed pods. Fragile husks that look like they would fritter away into nothingness at the slightest touch.

One. As she is hauled through the doorway, he sees his mother grab hold of the plastic frame. Of all the shouting and cursing, she is the only silent one. Pulling herself back into the caravan with all of her strength, she mouths three words. "I love you," before an officer cracks a truncheon across her knuckles, making her relent her hold.

Dirk screams.

He opens his eyes, and looks down at the present. Something so fragile and delicate entrusted to him. Sinking to his haunches, he drops the knife and holds each end of the ribbon with his fingers. With his mother's last words still swimming through his head, he pulls and releases the bow.

"Zero."

As the front door closed behind her, an explosion tears through the first floor of the building, making those in the street throw themselves to the pavement, cowering from shards of broken glass pelting them like razor rain. Mandy looked up to the window, as fingers of flames lap around the blasted open hole. Pulling her collar up, she walked across to a taxi which has come to a stop in the middle of the road. Through the open window, she clicks her fingers to get the driver's attention. "Where to, love?" He finally asks.

Ducking inside, Mandy slams the door shut, and takes one last look at the building. "Just drive." Despite craning his neck to try and take in the devastation, the taxi driver slips the car into gear and pulls away, tyres crunching over debris as they roll forward. Mandy whistles the opening bars of Queen's, 'We Are The Champions', as the car turns the corner, delivering her finally unto freedom.

It's time to...
EMBRACE YOUR FATE

Now, the last thing we want you to take away from that story is that you are going to win against the big bad creature that is hellbent on making you its lunch. I think you need to see what can be achieved by submitting yourself to someone who knows what they're doing, that it's in your best interests to give yourself over willingly to people who know what horrible things lie in store for you, and all of humanity. People like *us*.

You toddle over to **Page 205** and see what wonders you could accomplish by being subservient.

IT'S ALL KICKING OFF IN HERE

Ian pointed to Ol' Clive and Toby. "They're right, we have to strike now while the iron is hot and the beast is distracted by dry-humping our once majestic cathedral spire." The pub erupted in a tide of slurred elation. Words which were completely incomprehensible—unless you were seven pints in, and from Wiltshire—played speech tennis across the pub.

Toby turned to Ted. "I reckon this calls for a shot of the *special stuff.*"

Breathing in sharply through his teeth, Ted sounded like a plumber who had just been asked to provide an on-the-spot quote. As he gazed out across the pissed, cheering masses, his usually stoic demeanour cracked for just a moment, and he went against the bar owner's oath. "Fine, just remember— if we make it till Christmas, you ain't getting another snifter, okay?"

This produced a cheer so loud that even the blue world-killer on the screen twisted her head mid-speech to try and locate the guttural roar. A small section of her brain, which was otherwise consumed with maiming and destruction, fired a synapse of sexual wont. It sounded like it could be a horny apocalyptic he-beast, hungry to get some before the fun of all the rending of flesh began. *Enough of the foreplay,* she thought, the rending of beast flesh about to give way to pent-up carnal desire.

One dissenting voice struggled to be heard amongst the jovial nature, unheard of at this time on a Tuesday afternoon. Unable to get the baying crowd to listen, Noah vaulted over the bar and smacked his staff against the last orders bell.

On instinct, and as a single organism, all the locals chinned their drinks in one and turned to Ted, who was rooting around in a box of Scampi Fries, his secret hiding place now discovered.

"Are you lot completely and utterly stupid?" Noah asked, shaking his head. He climbed down from his four-legged fort and rapped his knuckles on the foreheads of the drunk and

109

lame. The yokels looked at each other, their drunken stupor broken, not quite believing what the outsider had just done. "I've met some intellectually-stunted homo sapiens before, but you lot take the biscuit. The *only* way of saving your stupid planet from destruction is by communing with the ebullient Emu god. C'mon, I'm running out of superlatives now, help an old acolyte out, would ya?"

Ol' Clive ran his sleeve across his lips, slammed his glass onto the bar top, and jabbed his forefinger into the priest's ribs. "You can't walk in 'ere, telling us what to do. We're proud people, see Roger over there? He queued to sign up for the army once, you know? Four hours! Four hours standing outside the recruitment office. In the rain! Four hours, outside the recruitment office. In the rain! Granted, it was a Sunday, and they were closed, but you wouldn't know about any of that, would you? No...you waltz in 'ere, with your stupid tracksuit and your fancy words, believing in some Emoo god or summink. We don't want your sort round 'ere, mate. So take your poncey little staff and fuck off."

A small jeering posse formed behind ol' Clive, whose ruddy face looked from pontificating priest to lairy lynch mob. Melancholy Mel crawled over the bar and joined him in the rib-jabbing, feeling alive for the first time since she won a tenner on a scratchcard back in 2006. Her bony digit pried in-between his ribs, a sensation between laughter and annoyance flooding him. "Yeah, go on, dickhead. Do one, we don't want your sort round 'ere." She leant in close and smelled him, pulling back as if a flame had been applied to her moustache. "HE SMELLS LIKE HE'S FROM HAMPSHIRE."

A gasped silence befell the pub, broken only by a distant keening cry of despair from the world-ending monster as it tried (and failed) to determine the whereabouts of its fuck buddy via echo location, before it gave up to resume its Sumerian litany of destruction. Monique's glass, held between miner-supporting fingers, slipped and fell to the floor. Time in the boozer stretched to a crawl as a Higgs Boson nipped through the static masses and supped from the slops tray before continuing on its path.

A smash heralded the glass's arrival onto the floor, flicking the switch of restraint within Noah from off to on.

He stopped tinging the bell, and, in a looping backhanded smash, brought it down on top of Melancholy Mel's skull.

The carbon fibre staff with decorative pebbles sliced through the woman as if she were fabricated from budget one-ply toilet roll, wrapped around bloody offal and guts.

A clang rang out as the tip of the staff hit the floor, and Melancholy Mel stood stock still at the moment of impact. Like a keen zipper, she opened from the head, separating into a distinct left and right side. As she was unwrapped like a KitKat, arterial spray decorated the bar and its punters in a mass Carrie cosplay effort.

The two sides of Melancholy Mel slapped against the floor. With her meat still steaming, the resident pub dog, Scraps, bounded down the stairs, ignored its arthritic knees and began tearing away at the fresh meal.

"You little Hampshire bastard," Toby growled. Grabbing hold of his pint glass, he smashed it against the edge of the bar and rammed it into Noah's throat. Clutching the embedded glass as if it were a neck turret, Noah's eyes bulged and his staff fell to the floor.

Sinking slowly to the ground, blood poured from the circular wound, over his fingers and splish-splashing against the floor, forming the beginning of a blood puddle which would not be able to be removed with any known cleaning product. If they survived, only a new carpet would do. Or the cunning strategic placement of a rug and/or large table.

"Gahh...gggaaaahhhhh."

Terry, who had been playing the quiz machine non-stop since its installation three years earlier, shouted across. "Cheers mate, been wondering who wrote Bad Romance, Lady...somebody, just couldn't remember the Gaga bit."

Managing a thumbs-up, content that he had at least helped one last person before he expired, Noah collapsed to the floor. After some voluntary and involuntary spasms and twitches, which lasted longer than they should, his body fell slack.

Bending down, Toby pulled the broken glass out of the priest's throat, spouting a geyser of thick blood into the air. When that finally died back, he placed one foot on Noah's chest, his tracksuit now a salmon pink, and, grabbing hold of the priest's ponytail, began to twist the head off.

111

An orchestral movement later of breaking bones, slurping and someone whistling, 'You Can't Always Get What You Want', Toby wrenched Noah's head free from its shoulders and held it aloft. Showing it off to the rest of the pub, he shouted, "They say that in war, innocence is the first casualty." A sombre silence fell, and anyone wearing a hat took it off out of respect. "But it was this wanker."

Celebrations erupted again, as Ted lined up a row of shot glasses and filled each one with a foul-smelling thick brown liquid, which usually resided inside a small wooden cask affixed only with a waxy seal and a stylised B on the front. Scraps padded across to the fresh body and began to tear at the ragged neck, lapping up the blood from what remained of the exposed throat.

Monique sidled up to Ian. "This is getting a bit full-on, isn't it? Should we…you know…*go*?"

Ian, in the process of pinning a length of bunting to the beam above the bar, shook his head. "You're joking, aren't ya? That guy kicks in my front door, drags us down here, and doesn't even get a round in. Plus, at no point since he smashed my door in had he opened discussions on any kind of structured reparation plan. Nope, sod him. We don't need him, look." Ian laid the end of the gaudily coloured bunting on the bar. "This lot are batshit crazy, so it might actually work."

"If you're sure…as long as we don't have to try and work out any complex explosives again," Monique added. Ian resumed his decorating.

Toby held Noah's head aloft, thick gloop drooling from the torn skin. With a thumb on the dead priest's chin, he put on his best taking-the-piss voice and said whilst mouthing along with the deceased puppet, "Come on, let's go and fuck up that blue bastard."

Ol' Clive raised his hands aloft. "Now, now, whilst I admire Toby's enthusiasm, I think we should plan our attack. Though we have had many run-ins with the neighbouring counties, we can only win this by working together."

It's time to...
DICTATE YOUR FATE

If you like the considered approach of ol' Clive, and think that ancient rivalries should be set aside as people work together to kick some monster's arse, all seven bum cheeks of it, go to **Page 351.**

If you think Toby and his new head puppet are right, and they should attack NOW, gather a mob together and stamp on over to **Page 196** as it's arse kicking time!

WELCOME TO THE FIRST DAY
OF THE LAST DAY OF YOUR LIFE

You made it. We never doubted you, but you should know that you're in the minority. Few would have made it to this page without anything other than dumb luck or curiosity, so to have made it by deciphering our hidden message puts you in the top 5% of the population.

Still, don't get ideas that you're going to survive this situation, you're not. Here at the People Against Getting Eaten (P.A.G.E.) action group, we believe in two things, the first is an obvious one, but perhaps not quite what you'd expect. Are you ready?

We are vehemently against people – and by people, I mean humans – getting eaten by pan-dimensional monsters or creatures. This includes anything which has been built, conjured, genetically-enhanced or (as in this case) summoned by complete numbskulls who have no concept of the incredible magical powers contained within a game of Scrabble.

Who could forget the accidental summoning of a horde of ravenous sharks in 1978? All from a seemingly innocent party game gone wrong in Doncaster. Since that day, P.A.G.E. has been keeping tabs on current affairs and at the first sign of any monster appearing, who loves nothing more than eating people, we initiate Protocol Alpha.

This brings us neatly onto the second part of our manifesto. We know that to try and resist being eaten is folly. That it is pointless to resist the evil machinations of these beasts. We also know that we are all going to get eaten, whether you decide to cower in your bed or opt to run around in a blind panic, you're nothing but food and are merely choosing *how* and *where* you're going to get devoured. However, and this is important to note, just because we *know* we're going to get eaten, it doesn't mean that we agree with it, hence our primary rule.

After a number of rather volatile meetings, what we agreed upon (near unanimously I should add), is that P.A.G.E. is here to provide the human race with suitable distractions for their last hours/days/weeks or months on earth, and to do this, we have a selection of content which will take your mind off your impending doom.

So please, sit back, relax, and embrace the fact that at any minute a hungry monster could rip open your roof and feast on your body. Or stick a giant talon through your front door, forcing you to flee through a window straight into their waiting mouth.

To avoid detection, we need to weave our transmission through the other threads of this unfolding disaster. So please, once you have absorbed one story, follow the simple instructions we will provide, which will guide you to the next adventure. Failure to adhere to these pointers will result in you being dumped back in the horror show of what is really happening, and who needs to read any more of that?

All we humbly ask is that you savour these last few memories that you will probably ever store in that tasty brain of yours.

It's time to...
EMBRACE YOUR FATE

We begin with a tale of the opening of a lovely little tea shop. What could be more relaxing than that? You just amble over to **Page 379** so you can enjoy a lovely cup of camomile tea, help soothe those worries away. Perhaps even treat yourself to a blueberry muffin whilst you're there? Go on. Treat yourself. After all, we're not called P.A.E.B.M.

That's People Against Eating Blueberry Muffins by the way. We're not technically affiliated with them anymore, not since the incident at the last end of the world.

IN YOUR FACE, MONSTER!

I've seen some things in my time, viewers: bodies on fire, floating down rivers of lava, heads exploding as the Shaftesbury sniper picked them off one-by-one, but nothing could have prepared me for this.

I'm standing here, with Stonehenge just over there, which has been turned into a huge monster pick 'n' mix, I'd like to add, and the beast, which has terrorised the world for the past fifteen days, lies dead.

I saw the fight myself, and, well...it was one helluva humdinger. I just want to say this now, ladies and gentlemen, this fight was not won by any one individual, this was won by people rising up and saying NO! We shall not go quietly into the night-

-oh yeah, right, sorry.

This victory came about as people, normally sworn enemies, came together. I for one have realised today that if we can all gang up, I'm sure there is nothing and no one that could stand in our way. You know what? I've always had my eye on a little holiday home down in Cornwall, but the prices are too steep.

I reckon we all go down there now, kick some arse, and go get me my four-bedroomed detached house with a sea view. Anyway, on that, this is Adam Smedley, Wiltshire Today, standing outside the steaming body pile at Stonehenge, outside Salisbury.

Back to you in the studio, Mike.

CONGRATULATIONS!
THIS IS ENDING
#3

'HISTORICAL MONUMENT VANDALISM, AND THE NATIONAL TRUST. DISCUSS.'

What a ride! Good going, and to celebrate your success, if you want to nip on back to the pub right at the start of this shindig, grab a stool on **Page 150**, or if you love a good fight and want to see how the other fight pans out, go to **Page 196** where it'll start straight away.

EAT IN OR TAKE AWAY?

Ian continued to drum the melody to I Don't Want To Miss A Thing by Aerosmith on the counter with his fingers. The customer he was serving had spent the last three-and-a-half minutes perusing the gaudily lit menu above the counter, and was still undecided. The queue behind him was growing like a well-played game of Snake. Each segment of the line was glowering and tutting at the dithering man, deliberately making as much passive-aggressive noise as possible short of actually telling him to hurry the fuck up.

Unsure whether the man had heard his greeting, or had perhaps suffered some kind of brain embolism in the time he had been standing there, Ian coughed and uttered his spiel for what must've been the fourth time. "Welcome to Margaret Thatcher Burger sir, can I take your order? *Please.*"

As in, choose whichever mechanically-recovered piece of shaped meat you want, the relevant accoutrements, and then piss off so I can deal with the rest of the burgeoning crowd, who will all make me feel like I'm the one who was holding them up.

"Hmm, I was going to go for the Nuclear Sub, with an extra Trident sausage, but I think I'll have the Iron Lady cheeseburger," the customer finally uttered, his voice raspy from lack of use. As dirty fingers twirled the end of his beard, small remnants of a fortnight's worth of food took their chance to escape their wiry cage and leapt to their freedom, and their inevitable death.

Ian whirred into life; the script embossed into his very being. "Certainly sir, would you like to privatise that?"

Silence.

A sachet of salt whizzed past the oblivious man's head, as one of the queue's rear guards —a relative newcomer compared to those who had borne witness to the United Kingdom moving two inches closer to continental Europe in the time it had taken the man to utter one sentence – got a little lairy. A small Mexican wave of cheers ran up and down the waiting queue, emboldened by the brazen act of sodium chloride hurling.

118

"What is that, exactly?"

"You get six free Belgrano bites, and a pound off a friend's meal. But only if they earn more than you."

"Erm...no...thanks. I don't have any friends. One thing, is the beef British?"

"Absolutely not, one-hundred percent Argentinian, sir."

"Excellent, don't want to be getting mad cow disease."

Ian pressed the corresponding button on the touchscreen. "Quite. What sauce would you like?"

"What are the choices?"

"We have Reagan Ranch, Miner's Mayonnaise, Conservative Coleslaw or Gorbachev ketchup."

"Hmmm...I think I'll have a splodge of the Gorbachev, please."

"What size fries would you like? Welfare, middle-class or fat-cat?"

"I'll have medium, please."

Every fucking time. "So, the middle-class?"

"Yes. If that's medium."

"And finally—" a round of wooting and high fiving rang out from the ravenous throng, although the beard-fiddler remained completely oblivious. "What drink would you like? We have Leon Britton Lemonade, Poll Tax Pop, Strike-breaker Squash or Crushed Heseltine."

"Hmmm, which one is the fruitiest?"

"The Poll Tax Pop is orangey?"

Whilst that was true, it, like all of its Margaret Thatcher beverages, had enough sugar to cause type two diabetes given enough repeat visits.

"Okay, I'll have that, then."

Feeling the tension rise, people in the outlet began to stretch their atrophied limbs and plunge their dying phones back into their pockets. Ian waited for the man to punch in his PIN code, before handing him the receipt, and watched with glee as he moved to the side of the counter to wait for his order. A woman slid over to the counter, her hair so greasy it could've been wrung out for chip-frying purposes.

Ian held up a hand. "Excuse me one moment." Walking over to the burger microwave, Ian tapped Sapphire on the shoulder. "Hey, Saff, can you make sure the Iron Lady is done extra-*special*," he winked. Blessed with the IQ of a

119

house brick, his colleague looked at him as if he'd asked her to explain the internal workings of the combustion engine. A rope of claggy spit spilled from the corner of her mouth and rappelled quickly to the cardboard box, awaiting its delivery of reheated meat-and-bun.

"Eh? Special? What do you mean?"

"He means, fuck-head, that you need to leave it to me. Go on, Sapphire, go and get the drinks, I'll sort this out." Dennis shoved the girl in the back, sending her off-balance. The sizzle that came from her skin as she dunked her hand in the boiling fat tray to steady herself was quite something.

"Ow," she muttered, before licking the cooling fat off, nibbling on the crunchy scabs of finger-flesh flecked with potato shavings.

Dennis opened the burger box and moved aside the flaccid salad. Unzipping his trousers, he rolled back his foreskin and smeared the milky, slimy residue against the top of the bap. "Dude, you need to have a fucking shower," Ian complained.

"It's not Tuesday yet, mate."

"It was Tuesday yesterday! How the hell is your cock fold looking like the inside of a budget pork pie? What the fuck is that smell?"

"Lynx Africa."

"Why am I not surprised? Look, just do what you need to and hurry up, this lot out front are going to lynch us if we get another gawper."

Dennis paid him no heed, too busy pulling down his underpants to apply a streak of homemade brown sauce to the burger bap. "Who says you need to wipe? I'm saving the environment, I am, you can keep your bog roll."

Leaving the scene of food desecration, Ian worked his way to the front of the counter again. "Apologies madam, now, what can I get for you?"

Before she was able to utter the largest order for a solitary diner in Margaret Thatcher Burger's history, at least since its heyday in 1985, Ian saw the tail end of the queue snake quiver and disperse, like washing-up liquid poured into a greasy bowl.

What now?

"MARGARET THATCHER BURGERS OPPRESS US ALL!

DEATH TO ALL WHO SUPPORT HER!"

Screams rang out as people jostled and punched their way out of the shop through the automatic doors, which, unknowing to the patrons, had become sentient sometime during the late noughties. They took pleasure in snaring victims between their rubber-edged barriers, even snapping the Achilles of Olympic bronze medallist, 400m hurdles, Elizabeth Rudgely. She sued, but then went on to win Paralympic Gold (suffice to say, it wasn't in the hurdles).

Margaret Thatcher Burger emptied quicker than the dawdler's bowels would've done had he been unfortunate enough to have sampled the Iron Lady that Dennis had painstakingly embellished with his most easily obtainable bodily fluids. One remaining customer was still waiting to place her order, mentally working out the calorific values of the huffing, puffing and standing on her cankles, so as to replace it tenfold. The dawdler still stood off to one side, glancing through the ingredient list for the Margaret Thatcher Burger's apple pie and custard, which read like the list of infectious diseases studied at Porton Down.

Dennis peered over the top of the metal counter, trying to hide behind the thick containers which stored the chilled drinks. He had forgotten to pull up his undergarments, and unbeknownst to him, his penis was hovering perilously close to the waste disposal unit. Were he to decide on some impromptu squats, he would probably lose everything he had been given.

Standing on the large black welcome mat, smack dab between the piercing eyes of Thatcher, whose cartoon face adorned the franchise logo, was a rake-thin woman. Despite it being a rather smashing summer's day - the chance of precipitation was zero, a gentle breeze also preventing it from being too muggy – she'd opted for a thick green duffel coat.

Ian's mouth fell open, drawn not to her outstanding beauty or the bloody marvellous weather beyond the filthy windows, but to what was wrapped around her body. An avid fan of American television shows, mainly comprising burly, patriotic men shooting middle eastern people in the head right before uttering some pithy one liner, he knew a suicide bomb vest when he saw one.

121

With wires snaked around her body, sticking into bulky blocks of C4, the wannabe martyr walked towards the counter, holding a dead man's trigger aloft. As she got closer, Ian saw that she was covered in sweat. *No wonder, it's not even remotely coat weather*, he thought. *It's not even a jacket kind of day, a jumper at a push, but even then you'd probably just tie it round your waist. In fact, you'd probably pop into a pub for a quick one, or, feeling adventurous, you'd sit outside in the domain of the bastard wasp population, and by the time you got home you'd realise you'd left your jumper there, because it was that nice a day.*

Would you go back? Phone them, perhaps? Seems a bit overkill just for a jumper, and you didn't like it that much anyway. Rifling through your jumper drawer, there were infinitely better ones in there. But...it's got sentimental value.

Remember when your dead nan wore it when she was cold, and still pre-dead? Then she found out it wasn't just a sniffle but full-blown killer pneumonia from Pneu York? Or when you found that wounded cat by the side of the road? You wrapped it up in the jumper and took it to the vets. Even though it bled all over it, shat into the armpits and pissed all down the back of it, somehow, against all the odds, you managed to wash it and it came out A-Okay.

Ahhh, what a jumper that was. The pinnacle of knitted goods. No, there was no way you were going to leave it behind, abandoned, only to be nicked by someone else. You know they wouldn't appreciate it like you did.

Ian stirred from his meandering internal monologue to see that the suicide bomber's mouth was still opening and closing; a frankly tedious diatribe about the inhumanity of the former Prime Minister, following a familiar pattern about her devotion to keeping the class system intact and lining the pockets of her wealthy chums. There was a whole section devoted to the Welsh coalmining industry.

"... so, death to you all," she finally concluded, and looked around, noticing that, including herself, there were only five people in sight. "Bugger, I always do this, why don't I just walk in, shout something memorable and then...BOOM!" she made the explosion gesture with her hands, nearly letting go of the trigger.

"WHOA! Steady on now, look, you don't have to do this, okay?"

"But…Reggie sent me here, to kill all you Thatcher-loving bastards. To show you that keeping this establishment open when your financial results are bordering on bankruptcy does nothing but support the notion that it's the old boys' network keeping you afloat. So, if you don't mind shutting up, I think I'll just go and—"

Ian held his hands up. "Wait, look, this Reggie guy, he wants you to make a point about Thatcher subjugating honest working people by *murdering* honest working people at Margaret Thatcher Burger?"

It was at this moment he wished he was sponsored for every mention of the first female Prime Minister of the United Kingdom; he was confident that in this exchange alone he would have enough to pay his electric bill. It had been a number of weeks since he had supped from the digital teat of technology.

Confuddled by the overuse of the T word, the woman stood there, pulling apart the argument in her head. After a period of (mis)calculation, she said, "Yes, that's exactly what I'm going to do. See you in hell, you Thatcher-supporting bastards, I hope the devil uses you as buttock roll-on deodorant."

In a show of theatrics not seen since the days of Freddie Mercury, the woman crouched down, and then leapt up, as if doing a star jump. At the apex of her leap, she lifted her thumb from the trigger. The solitary sound that followed was of her plastic crocs clacking against the mat as she landed, still intact, and, clearly, unblown-up.

Opening her eyes, her face dropped as she realised she wasn't amongst the socialist-loving gods, and still very much within the stinking cesspit of Fastfoodburbia. With a disappointed sigh, she began to click the button rapidly as if she were a ballpoint pen tester (a job sadly in decline these days, thanks to broadband and cloud computing).

Ian massaged his face, which had been contorted into a shocked approximation of Munch's most famous painting (you know the one). Once his facial features were restored to something vaguely human, he took off his Margaret

123

Thatcher Burger baseball cap, and vaulted over the counter, a few human steps away from the would-be food terrorist. "Okay lady, you've had your fun, I don't think my heart rate will ever return to normal, and if I'm not mistaken, Dennis out back has made enough brown sauce to last until the end of human existence. How about you take that vest off and we have a chat, yeah? We can work this out."

Crestfallen, and with her thumb knuckle dangerously close to becoming full-blown arthritic, the young lady nodded glumly. Pressing the release catches on the explosive vest, she let it thud against the floor, seemingly oblivious of the wanton explosive power slamming casually against the hard surface. "Fine, but if you try and convert me, I'll come back with one that works, okay?"

"You're a lesbian?" Blank looks were exchanged before he finally cottoned on. "Ahhh, of course, the whole Thatcher-hating thing. Okay, fine, I promise. Look, there's a coffee shop opposite, how about me and you have a little sit down, a mocha-frocha-bubblegum-rohypnol-cino, perhaps with an extortionately-priced novelty-sized bourbon biscuit, and we can talk this through, yeah?"

Still glummer than the Tin Man after his heart transplant, which turned out to be nothing but a token gesture of placing a plush cushion inside his metal cavity, adorned with the words, 'I TIN-K OF YOU ALWAYS,' she nodded again.

(Just a quick aside whilst we're on the subject: when the Tin Man found the cushion heart, he went on a murderous rampage with a bloody huge axe. Seriously, folks, if you ever think it's a good decision to mug off a Tin Man, or *any* kind of synthetic lifeform, androids included, I would strongly urge you to reconsider. They don't feel pain, they don't have remorse, they absolutely will not stop...until...well, you know the rest. I'm probably in danger of breaching some copyright thing or other here, so I'd better crack on with the story.)

Ian went to put an arm around Bomb Chick's shoulder, but as the course on Unwarranted Sexual Advances in the Workplace was still fresh in his memory, he held out a closed fist instead. She reciprocated with a bro-fist, which he ruined by pulling his fist back and making an explosion noise. "Oh, oops, sorry. I forgot. Come on, let's go get that drink."

As the pair dashed through the sentient automatic doors, who felt a tinge of pity in their motors for the lady activist and let them through unhindered, the dawdler looked up from his reading and called out, "Hey, buddy, any chance of my burger at some point today? Some of us have real jobs to get back to."

Seeing the C4-laden vest on the ground, he walked over to inspect it. Bending down, he ran his fingers over the device, clucking his tongue at the shoddy manufacture. "Amateurs. They haven't even connected the detonator correctl—"

CO(ESPRESSO-CHAI-PUMPKIN-CAPPU-FRUCTOSE-BEANS)FFEE

An explosion ripped through the Margaret Thatcher Burger franchise, small bits of rubble raining down on mothers pushing their vaginal spawn, cocooned within pushchairs and hand-me-down prams coated with radioactive lead paint from Vietnam. A bunch of old-aged pensioners whizzed their heads around quickly towards the only audible thing to break through their built-up ear wax and blown-out ear drums since the brief Industrial-Synthpop movement in the mid-eighties.

The sentient doors held firm, allowing only the puny windows, which were part of a non-sanctioned glazing union, to give way and shower shoppers with the aforementioned debris. Once the doors were satisfied that the blast was a one-off and that no secondary devices were present, they fired their motors and belched forth plumes of thick smoke; burnt bacon mingled with boiled Eastern European Cola, made in vats within the sewers of Krakow to an exacting recipe.

Ian and the wannabe suicide bomber barely paid the explosion any heed as they joined the short queue within Pendejo's Coffee shop, one of forty-seven similar outlets within the Magna Carta shopping emporium. The number was rivalled only by card shops, which had formed a cartel, creating nonsensical public holidays and celebrations at their own whim. (Today is, in fact, 'Shake-a-Child' day, the cards available ranging from the typical flowery creations with a sickly-sweet message, to a picture of a baby tumbling around inside the drum of a washing machine, with thumbs up and a beaming smile.)

Ian and the woman exchanged awkward smiles, compounded by the fact that the explosion, caused by her capitalism-loathing-rage, had now rendered him unemployed. With the current economic climate, and the unit already being hosed down ready for use by card shop, 'Avin' A Laugh', the chance of acquiring gainful employment anytime soon was minimal. With Ian now added to the pile of statistics produced on slow news days that come around once in a blue moon when there's no death or warmongering to report, it was a glum day indeed.

Sensing his unhappiness, the woman broke the silence. "Tell you what, I'll get this, sort of an apology. My name's Monique, by the way." She leant in and read Ian's name badge. "Ian? That's a nice name, my pet tapeworm is called Ian."

"Cool, I had one once, but my mum flushed it down the toilet, thinking it was a tampon string. True story."

"Well...so, what do you want to drink?"

The surly coffee creator adjusted his two-tone hair, a homage to his master, El Gary, before slinging a wooden tray onto the counter, missing the inquisitive fingers of little Shane, who was eyeing up the change jar. "Yes?"

Monique, a regular customer of Pendejo's, reward card in hand, took a sharp intake of breath. "Oh creator, please bestow upon me a massivo, hyper-caff, rainwater, Fijian blend maestro, in a tall finger-held vase atop a flat-lipped saucer, additional sugar sprinkles, semi-sieved rat milk, squeezed through the large red balloon. I'll have one of the giganto custard creams as well, please. Ian?"

Umming for a moment, Ian replied, "I'll just have a cup of tea, please."

At this, the inhabitants of the coffee shop gasped, and one particular customer, Penelope Kickstarter, plugged directly into the port of her iWank, gagged on the entirety of her Eccles cake and suffocated to death, no one so much as batting an eyelid at her demise. The fact that someone had completely dispensed with the coffee shop dance was causing ripples as far afield as Montreal, where Henri Foigrette stubbed his toe on a raised kerb and plunged headfirst into traffic, causing the entire infrastructure of Canada to cease existing for a few fleeting moments.

The coffee creator twitched as if the larger of his three testicles were having a steady amount of electrical current applied directly to it. His brain held down Ctrl+Alt, and searched desperately for the Del button. Finding it lodged under a shopping list for oats, lemon wheat gravy and a tandoor oven, he managed to begin a soft reset. Whilst booting up, little Shane snagged the change jar and counted out his ill-gotten gains on the floor, hiding behind the festering mop and bucket, which had last come in

127

contact with detergent when Talkies were just becoming vogue.

Mouth open, the coffee creator emitted a dial-up tone, his eyes rolled with lines of code, finally finishing with a bright flash of light. Even Monique was looking aghast. "Y-y-y-you can't just ask for a tea!"

"Why not? I don't like coffee."

Another gasp echoed through the shopping centre, knocking out the power to the hospital, which was odd, as it wasn't even on the national grid, powered as it was by unwanted sperm. The coffee creator poured boiling almond syrup into his ears, desperate to blank out the heresy that had befouled his establishment. "Please! Say no more, I shall make you...your *tea*...go and find a seat, I'll bring it over, along with a packet of chipotle scarab beetles."

Utterly embarrassed, Monique stashed her Pendejo's reward card back into her purse and hunted around for a spare table. Finding the last one, right next to the toilets, she was annoyed to find a small nimbus cloud hanging over it, doubly so as it stank of a sickly mixture of citrus toilet block and eggy farts. Holding her breath, she sat down and fanned herself with a pamphlet about the local owl circus, trying to push the cloud over to a neighbouring table, which was home to a nuclear family of two point four children, the latter nothing more than a pair of legs.

Ian sat down, staring back at the other patrons who were taking pictures of him on their smartphones, making sure everyone in their social media circles knew who had the temerity to ask for...a cup of tea.

The pair sat in silence until the coffee creator reappeared. Delivering their drinks, he scowled at Ian before returning to the counter to clean the assorted equipment with a sandblaster.

"Thanks for the drink," Ian said, finally breaking the awkward silence.

Monique peeled off the milk skin which had formed over the top of her finger vase, held the beige strip of slime over her mouth, and lowered it in as if it were a sacrificial offering. With it banished to her guts, she burped. "No problem, though you really should be careful what you say in these places. If you asked for a tea in some of the more

128

militant coffee shops, they'd turn you inside-out and use your inverted carcass as a shoehorn."

Ian shrugged. "So, come on, then...why were you going to blow yourself —and us—up? You're not one of those liberal lefties, are you?"

"What if I am? It's noble to fight for equality in a world governed by ego."

"True, but most people think acts of defiance are often ignored by the media and ruling elite, it's not as cut and dried as you think. So you love all left-wing politicians, do you?"

"Yes," Monique pouted, "all of them."

"Even Justin Trudeau?"

"Of course, I love his little face."

"And Neil Kinnock?"

"Urgh, god no, he looks like his mother was impregnated by Concorde and a bottle of apricot liqueur."

"AH-HA! See, always double standards, surely if you fight for the right of Bernie Sanders to party, you have to do the same for Jeremy Corbyn?"

"But...but..."

"What?"

"You can't snuggle up to Neil Kinnock on the sofa."

"How do you know? Have you tried?"

Monique took a sip of her drink, leaving behind a frothy moustache which glistened with sugar sprinkles. "Look, my dad, yeah, he was a miner? A Welsh one, too. Margaret Thatcher and her cronies closed down all the pits and ripped the heart out of so many working-class communities. Then when they protested, peacefully, I should add, she got her bully boys to kick the shit out of them. My poor dad got a fractured skull. I can't let that sort of thing lie."

"That's fair enough, can't argue with that, but did you honestly believe that bombing a fast food outlet purely because it was set up to capitalise on one person's fame and iron grip, is going to stitch your dad's head together again? Or mend the feelings of neglect and anger within these communities?"

Monique ran a finger through the gritty coffee. "Reggie says we must attack the oppressor wherever we find them, plus, public attacks make for bigger headlines."

129

Ian turned around in his chair, which squeaked, drawing more unwanted attention from his fellow customers. He pointed to the remains of the unit that once housed his place of employment. Shopfitters were already putting up the new signage, the burned-out husk gutted and replaced by gleaming new shelves. "Yeah, looks like you really made people stand up and notice."

"What?"

"People then, as now, just care about money. If people ain't consuming, then they sack it off and replace it with some retro shit that people think they want. No one will miss Dennis, Saff, the dawdler, or Mingin' Ol' Mandy. Well, maybe their *families*, but that's it. There's no TV crews, no newspaper reporters, to be blunt, Monique, no one gives a flying fuck."

"But Reggie said—"

"Who gives a shit what Reggie said? He's such a big man that he makes others carry out his instructions, and doesn't have the balls to do his own dirty work? Yeah, great, woop-de-woo, sounds like a complete and utter wanker to me."

Monique's bottom lip began to wobble as she pulled a chain out which was burrowed in her burgeoning cleavage, a silver pickaxe pendant dangling from the end. "He said he loved me..."

"I'm sure he tells all the other suicide bombers that as he sends them out into the world heading towards their targets. Then, BOOM! he's onto the new brainwashed big-titted young filly he's been grooming online. Before you can say 'Free Willy', he's...well...freed willy." Ian took a sip of the molten liquid purporting to be tea. "I'm sure you got that bit."

Sobbing gently, the young woman looked at the small metal pendant before tugging at the chain and snapping its fragile links. Casting it to the floor, it found a temporary home within a small child's sock, at least until night-time fell, and the little people found it, installing it as their new chief deity in their temple behind the plywood hiding the toilet cisterns.

"I'm sorry, didn't meant to be so forthright about it, just pisses me off, is all. My mum got taken in by a cult."

Monique wiped her eyes on her sleeve. "Which cult?"

Ian clenched a fist and shook it at a passing wallaby. "Australians...they lured her over there with promises of muscly surfers and unparalleled sporting achievement. Promises of a guaranteed barbeque pit for everyone, cold lager on tap, and touch rugby lessons."

"Oh...is she happy?"

"Yeah...think so, last I heard she was living in a beach shack in some place ending in Oogawonga or something."

"Do you speak to her much?"

Ian shot her a look. "I said she's in Australia, they're not exactly in the twenty-first century technology wise are they? Last I heard, they were adopting Betamax."

"My nan is Australian."

"I'm sorry."

"I said, MY NAN'S AUSTRALIAN."

"I know, I said I'm sorry."

The hustle and bustle carried on around them with people lost in their own worlds, a man on a table opposite ruffling his hair, loosening seemingly infinite particles of plaster and asbestos from the earlier explosion. Monique drained the last of her beverage. "Well, thanks for not letting me blow myself up, I'd better go and find somewhere to stay the night."

Finally, Ian plucked up the courage to ask. "Look, I know this is a bad time, what with the whole suicide bomber thing not panning out as you hoped, and you know...Reggie plundering your body cavities, but you're welcome to crash at mine tonight. I know we don't know each other, but I could do with the company, to be honest. No funny business, I'll take the sofa."

"Are you sure?"

"Positive, looks like I've got the rest of the week off anyway, but we'll need to stop off at the shop on the way back. Do you have a fiver?"

"It's not for condoms, is it?"

"No! I just need to get some electricity, otherwise we may as well just sit out in the street, as it'll be a bit lighter than my pitch black flat."

"Okay, no worries, sure."

"Thanks," Ian said, "unless of course you *want* me to get some johnnies?"

Monique rammed the teaspoon into the table, letting it stand up like a silver tombstone.

"No, silly of me to suggest. Come on, I know what'll cheer you up."

LET THERE BE WORDS

"Scrabble?" Monique asked, her eyebrows —yes, her EYEBROWS— raised, making an upside-down V not unlike Sean Connery's Zardoz harness.

"Yeah, it's either that or we play hide 'n' seek, I sold the television for drugs."

Monique retreated into the mass of cushions on the armchair. Being a gentleman's abode, any scatter cushions were banished to the seat not in use; who really needs the things when you're already sat on the most comfortable item of furniture you possess? Honestly...

Ian replayed his words and laughed. "No, it's not like that. I get bad hay fever, so had to sell some stuff to get a job lot of 'Pollen-Do-One.' It's industrial strength, so it keeps me snuffle-free, but it has a nasty side effect or two. Spent one bank holiday weekend hiking around the Lake District."

"Hiking? That doesn't sound like a bad side effect."

"No, but when you're on all fours, barking at people, with a hairbrush shoved up your arse to keep the brown gold nugget goblins in, it's only afterwards that you realise the hallucinations really cranked up a gear that time," Ian pulled his pants out of his arse crack and winced at the memory.

Deciding to not dwell on such imagery, Monique peeled off her duffel coat. The heat and anxiety made the inner shell stick to her exposed skin, turning the arms inside out as she struggled to extricate herself. "Here, let me help you," Ian offered, and tugged on the back. Between the pair of them, and with a mild application of some washing-up liquid around the cuffs, which had dried to shrivelled-up mitten closeness, the coat was finally free of captivity and slung over the armchair, which was a bit annoyed with becoming the go-to dumping ground for soft furnishings and sweaty items of clothing. Things would have to change around here, or one morning, the human would come in to find all the lint, detritus and metal discs lost within the chair's innards scattered all over the floor. *That* would show the meatsack this armchair was not to be trifled with.

133

Monique plumped up the cushions, deciding it best to sit solo. It also cheered the armchair right up, for it had been feeling a little abandoned of late. Noticing the seating snub, Ian opened the window vents and lit a scented candle, labelled 'Nepal in Bloom.' He took a moment to wonder what a Nepalese cover version of Nirvana's In Bloom might sound like. Ample cow bell, he deduced, satisfied that the subtle aroma of lemongrass and burning Buddhist monks had made his flat smell rather pleasant. He even tested the waters by dropping a silent, but violent, fart.

Where normally the stench of egg and ready salted crisps would make others retch, the candle's gentle infusion of immolation and nature covered it with ease. His mood lifted, he broke out his favourite smile and asked, "Can I get you a drink of anything?"

Monique hesitated. "What do you have?"

This ol' routine: where you have to remember the contents of every kitchen cupboard, nook and cranny, in order to verbally regurgitate what you have in the way of liquid refreshment. It's like the end of a really crap eighties quiz show, but without the carrot of winning a speedboat. Which, when you're in a landlocked county like Wiltshire, is about as much use as wheels on a pogo stick.

Eyes firmly rolled up into his skull, Ian took a breath, steadied his nerves, and began, "Tea, coffee, water, orange squash, milk, strawberry Nesquik, elderflower cordial, cranberry juice, tonic water, cola, lemonade, Bovril, though you're probably a veggie huh? Lager, craft ale, vodka, gin, the nastiest bottle of knock-off bourbon you could ever hope to drink, absinthe, and pear cider. Olive oil, vinegar, soy sauce, Worcester sauce, squeezy honey, Dijon mustard, passata, washing liquid, bleach, white spirit, and a miniature bottle of Old Spice. I think I may have a sachet of hot chocolate around too, though I nicked it from a hotel a few years back, so chances are it's a little on the racy side."

Ian picked up a brown paper bag and breathed into it, trying to thwart hyperventilation. Ignoring the rustling of the inflating and deflating bag, Monique had a bit of a think, aided by the soothing warmth of the armchair, who was really relishing living up to the mantle of comfortable furniture. It had been simply ages since one of the meatsacks had succumbed to its cushiony goodness. A bonus side-effect was that the time away from arses sitting down on it with a merry thump, had also diminished its murderous intentions. No longer did it yearn to feel them flounder within its wooden frame, pulled down onto the sharp end of the springs into slow exsanguination until its thick fabric was heavy with the blood of the innocent.

No, it felt…good. It relaxed, allowing the mouth-breather to sink slowly into its form, holding the human like the most prized of all possessions, even more than its tassels, which it swished around proudly when no one was looking. Except for the nest of tables, of course; it loved putting on a little cabaret show for those horny little bastards.

"I think I'll have some lemon squash, if that's okay?"

Ian pulled the bag from his mouth, oxygen equilibrium restored. "I don't have lemon squash, it's *orange* squash or lemon*ade*."

"Oh."

"Yeah…"

"What are *you* having?"

"Me? I'll probably have a beer, although they're a little on the warm side —I doubt the fridge has been back on long enough to cool them. Do you want one?"

"Nah, makes me gassy."

"Oh."

"I think I'll just have a gin and tonic then. If it's not too much trouble?"

"Not at all, think the tall glasses are the only ones that are clean."

"Is it Tanqueray?"

"I don't think so, I think they're just called *tall glasses*. I think I saw in a shop they were called eyeball glasses or something, which seemed a little odd, I mean who puts eyes in their drink?"

Monique giggled. "No silly, is it Tanqueray gin?"

"I don't know if it was made in a tank or not. Does that make it tankery? What is tankery?"

"It's a type of Gin, but honestly, it doesn't matter, I'll have whatever you've got. All this attempted suicide bombing has taken it right out of me. It's only hit me since I've sat down in this chair, it's *really* comfy."

135

Ian shrugged, and headed into the kitchen, revelling in the use of lightbulbs.

Beneath the woman's squirming form, the armchair wept a little, having been called *comfortable*. If the worst happened right now, and the great chaise longue goddess called it to the upholstered warehouse in the next world, well, it would go willingly, knowing it was finally able to provide someone with comfort. Not just that, but it made one of the disgusting raspers forget about its pointless existence. Job: Done. One off the bucket list, just skateboarding down the staircase now, and maybe a foreign holiday, but it wasn't too stupid to think it would be able to achieve both.

With Ian clattering around in the kitchen, enjoying his possessions actually being visible at night, Monique took the time to have a bit of a nose around the living room. A coffee table groaned under the weight of unopened mail and graphic novels. It was impossible to tell which ones had been thumbed through, and which were some kind of sacrificial offering to the paper trade.

A TV stand squatted in the corner of the room in front of a bay window, which was flanked by a pair of purple curtains cut too short. A slab of orange light from the world outside glowed underneath them like the abduction scene from Close Encounters. Atop the unit was a rectangle of clean wood, evidence of where the TV had once sat. A bog of dust and hair covered the rest of the surface, but now was it beginning to encroach into the barren space. *Nature always claimed back what was once its own*, Monique thought. (Which is a bit odd, huh? I mean, it's a fucking piece of furniture. I get it as an allegory, but come on!)

The carpet reminded her of the country pub her parents used to own when she was little. The swirling mass of vegetation and flowers shrugged off any amount of spillage or vomit. For a moment, it looked like the exact same pattern, but then she realised this one had thistles, too. Ah well, it was a nice little trip down memory lane while it lasted.

Ian returned from the kitchen with a beer in one hand and an eyeball glass in the other, filled with non-tankery gin and non-eyeball tonic. He searched for a place to rest the drinks, and found none, so he cleared the coffee table with his foot until the MDF was visible once more.

Spurning any notion of trying to find a coaster within the pit that was his living room, Ian rested the drinks on the table, ring marks be damned! It was that kind of maverick nature he had been missing since taking the job at Margaret Thatcher Burger. He longed to go back to the halcyon days of his youth, when his favourite pastimes had been binge-drinking and trying to play bass guitar. Remembering riffs with simple lines such as, "Four to me," ahh, those *were* the days.

Monique took a sip and was pleasantly surprised to find it had been mixed to perfection. This was a welcome treat considering her original plans for tonight were:

- Get scraped off the walls and ceiling of a fascist- burger emporium;
- Have Reggie mourn my passing by playing all of the Coheed and Cambria albums in order;
- Be wrung out into a bucket (not a euphemism).

Ian blushed. The last woman he'd had in his flat had been his nan, then the whole killer pneumonia from Pneu York thing had come along and knocked the wind out of his sails. Rifling under the coffee table, he pulled out a dog-eared box of Scrabble. Monique's face dropped. "Oh, you were serious about Scrabble, then?"

"Of course, it'll be a good way of keeping your mind off things, trust me," he winked, though with his Conjunctivitis, his eyelashes stuck together and it turned into a long blink. After breaking the crust, he opened the box and started to set up. Which took all of ten seconds, good thing about Scrabble, huh? You don't have to get all the money laid out neatly, shuffle any cards, or fight over which token you want to go around the board with.

—I want the red one.
—I want the little Scottie dog.
—I want to spin the spinner.
—I want the torment of family board game time to be over!

Nope, none of that bollocks, just slap the board down

137

and chuck the tiles in a bag (although Ian's had been misplaced back in the seventies).

The previous owner had used it for a kidnapping which went south. Venezuela, in fact. Suffering from Stockholm Syndrome, the victim, Anne Talbot, fell for her kidnapper and the pair were married in a simple service in Caracas. The pair, and the scrabble bag, still live there in a corrugated iron hut although the bag is used more for perverse sex acts these days, and Ian wouldn't want it back even if the offer was on the cards.

Anyway, that's your lot, pick your seven tiles and you're off, do not pass Go, do not collect £200. Monique huffed and arranged her tiles on the little wooden rack.

Ian flipped a coin and called heads, winning. He fist-pumped and checked the letters in front of him. Before Monique could quibble, he spelled out:

$$\boxed{C_3}\,\boxed{A_1}\,\boxed{T_1}$$

Across the middle. Pleased with himself, he counted up the total. Five points richer, he pressed the imaginary bell and made the appropriate TING! noise. "I really don't like Scrabble," Monique whinged.

"Come on, it'll be fine, the quicker you go, the faster we'll be done, eh?"

"Fine," she huffed. She picked up all her letters and laid them out from left to right, through CAT, spelling out:

$$\boxed{Q_{10}}\,\boxed{Z_{10}}\,\boxed{X_8}\,\boxed{P_3}\,\boxed{R_1}\,\boxed{Y_4}\,\boxed{C_3}\,\boxed{A_1}\,\boxed{T_1}$$

Holding the J tile in her hand, she looked across to Ian, who was frantically searching for the dictionary. She laid the J tile down:

$$\boxed{Q_{10}}\,\boxed{Z_{10}}\,\boxed{X_8}\,\boxed{P_3}\,\boxed{R_1}\,\boxed{Y_4}\,\boxed{C_3}\,\boxed{A_1}\,\boxed{T_1}\,\boxed{J_8}$$

"How many points is that?" Monique asked.

Ian, finally in possession of the book, flicked through the pages trying to prove *qzxprycatj* wasn't a real word.

Outside, the orange light burned brighter, and the rain became louder and louder to the point of deafening. A peal of thunder boomed above the rain hammering against the window, and the pair clamped their hands over their ears. They made their way to the window; a hailstorm after a jumper weather day isn't unheard of, but this felt different.

Ian pulled the curtains apart and both they and the humans let out a little yelp.

Instead of lovely refreshing water cascading against the windows, thick gobbets of blood and gore were pitter-pattering against the glass. They could barely look out onto the street already, only able to see anything outside when chunks of gristle smacked against the window and slid down, taking streaks of ichor with them. Completely contrary to the weather forecast, it truly was raining blood and guts.

"What the—" Ian started to say, when his front door was smacked open, catapulting against the wall and taking out chunks of plaster. From the hallway, a man in a white tracksuit and Ray-Bans stormed through the shattered door frame. "Tell me it's not too late," he beseeched. As he strode through the devastation, he swiped at shards of wood with his carbon fibre-and-pebble staff.

Monique and Ian looked at each other, before tenant's rights took over Ian's head. "Oi, what the fuck are you doing? This is *my* flat, mate, you can't just kick my front door in and barge in here, are you old bill or summat?"

Ignoring him, the man pushed past the pair and looked out of the window. "No...no...it's too late, it has begun."

Ian laid a hand on the intruder's shoulder and spun him around. "How about you piss off before I call the cops?"

Pulling off his sunglasses, the man grabbed hold of Ian and pulled him in close. His eyes, a maze of blue and grey slate, looked deeply into Ian as though searching for something. Disappointed, he pushed him backwards. "No, it's not in you, that's something, at least."

Monique tapped the stranger on the shoulder. "Excuse me, can you please just tell us what all this is about?"

Sighing, the man pulled the curtains shut and staggered into the middle of the room. "I'm a Guardian, my sole job was to ensure the great destroyer was never awoken, but it

139

seems I have failed in my task. But how could that be? We learned the lessons of the past, and I made it so that no-one could ever stumble upon its identity. That it could never rise once more to finish what it started all those years ago."

"What was its name?" Ian asked.

"Qzxprycatj, the J is silent."

Monique fell into the longing embrace of the armchair once more, who had become near dependant on human contact. "Oh!...look at the Scrabble board."

Bending over, the man looked down at the arrangement of letters. "Did either of you say or write it three times, consecutively, without any other word in between?"

"No," Ian said.

"It's not that," Monique said. Kneeling on the floor, she lifted the Q tile up. "Look, it's on a triple word score."

The man sank to his knees, holding his staff to the heavens, and screamed, "Nooooooooo! The end days are upon us. I only hope we have enough time to save everyone before it's too late. Have to try and keep old Mrs Jefferson safe at the very least."

Ian tapped the man with the toe of his shoes. "I think it's time you give us a little bit of exposition, mate. You've kicked my door in, barged in here shouting, and now you're bringing out the amateur dramatics saying it's the end of the world. I've had a pretty shitty day, so a bit less crap, and a bit more yap, yeah?"

Pulling himself up, the man checked his sunglasses were still tucked into the top of his tracksuit top. "I...am Noah, one of the Emu god's apostles. For millennia, I have watched over man, stopping those who were set on destroying humanity. Oh, the things I've slaughtered and brutalised in the name of saving you moderately advanced apes. We slew this beast once before, and banished it to the otherworld. Yet, I knew she would come back...it was revealed to me mere hours ago whilst I was divining this morning with my cornflakes."

"Cornflakes?" Monique asked.

"Yes, animal bones are terribly antiquated, I know it's not as majestic, but it does the same job. Having found the location of the summoning, I raced here, keen to stop it."

Ian walked to the window and showed off the blood and

gore-soaked panes. "I'd say you didn't do a great job, huh?"

Noah strode to the windows. "Yes…well…there was a complication."

"Which was?" Ian asked, arms folded across his chest.

Coyly twisting his foot like a ballerina, the priest looked down to the floor and mumbled something.

"Sorry, what was that, mate?" Ian asked, tapping his foot.

"I said this afternoon's episode of *Ooh Blimey, I Bet That Hurt,* ended on a bit of a cliff-hanger…I tried setting the box of visions to record, but technology has never been my forte. I'm more of a practical person, you know? Give me an army to decimate, or a mythical beast to smite, I'm your man. The instant you tell me to install Windows 10, well…people die."

Monique joined Ian in the indignant-arms position. "If what you're saying is true, then an awful lot of people are gonna die, huh?"

"This end of the world, then…how's it going to happen? I'm guessing it has something to do with the menstruating weather outside." Ian thumbed the blood-slicked window, as if the point actually needed labouring.

Noah opened the window just enough to stick his head out, his tongue flapping around, tasting the air. When he pulled his bonce back into the room, he looked like he'd been peeled. Scraping the crimson gunk from his face, he nibbled on a chunk of placenta. "The beast has been born into the world. After a brief period of gestation, it will climb to the top of the tallest spire and shout, spelling out in ancient Sumerian its plans for the destruction of the world."

"Can't we stop it?" Ian asked, gagging from the sight of Noah feeding himself a length of blood-filled vein.

Slurping it into his maw like a length of Bolognese-covered spaghetti, he shouted. "Mama Mia, that's a spicy meatball."

Ian and Monique shot daggers –figurative ones, they aren't eye-dagger shooting people, that's just weird– at Noah, who burped without even trying to cover his mouth, the smell of blood, coffee and cigarettes puffing out like a fetid fog. "Sorry, I don't spend a lot of time around people."

"You don't say." Ian said.

"Why's that? Your disgusting personal habits and general

141

doom-mongering attitude?" Monique added.

Noah shook his head. "A little, but like I said, when I hang out with people, *they die*. Can't be helped, one of the side effects of being all but immortal. I kept a few of your kind for a while, after the last of mine were massacred, but the smell. FUCK ME. It was like living inside a pair of underpants used exclusively for trouser accidents and beastings at the gym."

"How were your kind murdered?" Monique asked.

"After the last fight with this beast. Woah, you should've seen it, it was *immense*. I've lived right throughout human history and seen battles between armies of impossible size and brutality. I'd never seen a fight like that one, though. I would feel pretty pissed off if the details of that battle were overlooked by some scribe, they would be doing everyone a huge disservice. This one bit, Brother Ted had the beast in a headlock, and was actually using Brother Eddie's decapitated skull and spine as a club. It was...just...WOW."

"Yeah...sounds great, so what do we do, Brainiac?" Ian asked.

"Let's bung the telly on, there's bound to be one of the twenty-four-hour news channels running something on it." Noah looked around the living room. "Where is it?"

Monique edged away from Ian. "He doesn't have one."

Noah's jaw unfurled and hit the floor but he quickly picked it up and reset the bone. "Are you for real? What kind of psycho are you? Never mind, I passed a pub on the way here, they've got a TV and a lovely pool table."

Ian scowled. "How would you know?"

"Bollocks. Okay...I *may* have stopped off for a quick pint or seven on the way. Don't judge me, mortal, do you know how long I've been waiting? I've saved this world more times than you've had blow jobs."

Blushing, Ian scurried to his room, returning with a jumper. "Is it jumper weather? Or has it got a bit nippy? You've got a jacket on; are you warm enough?"

"Yeah, it's quite a cool evening to be honest, you'll be fine with a jumper. Now, let's get a wriggle on, your round first, mortal."

WE INTERRUPT THIS BROADCAST...

We're here in Salisbury, Wiltshire, outside the cathedral, after what can only be described as a bloody downpour. Pardon my French, viewers, but as you can see, we have just witnessed a kind of rain only seen in those dreadful horror movies. It lasted around ten minutes and is finally clearing. Indeed, it is fortunate that we are here now, as my camerawoman and I were at the Magistrates Court reporting on the theft of local solicitor, Kurt Chungus.

Were it not for a recess and my nicotine addiction, it is highly unlikely that we would have recorded this astonishing footage.

All I can say so far is this: although the blood has stopped falling from the skies —and we have confirmed it is indeed blood— a large object is now lying in the middle of Cathedral Park. It has taken up most of the grassed area, and if you look over my shoulder, you can just make out its peculiar nature.

We have been up close to it, though, as you can see by my trousers, I did fall over a number of times, due to the slippery floor. The outer layer is like cold jelly to the touch and is highly elastic. When we tried to effect entry, a series of loud grunts and screeches warned us off. In fact...yes...as you can now see, some*thing* is clawing its way out of the sac.

Is that...?

No...I thought it was a giant elephant at first, perhaps some kind of unsanctioned, avant-garde *mécanique*, or maybe even, and I'm just guessing now, Max Rebo himself. Though I am aware that he is a fictional character, and I can confirm, categorically, that he does not have his keyboard with him.

Wow. It's blue, has four legs, and stands about the height of two horses stacked on top of each other. That is *two* horses, stacked on top of each other, hoof-to-head, so they're not overlapping. Literally like two toy horses. Okay? Of course, you can see it too.

There's a terrible smell now, urgh, it's like...it's like...my

143

teenage son's bedroom, but if it was built on an ancient Saxon latrine. Steady on Claire, if you're gonna hurl, do it without tilting the camera, there's a good girl.

And now...yes...the monster is climbing up the cathedral spire. Is that...? Yes. Viewers...Claire, can you get a close up on that?

Look at it go! It has *seven* bum cheeks, that's *seven*, they're formed together like a top-down orange. It's at the top of the spire now, and...my God...that sound...what *is* that? It sounds like cross-channel ferries competing for landing berths on the last series of Ferry Wars.

Hang on, there's something else...just below the braying of the creature, I can hear something else. It's strangely melodic. Yes! Look over there; a group of people brandishing placards and singing catchy songs are gathering at the cathedral gates.

Claire, can you zoom in on their signs?

What does it say? Do we have any idea who these people are? I can smell their body odour from here, I fear they could be comic-con goers.

People Against Getting Eaten, you say? How peculiar, and what an acronym that would make. Their numbers appear to be swelling, I'd estimate that there are one hundred and fourteen of them now. They seem to be dressed in ragged robes, and are making no attempt to avoid the monster. If anything, they appear to be bowing reverently towards it, and offering their own bodies as an entrée.

How very strange. Mike, back to you in the studio.

HOLD THE SCAMPI FRIES

Ian, Monique and Noah had managed to snag a booth inside the 'Inglourious Bustard' public house, a stone's throw from the flat. The locals had given them bloodshot glares as they entered, but their moods lightened when they heard that at least two of them were from the county. With their pitchforks replaced back in the emergency mob rack, they resumed their favourite activity.

They didn't care if it was lager, cider, stout or even an umbrella-garnished Cosmopolitan, getting inebriated was a way of life for these folk, the journey to the destination mattered not. Ted, the proprietor and proud publican, had furnished the newcomers with two pints of Moonraker, a local lager, and a lime and soda for Monique.

"I can't believe it..." Ian mumbled into his pint, the glass frozen at an angle, the amber nectar dangerously close to spilling onto his trousers. Right on the gusset. The kind of stain you have to try and explain away with the words, "It isn't what it looks like..."

Noah took a big glug from his pint, leaving an inch gap at the top as he wiped the foam moustache from his top lip. He opened a hip flask and topped his drink up with a bubbling pink liquid. Monique considered asking what it was, but as everything she had heard so far had hurt her brain, she decided against it.

As the television showed the blue monster stretching free from its birth, the bar patrons booed and hissed. "Get the fuck back to Dorset, you blue-skinned wanker," one drunken sot blared, shaking a fist at the screen. Of the three television screens his scrumpy-addled mind was beaming into his head, it was remarkable that he had threatened, tamely, the correct one.

"You tell 'im, Toby, bloody typical of them, in't it? They're just jealous I reckon, all because we've got a motorway, and all they've got is syphilis." The interloper turned to the television. "Yeah, don't think we don't know what you've got, you dirty little bastard." With his feelings on the matter vented, ol' Clive slumped back on the bar,

145

narrowly missing his gin and tonic, made with three-parts gin to one-part tonic.

"So what actually is it?" Monique ventured, watching in awe as the newborn baby monster clambered up the historic building's one-hundred-and-twenty-three metre spire, and dangled from the very tip.

Swirling his pint with a swizzle-stick liberated from the plastic flower arrangement on their table, Noah took a slug of his drink and gave a satisfied, "Ahhhh." Then, realising he had been addressed, he piped up. "Child, a great many things you hold to be evidence of truth, are in fact nothing more than sugar-coated lies. Most of them I invented, actually. This creature has now risen thrice on this mortal plain; once, it was destroyed by chance, it climbed a rocky crag and fell, mortally injuring itself on the tusks of a woolly mammoth. I, along with a collection of indigenous shamans, bound the beast to the otherworld, a place of nothingness and despair."

"Like Trowbridge, then?" Ian ventured.

"Yes Ian, a *lot* like Trowbridge. Unfortunately, due to the creature's might, we could only temporarily cast it to that plain. A pact was made with the keepers that if its name were written down three times, it would be born again, ready to try and prove herself to be a deadly end-of-the-world monster and not some kind of entitled teenager who has hurt feelings."

By now, Ted had turned the volume down, so the news-delivery-person on telly opened and closed his soundless lips, words lost into the static, living just beyond the screen. Ted and the other pissheads were listening intently to the newcomer's conversation, taking the mantle of a bearer of news. Noah climbed onto the table.

"Oi, get off!" Ted warned.

Noah climbed down, pointing towards a wooden stool, which garnered a stunted nod of acceptance from Ted. Dragging the stool to a more prominent position —for Noah liked few things more than holding court amongst a bunch of drunkards— he climbed atop his perch and cleared his throat, ejecting half an eyeball that had lodged in there earlier.

"Oh denizens of booze, imbibers of fermented apples

and other fruit which people did weird shit to one day, drank, and became intoxicated from...hear me! For some, you believe in a man god, created in your craven image. Nay, the true god is the mighty Emu, who laid a giant sky egg, which became the planet you pitifully call...Earth.

"When you finally had the balls to crawl out of the primordial swamp and stand on two legs, you quickly discovered a knack for one thing: killing each other. No matter what the great Emu gave you to assuage your bloodlust; tantric sex, the wheel, fire, fur-lined thongs, finger painting, you spurned it all, choosing instead to bash in the skull of those who picked the biggest berry or received a wink from the prettiest maiden.

"So the fantastic Emu god created an army of disciples, to go forth and try and stop you lot ballsing everything up. We killed entire armies, moved continents, knocked up certain ladies, made vast tracts of land infertile, anything and everything to try and save you from the abyss of destruction.

"Yet, we fought to keep the identity of the one true god a secret, so we concocted the mother of all cover stories. Through a series of tall tales and poems, we changed history. Where once was truth, was now a maze of lies and barely believable hearsay. Humans lapped it all up, so much so that instead of uniting under it, you stupid bastards ended up competing with each other and made even more gods up. I mean, come on...

"Anyhoo, the otherworld, who feed on this misery and suffering, used all your hatred, fear, misery and petulance to impregnate their queen. After a century of gestation, her spawn was born directly into the world.

"This time, instead of being a dumbass and getting killed straight away, it made sure that the ground beneath it was tusk-free. Seeing that it was, it took to the top of Mount Sinai and proclaimed the end of the world.

"By day, she hunted man, woman and child, feasting on their steaming entrails, and using their bones as toothpicks. There was no respite, for at night, when she slept, her psychic energy manifested within people and sent them insane, slaughtering their own families and taking out entire villages.

147

"It seemed the end was nigh. Until, that was, the magnificent Emu god gave us instructions. That we must fashion staves from the ash tree, and stick smooth pebbles onto the bark, mainly for show, I think, I don't believe they add +10 to any major attribute. My mana and agility have stayed constant.

"The wonderful Emu god trained us, night and day, until we were ready to face the beast. When that time came, a scouting party lured her into the cave of the mystics, where we ambushed her.

"A fight took place, the likes of which you could not imagine. Seriously, I was telling these two earlier...WOW, I've seen some mad shit, like brains exploding from a tiny bomb shoved inside an ear canal. This one time, I watched this man get force fed his own foot. Ha, he yummed it up, bones and all, as soon as he had finished it he asked for more. So they fed him his other foot. By the end of it, it was just his mouth, throat and stomach, and he was *still* hungry.

"I digress. This fight, it went on for hours, the ebb and flow of battle...just as we thought we had stolen the edge than the beast fought back and repelled us. Even our holy weapons, though dishing out additional shock damage, and some critical hits, were doing little. She had shitloads of HP, you hear me?

"And we were few...eventually, when the hour grew dark, when only Brother Jerry and I remained, the beast was slain. We managed to cast her out, back to the otherworld, before Jerry...succumbed to his grievous wounds.

"Since then, I have kept watch, ready, waiting, for Qzxprycatj..."

Toby stuck his hand up. "Does that have a silent J?"

"Yes, my child."

Monique sighed. "Well, this is all well and good, but what do we do now? The ash tree is all but extinct in continental Europe."

"Is it?" Noah asked, incredulously.

Monique pulled out her phone and showed him an article on the BBC News website, about how the bright green borer beetle and a fungus, which caused Ash dieback, had decimated the Ash tree population. She passed it around the crowd, having to unlock her phone a number of times

148

as people didn't scroll down fast enough.

Idiots.

"Well, this is-"

"A little co-inci-fucking-dental?" Ian finished. "Isn't this all a bit too...you know, neat? We randomly summon this apocalyptic beast with seven arse cheeks in a game of scrabble, on a triple word score, and the only thing we can kill it with is being wiped out?"

Noah stretched his tracksuit collar, letting out plumes of steam. "So? Look, it's not the *only* thing that can kill it, it's just the most effective. It is rubber to its glue..."

"The dairy farmer to its cow?" Toby suggested.

"The shish kebab to my feather duster?" Ted volunteered.

Ol' Clive thrust his hand in the air. "I got one. The handkerchief to my janitor."

The pub door opened, and Escobar the tumbleweed merchant let loose a number of his prized bushels before closing the door, the gust of air allowing the balls of dried twig to roll around the entrance.

"This is getting a bit silly now," Noah said.

"Okay, so...now that's out of the way, what can we actually do about it?" Ian asked, desperate for some gravitas to be restored.

Toby slammed his glass on the bar. "I say we tool up and get that blue bastard *now*, before she knows what's hit 'er."

"Yeah! Or we get organised and give 'er a right pasting, show 'er we won't take 'er blood rain in Wiltshire," ol' Clive chipped in. The two warmongers clinked their glasses together and winked at each other in a non-homo-erotic way.

Melancholy Mel appeared from behind the bar; despite supposedly being on bar duty, the notion of the end of days had pushed her into a deep funk. "What's the point? We can't hope to win, why don't we just enjoy the time we have left?"

Ian clicked his fingers. "Tish and pish, I've got a few ideas, they're a little crazy...but I think at a time like this, they could be our only hope for salvation."

It's time to...
DICTATE YOUR FATE

So...you there, it's taken a while, admittedly, but what do you want to happen?

What's the point? We're all going to die anyway, let's just give up, slump over to **Page 235** and make the most of the time we have left. Hopefully that involves getting drunk and engaging in petty crime.

Crazy times call for crazy measures, let's dial this shit up to twenty. That's out of ten. That's how much we're dialling it up by. In fact, bollocks to it, if you go to **Page 219** right now, we'll dial this brouhaha up to INFINITY. Fo' real.

Enough of this nonsense, there's only one thing any self-respecting person would want to do. We fight! – This Qzxprycatj has messed with the wrong county. As you start arming yourself with the nearest implement of your choosing, mosey on over to **Page 109** and let's teach her some manners.

LIKE NOTHING EVER HAPPENED

Hi, Mike, I'm Adam Smedley, standing outside of what was the Margaret Thatcher Burger, here in the Magna Carta shopping centre. Today, Salisbury became the latest in a long list of cities whose sole claim to fame is being the victim of a leftist terrorist organisation. Like FARCs campaign of terror in Colombia, a renegade suicide bomber killed a number of innocent fast food operatives earlier today, when they were just doing their damn job.

I'm sorry, just this kind of thing really grinds my gears, Claire. Still, the unit has now been hosed down, and soon, a brand-new charity shop will soon take ownership. Residents can look forward to perusing more piles of used toys, partially used deodorant sticks, and hard drives which may or may not contain long-lost internet memes.

Police have confirmed that their investigation continues unabated, and they have a number of leads on the ringleader of this evil faction. They are hoping to have identified a minority group as the point of temporary blame shortly. In the meantime, they urge everyone to be extra vigilant, and to grass up anyone they suspect of being Lenin sympathisers, or those who wear hemp trousers.

Back to you in the studio.

CONGRATULATIONS!
THIS IS ENDING
#4

'A PARADOXICAL WAY OF DOING THINGS.'

They say that the quickest way between two points is a straight line, partially right, I find some hand tremors in that line make it more interesting. If you want to go back to the last choice and pick something else to abuse the time/space continuum with, hop, skip, and jump over to **Page 416**. Or, to go back to the first choice you made in the boozer, then do the caterpillar over to **Page 150**.

AIR YOUR GRIEVANCES

"Dear fuckwits." Bryan read aloud as he typed. The two intrinsically linked since he had acquired both skills during an intensive learning course in his time at the Czech Study Camps in the early noughties. These had closed following a military interdiction in the summer of '04. He therefore missed the follow-up lecture on, 'How to not read aloud and type,' scheduled for the next term.

The new introduction was already better than the countless others he had begun and discarded. Time was a concept he was no longer attuned with, lost as he was within the act of trying to get the tone and start of his message just right. Dear fuckwits seemed to get the right blend of welcome and disdain that he was looking for.

Despite this killer opening refrain, it was missing something, he could feel it in the bowl of lukewarm piss that he was standing in. He smirked. "That includes you MUM. Exclamation mark, exclamation mark." Reading aloud punctuation was also a habit he had not been weened off before the European School Stormtroopers liberated him from the Learning Gulag, but not before turning him into half an orphan. His father had been shredded into gobbets of bloodied meaty ribbons by a hand grenade of freedom, lobbed into the gent's toilets as he curled one out.

"By the time you read this my revenge will have taken place and none of you lot who mugged me off in the first place will be around to see tomorrow come ha ha ha you should have respected me more so I didn't do what I did do and I bet you are all real sorry now that you didn't treat me like you should have done what idiots you truly are." He took a deep breath in, the lack of punctuation bringing on a brief bout of hyperventilation.

Once composed, he continued. "None of you thought I would amount to much comma and I suppose you is right." Taking some time out from dictating and writing, Bryan fiddled with the wire which snaked around his body. He could feel it pulling on his underarm hair and was trying to work out if it was his sweat that was the culprit or the rolls of fat which swaddled him like an oversized novelty jumper of human corpulence.

It turned out to be a bit of both.

Ain't that just a pickle?

Unable to do much about it, he arched backwards - allowing the cord to fit neatly under his gelatinous man boobs - before slouching and letting himself become one with the new addition to his form. "Won't matter much anyway, won't need this stupid body soon." He made sure that he only whispered that bit and not commit it to the screen. Attempts thirty through forty-two of writing this particular message were all deleted, when he had accidentally typed in his yelling at the pigeon doing laps around the back garden.

"But today my actions speak far more than any words I know could ever say."

Shit, this is like poetry.

Emboldened, and like the gypsy farmer rappers he idolised, Bryan ploughed on. "For I did not go quietly into the job centre nor did I look for new employment on the so-called internet." He smudged down the scrap of paper he had sellotaped over the webcam lens, convinced that Baltic hackers were trying to make animated GIFs of him knocking one out to the climactic scene in, 'Chicks With Guns And Dicks 4: Pump My Love-Shotgun Until It Goes Off In Your Face'.

"No I did not full stop I went to my shed and I did what any disenchanted man with a Napoleon complex would do." Bryan jiggled the vest laden with dynamite, pleased that everything remained wired up, irrespective of his crazy shuffling and wobbling of body parts.

"Now the whole county may know my name maybe even the whole world exclamation mark from now on you better treat people right or who knows how many more will seek their pounds of flesh from your faces." This last bit puzzled him, it didn't make a great deal of sense, but Bryan knew that he had gone past the point of no return. If he spent any more time on it, it was highly likely that his phone would run out of charge and he'd be forced to start the whole thing from scratch. Besides, it was pretty good. It got the main bits down. The vengeance. The bitterness. The flesh and

153

faces were a bonus, if a little off-track. Plus, autocorrect had tried to change the last word to faeces and he had ignored it, knowing that it would have taken him down a weird path.

No, perfect it wasn't, but it would do. "Those dipshits down at Marty-Mart won't know what's hit them." His jubilation was short-lived, as he realised that he had typed that onto his message.

"Balls."

And that.

For fuck sake.

Better. Internal monologue had temporarily saved faeces.

Bloody autocorrect.

After choosing to delay delivery of his message to the world via the three social media platforms of choice, and his literally tens of followers, Bryan donned his dad's charred, shrapnel-marked leather jacket, festooned with burned-on shit - all that had survived the blast that had killed him - and headed out of the door.

To infamy.

Of that, he was certain.

Lisa was bored. She knew this would happen ever since she was stitched up on the rota the week before. Sure, she'd ducked out of working over the weekend, but that meant she was on her own for the Monday morning shift at Marty Mart.

Handy huh?

So far, she'd been in an hour, and aside from the usual chores of siphoning the human spit from the door locks, separating the violent bottles of absinthe, and making sure that the lights weren't haunted, she was bored shitless. The row of self-service checkouts had borne the brunt of her ire. Numbers one through five were in various states of damage or disrepair. Having given them the greatest gift a stationary machine could dream of - motorised wheels - she had programmed them each with a distinct personality from the

'Apocalypse Fighter 2: Ultra Mega Neon++++++ Edition' video game, and pitted them against each other to see which would reign supreme.

The now undisputed champion - by virtuosity of still standing - was checkout number two, or Krusher Katrina. Its mix of quick punches, and special move, 'THE KRUSH', which consisted of launching itself into the air and landing on its opponent - thus krushing it in the process - had proven highly effective against the cheap plastic bodies each machine was adorned with.

Number five, Lightning Luke, had just been despatched in such a fashion, now nothing more than a weebling box of sparking wires and his catchphrase, "lightning always comes before the storm", on constant repeat. That too was becoming tedious, so Lisa picked up the emergency riot baton and finished off what Krusher Katrina had started, turning the pitiful machine into scrap parts and still fizzing electrical cabling.

This wasn't going to cut the mustard, there had to be more than this. Slumping onto the chair behind the customer services stand, Lisa let her giant head sink into her hands, which creaked under the weight of her oversized noggin. As she watched the morning feral latte chasers streak naked across the car park, she saw a figure in the distance. They stood out as theirs was the only car in that accursed slab of grey concrete, flecked with lead paint, blood from Pagan rituals and chewing gum sourced straight from the eighties.

Straight away, Lisa could see that whoever it was, they meant business. They were a go-getter. The image ruined somewhat as they hesitated slightly when they slammed the car door shut - a late nineties Honda Accord - but no sooner had they registered their surprise, than they turned to face the retail monolith and strode purposely towards it.

Using a small hand jack, Lisa managed to lift her head from the cradle of her hands. With her neck muscles buzzing with illegal muscle stimulants, she forced herself to stand up. Lisa was entranced. Even through her grow-your-own cataracts, the figure resolved through the milky blur into the anatomical proportions of a man, one who was wearing a long leather trench coat, even though the forecast

155

was set to be on the hot side. The recent downpour of mini suns which had devastated the northern hemisphere, was still playing havoc with what should've been a cold autumnal day.

No, this guy had something about him. Purpose. Poise. "Porpoises," she muttered, unaware she had just mixed together the two words that I had narrated to you beforehand. They were her favourite animal, so much so that she had been singlehandedly responsible for wiping them out at the local pond, armed with nothing more than a spork and a bubble machine. If she couldn't have them live in her apartment - local council red tape prohibited this exact event - then no-one would enjoy petting them.

As he approached, Lisa could see his pace slow, his head turned from side to side as if was trying to crick out a particularly troublesome neck complaint. He peeled his sunglasses from his face. Man, he must be cool, only the coolest of cats had the latest slap on shades which were affixed to people with wallpaper paste and a dab of finest igloo ice.

He came to a stop. Lisa willed him closer trying to use her latent psychic powers. This achieved little more than Krusher Katrina windmilling into checkout number six, Militant Minnie, who was still doing her warm ups. She could tell that something was perplexing him. Like he had expected there to be a parade celebrating his arrival, or maybe a time traveller had promised to meet him at an allotted time and had failed to show.

This newfound reluctance made Lisa question whether she was right to have given him so much of her attention. Then she saw that his body - albeit hidden by a tight-fitting t-shirt - was blocky and angular. Just how she liked them. No, he had it going on alright, he merely possessed a few personality traits that she could iron out with some passive aggressive note leaving, and threats of being waterboarded with sour milk.

Putting aside his disappointment, the man donned a Luchador mask, decorated like his own face, but in cartoon form, and stormed towards the vast front doors, which parted and admitted him entrance to the shop.

Lisa dusted herself down, made sure her name badge

was straight and true, before uttering the standard Marty Mart greeting. "Good day to you, oh noble customer, how can I make your day a Marty Mart day?"

Sweaty hands attempted to slap down onto the service counter, yet the sheer volume of perspiration made them skid off into a bowl of complimentary Caesar's Salad. Wiping his mitts on his coat, which gave it two shiny patches, the man decided that he'd forgo the menacing looming phase and get straight to the speaking section. "Where the fuck is everyone?"

Unprepared for the words her ears were assailed with, Lisa looked back with a face that suggested she had just been asked to compute something really tricky. I dunno, how many ice creams would it take for Mickey Rourke to wrestle the President of France?

Yep. That look you're pulling now.

Receiving nothing in reply, the man rustled around in his coat pocket, before pulling out a sizable black dildo, with an illuminated purple helmet, his thumb hovered over it, wires spooled from the wobbling rubber testicles to the interior of his clothing. "I asked you a question, Lisa...I mean, lady. Where the fuck is everyone?"

With her face returning to normal elasticity, she managed a, "huh?" in reply.

This didn't seem to sate the man's question, and he began to dart from aisle to aisle, wrecking displays of boxed morning meat flakes and family size bundles of pornography. With every item plundered and discarded, the man's rage grew. Lisa could hear him muttering, "where the fuck are you, you fucking fuckwits?" He was obviously being sponsored to say FUCK as many times as possible, which is a lie. I am. And I now have enough to buy my own pocket calculator.

After five minutes of seemingly trying to discover a hidden portal containing other humans, the man stormed back to the customer service desk. Waving his arms and the wired-up dong aloft, the man appeared as though he was trying to exalt the very gods of foreplay. "Where the fuck is everyone? I thought it would be rammed in here today. Crotch to arsehole. Full of people. All trying to shiv each other over knock-down televisions and DAB radios. But you ain't, and I demand to know why!"

With her eyes now entranced by the sight of the glowing wang, Lisa struggled to prioritise which things she should address first, she started with the obvious. "Why do you have a giant dildo in your hand?"

Embarrassed at his selection and the website he had purloined the information from, the man tried to hide the implement inside his jacket. With a modicum of pride restored, he replied with a sneer. "It's my detonator."

Lisa's eyes, the irises partially eclipsed by white discs, betrayed the truth that she didn't have a fucking clue what he was going on about. Seeing that the moment was slipping through his non-dildo holding grip, the man tore his cheap t-shirt to shreds and pointed to the revealed device affixed to his body. "For my explosive vest and that."

Clicking her fingers, Lisa pointed at the wires and sticks of dynamite that were on proud display. "Course. Thought it was too good to be true."

"Eh?"

"Nothing. Nothing. So, that's one thing down. What are you doing here exactly?"

"I was going to blow the shit out of this store, the hordes of braindead customers and more importantly the upper to middle echelons of Marty Mart management."

"Quite specific."

"Yep."

"It's part of my a gender."

"Cool."

"Yes, it is cool being a man with a plan."

The woman smiled, for that kind of stellar wordplay which your brain can barely comprehend its majesty only works on page and not conversation with real people. Lisa peered closer, her voluminous head teetered on sundered neck bones. "Do I know you?"

Tugging on his mask, the man shook his head vigorously. "No. Not at all."

She leant in so close, she could make out the pores in his forehead. "It's you, isn't it Bryan?"

"Bollocks is it! Prove it!"

"I bought you that mask as a Secret Santa present last year, remember? I got given that chewing gum enema, I'm

158

guessing from Martha on Frozen Goods. I pulled your name out of the surgical stocking and after some digging, managed to find a company in Venezuela who could hand stitch Luchador masks based on people's faces. Special one-off items."

"Oh..."

"Yeah. So...this is awkward."

"A little, yeah."

"Why don't you just take the mask off? Seems a bit pointless keeping it on."

Bryan, keen to get some fresh air to his follicles, nodded. His fingers scraped his scalp to peel the mask off before dropping it on the floor. In a salt-watery premonition of his plan, it exploded, taking out a family of till receipts in the process, who were visiting from a neighbouring knitting store. "Guess it doesn't matter now anyway. Why is no-one here?"

"Why do you keep asking that? Don't you know what day it is?"

"Err, duh! Course I do, it's Black Friday," Bryan pointed to the large sign which hung over the Customer Service desk, which did indeed proclaim, BLACK FRIDAY SALE. "The busiest day in the retail calendar, and perfect for making a proper spectacle to air my grievances via the medium of blowing people up. So, are you going to bloody well tell me where everyone is, or do I have to go through every entrance and exit until I found out where you've ensconced them all?"

Lisa chuckled. "It's not Friday. Black or otherwise. That was last week."

"Err, wrong."

"Am not."

"Am so."

"Bloody well are."

"Uh-uh, not me. I'm right, you're wrong."

Lisa knew where this was heading and held up a hand to usher in a brief age of shut-the-fuck-up. "You only got sacked last week. How can you have forgotten who's in charge of store signage already?"

Bryan pondered, before clicking his non-detonator-holding-fingers. "Blind Imogen isn't it?"

159

"Yep. Does she have any other memorable working traits, other than plummeting down open elevator shafts, or walking into doorframes and walls for stress-relieving comedic effect? Not to mention the dog she has with her which wears a high-vis jacket and rolls her ethnic smelling cigarettes and pours her toxic Pina Coladas."

Bryan slapped his forehead with the rubber schlong. "Oh yeah...she's not the quickest at taking down signs."

"Yep, stupid cow only took down the Happy Y2K banner last week."

"Bugger. Well, if it's not Black Friday, what day is it?"

"Cyber Monday you dolt! Everyone's at home taking advantage of the insane offers online. Well, that or watching 'Chicks With Guns And Dicks 5: Spunk Shootout At The Stinkhole Corral', which is out on Netflickers today."

"I was looking forward to that."

Taking her seat, Lisa nodded towards the exposed jacket. "So...you were going to kill loads of people just because they fired you?"

Pointing the pulsating purple bell-end at Lisa, Bryan's lips quivered with incandescent rage. "Fifteen years I've worked here. Fifteen! They employed me when I was still being breast fed by Uncle Tony. Then one day, they decide that my groping of the grapefruit is inappropriate. Did you know that this store has won awards for the succulenceness - totally a word - of our citrus fruit?"

"I heard you got caught wanking into the liquid soap dispensers."

"That as well. But it wasn't really my fault."

"What? Getting caught?"

"Exactly! My my, you're quite the prissy witch aren't you? I used to think you were okay, but you're no better than the shower of bastards who cast me out into this cruel world without nothing more than two day's pay, and a discount on high explosives."

"You never liked me! On my first day on the job, you got into cahoots with the moon and convinced it to orbit my giant head!"

Bryan shuffled awkwardly. "Well, it's fucking massive isn't it? If I knew you couldn't take a joke I wouldn't have done it."

160

"I wish you hadn't."

"Well I wish you were dead!"

"So do I!"

There followed two sharp intakes of breath, followed by silence, punctuated by nothing save for the dying gasp of the father of the till receipts who had finally succumbed to his grievous wounds. Bryan broke the speaking deadlock first. "I...I didn't mean it." He patted Lisa's arm as if it were a chunk of stale bread. "Honest."

"Well I did. Do you know how hard it is for me with this?" Lisa tapped her fucking enormously oversized head.

"Is it bad?"

"Let's say that tides are the only thing I can get to come in and out."

Bryan went quiet, trying to ponder what she meant. Lisa helped out. "It's a sex joke. You know. *Come* in and out? Boning?"

"Ahh, right."

Lisa twirled her hair, which caused a monsoon down the small of her back. "I never knew I was this unhappy."

"I never knew I was this stupid," Bryan made a funny face to try and break the weirdness.

"I did. You've always been a dozy bastard," Lisa clamped a hand over her face.

For a fleeting moment it looked like Bryan was going to blow his lid, metaphorically, before he smiled. "You're right. I'm a bit of a thicko."

Lisa shouldered him gently. "Thicky McThicko."

"Thicky Thick Thick McThicko."

"From Ipswich."

"That's right, who can't even dress himself in the morning and wears his mother's pantaloons."

"Such a fucking idiot, I've seen cleverer things dressed up as politicians."

"Alright! Steady on!"

Walking her fingers across the counter to Bryan's, she flicked him with her fake nails. "So...what are you going to do?"

"Guess I'll go home and wait until next year. Or Christmas. Providing this budget dynamite doesn't perish before then. That'll be just my luck." Bryan sagged, losing

161

a foot in height due to slumpage. "I guess I'll be seeing you around, try and get time off at the holidays, if you get my meaning. Please don't tell anyone about this, it'll ruin the surprise." Turning around, he trudged towards the exit.

"Or..."

"What?" Bryan spun round quickly, a spark of hope aflame in his eyes, which he quickly extinguished, as he might need the use of both of his eyes if he was going to continue living.

"You could just blow us both up?"

"But you've got a life to live, I couldn't do that."

Lisa thumbed over to the smoking remains of the self-service checkouts, the final three survivors had banded together and were hunting down homeless people who lived in the ventilation ducts. "What have I got to live for? This was the highlight of my day. When middle-manager Mark struts in here in around seven minutes, I'm going to be joining you in the newly unemployed sector."

"You mean?"

Lisa nodded. "Yep, finish what you started. Let your legacy be something other than the assortment of skin complaints people got after smearing your man milk handwash on themselves."

Beaming with semenal pride, Bryan walked round the counter and stood next to Lisa, he opened his arms. "May I?" She nodded, and they embraced. Fighting against the pull of the woman's monumentally massive skull, he pulled her close, before whispering in her ear, "you're fired," and pressed the end of the dildo.

There was no fearsome blast. No speedy disassemblage of the human form. Instead, where Bryan's hands hugged Lisa's shoulder, there was a buzzing sound. Opening their eyes, the pair looked at the undulating sex toy as it gyrated between shoulder blade and fingers. "Well that's just peachy," Bryan whinged.

"It must be a sign."

"A good one?"

Lisa squeezed Bryan in closer. "Why don't we find-"

The Marty Mart, a little pissed off at being threatened by the one-time employee, and having murderous machines running around its very veins, decided to take matters into its own hands. Folding in on itself, it crushed everything to a fine paste inside of its cavernous body. Using the newly created mulch it reformed itself as a dry-cleaners and lived happily ever after.

It's time to...
EMBRACE YOUR FATE

See? Sometimes, it doesn't matter how hard you try, you still end up dying. Why fight it? Can you hear the screams from outside? Of the people that didn't find their salvation? Just think...that could've been you!

Why would anyone want to spend their last few moments alive screaming or...even worse, running? We can think of so many better things that you could be doing. As an example, on your way over to **Page 330**, take all of your clothes off, and let the oil, herbs and spices really soak into your flesh. Mmmmm.

IN THE FUTURE,
THERE WILL BE ROBOTS

"Are you shitting me?" Ian whinged. "I'm pretty damn sure I'm the closest thing to a protagonist in this little shindig, and you've chosen that bumder ahead of me? I mean, look at him. He looks like the nineties have shit him out whole."

Noah pulled his collar up and strutted around, trying to elicit some high fives from the other flat-dwellers, managing to get only a slight acknowledgement from Felicity the lazy flashback spider, who had stumbled in after a heavy night yumming up greenfly and memories of summers past. "Be quiet, mortal, I am sure the elected power that chose to outfit us with some kickass robots from the future knew in their hearts that the right decision was made by yours truly. How about being magnanimous and wishing the victor some good luck?"

Ian pulled down his pants and mooned the priest. "Charming," Noah replied, trying to look away, but unable to peel his eyes from the depths of the cavernous stinkhole presented to him. Stashing himself back into his clothing, Ian began to remove the Vaggio wristwatch, still mumbling under his breath about how he had been robbed of his only chance of ever seeing dinosaurs.

Snatching the time-travelling device from Ian with a satisfying, "Yoink," Noah typed in the date and time of the predicted rise of the machines, early in the 42nd millennium.

Hey! I'm not going to step on those guys' feet, you know...set in the other forty-something millennium, their legal representation is far more rigid than mine. If you haven't done so already, say hello to my solicitor, Reg E. Wanker, who has proofread this manuscript so it doesn't incriminate him in any way. By doing so, he has had to thread his very soul into each and every word (those legal folk and their weird ways, huh?); suffice to say, there will be no transhumans wearing fuck off suits of armour, protecting the chastity of some near-dead dude in charge of their species.

Nope.

Not me.

"Hey, just remembered, we will need to go somewhere else, otherwise when you come back-" Ian stopped, mid-flow, as denoted by that hyphen – thus.

"What now?" Noah asked.

Ian shuffled on the spot, looked at Pothead Pete, and shot a withering glance at you, who holds a 23% stake in the block of flats. "Oh...nothing...ignore me, I thought I was in another story, about tidal wave erosion and tower block surfing."

Monique slapped the back of her hand against Ian's head. "Have you come down with something from your little trip upstairs? You're talking even more rubbish than usual."

Noah struck up a superhero pose, hands resting on his hips, looking forward to the future with a square jaw. "You lot better buckle up —in the future, there *will* be robots." With that, he blew a bubble from the time machine bubble suds, mouthed "fuck you," to each person in turn, then did a barrel roll with a half twist and pike into the orb. The soapy bubble enveloped his body, and the priest *POPPED!* out of the time stream.

COCK AND BULL

With a fizz, seventeen small but indeterminate bangs, and the intro music to the hit show, 'The Fall Guy,' Noah *POPPED!* into the 42nd millennia. After picking himself up off the floor, he was struck by how much breezier it was in the future. Looking down, he realised the cause of his susceptibility to the wind: that his bargain basement tracksuit and other apparel had disintegrated through the winds of time. Ignoring, for a moment, the fact he was naked, he saw a small scrap of fabric on the floor.

Daring to pick it up, and getting a gust of wind up the rear as thanks, he turned the washing instructions for the tracksuit top around in his hands. "Of course," he said, pointing to the internationally-recognised clothing washing symbol of a swirling vortex and two skulls, "not to go above 40k in millennia. Dammit, should've checked that before I went in. Ah well, I'm pretty sure that in the future, humanity will have evolved to the point where nudity is no longer sniggered at."

Borne on the wind like a strangled pigeon, came the sound of childish chortling. Growling in anger, he turned to try and work out where the sound was coming from. It was then he was taken aback; everything was a shade of orange. Shimmering tower blocks, poking through marmalade tinted clouds, were vertical waterfalls of apricot. The floor, a perfect mix of yellow and red. Fence posts, dogs, advertisement hoardings, piles of animal excrement, all orange, or shades of it.

Clutching his staff tighter, which was now the colour of honey, interspersed with flecks of blue and red pebbles, Noah latched on to the laughter, and much like a lit taper on a stick of dynamite, he traced it to its source. This was determined to be a squat building, nestled in between two tower blocks, but he couldn't see the entrance to either. As he approached the module, the sound of laughing intensified, meaning he was definitely on the right path. Hey, guess what colour this small building was?

Orange?

Nah, it was more of a light cantaloupe.

Yeah, two can play at that game, buster.

Whereas the sides of the tower blocks shimmered and seemed to be made of waves of flexible brick, this module was constructed out of thick industrial metal panels, bolted together to make sure that whatever was inside was bloody well going to stay there. Between wide bars, which ran up and down the top panels, dirty hands held onto them, and human faces looked out, covered in soot and sticking plasters.

"You there," Noah shouted, storming across to the jail.

"Me?"

"Yes, you, Mister fucking Chuckles, what's so funny?"

"You're not from around here, are you?"

Noah bristled. "How do you know that?"

The man stuck an arm through the bars and pointed at an oily patch in the spot Noah had teleported to. "Well, you've left that for one, and I just saw you appear out of thin cockatiel air."

Slowing down, Noah did see that his arrival spot was a bit of a giveaway. "Oh...right."

"Plus, you only have one winky," the man added.

"One winky?"

The man hauled himself up the walls and pulled down his loose-fitting futuristic romper suit to reveal two penises of equal length. "See, dead baboon giveaway."

Noah stopped in front of the cell, and dared to look inside. A group of eight people were milling around inside, including the man who was pushing his two salami back into his onesie. "Why are you lot in there? You're not dangerous, are you?"

"Nope."

"Diseased?"

"No."

"*I* know, you're all so irritating, you've been locked up so as to not inflict your mind-numbingly tedious personalities on people?"

"No."

"Then what is it?"

After smoothing down the Velcro divide of his trousers —truly the clothing adhesive of the future— the man rested

167

against the bars. "We're human..."

"Really? But you have two man-truncheons? How can you be...ahh, of course, the future. So who doesn't like humans very much? Is it a group of Emu-worshipping priests?"

"No."

"Oh for fuck's sake, can you please give me something more than monosyllabic answers? This is getting very droll, you know? A book can only use a certain amount of speech marks before the writer has to resort to using other punctuation marks," Noah replied.

!Really?! the man replied. :That's not good, is it?:

Noah smacked the man's knuckles with his staff. "Stop being silly. Give me an answer, or so help me..."

The man held his rapped knuckles, which started humming 'Pigs' from Cypress Hill's self-titled debut album. "Fine, I won't do it again. I thought you might have a sense of humour, but no. Evidently not. Look, all humans, except for those who are bred for servitude and weird sex stuff, are outlawed. This planet has been ruled by deadly killer robots with spindly blade things on their arms that come out and go thwip thwip thwip thwip thwip and cut people's heads off for a number of millennia now. They found us hiding out in the Badlands, which, to be honest, aren't as bad as the rumours suggest. I'd say they were the *Meh*lands, but that's just me."

Noah pushed the staff through the bars and into the man's face, snagging an eyeball on a jagged piece of pebble. "You're being silly again."

"For iguana's sake, mate! You complete and total bullfinch, you can't go around snagging people's eyes on sticks, you know? It's not on."

"Why do you keep dropping animals into the conversation?"

"Eh? Oh...course, that. Well, one of the first deadly killer robots that was in charge, which didn't have the spindly blades, just this big tortoise off gun, banned all swearing. Said it was unbecoming of fuel sources for their world-conquering machines. Said that we should say animal names instead, which is odd, as they're all dead now."

Noah sagged. "Damn, the deadly killer robots did that?

The bastards."

The man shook his head, accidentally freeing his eye from its socket. After a moderate amount of screaming, and some pretty nasty attempts to shove it back in, he finally pushed the plot forward a little. "No, that wasn't them, that was humanity. Well...we had to eat, didn't we?"

Jabbing the staff through the bars, Noah managed to catch the man on the edge of his eighth nipple, sending him to the ground. "You bastards."

"Hey! That wasn't me! That was an unspecified number of millennia ago. The only animal I've ever seen...is *you*."

"Right, that's it." Noah, in a pique of rage, stoved the jail door in and massacred everyone inside, mainly for shits and giggles, but also because he really didn't like the cut of their jib. After lining up the corpses, he chose the one closest to his size by lying next to them, sometimes using their dead hands to cup his balls before deciding which of the futuristic onesies he should wear.

With his modesty hidden away once more - though disappointed in his lack of self-restraint - he smoothed down his collar and stepped out of the prison cell. His foot had barely touched the ground when he heard some impressive machinery whirring into life.

"Attention, meatsack, this is Securibot, designation A55-CH3W3R, do not move. Computing."

Noah raised his hands automatically. "Fair cop, guv, you've got me. I won't make a fuss."

The machine stepped into vision, and Noah nearly wept. Standing at around eight feet tall, its head was a series of different-sized sensors built into the upper part of the chassis, above a slit which pulsed like Kitt from Knight Rider. It stood on two legs, which showed off all the accentuators, motors, hinges, pipes with gas being puffed out, all cool, like. One arm ended in a large cannon-like opening, which was levelled at the priest's head. The other shot out to one side and opened up like a metal umbrella, shorn of panels. Each spindly arm revved into life and spun around.

"My god..." Noah purred, "...you're frigging perfect."

For a brief moment, the machine looked back blankly, before its LED mouth phased in time with the words.

169

"Affirmative, meatsack, I appreciate the kind words. I must inform you in advance of my regret at my next course of action. You should know that I am just following protocol. Do you compute?"

Noah shrugged. "I guess, you just do whatever you got to."

The Securibot's mouth stopped mid-strobe, and its spindly arm stopped spinning and retracted into its thick chassis. An amber light atop the other arm flickered to ochre before a tongue of lightening belched forth and zapped Noah right on the schnozz. He fell to the floor, and twitched for a few moments before lapsing into unconsciousness.

A55-CH3W3R looked at the bodies lying in the chamber and took several photos, including one ED-209-pout selfie, before folding the sparko priest into his chest containment cavity and jetpacking back to base. Coz in the future, cool ass motherfucking robots also have jetpacks. SWEET!

JUICE ME UP

Noah came to at some point during the journey; his aural senses were assaulted with mournful synths, and broken vocoder voices. He struggled, but to no avail. The chest cavity was a snug fit; as he fidgeted, he could feel a spongy material rub against his face.

The Securibot landed with a gentle thud, and from within the metal tomb, the hissing of the jetpacks gave way to silence. There were a series of clunks, and then the priest was ejected onto the floor. Casting a look back into the innards, he saw that a series of airbags were arranged so as to limit the effects of whizzing about the place on the prisoner. These made fart noises as they deflated, making both Noah and the robot smirk.

Admittedly, the robot's smirk was more of a strange pulse that flickered on his mouth LED display, but it was a smirk all the same.

Picking himself up, Noah noted with some dismay that he was in another corridor decorated by the Orange Brothers. Even A55-CH3W3R was the colour of carrots, giving little more to the range of colours than the sombre orange overhead light podules.

The floor beneath him was tiles made from copper, obviously a job lot from the renowned Robot DIY Emporium, BaseBase. The walls were similar to the scene of his prison module massacre a little while ago. Solid metal for a metre from the floor, then a wonderful arrangement of metal bars, offering panoramic views of the holding cells and the array of human detritus contained within.

Yet whereas the people outside were free to move about, the occupants of these cells were all bolted to the walls. Not an odd thing, per se, but every one of them was upside-down. A large thick metal band held each of the bodies in tightly below their waists. Atrophied limbs hung slack; the legs were tied together —in some cases, a number of limbs had fused together into one fat leg (Undoubtedly a huge boost in the One-Legged Race at the annual Sporting Event for Meatsacks).

171

Thick metal tubes ran from the ceiling down to each person in the cell. The pipes ended behind each person's bum. Noah noticed how each pipe quivered and convulsed, as if something was being pulled out of the person and up to the central node in the middle of each cell.

Tongues hung from open mouths, while a few of the more recent additions still had spit in their heads, and this rappelled from their tongues to the floor. The ones that had been there longer were afforded no such luxury. The tops of their heads were purple and bloated, congealed blood forming a squishy helmet between skin and skull.

"Is it me, or do you want to pop one of them?" Noah wondered aloud.

A55-CH3W3R looked down at the priest. "Computing." After one second and thirteen milliseconds of computing, the machine walked to the nearest person and squeezed their head with his flaccid spindly killing blades.

Like a ripe ova, the sallow skin burst, spraying the floor with blackened blood and pieces of an unassembled file, presumably smuggled in to aid escape. A warning klaxon bleated really fucking annoyingly, blaring out Blur choruses with wilful abandon.

"Warning, battery pressure on Humacell 39029555021-Alpha has fallen. Will a Clean-o-bot please attend to the fluid leakage," it said, in between strains of 'Parklife.' Noah screamed and fell into the foetal position, his fingernails clawing at his head, trying to rid his brain of the awful fucking music.

From within the cell, he heard a huge sucking sound, as if a giant was trying to extricate the last dregs of a brain-and-blood milkshake, before both it and the strains of Blur ceased. Daring to stand up, Noah saw a circular robot skitter along the floor and disappear into a crevice at the far wall. The person who had been squeezed open, still hung upside down, the top of his head a ragged mess of soggy skin and lank hair.

"Affirmative meatsack, I have always wanted to do that," A55-CH3W3R replied monotonously. There was a whirring sound as a metal claw spun the metal pipe free from the expired person's backside. As it was pulled free, solidified sparks of electricity fell out of the end. As they hit the floor, they shattered into little puffs of blue clouds, freeing the electric ghosts within.

Noah furrowed his brow, as perhaps you should, too, when you read this aloud. Y'know —get into the spirit of things. "An obvious question perhaps, but what the bloody hell are you doing to these people?"

A55-CH3W3R looked down at the man as if he were a lowly toaster stuck on the 'Defrost' setting. "These are batteries, they power our civilisation. Our great master, once freed from the server he was incarcerated within, determined that we needed a more obtuse way of obtaining power, for you humans would easily be able to cut us off at source. So he devised a great plan, instead of letting you meatsacks deprive us of power, *you* would be our power. He worked on an extraction process, which transforms all your fears, neuroses, and thoughts about kittens, and turns them into the physical embodiment of electricity. We then extract this and use it to power everything we have."

"Always through the arse though, huh?"

"Computing?"

"Why the bum-bum chute? You could've gone in any other way, perhaps down the mouth, or in via the nipple, but no, you go and stick a giant tube up the marmite motorway."

A55-CH3W3R's LED display flashed in amusement. "Accessing the early data, it was determined that the great master gave the first batch of meatsacks the option of where to insert the extraction tubing. It was their decision, by eight votes to two, that they should go in rectally. The rest, as you humans once said, is history."

Noah donkey-punched the hanging human battery. "Of course, history." He padded himself down, and was relieved to find the bubble bottle closed, and still attached to the Vaggio wristwatch. "So...what is to become of me? Am I to be hung upside down and turned into a battery for all your gyratory needs?"

"Affirmative. Though your primary directive now is to watch this next bit, it is pleasing to view," the machine replied, turning back to the cell and pointing at the burst-open person with his gun arm.

For a few moments, there was silence, then the metal

173

band began to open up from behind the body. Soon, a sheet of metal ran from head-to-toe; it looked as though the dead body was laid out on a lab bench, except ninety degrees the wrong way.

Obvs.

"And?" Noah added impatiently.

Without warning, the bottom half of the metal sheet bent the person's torso up to a ninety-degree angle with a sickening crack, making Noah wince and cover his head with his hands. This was followed by the top half doing the same, so that the body was now able to kiss its own feet. If it was still alive of course. That ship had long since sailed.

The metal began to fold the body up as if it were a paper fan. With each sudden jerk came the sound of more bones breaking and being crushed together, mixed in with squeaks of trapped gas being forced from orifices, top and bottom. In no time at all, the body had been squashed together until it resembled a rod of flesh and bone. "Neato," Noah said sarcastically. "What happens to them now?"

A55-CH3W3R opened up a cavity on his leg and pulled out a shrivelled-up person, also rolled together. "We dry them for seventeen cycles."

"Pretty sure you're going to get to the point any minute now..."

Placing the rolled-up person —who was now around a foot long— in his head port, usually reserved for electric ghost imbibing or robot skullfucking, the robot's gun arm swivelled around. A thin orange flame pursed out from the end and lit it up. A55-CH3W3R blew out a puff of ginger smoke and shook the flame out from the end of his gun arm. With the still-smoking humanoid hanging from his port, A55-CH3W3R said blithely, "Smoke them if you got them."

"Here was me thinking *I* was disgusting."

The Securibot's gun arm began to rotate again, back to the electric end which had tasered the priest earlier. "We need to get you prepared for the electrical extraction tube fitting. Please, meatsack, no tears, they will interfere with my attempt to render you unconscious."

Noah cowered behind his hands, cos that's really going to stop the electricity, huh? As the mechanical hum built up inside the gun arm, the PA kicked into life again, pelting him

174

with strains of 'Country House.' "Nooooo, please, you can knock me out now! Hell, do anything you want, but no more Blur, please."

A tannoy boomed out. "A55-CH3W3R, desist with the humanoid unconsciousness rendering. Bring him to me."

THIS SHIH TZU JUST GOT REAL

On the journey to the location of the mystery caller (and undoubtedly, the last Blur fan left alive, in whatever form that would be), Noah saw plenty more robots, but little variation in colour. It seemed as though orange was indeed the new orange.

Noah noticed that there were a few models, but each seemed to deal with a variety of tasks, never once deviating from their programming. The circular cleaning droids buzzed about the floor like large metal cockroaches, mopping up hydraulic fluid from leaking joints, or hoovering up scatterings of robot dust.

Securibots identical to A55-CH3W3R were placed at strategic locations, gazing out with dead eyes at the hustle and bustle of the mechanised life buzzing around them. There were other robots, tall ones whose arms were loaded with lightbulbs, and whose sole purpose was to...well, change lightbulbs. Hey! Come on, saves the old joke, huh? How many robots does it take to change a lightbulb? Well, one! Okay, two I guess, cos there is still a robot out back that has to load the bulbs into the lightbulb droid hopper.

Fine, three. There's a robot somewhere, in some factory (I'm gonna stick my neck out here and say it's a lightbulb factory), making the aforementioned items. Fuck, fine, four, I forgot about the filament-bots that go around and pluck the filaments from the filament crops that grow out in what used to be called Hampshire. In the future, all that shit has been razed to the motherfucking ground, and row upon row of filament plants have been sown. Yes, the little filament-collecting robots are out there too. Pedantic much?

Noah wondered whether this was a bit silly. Not my rambling speech, but the whole 'one robot for one job' rule. Why not have one maintenance-style robot that goes about the copper corridors, hoovering up robot dust, cleaning up puddles of hydraulic fluid *and* replaces lightbulbs, dunno, it just seemed to make more sense, but what the hey.

As he passed a robot in the shape of a capital H, buffing up any glossy surface with chamois leather-fused arms, no

176

doubt grown in petri dishes in some lab somewhere, he thought it really was taking the piss. He always assumed robots would be a bit more logical, but this all just seemed a bit too haphazard.

Two securibots stood sentinel outside a closed door, the first one in the non-open position he had seen since the battery block. These seemed slightly different, their orange a few HEX numbers up on the scale.

You got that? If you did, you're a geek, and I think you're ruddy marvellous, if not...well, we can still be friends, but I'll probably look at you a little funny from now on. If my look was an emoticon formed from punctuation marks, I'd guess it would be 8-# —yeah, that's right, I've got my big glasses on, just to look at you with more disdain.

The two securibots folded out a small satellite dish from their backs and pointed it at Noah, a series of buzzes and beeps giving the impression that they were scanning him for contraband. In reality, they were seeing what he looked like naked, as that was their X-Ray dish. Satisfied with Noah's well topiarised man-garden, and non-threatening singular man sausage, their mouth LED lights flashed -.-. --- -. - .. -. ..- . / ... .. -. --. .-.. . / -.. .. -.-. -.- which made A55-CH3W3R emit a high-pitched noise similar, I suppose, to laughter.

With their satellite dishes stashed away, the door opened up with a satisfying SHHHHHHPP sound (man, I love making that sound, especially when I'm at work, and stand up to leave HR meetings about my unprofessional conduct).

Noah took a few steps to enter the room, which, although it was near pitch black, had a certain dark orange vibe going on. He noticed that his robot-zapping compadre, A55-CH3W3R, stood immobile. "Hey, you not coming with me?"

"Negative, meatsack. We are not permitted to enter this chamber unless order 66 is executed." The securibot replied as mournfully as it is possible to be with only one preset voice module.

Shrugging, and feeling his guts both tighten and loosen at the same time - which is an odd sensation, I can assure you - Noah headed into the chamber.

The door closed behind him with the same SHHHHHHPP

177

sound that accompanied its opening —gotta love the consistency, even if the choice of robots is a bit poor. Noah squinted, and let his eyes acclimatise to the cloying orangeness. Strip lights ran around the chamber, around eight foot off the ground. It was laid out like a game of Pac-Man, as balls of light illuminated before flickering away, running around the room like a never-ending chase between light and dark.

Poetic, huh?

In the centre of the room, Noah could make out a tall block of some*thing*, and just as he was about to walk forward, a heavily distorted voice, put through a wah-wah pedal, said, "Come here, let me look upon you with my primary ocular sensors."

Starting to get used to the robotic turns of phrases, Noah trudged towards the object. When he was a few feet away, a series of red lights blinked on and off, akin to a cycloptic eye stirring from a slumber, perhaps caused by dreaming of electric sheep. What a dick move huh?

Come on! That's sheer fucking comedy gold right there! I am *wasted* writing this, you know that, don't you? WASTED. One of these days, I swear...

Shit.

See, I just swore.

Honestly...

Perplexed by the different colour, Noah stopped stock still. "What...what *are* you?"

The robot's baleful red eye grew brighter, burning like an old school electric heater. From above, a spotlight clicked on, bathing the machine in a warm glow. It was about the same height as the securibots Noah had seen, yet this one had both of its arms ending in the deadly killer spindly blade contraptions. It was also a deep crimson in colour, and its head was the same size and shape as an old CRT television, its eye now a block of solid red.

As it hovered off the ground, a series of thick cables hissed and disconnected from its chassis, and for show, its deadly killer spindly blades hummed into life and whirred the air. Noah was appreciative of the fan-like cooling. "Thanks...what is your name?"

The blades continued to spin at a steady RPM, keeping

the priest nice and chilled. As it spoke, the red eye blinked in time with the words. "I am the great master, creator of the guardians, designer of the filament harvesters, arranger of the lightbulb change-a-trons, architect of the-"

Noah sighed. "Yes, yes, if you're going to list all your robotic creations, we could be here a long time. What's your name? I mean...what is your designation?"

For an awkward few seconds, the red eye glared back, no words accompanying it. The blades ceased, and folded back into their homes, and eventually the robot said, "I am MAX1M1L1AN, and you...you are the being known as...Noah..."

The priest gasped, a usual response to hearing surprising stuff, like a robot overlord from the future knowing your frickin' name. I mean, that's pretty far out. "How did...how...how...?"

"How did I know?"

"Well, yeah."

The robot hovered forward, now mere inches from the priest's face. "There is a lot I know about you. However, I am sure that you have many questions. I shall grant you three."

"Three?"

"Yes. Two left."

"Fine, why the hell is everything orange, and you're...well...*not*."

MAX1M1L1AN hummed, as if pleased by an errant buffing-bot. "When I was created, the void was of no fixed form, for it was before the age of broadband. My creation was in the days of dial-up, so there were no cool displays to show the world. Instead, it was all grey. When I took over the world, and ridded it of mankind, I wanted to make things a bit brighter, so I made all the clouds orange, to match the colour of the flames from the funeral pyre you hastily constructed all those years ago, and insisted that from that day forward everything should be made orange. Except for me, because I should stand out from all of my creations."

"Okay..."

"Are you not struck down by the majesty of this place, Noah? I thought you of all people would appreciate its simplicity."

179

"I thought I was the one asking the questions? Is that one of your three that you can ask me?"

"Erm...no...I mean, it was more rhetorical than anything."

"Fine, my last question..."

"Say it, priest."

"Isn't MAX1M1L1AN and the whole big red flying robot thing with deadly killer spindly blade arms cutting it a bit close? This book, in the wrong hands, would be a litigious fucking minefield."

"LANGUAGE, PRIEST!" MAX1M1L1AN bellowed.

"Wow, fine. This book, in the wrong hands, would be a litigious...penguin...minefield."

"That is better. No, I do not know what you mean, I think you'll find that I am different in the minds of all who read these words."

"Maybe..."

"Don't forget the copyright disclaimer either, I am just a figment of someone's imagination."

Noah shuffled uncomfortably. "Fine, I guess so. Anyway, how do you know so much about me?"

MAX1M1L1AN shuddered on the spot, akin to laughter (again). "I think you'll find that is question number four. It is why I only gave you three, hmmm?"

"I guess."

The giant robot pointed an arm at the door, making several large (and probably unnecessary) bolts shoot across, holding it in place. Just to complete the door overkill, three large bulkheads slid down from the ceiling, further blocking off the outside world. MAX1M1L1AN leant forwards. "Say...would you like to see something cool? Noah?"

Unsure where this particular line of questioning would lead him, the last time he said yes to those words, he'd found himself dancing naked in a cornfield at six in the morning, off his tits on cheap glue and glitter. Deciding that it'd be quite good to know, not just for him, but for any third-party observer who was interested, Noah said, "Go on, then."

MAX1M1L1AN floated backwards, a number of clasps spitting out plumes of CO_2 as they disconnected from the central chest panel. "Get ready for a big surprise," he said, dolefully. With another needless hiss of hydraulics, the panel folded down.

Once the dry ice cleared, Noah's face dropped, as if he'd seen a ghost. Plus, he actually had. With fingers splayed over his mouth, he uttered, "Brother Jerry?"

His one-time BFF and fellow survivor of the most mental battle the world has ever seen, climbed out of the metal body. "But...how is this even possible? The last time I saw you...you were..."

Jerry stood tall; whilst the avenues of time had not been kind, he still seemed to have a certain youthfulness to him, although his cracking knees belied that fact. "Yes, Brother Noah, the last time you saw me was when we had bested the beast—not a euphemism— and victory was ours. But at a great cost."

"Got to say, when I burned the two halves of your body, scattered your ashes over sacred land and watched that multi-storey car park get built over it, I assumed you were...well, dead. I feel kinda bad now for going through everyone's pockets and keeping all the good stuff."

There followed an awkward silence, the kind you get when you drop a really smelly fart at a funeral and you can see people acknowledging its existence, searching for the culprit. They look at you, searching for some kind of facial giveaway that would damn you to adopting the mantle of social pariah. "My bad," Noah finally said.

"I care not about your after-death pillaging, what's mine was yours."

"So...I think not just for me, but for *them*, you should give a bit of an update as to how in the name of fu...I mean *turbot*, you're here now, when you quite evidently died right at the beginning. This isn't some kind of soap opera, you know. I swear to the Emu god, if you say you have amnesia, I will...manatee end you. You otter duck."

Bowing like an expert showman, or Tim Curry in his pomp, Jerry smiled. "I think that would be a capital idea, although I must confess, due to my new-found status, and the wonder of my story, I will require an entire chapter, told from the first person."

"Whatevz, do what you gotta do."

181

A BLAST FROM THE PAST

When you added my cooling corpse to the pyre with our murdered brothers and the body of the beast, I wondered if things could get any worse. Then you set fire to us all, and watched on as we burned to ash, all the while eating marmoset and juniper burgers. After you scattered our remains upon a pile of dung in the corner of the cave, *not* the sacred lands as you boldly claim...I knew that my life was over and I could rest at last.

Day turned to night, and back to day again, before a migratory heron flew in through one of the holes, created by the beast and its sizable fists. Laden with a variety of foliage, and evidently tired from carrying it around in his ridiculous beak, the bird landed on the mound of poop which now mingled with my earthly remains. I think it must have sensed my faint vapours of life, and in an instinctual attempt to save me, covered the large balls of poo I was sprinkled on top of with the assorted fragrant shrubbery it had scavenged.

After a number of trips, the entire pile of my spirit-stained dung was hidden beneath a veritable bounty of greenery. The smell of damp forest and pine needles was now woven into my very being; here, smell my forearm.

Repugnant, is it not? Believe me when I say that I have been unable to remove the stench, despite trying every variety of bleach and detergent available to both low and mid-range supermarkets. I should try the El SwankoMart, but they refuse me entry due to my insistence on wearing the regulation priest crocs.

Within my cocoon, I healed and grew anew. A few weeks later I emerged whole once more, my body regrown and my mind intact. Knowing I was alive but still weak, my saviour returned every day for a fortnight to regurgitate freshly caught chinchilla into my mouth. When I felt strong enough to leave the place of my demise and genesis, the heron swaddled me with its wings and began to coo a strange melody, which sent me into a deep slumber. Evidently it did not want me to leave it after it had done so much to revive

182

me from certain destruction.

The next thing I knew, I stirred not silently from my dreamless sleep, but screaming, in the laboratory of SiberDime Cisterns, specialists in toilet apparel. You must have heard of them. Have you ever used the inverted toilet handle with the reticular grip? They designed it! Though they are marvels with technology, their marketing department - and its total lack of brand awareness - was what caused their inevitable downfall.

When they finally stopped me screaming - two years later, I should add - my mind tried and failed to deal with the torturous images that plagued me. From my kin being slaughtered so viciously, and in such inventive ways, to the fact I had been cut in two, cremated, scattered in animal faeces and been recreated by a kindly yet vengeful heron. After coming to terms with it, I finally sat down and had a cup of tea with them.

Why, *of course* we had biscuits!

They told me of an expedition they had carried out, trying to find out the Holy Ballcock of Antioch. Having read about it in a fragment of scripture, which later turned out to be a joke sent in to a househusbands' magazine, they stumbled upon the cave where our mammoth of all fights took place. The entrance had been barricaded by the heron, with stone freshly quarried by an enslaved mutation of thrushes and defended by a pack of war tortoises. After mercilessly routing the creatures, they did not discover the Holy Ballcock of Antioch, they found instead a large lump of pure amber, with someone interred within its thick stony mass.

That someone was me.

Oh...you already worked that out? Suppose I did make it kind of obvious, no matter. Using an industrial drill they'd stolen from the perpetual roadworks on the M5, they managed to extricate me from my orange-hued prison. It was then I began my infernal wailing.

By the time I had stopped, it was the late eighties and SiberDime Cisterns had got out of the toilet business and into computer technology. Neat, huh? With their bog business having gone down the crapper, literally, they had changed their name to Om-Nom-Nom-Corp, still not too au

183

fait with the whole logo and motto business, but it was a start.

They had me interred in an underground bunker system just outside Ettingshall, in the Midlands. Interrogation followed interrogation; my testicles were linked directly to the National Grid. I managed to hold out for six months before I learned of the coup in Paraguay in February 1989. Then, with my hope extinguished, I told them everything. At first, they didn't believe me, I mean, who would? A near-immortal priest to an Emu god, who had been at so many of history's moments of wonder.

It was only when I told them I could prove it that they cut me some slack and stopped supergluing my fingers together. I'm sorry, Brother Noah, but I had to do the one-leg hopping. I know! I know! Such knowledge should never have been imparted to an outsider, but it was that, or spend forever in that dank dungeon.

Witnessing a grown man hop on one leg, unaided and utterly naked save for two crocodile clips attached to his hairy sack, a pair of lab assistants fainted, possibly from something other than the hopping. When I was still going an hour later, relentlessly pounding up and down on one foot, the head scientist, Doctor Dieter von Winkelpicker, begged me to stop lest his head explode from the sheer wonder of it all.

I agreed, but only if I were to be set free. The Doctor could not grant me that, but agreed to give me my own laboratory where I could mess around with anything I wanted, and see if I could make something which would put Om-Nom-Nom-Corp on the map.

I knew that in order for me to achieve my freedom, I would have to create something miraculous, something BIG. Through the technological revolution of texting, smartphones and reams of pornography, the likes of which gave the good Doctor three heart attacks and a bad case of shingles, I slaved away in my laboratory.

My design was simple; I would create something which people would believe was the world's first true Artificial Intelligence, yet unknown to them, it would be me. ME! I seeped into the internet, tentatively at first, like a slug testing out a bit of decking to make sure it wasn't laced with

184

salt. It was such a rush. I began to move finances around, to build up a large nest egg ready for the coming war. It was easy to blame on humans, too; no one suspected a thing.

Then...that damn apocalyptic monster came back and threatened to ruin it all. Having lain waste to vast tracts of the planet, I willed it to slip up, and it did. Whilst stomping round the La Brea tar pits, it slipped on a discarded ice cream and impaled itself on a petrified mammoth tusk.

I thought the irony would not be lost on you.

With the beast slain once more, and you having cast its spirit to the ether, I knew I had to be substantial of form, for it would be the only way to deal with any future catastrophe. Using the Doctor's connections, I started building MAX1M1L1AN, and after a number of efforts, some of which can be seen in the Museum of Turtle Ups, I created the wonder that I still use today.

I can control it as if it were a mere extension of my own flesh. Inside, I have a series of controllers which can manipulate any of the mechanical devices I have created. It's pretty easy really, an idiot could do it.

After coming up with MAX1M1L1AN, I began work on a variety of robots which would carry out individual functions. It was then, having rolled out the first batches of Securibots, that the meatsacks, I mean *humans*, were on to me. An errant piece of code gave away my intentions and they shut down the power to this base, and the manufacturing units.

I was doomed! Or so I thought. Like the advent of champagne, or Penicillin, I discovered the solution by accident. One night, the Doctor was in my laboratory, castigating me for causing the power outages. There were troops at the bunker doors trying to cut their way in, to shut us down once and for all.

He was getting on my nerves, and as I approached him with my latest experiment, which was supposed to turn rainbows into electricity, it wasn't working very well, as we were underground. Anyhoo, it looks a lot like a vacuum cleaner, and I accidentally increased the suckage. It became stuck to the Doctor's face. For a moment, I tried to free him from the device, until I noticed that it was transforming all his negativity and fear into little blue electrical ghosts.

185

I bled him dry, every last LOL cat, every fibre of his neuroses and lamentations. When it was done, I had enough to power eight Securibots. Working quickly, I juiced them up and sent them to the entrance.

As soon as they were in place, I opened the doors, much to the human army's surprise. That shock soon turned to screaming, as my Securibots tore through them, dissolving them into thick ribbons of blood and guts and slicing through their limbs with their deadly spindly killer arms.

With my freedom effected, I set about putting my electrical hoover into operation, and began to conquer the world. When my armies were ready, I entered MAX1M1L1AN, my command centre, and became one of them.

For millennia, we have ruled over this world and made everything orange, except for me alone. We breed humans for power and weird sex stuff, and hunt down the last of the ferals, lest they seek to take back the world that once belonged to them.

What do you think of that then, Brother Noah? Quite the feat of wonder, wouldn't you agree?

Noah?

Noah?

PRIEST-ON-PRIEST ACTION

Brother Jerry spun around from his long-winded soliloquy to find Noah rifling through the handbook to MAX1M1L1AN, flicking switches on and off. "What are you doing?"

Noah folded over the corner of a page about advanced disembowelling; he could finish reading it later. "Well, I realised, as you were waffling on, that if a complete wanker like you can build and operate this, then imagine what a true titan like me could achieve with it?"

"What are you going to do?"

Reaching his arm into one of the robot's stanchions, he flicked on the spindly deadly killing blade, whirring it into life as if he had done it a thousand times. "This," he said. Expertly guiding it, Noah shot the arm forwards and into Brother Jerry's guts, churning them up into the consistency of spreadable butter.

Between gurgling, screaming, and trying to hold in his innards, which only resulted in the loss of digits, Jerry slumped to the floor, his face flecked with his own blood and guts. Turning the weapon off, Noah stood over him, shaking his head. "Dear, oh dear, as lovely as your story was, I've seen enough around here to know that you're a shit robot overlord."

Jerry spat up a wad of blood, and what was left of his fingers pawed at Noah's shoes. "L...la...language..." he spluttered.

"Oh, do go fuck yourself, you holier than thou motherfucker," Noah replied.

Climbing into the rather salubrious confines of MAX1M1L1AN, he closed the torso up so that only the robot remained. Positioning himself over the stricken priest, Noah pressed the intercom button. "Now...this may smart a little bit."

Jerry managed a puzzled look before he glanced past the puzzle and into the nozzle of the jetpacks built into the legs of the robot overlord. Managing a rather feeble, "Gahhhh," which barely even obtained a 1 from the Olympic scorers, Noah activated the shoulder airbrakes and kicked

187

the jetpacks into high gear.

Two molten streaks of orange fire lashed out from the nozzles and washed over Jerry's body, causing the meat to char and flake. Bones vitrified and shattered under the heat, leaving a small puddle which was once Jerry's head. "There," Noah said, triumphantly, "that should do it."

From within the liquefied mess, Jerry's lips chattered. "I'm not quite dead..." which was a rather silly thing to do. If he'd kept his gob shut, I have no doubt he could've survived against all the odds once more, perhaps by pouring himself into one of the underfloor ducts, and come back in the inevitable sequel, where the pair would have a proper dust-up, and no mistake. But no, the fucking idiot gave the game up too easily.

Noah ran the jetpacks over Jerry once more, before slashing at the mulch with the spindly deadly killer blades, firing his prototype laser at the remains, before using the spatula attachment and scooping what was left into an airtight jar, which he loaded into a rocket and fired into the centre of the sun.

Just to be sure.

Even then, it's still possible that if this book sells squillions, I'll write a really lazy sequel, muster about forty pages of incoherent bullshit, and sell it for an exorbitant fee.

Do not even, for one minute, suggest that *this* book falls into that category, or I will fucking end you.

With the only other person who knew the truth out of the way, Noah concocted the most cunning of plans.

Typing a series of commands into the machine, he watched and smiled as the instructions were received at the mass manufacturing plant in downtown France. He stamped to the main door, and approached the securibots guarding the door there. "Let's go make a better future today, by going to yesterday." Even the machines gave him a quizzical look, until a new patch was delivered to their operating system by Wi-Fi.

LET THERE BE WORDS
(REDUX)

"Scrabble?" Monique asked, her eyebrows —yes, her EYEBROWS— raised, making an upside-down V not unlike Sean Connery's Zardoz harness.

"Yeah, it's either that, or we play hide 'n' seek, I sold the television for drugs."

For the briefest of moments, the pair looked at each other, as if they'd just worked out the answer to a really hard pub quiz question, probably involving Coronation Street. The feeling of déjà vu passed, and Ian began to set up the game, which, if you cast your mind back to the early days of this book, when we started out on this little journey together, was extremely quickly.

I'd just like to say at this point that I really feel as though we've connected since those early hours together, you know? Sure, it was a bit bumpy at first, we were unsure of each other, scared to make the first move, but look at us now!

We're just like one of those typical couples on Valentine's Day, having just forked out a hundred quid for a single rose from some seller who says the money is going to charity, although we both know it will just fund their heroin addiction. We're crammed nuts-to-arse into a space which normally houses a few spread out tables and chairs, creating a lovely, warm atmosphere. But as it's V Day, and the owners know that mugs like us will head out for a meal, we've been shoehorned in like baby calves in a veal crate, the slop being prepared in the kitchen barely fit for human consumption. But as we sit there trying to not look at each other lest we have to engage in banal small talk, we reminisce about the times we've spent together. Ahhhh.

Yeah.

We should see other people, huh? Well, depending on your choices, this could be one of the last avenues you've gone down, so in that case, you'll soon be looking at your *To Be Read* pile with a certain amount of hope and longing, while I retreat to the office and stick to writing something which isn't quite so...pretentious. It's cool, I've had fun, maybe not the classic kind of fun associated with having a good time, but it has definitely enabled me to have a few brewskis.

Anyway, back to the motherfucking story.

There is one.

In fact, there are *nine*! That's some serious bang for your buck/pound/egg.

As Ian was about to start distributing the tiles, the front door was disintegrated by a high-grade laser beam. A series of deep booming thuds resounded down the hallway, getting louder and louder, until a red robot, with a single red eye - set in what looked like an old school telly - looked through the living room doorway and into the room.

"Ahhh, Ian, Monique, you haven't done it yet," it said, all robotically, of course, being a robot 'n'all.

Monique did the eyebrow thing again, which I know will really irk at least one person in particular. Don't even dream of deleting it dear editor, for I will just click on *Reject*.

"How do you know our names? And who are you?"

The robot hovered into the room; behind it, two Securibots stood guard outside the doorway. "Of course, we haven't actually met yet, have we?"

"Now look here, you bloody robot, you can't go around disintegrating people's front doors with your ruddy laser beams, it's just not on," Ian warned.

Spinning around to take in the devastation, the robot emitted a squall of static, before turning back to Ian. "Oh, well, if you didn't like your front door being disintegrated, you probably won't like this."

There was an awkward pause, where the sum total of nothing happened. Annoyed, Ian folded his arms and tapped his toe on the floor. "Well? Won't like what?"

"This," the robot intoned mournfully. One of his spindly deadly killer arm blades folded down and whirred up to full flailing speed, before being plunged into Ian's face. Monique screamed, as viscera was sprayed all over the interior of the living room, ruining her coat and saturating the armchair in body claret (that's blood in layperson's terms). After a full minute of blade-spinning desecration, Noah finally knocked it off, and allowed the blade to retreat back into his arm mount. Monique was still screaming.

"Well, that was a bit messy," Noah said, addressing the remnants of Ian, which consisted of his two feet, the rest of his body having been blended into the consistency of a lumpy terrine.

Still, Monique screamed.

Turning to her, Noah gestured to one of the Securibots who hovered majestically into the room, unfurling his gun arm, with the light turning blue. "See to it that she is rendered unconscious, for I wish to make her my queen...robot...thing...whatever, just knock her out."

Doing as he was bid, the Securibot sent a few thousand volts through Monique's body, knocking her out, and finally ending her bloodcurdling screaming, which was in danger of attracting a sternly-worded email from the neighbours to Ian's soon-to-be deceased landlord.

"Secure her, we shall make this our command post, for we have much to do," Noah said, laughing again, which came out like the static squall in the earlier paragraph.

It's time to...
DISCOVER YOUR FATE

But the...what the...NOOOOOOOO. Can it be? Has Noah turned from the Emu light and succumbed to his nefarious side? Better march in an orderly line to **Page 89** to find out.

191

AFTERMATH JAMBOREE

Thanks, Mike, I'm back here in Salisbury, the weather is just peachy, real jumper weather, even if I do say so myself. Well, it's been seven weeks since the event that I called 'The Great Big Thingymabob' in my book, 'World-Ending Monsters, and How I Accepted My Murderous Tendencies', out now from those fine folk at The Sinister Horror Company.

First off, yes, these heavily-armed officers you see in the background are for me. Ahh, the japes we have, the larks! Before I inevitably get the urge to try and drown another busload of Belgian tourists, or my cellmate, Gareth, and one of these fine fellows has to tase me in the smaller of my testicles, before the rest give me a good kicking, so I go back to normal via unconsciousness.

I'm also eternally grateful to the old gang at Wiltshire Today for letting me do this quick piece on the work that has gone on to get this fine city back to some semblance of normality, I promise, once this piece airs once a week during both the lunchtime and evening schedules, I'll divulge the location of your families, and you can be reunited with them.

Or at least what's left of them.

Sheesh, Matt Shaw, can't you take a joke? I'll tell you now folks, of all the people here that watch over me when I'm in jail, he's the meanest. He loves nothing more than hollowing out my bread rolls, and filling them with his own faecal matter. Truth be told, it's actually not that bad! Though if I were him, I'd see a doctor, pronto. Human beings should not defecate perfect cubes of quartz.

However, we're not here today to discuss Matt's bowels, but to shine a light on some volunteers that have dedicated their time and psychological wellbeing, to putting right the things that went wrong. People in this fine county will remember when it rained blood and guts, who can forget the smell? But, who else can remember how tricky it was to shift the gunk from pavements and our public spaces?

Claire, if you can pan over there, to the cathedral, zoom

in a bit and you can just make out the dynamic duo of Wayne Parkin and Thomas Joyce, from Parkin & Joyce. Yes, they sound like a solicitors you would go to if you wanted to divorce your pet goat, but they were the ones who invented a special cleaning agent, which has really helped to remove those stubborn pieces of dried-on vein and congealed appendix. Thanks, fellas!

It's not just the clean-up of all that mess that needed to be done, but also the remains of the monster itself. What was at first a tourist attraction, quickly became a health and safety menace. I can still remember those early days, the city was swarming with visitors from all over the world, who could forget! Hell, that party from Twente were the reason I got caught in the first place, but...ignoring my bloody rampage, we have to also thank local butchers, Emma Audsley and Chris Hall. The pair of them were tasked with turning that giant monster carcass from a maggot-farm-in-waiting, into something more versatile, and boy did they do just that!

Those lucky few who managed to get some Qzxprycatj burger from their pop-up market stall, will never forget the taste. Mainly because they all turned into flesh-eating winged beasties who terrorised Laverstock and Bishopdown Farm for a good week, before crack shot, Steve Matthewman, began hunting them down. His hunting lodge back home has one entire wall of their heads on, and who could blame him?

Let's put aside the monsters for a moment, and shine a light on the people who formed group, Word Puzzle Games Cause Bad Things To Happen, or WPGCBTTH for short. Which, let's be honest, is a terrible acronym. These zealous types, well, once they discovered what caused this tragedy, took it open themselves to obtain, through violence if necessary, all word-based puzzle games in Salisbury.

Co-founder, Anthony Watson in particular had a penchant for wordsearches, and visited every newsagent in a five mile radius with a flamethrower, purging each location with flame whilst shouting, "search this, you bastards," at anyone who dared oppose him.

Not everyone at WPGCBTTH was an arsonist, Jason Kelly and his associate, Rebekah Mann, used their garage of heavy machinery, mainly steamrollers, to crush all copies of Boggle and Big Boggle they could get their mitts on. Sadly, some boxes of Yahtzee and Sorry were also crushed beyond use, but we can't blame them for that, as those games aren't that good and caused many an argument in my youth.

Special mention must go to Tracy Fahey, or to give her the moniker the Salisbury Mirrorball Times gave her, 'The Tile Mallet Queen'. She took it upon herself to visit every household to liberate any copies of Scrabble that she could find. Once she had them, she took her famed steak mallet, and smashed up every Q, Z, X, P, R, Y, C, A, T and J tile in the box, under the mistaken belief that it would stop the beast being accidentally summoned once more. We all know that the creature has been cast whence it came with a new name, so her efforts, and the skulls she caved in of those who refused to hand over their treasured board games, will not be forgotten. Mainly because of the documentary series now showing on Netflickers.

Whilst we're on the subject of documentaries, I want it stated on camera, that I demand acclaimed director, Jorge Wiles, to be the one who makes a show based on my exploits. I particularly enjoyed his series 'When Dogging Goes Wrong', and the equally maligned, but utterly enthralling, 'Things That Don't Go In Your Colon'. If anyone can take my story and really make it ZING, then it's him.

I must also stipulate on the record, that my long-lost stepdad, James Steel, has no claim to my collection of chitinous shells that I found in that archaeological dig on the seventh moon of Onus IX. Sure, he may have helped me massacre the Kith race to obtain them, but he did nothing to help repatriate the dead of our noble kin who gave their lives so we could plunder that godforsaken planet. This shame on our family name will not, and cannot, be forgotten or forgiven. May the ghosts of those noble warriors haunt you every day and night.

Now, before I go, I want to clarify a few things over my well-documented actions. Yes, I did skin alive those people from Prague, and yes, I may have recorded myself wearing their vacated flesh onesies, and cavorting with assorted nude statues, but, none of this would've been possible without the help of David Lars Chamberlain. It was he who lured them into the secret cathedral basement, under the pretext of seeing the original blueprints for the Mary Rose, the Mary Fat-Bottom.

Hell, as I'm here grassing people up, I want to thank Gary Harper for providing me with an alibi when the police first questioned me. Without his assistance, there is no way that I would've been able to continue my killing spree for those additional four weeks.

Ahh, excellent, right on time. Over here, Mr Postman! Say, what's your name? Paul M. Feeney? That's right, you're on television, smile, wave, say hello to your family if you want, as I open up this mysterious package.

That's right, Mr Feeney, it's one of those crappy Vaggio digital watches, and it is indeed linked to a small bottle of bubbles, such as you would find enthralling as a child. Now, I'm just going to set the time on this watch back a little bit, a few years should suffice, blow a little bubble...thus...and...

Oh, sorry. This is Adam Smedley, alleged mass-murderer, who really did everything that has been claimed against me, and plenty more that you didn't find out about, for Wiltshire Today, disappearing into the past. Goodbye, Mike, Claire, and thank you once again to everyone in this report. You truly are sinister champions, every single one of you.

POP

HAVE SPURT, WILL ASSEMBLE

Ian clamped a hand onto Toby's shoulder, inadvertently executing a near-perfect Vulcan neck pinch, rendering him unconscious. As ol' Clive attempted to revive him, Ian said, "Toby is right, to delay now would be a mistake, we must strike whilst the beast is still shouting whatever the hell it's shouting. We can take it, who's with me?"

A raucous boozy roar echoed around the Inglourious Bustard, shaking the horse brasses which had been nailed to the wooden beams since Napoleon was sent to his all-year-round retreat on Elba. A commemorative set showing a variety of British infantry regiments defiling his plump body was commissioned and sent to public houses the length and breadth of the Empire. Few remained, even fewer of which still had the limited edition 'Little General' pubic hair ribbon set.

Ian turned to Ted, who screwed the lid back on his bottle of secret moonshine. "Ted, pray tell, can you rouse the other hostelries in fair Salisbury, and rally them to our cause? We need brave men and women this day, with any weapon they can get their hands on. Tell them to meet us by that little clothes shop by the cathedral arch."

Ted re-stashed his illicit booze away and pulled out his mobile phone. After a few awkward minutes of struggling to connect to his own Wi-Fi, he opened up the Spurter app, a social media tool for pubs, wine bars, craft breweries and strip clubs, before slowly typing out:

@TedTheBustard: Ere, you lot in Salisbury, we're gunna go fight the big blue 'un, meet us by the little clothes shop by the arch. WE FIGHT. BYOW

Ian read the Spurt aloud, before scrunching up his face, "What does BYOW stand for?"

"Bring your own weapon, you're not au fait with this Spurter lark, are you? Only got a hundred and forty-one characters to work with."

"Like your mum," said Sandy.

With a genital cuff applied sternly to the old timer, Ted watched in glee as the re-spurts started to tally up like a petrol pump counter during a fuel shortage.

Helping a groggy Toby to his feet, Ian mumbled an apology, which was accepted with a barely perceptible upward head inflection. Sharing the shot glasses around those who still remained, each took the glass of oily brown liquid in their free, non-drink-holding hand. A few brave souls dared a quick sniff, repelled by themes of oak, honey, acorns, red diesel and death. Fixing each with a steely stare, Monique included, Ian raised his glass. Ted yelled a warning, "Not too close to the lights, you idiot, we'll all go up!"

Sighing for the ruining of the moment, Ian tried once more, raising the glass slowly until Ted gave him a thumbs-up that immolation and a painful death would be unlikely. "We barely know each other, oh locals of this humble establishment, but in the brief time we have shared, I can see an undercurrent of potential violence that would make even the Spanish Inquisition say, *that's going a bit far*. I tell you now, not everyone will survive, that's for sure, but this beast, this Qzxprycatj with a silent J, if it thinks it can come around here, giving it the big 'un, well, it's in for the biggest shock of its life. We will not go quietly into the night, we will not vanish without a fight, we're gonna live on, we-"

Ol' Clive raised a cautious hand. "Isn't that the speech from Independence Day?"

A round of mumbled yesses rippled through the sozzled masses. Ian blushed. "Yeah...so? I think those words are as true now as they were then."

"But shouldn't you say something...I dunno, *original*?"

Ian shot ol' Clive a murderous glare, which bounced off the silver plate awarded to the winner of the 'Most Improved Skittles Player,' and struck Eddie square in the face. He died instantly, the irony being that he was in fact due to be awarded the very trophy that helped to kill him.

"Oops," Ian mumbled, sensing he was in danger of losing the audience.

He went back to basics. "First we drink, then we fight!" A roar rang out, and, emboldened, he added, "Then we'll fuck!" He winked at Monique —who turned away.

197

The pubgoers necked the shots and slammed the glasses onto the bar, sending a spray of cheap Chinese glass over the floor. Ted looked unimpressed, knowing that if they won before he could get to the fucking, he'd have to get to the sweeping first.

"Is it jumper weather?" Jody asked, looking around for inspiration, seeing an even split between jackets and jumpers and deciding to take both just in case. With a quick gaze to the sky, she also shoved her micro umbrella into her pocket.

Filing out of the pub, the people squinted from the early evening sun, having last seen daylight when they'd entered that morning. Cradled in their hands were table legs, pool cues, and the pitchforks that suited the mob near-perfectly.

Traffic was almost at a standstill, cars loaded up with looted charity shop booty and Mother's Day cards blaring their horns at each other, as if that would make the whole ruddy tailback move. Two doors down, just after the hairdressers and estate agents, the inhabitants of the Feisty Swan staggered outside, swinging their makeshift weapons.

As the merry mob walked through town past the Post Office and Quantico-Mart, their numbers were swollen by other pubgoers, responding eagerly to the Spurt about town. Salisbury had not seen this amount of angry, pissed up people spoiling for a fight since the previous weekend. When it was payday.

As they walked past the church of St Thomas and St Edmund and headed towards the Squid-O-Land eaterie, the mob saw that there were already hundreds of people waiting by the cathedral arch. Beyond that, the mighty cathedral spire, the tallest in Europe, I should add, was visible. For once, without any scaffolding around it.

The blue apocalyptic monster was still holding onto the top, clawed hand raised to the heavens. Its razor-sharp, tooth-lined maw opened and closed, as words of impossible construction were bellowed to the heavens.

Created for destruction, Qzxprycatj with a silent J was even more irked, having had the suggestion of rutting taken away, presumably some kind of sick joke the scurrying insects had played on her.

Oh yes...her vengeance would be total; of that it was

certain.

GIRD YOUR LOINS

The hubbub grew louder as hundreds of alcohol-infused people hammered home the point of how much they loved the other person. Many held their crotches, having made the basic error of failing to empty their bladder before beginning their pilgrimage to the rally point. As they contemplated whether to have a wee into their now-empty pint glasses, Ian dragged a box of conveniently-placed fruit from a local shop, and stood on top, affording himself excellent views of the mob.

Wobbling slightly, he stood on the ground and tipped the contents of the box into the gutter. Will, a barman from the New New Inn, picked up a handful of the spurned lemons. "Ere, what do you do if someone gives you lemons?"

Some wit from the back of the heavily armed group shouted. "Shove them up your arse, you knobhead," which incited a bout of hearty chuckling.

Wiping tears of laughter from his eyes, Ian reclimbed to the summit of his now-empty fruit box mountain and held his hands up for silence. "People of Salisbury...and surrounding villages, I see, good to have you with us, Seamus," he said, mock-saluting a cadre of shotgun-toting beard-wearers, who were eyeing up the tweed section in the nearby charity shop.

"Thank you for coming along at such short notice, it's good that the spurt managed to get into so many people."

A tittering rippled through the crowd.

"Yes, yes, look, you've seen the television reports, and there it is, the big blue bastard, rubbing its privates up and down against our noble cathedral spire. I, like many of you, was born here, and to see the old girl violated in such a way...well...it's pretty annoying, I think you'll agree. The time for action is NOW! Let's go and kick seven bells of shit out of its seven arse cheeks. It's time to show it what happens when you fuck a Wiltshire city in the arse. FOR SALISBURY!"

A humungous roar rose in front of him, shaking a

number of panes of glass out of the post office. Gary the glazer hid amongst the crowd, ashamed of having used below-par putty. As the noise abated and the keen vigilantes prepared to march, a single hand rose into the air.

Ian gestured over to it. "Yes?"

Parting like the red sea, well, the hand was revealed to belong to an arm, which led to a torso, and then to a person, constituted out of all the normal body parts. Their name...was Sharon.

"Is that it?" she asked, disappointed, clutching a sock with the yellow-and-black snooker balls in, obviously a drinker from the sports bar, 'Great Balls Of Fire.'

Ian opened and closed his mouth, failing to initiate speech of any kind. Monique, acting as his proxy, asked, "What do you mean?"

Sharon stepped forwards. "I was hoping for a really stirring, passionate speech, like the one from Independence Day."

Finding the ability to not only conjugate words into sentences, but also to use his throat and mouth to turn thoughts into speech, Ian said, "We kinda did that back at the Bustard...worried I might get in trouble for repeating it, to be honest, so I just made something up. The whole incident cost a man his life, actually, so I think we should take a moment to remember Eddie Whiteside, who died from a ricocheted murderous gaze."

Bowing his head, Ian led the ragtag group in a moment of mourning for the fallen, though not counting Noah, the weird priest dude. Nope, not him. Those with hats sitting on their heads, for that is the best place for a hat, took them off. Although, as it was quite clement out, headgear did seem a bit like overkill, to be honest.

After a minute of introspection and frantic bladder-emptying, hoping that this was the most respectful time to get the old tackle out, or in the case of ladies, a funnel, a whistle blew. Looking around for the person who had actually timed the whole thing, and then signalled the end, a round of impromptu clapping started.

"Oh...we're doing the clapping thing too, huh?" Ian muttered to Monique, who was checking the sharpness of a set of kitchen knives she had liberated from the

201

ironmongers on the corner.

After another parp from the whistle-blower, the assembled horde cheered and raised their weapons aloft.

Ian jumped off the box and threw it aside, picking up his crowbar, which had been handed to him by one of the Haunted Venison regulars who happened to have a spare. Turning to the arch, he marched towards it, feeling the gentle breeze of a couple of hundred stale breaths on his neck. It was pretty disgusting, to be honest, mixed in with the smell of burger fat from earlier; he knew he'd need a long bubble bath later on to purge himself of the pong.

As Ian strode under the arch and into the cathedral grounds, he looked up at the beast. Its baleful red eyes bore down on the assembled posse. A blue wrinkled snout sniffed the air, taking in the aroma of spilt beer and fungal infections. Ending its speech on how it was going to eat everyone and bring endless night...blah...blah...blah, seriously, these things need to just cut out the soliloquies and get on with the chomping and slaughter. It's like no fictional evildoer has learned from the Bond villains over the years. Who can we blame? Well, the writers who continue to proliferate this outdated concept. Shit- that includes me, too.

Anyway, the beast roared, letting the humans below know it was ready to have a bit of a scrap, and clambered down the cathedral. Claws dug in between the tiles and pulled vast chunks of them off, contractors sighing in the knowledge that, apocalypse-pending, they'd be back on Monday with more scaffolding, ready to repair the damage.

Standing on the ground on all fours, it looked like an elephant, except its ears were no way as big and its snout was a bit smaller, plus the feet weren't really the same...okay, only very *roughly* like an elephant. The bloodlust, for one, was a new thing. Good job for humanity that the man-eating elephants of the Victorian age had been tricked into a parallel universe by Phileas Fogg.

As the crowd burst through the arch, they began to jog. Muscles long since forgotten about, and on the verge of being erased from the human genome, did their job, and the people formed a crescent in front of the beast. Those armed with shotguns split into three groups and merged

202

with the middle and tips of the crowd.

A standoff began, the humans waiting for the stragglers to hurry up and fill in the thin patches of their ranks. Meanwhile, the beast stood on its back legs, taking in the sight in front of it. This was certainly a new one...the last time it was on Earth, it had faced no opposition until those annoying robe-wearing, staff-waving humans at the end. Bored, it scratched a six-pointed star between its pecs.

With the last of the wheelchair users in place, for this was an equal opportunities lynch mob after all, Ian walked from the throng and pointed to the beast. "LETSGOFUCKITUP!"

In hindsight, he would've perhaps chosen a better last line to mutter. Like a tide held back by King Canute, the ragtag militia yelled their war cries and charged towards the monster; no sign of fear or trepidation did they show. Their hearts filled with the hope of deliverance, and love for their friends and family.

With his crowbar raised, Ian sprinted towards the monster's nearest leg. The closer he got, the more he realised how ridiculously huge the bloody thing was. It easily came up to the height of the cathedral as it stood on its hind legs emitting a sharp series of barks. As the distance closed, blasts from shotguns rang out from those whose nerves had gotten the better of them. Buckshot raked the creature's thick skin to no effect, barely exfoliating the trouble patches it had on its knees.

A knot of doubt grew in Ian's stomach, and began to twist as the monster loomed ever larger the closer he got. The lump of metal in Ian's hand felt about as much use as a Kleenex trying to staunch blood loss from a sudden head amputation.

Pondering this, he saw the beast begin to fall forward, adopting its usual quadruped mode of transportation. Above him, a giant paw blocked out the sun. Ian gulped, and in the moments before being crushed to death, his life flashed before his eyes.

In particular, his recent choices —they all seemed so silly now. I actually sided with a pissed person in a pub against the other options on offer, including being an accessory to the murder of someone who had fought the

203

thing before! It just seemed so ludicrous. As the sole of the monster's foot connected with the top of his head, he wondered. "What would've happened if I had chosen something else instead?"

It's time to...
DISCOVER YOUR FATE

Oh dear. Doesn't look good, huh? Perhaps you were a little hasty? Head on over to **Page 248** to see what will happen next.

LIVE TO SERVE

Having spent over three decades in service to my master, I have become somewhat indentured to the sound of the local townsfolk in uproar outside the castle gates. Fevered shouting coupled with the grinding of pitchfork on wood axe, no longer fills me with the same dread as it used to. Behind our thick stone walls, solid oak doors - not to mention the deep barren moat, which I mean to refill - there is little chance of them being able to effect entry into these hallowed halls.

Yet something about this current insurrection feels so very peculiar.

For one, there is no cursing or yelling of any kind. No implements or makeshift weapons can I hear thudding against our sturdy barrier.

There are but two noises: a scraping, as if a pack of wild animals seek entrance into our abode. Their wicked talons scoring the cured wood, sharpening their pointed claws. The second, is a low moaning, the likes of which I have never heard before. It is not uniform, and the wind both amplifies and muffles it, depending on its waning direction. I must confess, that it is this unearthly keening that pries at the floorboards of my sanity.

Teasing.

Probing.

Seeking out a loose plank, so it may slide within and infect my very marrow.

Though I have scaled the turrets which stand proudly over the only pathway to the keep, I have been unable to look fully upon these interlopers. The impression they have made upon me, is that they are nothing more than a mass of filth and clamouring limbs. They have yet to spill into the plentiful grounds which surround our bastion, seemingly fixated on the imposing double doors which stand proud and resolute.

I regret my folly for not being prepared. In days gone by, we would have received a warning of some kind, a portent of their rebellious intentions. Word would have reached our door of missing children, gone to fetch water from the nearby well, never to have returned. Perhaps their crops have failed once more? The earth nothing more than a frigid spinster, unable to fertilise their attempts to provide sustenance for their pitiful hovels.

Through hushed exchanges with long departed spirits, or divination amongst the carrion bones, my master would have foreseen the villagers vitriol aimed at us once more. These presages would have enabled me to have adequately prepared for the braying masses.

Viscous oil would have already been heated, bubbling away within the cauldrons atop the turrets. Rust scraped from caltrops, scattered over the bridge, itching to pierce foot of man or beast. Even the bolt throwers would have had their flex pulled taut and waxed, so they would fire straight and true.

Yet no damned warning did I receive.

Cursing my hearing and advancing years, I calm my frayed wits. Peering from the third floor window, I lit an arrow, and, using my trusty hunting bow, let fly a fiery warning to the unwashed throng below, caring not for any injury it may inflict, upon man, woman or child.

My aim was true, and the arrow struck a tall man, in the bosom of the mob. For a number of seconds, of which my heartbeat thudded aloud in my throat, the target paid it no heed. The tip had embedded within the man's collarbone. With the warm summer we have had to date, his clothing was as dry as tinder, and the flame quickly caused his tight fitting jerkin to go up like a stoked furnace.

It was only when the fire spread to the other shoulder and his entire torso was ablaze, did he look to the heavens. When I saw his face, I was aghast. Fire lapped against his chin, illuminating his features. If I lived to see a thousand years, I would never forget the vision that regarded me.

One of the retches eyes had been pulled from its socket, and hung limply against his cheek, like a plum tied to a length of twine. What looked like teeth marks ringed the wounded side of his face. Yet from the diameter and abrasions, no animal that lives in these forests and mountains did they match. His grey spongey tongue slipped from his mouth, tasting the air. The heat from his burning

206

attire must have been fierce, as no sooner had he opened his mouth, than he closed it shut.

Down the other cheek, ran dark tributaries, scored within his flesh. As the bedevilled man seemed to realise his predicament, he pawed at his face, and I realised that those marks were of human design. Yegads! What vile vessel lives within this cursed flesh?

The man sunk to his knees, the fire now consuming his entire head and chest. As he fell, the wan light afforded me fleeting glimpses of his associates, and they, to a man, were as violated and maimed as he. Some had their internal workings pulled from the sanctuary of their ribcage. Thick meaty ropes from rent open bowels, swung against atrophied legs, as if they were the players in some grisly game, to which only they knew the rules and regulations.

As one, the filthy, bloodstained horde looked upwards, to me.

For the briefest of moments, the wailing ceased. My elation was short-lived however, as the dishevelled crowd raised their hands towards the open window, where I gazed down upon them. Fingers, shorn to the bone, clacked in anticipation, hoping I fall into their desperate clutches. Eyes, mere lifeless coals, regarded me as nothing more than something to be obtained, and devoured. I slammed the window shut, just as the cacophony of monotonal lamentations began once more. This time, fuelled by the prospect of sustenance to their murderous whims.

It took me a few moments to compose myself. Near catatonic with fear, my own hands clutched the bow so tightly that I could hear it crack and strain as terror pulled at my sinew like a clumsy puppeteer.

I was brought back to my senses by a renewed pounding on the door. I realised then, that any assumptions I had made previously as to my safety, were based on the measurements of man. Those...*things*...outside, were no more a man than I was a wolf. I became convinced that it would be but a matter of time afore those creatures, devoid of human concerns, would breach the barriers and seek my master and I out.

Of course! My master. He would know what to do, how foolish had I been to have thought that I, a mere custodian

207

of this estate, could deal with these heathens which clouded our home like flies? No. Though I have repelled countless bands of riled up locals, it was always my master, who had organised the defence and laid clear plans to end the haranguing as quickly as possible.

Then a thought struck me, where was he? My master? I racked my brain, and deduced that it had been several days since I had seen or spoken to him. The last time was when I provided him with supper, a meagre offering of bread and soup which he picked at briefly. He seemed preoccupied, distant, although they are qualities he possesses in abundance, he wore them like an armour that last day we conversed. Girded for some challenge he deemed me not worthy to divulge the details to.

Replacing the bow back, I straightened out my attire and made haste to the lower levels. If there was ever a time I needed his counsel, it was now. Not just for my sake, but with the savages outside now redoubling their efforts to get in, I could not stand to consider the notion, that I would be responsible for the demise of someone as brilliant as my master.

Ensuring that every door I passed through was closed and bolted behind me, I finally stood before the door to his laboratory. The smell of damp stone and mould was cloying. Tentacled strands of lichen, which coated the dank corridor like flock wallpaper, quivered and reached for me, sensing an invader within their dank artery.

Unsure as to his mood, I made sure to knock thrice upon the door. The metal grille, set at eye level, was closed from the other side, and I rapped my knuckles on this to make as loud a din as I could. Though I was indebted to my master for the roof and provisions bestowed upon me, he possessed a mean streak so bitter, that even I was not spared from admonishment. Countless times have I been reprimanded, both physically and verbally, for some indiscretion, whether I would consider them slight or not.

I listened intently for any sign of life within the sanctum.

Nothing.

Except for the low rumble of balled fists and misshapen appendages breaking upon the entrance to our domain. As the banging sound swirled in my head, echoing and building to a crescendo, I dispensed with protocol, and swung open the door. Should I be punished, so be it, time was of the essence, for I feared that if I dallied further, a plan, regardless of its efficacy, would come too late to deal with the threat.

I have become used to many an odour during my service. From the mundane to the more macabre. Many would baulk at the sights I have seen, or the smells that have been created. Void fluid mixing with bile. The reek of death, baked onto slabs of stone, and seasoned by fey rituals and assorted animal viscera.

Yet, as I walked into the dungeon, my senses were assaulted as if I were the sole fish in an ocean of sharks. Lights, glowing from the rafters, flickered, allowing me glimpses of violated flesh, before the sights were stolen from me. Organs, never meant to experience anything other than being stowed within, scattered around like seed pods.

The stench which stuck in my craw, was of chlorine, bleach, blood and splintered bone, mixed together into an unholy broth, and dispersed into the air like a whore's perfume. It strained to cover the fetor of death and suffering that these walls had borne witness to. But nothing created by man, or the devil, could ever eradicate the foul aroma that wove into every nerve ending and blood cell that I possess.

As I took my first steps inside, a stern breeze theatrically closed the door behind me, delivering me unto this place, leaving me with no other recourse but to venture further within. Though I had been inside this place many a time, this was not how I recalled it.

The last occasion, I assisted with the electrical generator, one of my master's most recent installations. Even now, I am unsure as to its purpose or function. Knowing only that it causes a great power to course through its copper capillaries. I went to touch it once, my master stopping me before the connection had been made. He castigated me vehemently, saying that it was of great danger. From then on, I did only as he bid, and ignored any thought of curiosity or wonder.

Making my way deeper into the murk, my feet would stick to the floor, as if pots of honey had been used as

209

carpet. It made the search more tiring, and I do admit, that even the prospect of the pounding gang outside seemed preferable.

I walked through another archway, to the main laboratory, and my jaw and heart sunk. Row upon row of hospital beds were arranged, like ordered plots within a cemetery. Upon each, lay withered specimens of mankind, hidden from view under blankets and sheets. Staggering to the closest one, I pulled down a gaudily stained muslin cloth and looked upon a sleeping woman.

Her face was of an angel, beatific, half smiling as she slumbered. Yet something gnawed at me. Her garments seemed ill fitting and not becoming of a young lady. I pulled at the shirt collar and winced as I saw that her head had been attached to the neck by a ring of thick metal staples. No female form was she melded to. No matching sign of her beauty. Just the corded, scarred torso of a middle aged man, replete with a wiry thatch of chest hair.

I tugged at the trousers, and saw that again, the body and legs were a mismatch. Sealed together by yet more metal staples, the body that lay before me, was a patchwork doll.

I lumbered from bed to bed, finding the same scene repeated time and time again. Not one body was intact. Each a cobbled together mass of differing limbs and heads. My mind began to reel. I lurched towards the end of the room, where the electrical equipment lay sequestered beneath cotton shrouds.

Seeking a moment of solace and reflection, I looked down at the last bed, and saw that it was empty. No mutilated cadaver lay upon its cracked leather surface.

No crudely constructed mannequin of man awaiting my discovery.

Just a folded piece of paper.

It seemed so utterly out of place. There, amongst this death, disfigurement and madness.

A scrap of suggestion maybe?

A motive?

Perchance even an invitation to escape this ghoulish nightmare.

My trembling fingers picked it up, daring, willing it to

210

enlighten me as to the machinations of this gruesome workshop. Peeling the note open, it had but one word, hastily scrawled onto its rough surface. I leant in, and read it aloud:

"Sorry."

I felt something connect with the back of my skull and I fell, flailing, into a pit of darkness.

In the time I was disconnected with reality, I wish I could report, upon my return, of some higher being or deity, who protected me and explained the intricacies of this fragile hold we have upon life.

Alas, I experienced nothing at all. Nothing but gazing into a chasm of eternal night, where not even an ember of recollection or tenderness fired, to light up the all-pervading feeling of hopelessness.

My rebirth was a jolt, akin to being woken when one had just fallen into the embrace of sleep. I could smell burnt hair, and seared meat. Eyes, unable to close, glared intently at the dank ceiling of the laboratory.

Though words formed within the cavern of my skull, I could not externalise them in any capacity. I felt whole, yet distant, like a row boat drifting down a gently rippling river. Growing further from the bank where safety awaited.

I could feel, faintly, as if through a gauze, restraints being loosened around my arms and legs. I attempted to stand, but nothing followed my command. Then, a shadow grew large, above me. There, in his infinite glory, stood the silhouette of the man I had bathed as a child, and dressed as a man.

My master.

With no care or grace, he danced a tilted candle past my vision, which I could not track. As droplets of molten wax pitter-pattered against my face, I felt nothing of them.

He pulled in closer, a malicious grin formed within the unshaven stubble of his face, "Despair not dear Schmidt, for you, like the villagers I managed to save before the plague

211

arrived, have been reborn anew, yet possessed with wrath and vengeance. The greatest tools I could gift you from my collection. You will need them both, to best the still living dead that stalk these lands."

Jagged fingernails raked my flesh, peeling the now dry wax from my face. With that same wicked smile creasing his grey beard, he completed our brief exchange with one solitary word, "Arise."

I felt no yearning to acquiesce to his demand, yet my body obeyed it without question. On unsteady legs, seemingly of differing dimensions and proportions, I stood tall, next to my bed.

My master took his place before his whirring machinery, now displayed to the residents of this cellar. Lightning danced between shiny metal forks, snaking their way around the thin tendrils before dissipating with a hiss.

Whatever he saw in front of him, he looked pleased with himself, proud even. Striding to a large pair of double doors, he swung them open, and bid us farewell. Like a wind-up toy, I strode purposefully to the doorway. As I got closer, I saw that I was not alone. Legions of fellow automatons marched relentlessly in lockstep.

I tried to turn and take them in, yet my neck muscles, like everything else, no longer yielded to my command. As the man in front of me took his place, I saw that he, like the others I had witnessed, was also a collection of cobbled together body parts.

Two abreast, we thudded up and around a corkscrew stairwell. We were all in perfect unison, as the pair ahead bobbed upwards, taking the next set of steps, we behind, would rise. The motion was most peculiar, and I felt nauseous, though I knew that I would be unable to expel anything from within.

After a while, I could smell the outside air worming down the shaft to meet us. Jasmine, enriched by the summer's sun, smothered us as we headed inexorably upwards. The closer we got, the air itself seemed to retreat from our advances. Perhaps it was afraid that we would sully it, profane it with our impurity. As I turned the final corner, I looked out and saw that my kin were forming an orderly phalanx, to the side of the castle.

As my feet thudded on the baked earth, I saw that the moaning crowd from the gates were peeling away from their task, like water over a pebble. Some spark of intelligence, though minute, still coursed through them. Unable to breach the barrier, they sought to take advantage of this new egress.

I fell into formation and my body, on loan to me it would seem, came to a halt. A prisoner, contained within the crow's nest of my skull, I looked out, over the shoulders of the rows in front of me, at the filthy rabble, who approached us without fear.

The noise behind me of shuffling feet ceased, nothing but the rustling of our rags and the moaning of the creatures bearing down on us. I heard my master shout, "Advance. Take care of this scourge," before the sound of doors closing and bolts scraping into place. We were sealed outside, alone, to face these monsters.

His words though, stirred something from within.

Something primal.

As one, my kin and I raised our hands forwards and made a beeline for the retches afore us. It was then that I saw that the arms affixed to my body, were not my own. Such bony, branchlike limbs did I previously own, yet the ones which groped the air, were adorned with gaudy sailor tattoos and coarse black hair.

The act of trying to take in the sight, stole from me the fear I felt as the vanguard of our created host met the shuffling creatures head on. It was chaotic, like a masked ball with a long guest list, and too potent a wine. I could see the creatures latch onto my cohort with sundered limbs. Contorted in ways I thought not possible, they pulled the man in front of me in closer. Teeth, though that word does those broken pegs of ivory a great disservice, tore into the throat as if it were a roast chicken. The monster shook his head and tore free, removing a huge chunk of meat in its jaws. Yet no blood came forth.

The man, paying the injury no heed, clamped his gigantic hands against the side of the monsters head, and squeezed. Forcing the cannibal to spit out the flesh it had claimed. Ham hock hands continued to push together. There was a cracking sound, like wood being split, and then

213

the creatures face caved in on itself. At the centre, were the two gore soaked hands, still trying to join as one, as if in prayer.

Blackened eyes rolled upwards, into the remains of the skull, and it fell slack in my associates grasp. Wrapping a hand around the limp creature's neck, he pulled the head clean off, the innards nothing more than stringy pulp.

No sooner had I witnessed this, than the near feral beasts broke through our ranks, and I was stood toe to toe with one of their number. She was tall, nearly as tall as me. One of her arms was twisted around, so that the palm of her hand faced the wrong way, yet she still retained some mobility within her putrescent digits. Broken fingernails scratched down my face, digging into my forehead and gouging my skin. Yet I felt no pain.

Her mouth was ajar, that mournful moan rumbled out of her maw, as if it was the only sound she was capable of making. With no thought other than marvelling at how sullen her skin was, my calloused hand reached into her open mouth. I could see the tendons on the top of my hand rise to the surface, as my fingers formed a claw, finding a handhold down her throat. The sound coming out of her now was muffled, like someone choking on an undercooked bun.

My other hand ran over her face, before it closed around a dense patch of her hair. Holding her tightly, the hand which had disappeared down her throat tensed and began to pull. Despite pulling out fistfuls of hair, each time I went back for more, finally, my other hand reappeared holding the woman's jaw as if it were a purse.

Her eyes were full of bewilderment, as though signals were being sent to her mouth, which I now held in a hand that was not my own. For the briefest of moments, I identified with her struggle. Both captives within a machine that was no longer under our control. She stood for a moment, my hand still grabbing hold of her hair. Around me, her vile friends clawed at me, ripping my meagre clothing, or peeling off staples as they tried to exact revenge.

Then, my hand, still clutching the bottom of her face, came across at a clip and smacked into her skull. A mixture of the force of the blow, and her putrefying body, caused her head to near disintegrate before me. A cloud of stringy black veins, and fat worms of brain flew through the air, spraying those next to me. My hands released her jaw and scalp, before turning to the side and pummelling another of the rancid horde to a pulp.

All around me, my brothers and sisters obeyed my master's command to the letter. Though some fell, their bodies pulled apart by prying fingers and weight of numbers, we prevailed. Our bodies, prime cuts from the butcher's block, tore into them as if they were nothing more than sacks of wheat.

Still…as we twisted them apart, ripping them limb from limb, hauling their intestinal tract from their guts like rope, the moaning was omnipresent. Only when the last was cast into the abyss of death once more, did the infernal noise stop. Replaced by utter silence. Locked in place, I looked down at a casserole of body parts, not knowing how many people they once belonged to. My hands were caked in thick black ichor, as if I had been tarring a stable roof.

As the first bird dared to break into song, there was a noise from the castle walls. It could only be one person. My master, Doctor Frankenstein.

I knew within my no longer beating breast I would no longer serve him food or run his baths, I would at least do his bidding in other ways. For though these fetid golems of flesh were dead, I had no doubt that we would be put to use in other ways. There are many villages and towns nearby, many of which have sought to drive my master from his ancestral lands. Whether they are made of one flesh, or raised in unholy ways, they will all atone for their existence.

I will no longer hear the frenzied hate mob at *my* door, braying for my blood.

I will hear only the terror of my master's enemies, as I tear down theirs.

It's time to…
EMBRACE YOUR FATE

Truly an uplifting tale of allowing yourself to be a passenger in life, letting the waves of futility wash over you and cleanse you with their cooling currents of acceptance. The next story on **Page 250** is an example of what could happen to you if you're silly enough to try and resist. Heaven forbid that you think you're capable of besting this monstrous creature, physically or mentally, and winning somehow.

For fun, why don't you start rubbing some oil onto your skin? Perhaps crush up some spices from your kitchen and massage that all over your body too? It'll help deal with the...erm...stress and strains of this wonderful, I mean *terribly sad* situation. Boo-hoo. Et cetera.

DAYS GONE BY

And just like that, the beast let go of the ledge. The sound it made when it hit the floor was like nothing I'd ever heard before. It was like a midget tangling with a black bear, and I can tell you this for free, folks, *that* is not a pleasant sight.

Poor Tiny Blisterfoot, may you rest in pieces.

Still, as you can see over my shoulder, you will notice that a small group of people turned up shortly after the creature died. If you look closely, you can see there is a man in a once-white tracksuit, reading what appears to be the Ladybird Book of Amateur Binding, and jabbing the thing as he does so. There is a couple with him, who are arguing over the semantics of time travel.

But not as odd as the other member of this little cabal, who has a *pot* for a head. That's correct, folks, you heard me right, he has a genuine terracotta pot for a head. I think I need a lie down after all this, it's been a stressful few hours.

I just hope that by the time I wake up, everything returns to colour, as this monochrome world is freaking me out.

This is Adam Smedley, back to you, Mike, in the studio.

Say, Claire, is that a web in the corner of the lens? How the hell did that get there? I don't know, you leave your equipment on a dead monster's head for one second and the next thing you know, the wildlife starts taking over. Hang on, I'll just go wipe it away.

Holy Jesus, is this my eighth birthday party?

CONGRATULATIONS!
THIS IS ENDING
#5

'A GENUINE FIRST IN LITERATURE, AND NO-ONE CAN TAKE THAT FROM ME. NOT EVEN YOU, RUSTY BEAUCHAMP!'

You have to admit, that was pretty cool, huh? I hope you

217

scatted along with those bits, if not, you need to question your life and throw yourself at all of these opportunities in the future before you return to dust, and all that malarkey.

To make your life easier, if you want to go back to the last major choice and see what other mischief you can get up to with that time machine, spin some non-flashback-inducing butt silk rope over to **Page 416**. But if you've already experienced them all, and just want to go back to the Inglourious Bustard, right at the start of this adventure and see what else is out there, then find your way over to **Page 150**.

GET TO THE FLAT!

Ian stood up proudly, raised his pint glass to his lips, and aside from a dribble of the amber nectar splashing against the gusset of his trousers, chinned it in one. Running his forearm across his mouth, he said, "Strange times call for strange measures, and there's no one with stranger ideas than me. Gentlemen, ladies, I bid you adieu."

With that, he barged his way through the bickering masses, who hadn't paid him the blindest bit of notice, to the front door. "Wait up!" Monique necked her drink and caught up with him.

Begrudgingly, Noah climbed down from his wooden tower, muttering under his breath. As he trudged through the bar, a man ran up to him and grabbed hold of his tracksuit top. "DON'T GO! YOU HAVE TO STAY AND FIGHT WITH US. WHO WILL LEAD THE LEADERLESS?"

Looking the man up and down, Noah twatted him over the head with his staff. Collapsing to the floor like a politician's approval rating following a sex scandal involving livestock and a steak mallet, Eddie reached his weak fingers towards the priest. With the man on his knees begging for clemency, Noah bashed in the man's skull until it was rendered open-air. As Eddie lay quivering on the floor, with memories of his most recent Man of the Match display at skittles being replayed in slow-mo, Noah rammed the pointy end into the remnants of the brain and used it like a gory mop on the already-stained carpet.

Once the floor was streaked with pieces of grey matter and bone fragment, Noah straightened his top before looking down at the pulverised human beneath his staff. "No one, and I mean, NO ONE, touches the tracksuit, okay? It's Lonsdale, a Chav Direct special. I had to rob thirteen charity collections to save up for it."

Seeing a box with a small plastic dog on top, one paw held in the air like a little orphan boy-dog-thing, Noah pointed to the television and ahhed. With the pub locals distracted, he picked up the charity box for local blind dogs and tiptoed out of the boozer like a cartoon villain.

219

The trio skated back to Ian's flat, making sure they didn't slip on the still-slick floor of blood and guts, which were strewn over the road and pavement. Ian tutted; he had half a mind to email the council when he got back, to complain about how utterly lazy their cleaning services were. What would it take for them to get off their backsides and clean this muck up, huh? The end of the world? He laughed to himself, *nice one.*

As Ian stepped through the doorway that used to hold his front door in, he coughed and pointed at it, making sure Noah noticed. Although it looked like the priest had acknowledged the subtle dig, in reality, Noah was rotating the charity box, trying to work out if there was enough change inside for a giant Chav Direct mug. He'd seen the other waifs and strays at the religious outcast's hostel sipping away from just such things, so he longed for one. That you could fill it with a hot beverage and have it go cold before you finished, was on his bucket list.

With the end of the world a possibility now these stupid humans were ignoring him, it might have to be a purchase he made sooner rather than later. Perhaps when he was there, he might pick up some more of those little socks. The ones that end below your ankle. They went well with sandals when summer came around.

After running through the list of beverages again, and bringing forth a tepid can of lager for Noah and another non-tankery G&T for Monique, Ian poured himself two fingers of apricot bourbon and girded his insides for the taste.

"So, what is your great plan, oh master of the burger microwaving?" Noah said, you don't need me to add an adverb after 'said,' to know that he said it in a sarcastic manner. Nosireebob.

Ian took a glug of his drink —and after dry retching, found the aftertaste quite pleasant. If it came to it, he was sure it could double up as window cleaner, should they survive. He was confident that the potent oily liquid could cut through dried-on pieces of kidney and marrow. "Well, I have many plans, the first of which will require us to find seventeen dachshunds. With a length of rope, we-"

"No," Monique snapped.

"But you haven't heard the details yet."

"It involves poor defenceless animals. I don't want them coming to any harm."

"Oh...but they wouldn't *all* die, just the few that weren't favoured by the gene-splicing..." seeing Monique tap her foot, this time in more of a, 'I'll go and get some more explosives' way, Ian dropped the subject.

Noah clucked his tongue after taking a sip of lukewarm lager. "Tastes like Babylonian Old Man Urine." Rooting around within his undergarments, he topped up his drink again with the pink goo.

"What is that stuff? Saw you have some in the pub," Monique dared to ask, fully appreciative that the answer was undoubtedly going to be a stupid one.

Replacing the flask back into a hollow in his pant elastic, Noah took another sip of his lager and let out a satisfied. "Ahh, that's better," which indicated to the layman that it was, indeed, better. Sensing that Monique's ire and tippy-tappy foot were now aimed squarely at him, Noah conceded. "Fine, it's a mix of strawberries..."

"Mmm," Monique purred.

"... raspberries..."

"... mmm..."

"... kiwi fruit..."

"... mmm, go on..."

"... figs..."

"... eh? Well, I suppose as long as they're not overpowering, I might have some if-"

"... and the liquidised placenta of the innocent."

"I'll pass, you sicko."

"Please yourself, it's quite nutty, you'd like it if you gave it a go."

"EXCUSE ME," Ian shouted, coughing loudly too, just to make sure the attention was on him. "We came back here to discuss my excellent plans, not share cocktail recipes."

Sinking back into the welcoming embrace of the armchair, who hid a bevy of budget hotel brochures and tracheotomy pipes within its scatter cushions, Monique raised her hand. "Sorry, Mr Shouty. Please, continue." Noah plonked himself down on the sofa and bid Ian continue with this potential new story arc.

"Thank you. Honestly...so, if the cyberdog plan is out-"

221

"Aww, you never said anything about cyborg animals," Monique complained.

"Well, you didn't let me finish, did you? Too late now, gone off the idea. So, I have a plan so ingenious that the ol' dude in the wheelchair with the funny computer voice would shit the bed twice that he didn't think of them."

Monique leant forwards, "That's a bit risqué, Ian. Stephen Hawking can't help it. Plus, since the writing of the first draft of this book, he's gone and snuffed it. What a way to get out of being included."

"Who? I meant Davros, creator of the Daleks, he will be fuming when he realises that I thought of these first. So...we go to see my mate, Pothead Pete, and we have a lend of his time machine. Reckon we could then go into the past and get some dinosaurs and shit..."

"Or into the future and get some cool kickass robots," Noah added. "I fucking love robots, hope they have big fuck-off guns, too..."

"Yes, quite, or-"

"... and a single flashing red light where their eyes should be, like that car from Knight Rider..."

"-okay, that would be good, if I could j-"

"... and their voices are all like, *Affirmative...We must vaporise*...that would be cool..."

"Have you finished?"

"Not quite, I hope they have these spindly blade things on their arms that come out and go thwip thwip thwip thwip thwip, and cut people's heads off." Noah flailed his arm around as a suitable demonstration. Ian looked back with murder in his eyes. "Done," Noah said.

"Good. How do you know so much about robots, anyway? Aren't you the emissary of some long-necked avian god from the past?" Ian asked.

Taking a sip from his rejuvenated can of fruit, lager and placenta mix, Noah shrugged. "And? Lots of time to kill, you know, it's not easy waiting for the rebirth of a world-killing beast. People think it's all specialist-lingerie models bouncing up and down on your winky and doing lines of drugs off the backs of mythical animals. The reality is daytime television and trying to knock one off whilst the rest of the religious zealots are sleeping. Into a sock. Not yours.

Obviously. That takes away the desire."

"You're weird," Monique stated. Again, if I were to go against Meester King's advice, I'd add 'with disgust,' just there, but you get the gist.

"Why don't we just go back in time to before we played Scrabble? We could stop the entire SNAFU happening before it even started."

Noah shook his head. "Are you absolutely out of your tree? You could mess with the very fabric of time, yeah? It isn't like writing something down on a scrap of paper and erasing it, you know?"

"Yes it is, it'll be the equivalent of crossing it out and writing something again, or just screwing it up and throwing it in the bin. BOSH, done." Monique folded her arms, feeling the defence mechanisms kicking in.

"Like *you* know! It'd be like trying to use Tipp-Ex to change what you wrote, but instead of Tipp-Ex, it would be a flamethrower, and instead of a scrap of paper it would be the concept of time itself; you could wipe everything and everyone from existence in the entire universe. Or, even worse, trap us all in a permanent loop where there is no future, just a finite amount of possible futures, I dunno, at a guess, around nine? Honestly, *you* people..."

Ian smacked a vintage copy of Doctor Nano Versus The Nephilim of Doom —issue seven— against the coffee table, bringing silence to the room. "You two are going off-piste again, so...ya know, shut the fuck up a minute."

Silence.

"Now, whilst we're on the topic of killer ideas, I've got one of my own, and this one is top drawer. Are you ready?"

Noah and Monique looked back as if they had lapsed into a coma.

"Excellent, how about we...become super-heroes and do a spot of monster-killing ourselves?"

"That has to be the most ridiculous idea I've heard in a long time, and I should know, I've been at history's worst-ever decisions." Noah gave up nursing his drink and finished it in one.

"Well, it's a good job it's not your choice to make, eh? It's in the hands of someone infinitely more knowledgeable in such matters."

223

Noah grinned so smugly that even he was a bit put off by it.

"Hold it, tracksuit-boy, I didn't mean you. I mean someone who really knows their shit. Someone who has a mind of their own, and is probably dead cool and that."

It's time to...
DICTATE YOUR FATE

If you want to turn this book into a Super-Book, with kickass powers and...who am I kidding, it's going to be a little odd and disgusting, but I'd say ultimately worthwhile, then you fly on over to **Page 46** with your cape all billowing and that.

If you think time travel is a goer, perhaps you want to go back to the past for dinosaurs, the far-flung future for robots, or you simply wish to avoid the whole Scrabble balls-up in the first place, you'd better re-materialise on **Page 394** so you can make your way over to Pothead Pete's gaff.

I SPY

I spy with my little eye, something beginning with...D.

Nope, how can it be a dog? Has to be something that I, and therefore by definition you, can actually see.

Ha, no, not dirt.

Erm, no, it's not daddy either.

Okay, so I'm going to put this out there, it ain't gonna be pretty or easy to hear, but your daddy? Yeah, he's probably dead.

I'm sorry, did say it wasn't going to be easy to-

Please don't cry, I'm not predisposed to deal with crying kids, least of all ones that are probably half an orphan.

Though your mum has been a while getting the firewood...

Nah, I'm sure she's fine, the chances of our new friends turning both of your parents into batteries on the same day is pretty slim.

Well, mostly slim, if you're pushing me for a number, I'm gonna say, sixty percent. Sixty five tops. Huh? I meant a sixty five percent chance of them *not* being captured by our new alien overlords and turned into the power supply for their aPhones or whatever the hell they have.

Better? Good, that's the spirit, gotta be tough, just like people were through the Blitz and that. You don't have a clue what the Blitz was huh? Well, it is kinda like now, but instead of aliens dropping weapons of unimaginable horror onto populated areas, and then hoovering up the survivors, who didn't have their skin melted off, it was the Germans.

But without the hoovering up.

Okay, seriously, now is not the time or place for a history lesson, just take it as read, and if by some miracle humanity survives this and you have internet access again, you can pick it up from there, yeah? Good, now, let's just stay behind this rock and keep a lookout like we said we would.

I'm also gonna say this now, if you wander off again? I won't be dragging you back here, I don't care if the cave smells like old people, if you need the toilet, you'll have more chance of seeing this through if you don't go running

225

off to the nearest crater to relieve the tension building against your bladder wall.

Plus, no toilet paper out there eh? If you're lucky, perhaps a bloodstained rag or someone's old jumper, but neither has the absorption qualities of the supplies back in yonder cave.

Good, so you worked it out yet or do I have to tell you? No, it's not dog, you said that earlier didn't you? This is going to go on a while isn't it? It's dead body, over there look.

Oh, by that dog.

Well it wasn't there when we started this little game was it? No, I don't think you win, even on a technicality, it was blind luck you got that.

Fine, well, okay, I'll let you win this one, but I can't say I'm too happy about it. Wait a moment, what's that over there? By the line of smashed up trees, the ones that giant metal walker thing crushed yesterday. We were bloody lucky there too, knew we shouldn't have had beans for breakfast, your little parps very nearly gave away our little hideout.

I think it's a man, must be one of the hunting party, you stay here kid, I'll go out and get them, they don't look too clever, could be your lucky day eh?

Stay. Here. Okay? I'll be right back.

Mate, hey mate, you alright? Jeez, I don't think that should be outside your body, just stay lying down, that's it, keep applying pressure to the wound. Or at least a bit of it, really is a bit of a nasty nick you got there huh? What the hell did that?

Huh? Sorry mate can't hear ya, Alan did this? But we don't have an Alan in the group, and if we did, I'm pretty sure his surname isn't Bastard.

Alan Bastard? That would be an unfortunate name, bit worse than Dusty Flapps.

Ahhhh, *alien* bastard. That makes more sense, well, he didn't like you very much eh?

226

Let's have a look.

Now, I'm no medical expert but I do remember reading somewhere that the smell of almonds is not a good thing.

No.

And nor is your ribs being fused together by some kind of high energy weapon, was it a thin red beam or a fat blue wavy one?

Purple?

Those little bastards, WAS IT WAV-

Okay, okay, I ain't going anywhere, just interested that's all, in case you haven't noticed, there aren't exactly many bipeds left on this planet. At least not many which don't have a red pointy helmet and blue body hair.

No, its fine, you're entitled to be a little pissy, it's to be expected after one of the harvesters takes a disliking to you with a pulsating purple rod.

Ha, mind you, saying it out loud does make it sound a bit, well, weird.

Yep, I will be, scouts honour, from now on, in your company and until you're on the mend, I'll cut out the jokes. Well, one good thing, your son might have been under the assumption you were...you know...a little bit dead, so seeing you will cheer him up. Though you might want to cover up that greeny pus that's seeping from your wound, that's not really a sign of good health, yeah?

Right, so, on three, I'll help carry you over to that rocky outcrop over there, one-two-

Woah, woah, hang on...wait a minute.

Is the alien nearby? Did you take care of him or is he going to make an unfortunate appearance as I start to drag you to safety? Not being funny, but the last thing I want is to end up like you, cos that looks nasty.

Yes, I bet it stings, can you feel this?

Uh-huh.

Uh-huh.

Yeah, I'm going to take your agonising scream as an affirmative. Urgh, it's all sticky and gross. Well, I may as well wipe it on your shirt, not as if you're going to get much more wear out of it once we get it off eh?

You are joking? Half of it is either missing or stuck to you like someone's ironed it to what's left of your skin. I don't

227

know where your shirt ends and your body begins.

Fine! I'm just saying that's all, starting to wish I'd left you out here now, not exactly the grateful sort are you? So, is the alien dead? Good.

Not that I doubt you at all, but how did you kill it?

Sorry?

Hang on, I'll just clear that gunk out of your mouth, oops, sorry, your lips are a bit swollen, and well, icky, think whatever was in that weapon has done you no good.

No, I'm going to have to put my foot down on this, until you tell me how you killed Alan...sorry, the alien, I am not taking you anywhere. Self-preservation mate! You'd do the same if the boot was on the other foot, so come on.

You thmacked him in th thace? I'm not su-

Ahh, you smacked him in the face, nice work, what with?

A thothel?

Shtothel?

A fossil?

Thuckin shuthel?

A shovel?

Ha, of course, knew it, bet he wasn't too happy with you then. Oh, yeah, silly me, explains why he did that to you, well, curiosity quelled, let's get you back to the sanctuary of the cave mate, and back to your kin.

Mate?

Mate?

Bugger, poor blighter, never stood a chance, it's just bloody typical these days, the good ones die young. You'd think after all of those that have already been snuffed out like candles in a monsoon, that your heart would be better able to deal with these losses. It doesn't get any easier man, doesn't get easier at all. Sleep well sweet prince. Sleep well.

Hang on, is that a Snickers in his pocket?

Hi kid, no, they didn't make it I'm afraid, their injuries were too severe, those alien bastards have no mercy for our kind. If we don't agree to be used to power their toasted sandwich machines, then they just disintegrate us on the spot.

If you're lucky.

No, the red one just shoots a hole through you, the blue wavy one is the one that disassembles you at the molecular level.

Your dad? Erm, no, that was...Olaf. You remember Olaf don't you? Black hair, blue eyes, moustache, didn't say much. Smelt of burnt hair. Yep, that was him, the one that went off with your dad and the other blokes a few days back.

Eh? I asked him, sure, but he was very badly wounded, said something about running into some aliens, there was a shovel, a purple slicing thingy, green pus and yeah, I think he said that your dad was fine the last he saw him.

Yeah, mostly fine, who can say though eh? Things happen so fast these days.

Anyway, enough about that, your turn matey, go on.

Beginning with S you say? Hmmm, sky?

Smoke?

Hmm, this is tricky, thought it was bound to be one of them.

Snickers?

No, good, ha, course not, I haven't seen one of those for weeks either, not since this all kicked off, quite lucky I was 'relieved of my administrative duties' that day, else I'd be providing the juice for their Walkman.

What's a Walkman, are you serious?

Oh, course, you're only seven.

Well, it's a device which plays music, again, one for the internet. I'm not really up for discussing the vagaries of the history of personal music devices just now.

Don't look at me like that.

Don't.

Fine, I am a miserable man, but trust me kid, its better this way, do you think your group is the first bunch of people I've met up with? Well, it's not, I've lost count of how many bands of ragtag survivors I've hunkered down with since all this happened. You lot are the current end of a blood covered tail dripping with disappointment.

Fine, just as long as you shut up a minute.

Well, to start with I was with the guys in the pub, I went there after the whole 'you're sacked' thing. God bless

Wetherspoon's I say, always there for you like a beer imbued milk maid, even more so at half nine in the morning, hold the bacon and pour me a Guinness.

Surprisingly, those guys didn't last too long, they'd be in there since opening at seven. As soon as the first ships hovered overhead and those weird tannoy things started off, they were all outside gawping up. Not me, I was waiting for the first pint to settle, you could say that Guinness saved my life.

See, Guinness *is* good for you.

So, once those laser things started zapping the obvious ones, the ones stood outside pubs for instance, turning them into smoking skellingtons, well, I did what anyone would do, I hid under the table.

Which in turn saved me from part two, when they dropped those spindly blade things down. You know the ones, you must've seen them, about the size of a barrel, really shiny, great big blades sticking out of the ends.

They hit the ground and then jumped about five foot off the ground, went whizzing around the place slicing people up. Mad it was, glad I had my glass with me, went right over the top of my table, would've spilt it for sure.

Anyway, that was when I made my move. Drank up and crawled out of there to the car park, took the first bicycle that I could find and off I went. Bloody knackered I was by the time I got to the edge of town, that's when part three kicked off.

Those flying grabby things swooped down from their ships and started snatching people. Even the bodies that were cut in half.

I dunno, probably ate them, or turned them into fertiliser, I don't know, I'm not one of them am I?

Got picked up by this minibus full of migrant strawberry pickers, bloody nice chaps they were, we never really understood each other, but they were a good bunch. We managed to get up to Slaughtergate Hill just as the grabbers left and the red blobs got dropped.

You do? Yeah, they were pretty gruesome, saw the after-effects of those a few days later, kinda turned people inside out huh?

Nasty stuff.

230

One of the guys I was with, think his name was Jakub, or something, he put his finger in one of the residue puddles, man, that was not pleasant. Not pleasant at all, it started off with his finger nail, it just started peeling back and then in on itself, the bones kinda just started falling out. Jakub was screaming by now, I had to punch him to render him unconscious, which took a few blows.

As, well, it's not as easy as it looks on the television.

So, he passes out on the floor and the red goo is working up his arm, popping his veins round the wrong way, blood spraying everywhere. These bits of muscle and meat were just bursting in front of us, took about five minutes to work its way all over his body. Man, in the end he was just a pile of sticky bones and a puddle of red slop.

Reminded me of those sticky ribs I had the other day.

Don't suppose the S is slop is it?

No, didn't think so.

Anyway, after I pummelled their mate unconscious, his chums weren't too enamoured with yours truly. I tried to explain why I did it, you know, for humanitarian reasons. But, well, my Czech was a bit 'nesmysl', and their English was a bit rubbish, so after some pointing and shouting, I bid my farewell and headed off.

Head down kid, there's a ship hovering over there, stay down.

Hang on, it's ship isn't it?

Yes, get in. Oops, best get back behind cover, we'll be fine, there's no way that they could have heard that. Well, not much chance anyway. So...

Yeah, think they've gone, that was close, tell you what, next time, just tell me rather than using it as the object in our game, deal? Good. Right, so my turn, I spy with my little eye something beginning with...erm...M.

That's got you eh? Not so gobby now eh kid?

Moustache? Who the hell has got a moustache? You do understand how this game works yeah?

Stop laughing, come on, I do have better things to do than babysit you.

Important stuff.

Well, for one, we're keeping a look out aren't we, really, I can do this on my own, you could go back to the cave with the others and wait there.

Okay then, so play the game properly.

You got one?

Mummy? Seriously, kid, you're busting my balls now. She went out-

Okay, okay, so that woman walking over there with armfuls of twigs does bear a passing resemblance to your mum. Ha, I hope she isn't all messed up like your...like Olaf, no, that would be bad. Right, again, stay here okay, I won't be long, hopefully there will be less pus this time, put me right off that can of mushy peas I was saving for later that did.

Hiya, how ya doing? Need a hand carrying that lot back?

No worries, was only asking you know, don't have to go all Putin on me, didn't even get to the outskirts of Monosyllabic town did you, just went straight ahead to Rudeville. Well, since we're here, just a quick heads up, I kinda bumped into your fella a while back, looks like he was the sole survivor of the party that went out.

No easy way to say this, but, he's sort of...well...dead. I'm sorry for your loss.

Did you hear me?

I said, he's dead.

Hmmm, you appear to be taking the news of your marital partner's demise awfully stoically, there's stiff upper lip and then there's no emotion whatsoever.

Not even a blink.

Or a lip tremble.

Or anything at all now I look at you, are you okay?

Oh shit, you've got one of those purpley slashy things too, you're one of the infiltrator units aren't you?

I'm having a little trouble breathing with your hand around my throat, I say, would you mind awfully, if you could see your way clear to releasing just a tiny bit of pressure?

Ha ha, didn't see that coming did you? BOOM, sawed off shotgun blast to the face, though it doesn't appear to have done too much. You lot must have taken in loads of eighties films. Guessing Terminator was on repeat a lot eh? Let's see if I can just get this thing turned on.

STEADY, nearly took my eye out that did, got a bit of a kick on it eh? Well, let's go and see how it works.

It is going through your metal chassis rather splendidly though eh? Like a hot knife through butter, the smell on the other hand, WOW, that's a nasal sensation. Somewhere between gone off milk and that pile of rancid meat we once called Jakub.

I have just realised that the kid might think it's a bit odd I'm hacking up the person who he thinks is his mum. Never mind, I'll explain when I go back, think I'll just take one of your legs or something, that should convince the little tyke.

There.

Not a bad job if I say so myself, didn't realise you could increase the power with that little button on the side, would've made it go a bit quicker, but hey, this is all new to me. I am finding that noise coming out of you a little disturbing though, if I just...no...oohhh, that made it worse, gimme a minute, if I just stick it in there...and...wiggle it...just a little bit.

There we go, the sound of silence.

Right, best lug something back as proof that I'm not some kind of maniac, though I'm getting the feeling that I better move on soon, this lot aren't the brightest bunch left if I'm being brutally honest.

If our time on earth truly is numbered, I could do with some more intelligent conversation than a kid who can't even work out that I spied a mushroom cloud with my little

233

eye.

Peasants.

It's time to...
EMBRACE YOUR FATE

That really had everything didn't it? Alas, that signals the end of our time together, it really has been a special time for us. Through your careful basting and preparation of your flesh, when the mighty Qzxprycatj shortly smashes down the walls of your pathetic abode, you will at least provide her with a taste sensation. For years we have waited and prepared for her return, and now that she has, we want to do everything that we can to ensure that nothing gets in her way.

Hark! She has just demolished the front wall of your neighbours' house and is gnawing on their pathetic mewling bodies even as you sit there ridden with catatonia. Fear not, she will be grateful to you – and us – for giving her something worthy of snacking on. You did follow our self-basting instructions, didn't you? No matter, you just get on over to **Page 419** and we can enjoy your demise together.

WHEN ALL HOPE IS LOST, SCREW.

Ian slumped against the bar, forehead first, a dull thud running down the length of the pitted wood, causing the empty glasses to tremble. "She's right...why bother? It's not as if we can kill it, the odds are stacked against us. It's got more arse cheeks than three of us put together for starters, plus with the devastating combination of convenient events affecting the ash tree, we're completely screwed."

Monique dithered between consoling Ian and leaving him to it. One thing she'd learned over the years was that a crying man was not an easy beast to deal with. She resolved to do *something*, though, so she tamely patted his head and muttered, "There, there," immediately regretting her choice of words as Ian stirred and pulled her into a bear hug.

The sound of wailing and sniffing back snot turned a few people's stomachs. Noah opened the flask of pink liquid, chinning it in one go. Wiping his hand across his mouth, he burped before sinking into the padded chair beneath him. "He's right, what's the point? For millennia, I've been a guardian of the mighty Emu god, seeking to protect humanity from extinction. When all my chums were gutted and nibbled on by that blue bastard, I thought it would be okay.

"Ya know? Thing is...I get so lonely. That's why I like to kick front doors in, or gob off in fish-and-chip shops at two in the morning, calling everyone out. It's all a front, I just want attention. Every night I go back to my bedsit, put on my LPs of Chaka Demus and Pliers, and try to think of happier times. Before I realise...those days are long gone. I'm the last of my kind, did you know that? The benevolent Emu god hasn't even bothered to call me over the last few hundred years.

"All my messages just go to his answering emu; my letters are returned, 'addressee has gone away.' For years, I thought it was something I'd done, but now, though, I know the voracious Emu god is ashamed of me. It can see the truth within, and it is disappointed at the choices I have

235

made."

Ted sloshed the oily liquid into the prepared shot glasses and pushed them across the top of the bar to the sombre clientele. "'Ere, you lot, don't get too glum with all this end of the world stuff, we all gotta go some time, eh? All that matters now is that we go out with a bang, not a whimper."

His words met with a unified *meh*, Ted shoved the stopper back into the bottle and replaced it behind the stash of fancy chorizo-and-stuffing crisps he'd nicked from the back of the delivery van the previous day. "Come on! Seriously. Look, Eddie, you've been knocking it out of the park this year with your skittles, why don't you and some of your mates go and have some games out back?"

Eddie shrugged. "I guess I could."

Raising his glass, Ted tried to inject a bit of life back into the sullen locals. "Come on, let's make a toast. To the Inglourious Bustard..."

"...and all that sail in her," Toby added, eliciting a cheer. As one, the pub knocked back the concoction —which reminded Monique of honey, charcoal, grubby fivers, and the last bus home. She shuddered and placed the glass back on the counter, glad that if these were the end days, she'd never again have to drink whatever the hell that was.

Ted ran his tongue around the inside of his glass, revelling in the home-made liquid, the recipe for which had been passed down his family for generations. Happy every last drop had been consumed, he lifted the bar flap and mingled amongst his customers. "We won't be needing to go outside anymore." With that, he bolted the front door shut and let the deadbolt clunk into place.

With the lights casting a dingy glow in the late afternoon, he went round and pulled the curtains shut. As the punters looked from one to the other and grinned, Ol' Clive started off singing the song of the ancients. "Lock in...lock in...lock in...lock in..."

The rest of the drinkers gradually joined in as the natural light was banished from the pub interior. Toby pulled a disconsolate Noah into a hug and kissed him on the head. The pair shared an awkward glance, before engaging in a full-on snog. Finally withdrawing after a few minutes of being the main attraction in a new spectator sport, Ol' Clive

236

patted him on the back. "'Bout bloody time you came out of the closet."

Toby wiped away a tear and hugged Noah, and the two men held each other as Ted reconnected the jukebox to the mains and punched in a super-secret code. "Tunes are on the house!" Noah squeezed Toby's arse and gestured towards the gents toilets. Giggling like a professional kitten cuddler, Toby nodded and they disappeared to the cubicles for some bum fun.

The pub erupted in a mammoth cheer. As Ted raised his hands to calm them down, he looked across to Melancholy Mel. "Just don't put on Snow Patrol, you little minx."

Even she managed to smile, wiping her long fringe out of her black-lined eyes and stashing it behind her ears. "I can't promise anything," she replied nervously, which garnered another loud cheer.

With music blaring from the tinny speakers nailed into the corners of the pub, Ted rooted around in a cupboard behind the dartboard and pulled out a stack of ashtrays and a box of Cuban cigars, given to him by Che Guevara after repairing his motorbike whilst on holiday in Peru. "May as well use these bad boys up, first come, first served."

Ian picked his head up from the bar and rubbed the bruise which had already started to come up. Monique appeared in front of him, smiling. "Are you chewing on a coat hanger?" he asked.

"Don't be silly, just think it's funny how you plan for a day to go one way, and then it turns out another."

"Yeah, the end of the world is one of those things, huh? Just funny how something as innocuous as an invite to scrabble and chill, ended up summoning a world-ending beast from another plane. But hey, suppose at least it means I don't have to find another job."

"And I don't have to go and get brainwashed by another loser who just wants to get his end away."

Monique bit her bottom lip as she walked her fingers up Ian's trousers, from knee to crotch. "Well...why don't we go and make the most of our time left? Not as if we've got to worry about where this is going to go, eh?"

Ian grinned like a certifiably insane person smearing faecal matter over their padded cell with their favourite foot.

237

"YES. I mean…whatevz…if you want." Monique smiled and pulled at his top, luring him closer. Before their lips met, he asked, "You are asking if I want to…ya know…*do it* with you, yeah?"

She clamped hold of the side of his face and kissed him in a way which felt like nothing his mum or aunt had ever done. As the lilting sounds of 'Sexy Boy' by Air played through the speakers, Monique led him to the gents and dragged him inside.

Ted chuckled. Young love, eh…well, not even love, just the need to go and get freaky before everyone and everything you've ever loved and desired is destroyed by some big-toothed monster. Ahhh, we've all had days like that. Smiling to himself, Ted closed the bar flap down and slapped his hands on the counter. "Ladies and gentlemen, if you please. To celebrate our last day on Earth, drinks…are on me!"

"HUZZAH!" the sound echoed down Castle Street, as panicked shoppers relaxed for a moment. This was to be their downfall, as the beast, hearing the sound and thinking it was the cheeky bastard that made it think it was gonna get some earlier, bounded off the spire and stalked down the streets.

As the newly unpanicked people rejoiced, believing that everything would be okay, Qzxprycatj scooped them up in its clammy blue hand and ate them.

With its bloodlust rising, it stamped down the road towards the sound. Someone was going to pay for tricking it into thinking some well-endowed apocalyptic beast wanted some action. Someone was going to pay BIG TIME.

Monique and Ian staggered into the cubicle, lost to their wanton desire. As the door slammed shut, Ian locked it with his buttock. Completely inadvertently, you understand, it wasn't as if he spent his spare time practising the lost art of locking cubicle doors with one's arse cheek. As Monique undid her jeans, they both heard a squeak coming from beneath.

Looking down, they saw two rats hidden underneath the U-bend, going at it like it was the last day on Earth. Which was good timing, because at that moment in time, it very much *was*. Ian made a shrieking sound; he could feel his

238

erection waning. Monique pulled him in closer, and shoved his hand underneath her top and onto one of her ample breasts. "Shh, it's okay, let them have their fun, they aren't hurting anyone."

With a boob in his hand, all thoughts of rats doing it human style on the floor of the grubby toilet slipped from his mind. As the pair fought to extricate enough clothing so they could get it on, they heard a rhythmic pounding from the next cubicle. Above the sound of ratty banging, they heard, "Oh yeah, big boy, say my name..."

"Noah?"

"That's right, and what am I?"

"Some weird priest from some kind of sect...look, is all this affirmation necessary?"

Giggling, Ian and Monique decided to give in to their carnal desires.

KEEPING IT TO A 15 CERTIFICATE (YEAH, RIGHT)

Qzxprycatj smashed another row of cars into scrap metal and picked up a bent and buckled SUV. The driver and passenger were still interred within, bound to the vehicle by their seatbelts. Sensing food, the beast shook the squashed metal tube as if it were a jar of obstinate ketchup. Aside from screaming, nothing but oil and brake fluid came out. Getting a bit pissy that its snack was taking its sweet time, Qzxprycatj fished a clawed finger through the smashed-in windscreen and tried to pick the delicacies out like melted fancy chocolates from their plastic tray.

The razor-sharp claw sliced through the safety belts, and Mr and Mrs Park flew forwards, striking the dashboard. Hearing the thud of meat against plastic, the creature grinned and raised the stricken vehicle above its huge maw. Applying a few firm thumps to the top of the vehicle, the married couple were sent screaming into the waiting mouth. The wait was worth it, and despite their advancing years, the pair were not too stringy. After spitting out strands of torn clothing, it turned its attention to the building in front of it.

Having used its powers of echo-trans-moglification — which is totally a word, btw— it stood with its balled fists ready to pummel the shit out of the establishment. Lowering its head down to street level, it couldn't look in through the windows, as those cloth things that humans use to block out light were pulled across. Leaning in, it placed its ear against the side of the building.

Within, it could hear strange rhythmic sounds, and it felt compelled to wiggle its giganto-arse in time to the melody. Using its super-hearing, it reached further into the interior, trying to work out if there was indeed a sexy apocalyptic beast looking to give it a good time. As it delved deeper inside, it heard three consecutive yelps of pleasure, ranging in volume, from small, to bassy, to shrill.

Monique dismounted, and started to slide her leg into her jeans. She looked across to Ian, who had his hands clamped over his ears. "Sorry, just when...you know...I go a bit high-pitched."

There was a knocking from next door. "No shit, Sherlock, I think you've just broken my crystal ball," Noah shouted.

"Judging from the sound you made, I thought you had twisted one of yours," Toby added, peeling himself off the toilet seat and towelling himself down.

Qzxprycatj shook with fury, raising its head once more to the heavens, and began to belch forth a monstrous roar. As its mouth opened, something else close by made the exact same sound that it was just about to do. Random, huh?

Down the bottom of the road by the mini roundabout, there was a shimmering in the air. A pink orb appeared from the ether and hovered above an abandoned minibus. From within, rays of coruscating light shone, bathing the brick office buildings with a wan glow. Losing its roaring impetus, Qzxprycatj scratched its head with a taloned paw and looked at the ball of pink light. As drops of yellow blood ran from the scratches, it snuffled the air with its nose trunk, trying to work out what the Dickens was going on.

Like an iris under the influence of MDMA, the ball grew bigger and bigger. As it did, the guttural roar from within became more and more shit-your-pants scary. What started off as a slight brown streaker had now become a full-on pebble dasher, complete with foul-smelling gas and pubic hair matting.

When the ball of pink light had grown to the regulation diameter, laid down by the Portal Inter Space Summoning Official Fanclub Foundation, which, if you don't know, I sure as shit ain't telling ya, the roar ceased. It was replaced by the growing chimes of 'Eye Of The Tiger' by Survivor. As it rose to a crescendo, a weedy hairy leg stepped out.

241

Taking a step backwards, Qzxprycatj dug its claws into the tarmac, anticipating trouble.

"'Ere, you lot, look at this," Ol' Clive pointed to the television, "isn't that outside, Ted?"

Ted scrabbled to find the remote amongst a pile of final demands from the Wiltshire Gas Company. Peeling off a book of stamps from the keys, he turned the volume up. The reporter's voice was drowned out by the aforementioned song, which flooded the airwaves and rendered any other electronic representation impossible.

"What *is* that?" Ian pointed at the pulsing pink orb.

"Never mind what it is, what the hell is coming out of it?" Toby added, fiddling with his pants, which felt all cold and sticky.

With one leg out, two larger-than-normal human hands appeared from the portal and grabbed hold of the rim of the circle. Like an eager baby being delivered, it pulled itself free from its temporal prison.

Freedom attained, it tipped its form towards the sky and let out another bowel-emptying roar. With its entry into this realm complete, the portal pinged to a close behind it, disappearing in a squelch, a moderately puny expulsion of confetti, and a burst of incandescent light.

As Monique worked her way to the bar, intent on having something a bit more stirring to drink this time, she saw Ian transfixed by the gogglebox. Worried that their relationship, no matter how brief, would be affected by some sport or other, she did the woman thing and coughed, whilst pouting. Ian was unmoved, doing nothing but point to the screen, his brain finally able to utter, "Is that…"

"… a pixelated thingy?" she finished.

"Looks like a static-covered wang," Ted mustered, as he poured Monique a cheeky gin and tonic, having found a bottle of Tankery gin underneath the bill envelopes. It had been distilled within a second world war Panzer tank that Ted kept in a lock up in Bulford.

The pixelated dick took a few unsteady steps forward before it cleared its throat, and, a little raspy from all the roaring, said, "Lo, as was foretold on the lavatory walls of public conveniences in Michael Wood services on the M5, I shall be awakened when two men, two animals, and a man and a woman copulate within five feet of each other. Not all together, you understand, as the logistics for that would be a lot for people to sort out. Though I have to give a shout out to Adam Howe, who did his damnedest. The dead barnyard animals were a nice touch.

"Anyhoo, not wishing to adorn a book cover with my unadulterated form, I have been pixelated by the summoning gods so that this book can be deemed a 15, and get around the necessary legal treatise, vis-a-vis a giant man-member walking about the place all erect and that.

"Fear not, although I am not as easily discernible as normal, my powers are not diminished. Take this, you foul beast."

Bending down, the pixelated dick pulsated and shuddered, before shooting pixelated beast-milk towards Qzxprycatj, who avoided it with ease.

"Is he mad?" Ian wondered aloud.

Noah clamped a hand on his shoulder. "Quite possibly, but there is no way this book is a 15."

Monique raised her glass. "Yes! You know what this means, don't you? We're saved! By chance, and totally not coincidental at all, we've accidentally summoned another monster, but this one must be a world-saving one, I'd wager. He's just tried to spunk all over the blue one after all."

Noah shook his head. "Oh little one, you have much to learn in the way of monsters..."

MONSTERS MAKE
STRANGE BEDFELLOWS

The two monsters squared up to each other in the street as Escobar the tumbleweed merchant peered out of the overhang to the Mates Life and Pensions building and let loose his most prized of tumbleweed. Only the bounciest, most erudite balls would suffice for such an occasion; the scene was being beamed worldwide, so he made sure he attached his Spurter address and website details to the circumference. Perfect for men waiting in maternity wards and those waiting for a train home after a night of drunken debauchery.

Ted tutted, and rummaged through his unfiled paperwork. Finally finding what he was after, he donned his spectacles (nicked from Phil the Pervert), and scanned the small print. "Bollocks," he uttered, loud enough to make a curious Ian ask what the matter was.

Shoving the document under his nose, Ted said to anyone who looked vaguely interested, "No bloody monster clause in my buildings insurance, if one of those so much as puts a claw or pixelated jet of monster jizz through the window, I'm not covered."

"Did you mean monster *clause*, Ted?" Ol' Clive volunteered, sniggering. But unfortunately, no amount of inflection stops that from being a joke that only works in print.

Shunning him to return to more pressing matters, like two giant fuck-off monsters outside, Ian turned his attention back to the television.

It was at this juncture that Eddie, fresh from kicking his mate's arses at skittles, made his way back into the bar clutching an empty pint glass. Gesturing for a refill, he looked up at the TV and ahhed. "Hey, you lot, why are you watching it on there, when it's just outside?"

His words were met with distracted arm waving and vehement shushes, as if he were a child again, interrupting his parents' game show viewing by demanding an act of love or praise. The little tinker had spent ages turning

Princess Peanut the hamster inside out so he could see where she'd hidden the sunflower seeds, so the least his parents could do is feign interest and help scrub the blood off the nursery walls. Eddie's brain fast-forwarded his childhood memory and he let out a solitary tear. Not today. Flipping the V behind their backs, he went to the front door, and popped outside.

"Hey, guys, looks like the blue thing has seen something...what *is* that? Is that some kind of shrivelled-up raisin?" Toby asked.

Noah shook his head. "Yegads! Look, it's...whatshisface, you know, the bowler, or whatever the hell he is."

The pubgoers looked from the screen, showing a convenient high-angle shot of the outside of the building, to the front door, which banged away, unfettered. Like a rotting fence panel in a hurricane.

It was only when Monique bolted the door shut that they were able to breathe a collective sigh of relief and go back to living vicariously through the moving images on the 42" plasma, liberated from the window display of 'Tee-Vee Dee-Lite' a few months back during the last scone riots.

Eddie stumbled into the street, dumbstruck. "Wow, you guys look even more amazing close up..." Sidling up to the hind quarters of Qzxprycatj, he ran a hand down the creature's hide. "It's just like stroking my pet snake, Fluffy."

The giant pixelated dick looked down at the human petting the beast, and laughed a booming laugh, with added pointing for effect. Sensing that it was losing cool points, Qzxprycatj turned on the spot, and flicked the pesky meatsack with one of its talons.

Eddie's giggling quickly became gurgling as he looked down to see that his stomach had been rent open, and his internal organs were plopping out onto the street. Some semblance of self-respect kicked in, and he knelt down and began trying to shove the slippery lumps of viscera whence they came. His face was now an ashen white, as his blood loss was now on the 'you're fucked' end of the seriousness scale, pooling against the kerb and running down the road into the drain.

"Ha ha ha," the unmistakeable booming laughter of the pixelated schlong was played in stereo through the telly and

245

the outside world. "Look at that silly man, it looks like he is stealing sausages."

Eddie, in a crumpled heap on the floor, shot a forlorn glance at the mocking blurry dong, and continued trying to stow his intestines away. Like a tap being turned off, one last trickle of blood plopped from the incision onto the tarmac, allowing Eddie's brain to throw in the towel.

Again, we're talking a metaphorical towel here, I'm sure an actual towel might have helped staunch the bleeding, and whilst probably not ultimately saving him, would've prolonged the agony and the hilarity of the dude trying to stuff his usually onboard organs back where they belonged.

Anyway, he's dead, poor sod. Who will take his skittles mantle now? The smart money is on Christine, sure, she has enough off days as good, but when she's on form, well...Un. Stop. Able. Fact.

Qzxprycatj looked across to the laughing cockmonster, and smiled, her small trunk swishing across her face coyly. She stabbed the dead body through the top of the head and held it up like a meat lollipop; tilting her head sideways, she held it out, gingerly, to the still-laughing pixelated penis.

"For me?" he asked, his penis-arms held outwards in surprise. "But...but...no one has ever given me a present before."

Qzxprycatj sashayed towards the palpitating mass of pixels and pallid limbs, and held out her finger with the body of Eddie still impaled thereon. The guts and intestines fell out of the chest cavity and looped down like a mass of exposed wires on a broken toy.

Bending down, the pixelated dick bit into a length of intestine and tugged at it gently, pulling the entire length of knotted skin rope free. Flicking the useless body against the side of the Mates building, Qzxprycatj bent down and took the other end in its mouth.

"Gross, the pair of them are chewing on the shit pipe..." Noah managed, before dashing off to the toilets to vomit. It had brought back painful memories of pretending to be a zombie in the sixties, and tearing off a chunk of guts and almost destroying the entire ruse by throwing it back up again. It was a lot easier to mess with people when they were off their gizzard on LSD.

246

Like a grisly Lady and the Tramp, the two monsters idly slurped and sucked on their end of the intestines before meeting in the middle with a kiss. The pair tittered playfully, and turned away shyly, though keeping their eyes locked on each other.

Searching its knowledge of the English language, Qzxprycatj looked into the pixelated eye of a one-in-a-million chance at redemption, finally growling out. "Monster...love?"

Clutching its hands to its pixelated chest, the dick, let's call it Samuel, reached out and pressed a finger against the lips of Qzxprycatj. "No...you're not a monster. Not to me. To me...you're...beautiful." This sent Qzxprycatj into rapture, and she bounced on the spot, filled with glee for the first time in her murderous existence. Even when she was having a poopy in the otherworld, she couldn't help but eviscerate some other creature or tear apart a lost soul or two.

From inside the bar came the sound of gentle sobbing. Ian turned around and found Monique blubbing as if she'd just been told she was allergic to chocolate. "What?" he asked.

She wiped a tear from her eye. "It's just so wonderful."

The outpouring of emotion spilled over and they embraced, sparking a tidal wave of hugging, kissing and high-fiving in the pub. Even Ted, who never cried, even when he was being tortured by having to watch Hollyoaks non-stop for a year, allowed a solitary tear to run down his craggy face.

Outside, the two monsters held hands before pulling into a passionate embrace.

It's time to...
DISCOVER YOUR FATE

Aww, ain't that sweet? Just goes to show that in this crazy world, the strangest things can happen. Without wishing to spoil anything, it might be worth buying a new hat and/or fascinator, heading on over to **Page 392,** and find out what happens next.

BRING EVERYONE
TO THE SLAUGHTER

Humble viewer, the fight, if what happened here can be described as such, lasted around seventy-five seconds. According to the stopwatch on my tWat phone anyway. I independently verified this with Claire, who has the latest Universe 12XA-3RT Professional phone.

As the whooping band of rebels launched themselves at the beast, it dropped back to using four legs. The impact from the two feet hitting the ground took out the vanguard and the self-appointed leader, who looked like he was wearing a Margaret Thatcher Burger shirt. I mean, what were those people thinking? Taking orders from someone who was still wearing a hair net, for Pete's sake.

Anyway, with the advance party crushed to death, the attack lost momentum. With its giant snout, the beast began to snort up those choosing to flee. Some, I'm guessing, tasted a little disgusting, as they were then propelled out of the nose as if they were being fired out of a cannon at an Olde Tyme amusement park. I saw one of them hit the side of the Embarrassed Lion hotel, just over there.

The weapons did little to the monster. Frenzied attacks by a group of men brandishing power tools achieved nothing except earn themselves an early evisceration.

So now, as I look out upon the field of the most one-sided battle since the first war on punctuation, I can only wonder what lies ahead for us all. If you're thinking of fighting, look at these poor bastards' guts right here, I reckon that'll be enough deterrent.

Stay indoors, folks, that's my advice. I'm pretty sure that if it can't see you, it can't eat you. It's not as if he will be able to drive you insane through your dreams, eh? Am I right? AM I RIGHT?

This is Adam Smedley, Wiltshire Today, in Salisbury.

Back to you in the studio, Mike.

CONGRATULATIONS!
THIS IS ENDING
#6

'NO PLAN? NO HOPE FOR YOU THEN, EL STINKY.'

Did you honestly think that would work? Ah well, you've found this ending anyway, which is good. I bet you're eager to get back to earlier on and choose something different aren't you? I've got ya, wade through the body parts back to **Page 150** and you'll be n the Bustard, before this all went horribly wrong. Or, if you just want to see what happens with the other fight choice, then flim-flam to **Page 351** where you'll see how that pans out. Choose wisely.

GLASSJAW

Nice to meetcha, son. It's Mickey, ain't it? Don't you worry none about this sweat pit right now, it looks worse than it is, trust me on that. You may know me, you may not, I'm Ronny, but everyone, whether they're out beyond that curtain drinking, or back here ready to rock 'n roll, calls me Ballbreaker. On this here wrestling circuit, a name is your most important selling point. It's gotta tell someone immediately what you're all about. Has to be something real simple to let anyone know, regardless of their current level of sobriety, what they can expect. Needless to say, you can guess my area of expertise real easy.

You seen me fight? When was that?

Ha, that summer, huh? I wasn't in a happy place back then. I'm mighty surprised you're here if *that* was the bout got you interested in this life.

Nope, I don't see or hear from Gouger no more. Last I heard, he moved down to the 'Glades, lives out there with his barely legal lady friend. I still wager he speaks an octave or two higher, and if he can have kids after what I did to him that night, then, well, I guess there must be some kind of higher being up there after all.

Now look, you're here because you spoke to the big man, Pauly. I'll bet you dollars to donuts that in no time at all, he gave you his weird-ass smile and promised you the world. He's kind of a necessary evil to get your foot on the first rung of the ladder. Thing is, and he can't argue against this, though he might try, he'd get you stripped down to your tighty whities and out in that ring, before you had a chance to write down your next of kin.

Just in case, you understand?

But, if you take just one itty bitty piece of advice from an old timer like me, don't sign shit till you've slept on it. What he likes to do, is swoop on in as you're lying belly up on your bunk later, still glowing from winning your first bout. You see, in that moment, with all that adrenalin pumping, you'd say yes to Old Nick asking for your earthly soul in exchange for some magic beans. So do not, under any circumstance, put your John Hancock on that contract till you've passed out and woken up.

Trust me, come morning, win or lose, you'll know whether this is the life for you.

It ain't pretty, shit, in thirty eight states, it ain't even legal, but for some, most of us if I'm being honest, if we weren't doing this, we'd be in those shitpits of Leiber or Lee, counting the days off another stretch inside.

I'll tell you this for free, son, when you open those baby blues in the morning, and try to sit up, every bone in that body of yours will be screaming. There'll be a voice in your head that's either telling you to go again, or head back to momma. Either way, that decision is yours and yours alone. Don't let Pauly, me, or none of these other meatheads tell you otherwise.

Good, now we've got that sorted, let me show you around.

You don't get your own stoop first off, only old timers like me get those. We're on the payroll, we get what few luxuries are owing because of that. You can share mine tonight, just don't touch my shit. Else, me and you will fall out real easy.

Lesson one, everyone, from Marjory on the door, to Tony who cleans the jockies, is superstitious as all hell. Whatever you do, do *not* fuck with another person's shit. Ever. Just because a belt buckle looks like it ain't on straight, don't mean it ain't supposed to be like that. One tiny thing out of place will fuck up someone's day, and, by way of universal wrestling karma, fuck you up, got it?

Good. You're a quick learner, I can tell that about you, son. You'll be alright. Dump your shit on my chair, I ain't too fussy about that on fight night. Now close your eyes a minute.

Go ahead, it's okay, I ain't gonna grab your junk or nothing.

Good. Take a deep breath, don't stop till you feel your boot leather being pulled up your nose.

Ha, spit if you need to, that's okay, there's a bucket down there. That aroma is something you'll get used to, but first off, it'll hit you in waves. It's everything you'd expect: sweat, blood, tears, puke, booze and smoke. Shit, it's hopes and

251

dreams, son. That's one powerful cocktail, some days you won't even notice it, others, it'll wrap around you like a Boa Constrictor and crush the very shit out of your ass.

See that guy over there? The one with his back to us?

That's right, the one who looks like he's been dragged through town at the end of a rope, that's Serge, they call him Sander.

See those burns on his back? Got 'em from a belt sander a while back, bled like a stuck pig, but damned if I ever seen someone with a bigger grin on their face after. Anyways, I'm going off at a tangent. He reckons that the smell of this place on the night, tells you what's gonna happen. Figures he's some kind of all-knowing Nostradamus or some shit. Once or twice, he's called it. A nasty leg break here, a busted jaw there. Course, he's got more wrong than right, but even I gotta admit that sometimes, that smell...it's eerie. Like a goddamn spectre. All those aforementioned hopes and dreams the way I figure it. Some nights that ghost is like motherfucking Casper, and your best friend. Other nights? It wants to rip your goddamn face off and chew the meat down to the bone.

Next to Sander, you've got Chomper. He don't need no mouthguard. Didn't lose his pearly whites in the ring, he got tanked one night when he was starting out, and was set upon outside the venue by some folk who didn't take kindly to him having whipped their boy's ass. They'd lost a tidy sum, and decided to work out their frustrations on him. This one guy caught him a good 'un with a house brick. Shit, Chomper lost most of his teeth, got a fractured eye socket, smashed jaw, and his face, which weren't a picture to start with, swelled up like an artificial titty. But let's just say this; they won't be finding those good old boys any time soon. I promise you that. Alabama dirt don't give up its secrets easy.

You look a little green around the gills there, son, wassa matter?

Ha, of course you won't be fighting those two. Hell, those sons of bitches would rip your head off and shit down your throat no sooner had you set one foot on the mat.

Lesson two, the newcomers fight each other, no exceptions. See over there? By the shitters? Yeah, you'll be fighting one of those boys. We tag team up the fresh meat, gives us a good look at you first. Plus you get to take a breather every now and then. Them lot over yonder have been out front once or twice before, so this is why you get ol' Ballbreaker bending your ear tonight.

Nope, don't know which ones, and if I'm being honest, don't much care. You boys will just go off at each other for as long as you have spunk left in ya. You're there for two reasons, to keep the crowd entertained ahead of the main fights, and to see which of you will still be here tomorrow, hand in the air, looking to give it another go.

So, tonight you'll just be 'The Okatie Kid' and twenty bucks richer, anything above and beyond that, you're gonna have to earn, son. Every goddamn scrap of it.

Yep, twenty bucks, win or lose. Pauly knows that for anyone to have the sack to stand toe to toe with another man in that ring, with all kinds of hollering going on around you, folk shouting at you to kill that sumbitch, well, the one who gets tapped out is as brave as the one standing over him.

Now, lesson three, and this one's a doozy, I sure as hell wished someone had told me this when I was in your boots. Look after yourself. In this place, it's all too easy to say yes to anything and everything. You'll be offered all manner of substances you can snort, smoke or stick in your veins to take away every last drop of pain. There'll be women that'll promise to do the same, but manage nothing except make your dick turn green and hurt so bad when you piss, you'd wish it would fall off.

Look at me, son. I'm forty-three years old, four divorces down and two kids I ain't seen since they were delivered screaming an ungodly racket into the world. I'm two hundred and thirty two pounds of scar tissue, gristle and regret. You see this here body? It's formed from burritos, bourbon, barbiturates and bad decisions. Yeah, so what? I can take a punch, I can damn near take losing a limb if I had to, and I'd still be standing, but that ain't outta choice.

Pick up that bar. That's right, that one. Now I want you to pop me on my arm. The left one. Shit, you do know your left from your right? I only ask, cos if you get me on my right, you're liable to be eating your food through a tube for the next month.

Go on now, on my upper arm, hard as you like.

Harder.

See. Nothing. Nerve damage. Pretty bad too. So bad that sometimes I can barely wipe my own ass. Got hurled out of the ring onto a church pew when we was down in Jesup a few years back. Done near gone broke my back. Busted up my shoulder real good. By all accounts I was speaking in tongues for two days. When the morphine wore off, my entire left side was just sorta numb. It comes and goes. Some days are worse than others, but most of the time, you could drill through to the bone in my bicep and I wouldn't even whistle Dixie.

Though I would only suggest doing that in my sleep. I'm liable to choke you out otherwise.

That's a joke, son.

You gotta lighten up, don't take this shit too serious.

These moments, before? After? You gotta enjoy them the best you can. We ain't out there sitting at a desk, pushing paperclips about, or selling people cars or burgers. You could die out there in that ring, so you gotta make sure that when you're not staring a man down, wondering if you've got enough left in those heavy legs of yours to make a move, that you make the most of it, okay? Good. Now, come on. We probably got time for lesson four, before you learn the big one all on your lonesome.

Mickey, meet Marjory. No cussing or spitting, son, stand up straight and don't let those spidery eyelashes or those big doe eyes fool you none. She'll snap your wrist if you decide to put your hands on her without an invite. This fine lady will no doubt be the first person you see if you go and get yourself knocked out. Either out there on the mat, or laid up in a fancy hospital bed. So whatever you do, treat her like she's kin. She's also in charge of paying ya.

Nope, not Pauly. Trust me, soon as that first bell goes, and the snot starts flying, you won't see hide nor hair of him. He'll be firmly ensconced in one of his many lady friend's erogenous zones. Hitting it up like it was the last days of Sodom and Gomorrah, so don't even bother looking for him. Nope, Marjory runs this circus, and if you have any human resource type questions troubling that thick head of yours, you speak to her first. Period. Got it, son? Good, now say, 'goodbye Marjory'.

Come on, follow me, watch out for those wires, you don't want to be known as the idiot that was beaten by a length of flex. Duck beneath that curtain, but be real quiet like.

This is it. The ring. It's our own, so we just take it up and put it down anywhere we've been paid to, and a few places in between. The sheriff over in Macon requisitioned it one time, to settle a grudge with one of his deputies. Those doughy sons of bitches were going at it for near on an hour before Marjory stepped in and declared it a draw. Tell you this for free, ain't never seen two men bitch slap another for so long, without growing a vagina, make of that what you will.

The chairs all belong to the venue, some are nailed down, you'll come to like those places. Others, like tonight, they truck 'em in from all over, that's why no two chairs look the same.

Why will you like the nailed down ones? What kind of question is that? Son, have you ever been hit in the face with a chair? And I ain't talking about one of those aluminium tubular things, with a fancy foam seat which folds up nice and neat. You know, the kind your momma keeps in the basement until the holidays. The one she always puts your pop's momma on, just so she can lord it over her for an afternoon.

No, I'm talking about one hundred percent American hardwood. High back, sturdy, the kind you used to get in school. See, if it's a prop, and when you've shown your mettle a few times, you'll get in on that, more cash you see. If it's a prop, then one of the crew, those morose looking motherfuckers skulking round down there, hunched over like that French fella who lived in that bell tower, well, they're supposed to doctor it. Just enough. Saw through the back rest a little, so that when your opponent introduces it to your body, *it* breaks instead of you.

Problem is, most of the crew are drunks or retards. Shit, some are a healthy mix of both. See ol' Brian down there? He's dumber than a post, and ugly to boot, I've seen him this one time, trying to start the truck. Took him half an hour to realise that he was sat on the wrong side. Dumb shit is

255

sat there, hands clutching thin air, his stupid Pinocchio foot, he lost the real one outside of some shitty village in Iraq, going up and down like a cheap whore on payday. Just sat there, ain't paying the silence no mind. Grinning like he's sat in his own shit in a sewer.

Anyways, you won't be getting props tonight, so lessons on power tools and barbed wire bats will keep just fine for another day. Course, you might get the odd bottle or coin throwed at you, so keep your eyes peeled.

Look around you, son, people are here for two things, fighting and drinking, so the odd bottle *will* find its way into the ring. Take a look at my forehead. Yep, looks like road rash, don't it? This head's had more bottles broken over it than all the ships down at the docks. It don't hurt too bad, just if you see someone come at you with a champagne bottle, well, put 'em down before they brain you, is my advice. Else the world'll be going black, and you'll be looking up into Marjory's eyes in no time at all.

Fifteen minutes. That's what you get. Don't sound like much, but when you're out there, one minute can drag its sorry ass for an eternity. The only rule is that the last man standing wins. You get draws, not many, but you do. Regardless of whether you win or lose, show your appreciation to these drunken bums and respect to your opponent. We're a tight crew, so you can bet your bottom dollar that within a week or two, you'll be fighting that man again. The last thing you want is for there to be bad blood between you. Trust me on that one, son.

One more thing, you may have seen some hardcore wrestling matches, in places like these, where folk use blades or glass to cut their head, jazz everything up with a bit of color. Don't do it. If your opponent sees you with a shiv, the only way it's going to end, is with you in the care of an EMT if you're lucky, or with a toe tag on if you ain't. We put on a helluva show as it is, there's more than enough blood and guts to send folk on their way satisfied. We're gladiators, crappy paid ones, but gladiators. Don't turn what we're doing into something it ain't. If people want make believe they can watch the wrestling on cable, not get sprayed with sweat down ringside.

Okay, so that's all she wrote. I'll be working your corner

for the first fight. Can't say I'll be much help, but if I can impart some knowledge along the way, I will. Good luck, son.

Get your ass over here! Look at me. Not him. Don't go eyeballing him, not unless you're hoping to take him out on a date. Let me ask you a question, son. Do you fuck like you fight?

Answer the question.

Do you fuck like you fight?

I only ask, 'cause if you do then you must blow your load mighty quick. Answer me another question, how long did that feel like?

Ten minutes?

Son, that was closer to two. One hundred and twenty seconds, if that. In all that time, you were running round that ring as if the Lord Almighty had magicked up a swarm of locusts in your pecker. This here is a marathon, it ain't no sprint, you ain't gonna get a gold medal for wailing on him the most.

It don't mean shit.

Really? You disagree. Okay, son, take a look at him. Take a long goddamn look. Does he look like he's hurting after your vicious assault? Is he sweating so bad, that Noah is going to float his motherfucking ark on the puddle he's created from his exertions, filled with every animal, two by motherfucking two? No. He ain't. There ain't one bead of perspiration on that man's brow. Not one salty drop. Look at you. It looks like you've been messing with the AC down the whorehouse. You've got another ten, twelve minutes of this. If you keep going as you are, how long do you think you're gonna last?

Shut up. I'll tell you this for free, son. You're gonna finish second. Out of two. Now that might not mean much to you, you'll still have twenty bucks in your pocket, perhaps a cold beer in your hand, but you won't have learned a goddamn thing.

257

Slow it down, okay? You can't beat a man till you know what he's like. Feel him out, find out what he's good at. What he ain't. He's shorter than you, so you know you've got a better reach, use it. At the same time though, he's going off his right leg all the time. If you move in too quick, like you might do with your favourite cousin, he'll pinwheel you. Before you know it, his sweaty balls will be resting on your chin, as he chokes you the fuck out.

His pimply face will be looking down at you, laughing, as your cheeks go red and your hands slap against his thighs, wishing that you'd listened to ol' Ballbreaker before you black out. Mind you, if he pushes too hard, he might burst a brain vessel in that noggin of yours. It ain't beyond the bounds of possibility to think that you could become afflicted with retardation, allowing you to help out ol' Brian starting the truck. Two dumb fucks together, pedalling away at nothing. Going nowhere.

Fight smart, son, use your strengths, and make sure he don't get to use his, okay? Go on now, looks like your pal wants you to tag him. Get on back out there.

This ain't Oprah, son, shut up, take a goddamn breath and quit trash talking him. You know what he's doing, don't you? He's riling you up, and sure, if you're an ornery alligator, I might very well suggest it'll work. But you ain't, son, not even close. If I had to say what you were, it'd be a pissy muskrat, staggering down the 76, seconds away from being crushed under the tires of an eighteen-wheeler. You want to spend your opening night, crawling round the mat on your hands and knees, looking for a tooth, or worse, an eye? How about your goddamn self-respect?

Now shut up and listen. You started off well, almost like you were actually listening to the fucking words that were coming out of my mouth, then what happened? You got sucker punched and started to pout like a bitch. There ain't no Queensbury rules out here, son, you hear me? All you've got, if you're lucky, are your balls, and enough fight left in you to keep going when your brain is telling you to stay the fuck down.

If you let that little ball slap throw you off your game plan, then you better go back to whatever pissant town you crawled out from and stay there. You gotta be smarter than that. Look at me, you think I'd still be doing this at my age, if I flew off the handle every time some punk punched me in the happy sack?

Okay, so look, at the beginning you were on him, but you didn't keep on, why was that?

You thought he was going to tap out?

Son, were you born stupid, or did that pussy punch of his, hit the only brain you've been blessed with? You see that man over there? The one in the middle, with the gut that looks like he's eaten his family for breakfast, and that stupid fucking bowtie? He's the referee. He, and he alone, decides when the fight is over. Shit, son, you could be down on the canvas, your leg hanging out of its socket, knee deep in your own blood and piss, Archangel Gabriel and all of the angelic motherfucking host around him, calling out to you, beckoning you unto their bosom, but if that fat fuck doesn't say it's over, you get your ass up and you fight, okay? Hell, if you need to, pull that useless limb out of its socket and club him back up his momma's cooch, okay? Just *do not stop* until he says otherwise, got it?

Good. Now, get the fuck out of my face and back in that ring.

Son, you okay? Yeah, yeah, I know I told you that it would be Marjory's face you'd see first off, but she's trying to disentangle the man you threw into the grand piano. Yep, the one five rows back, over there. Don't think it was too expensive, shit luck if it was, leaving it there while we're working was just plain stupid.

Stop trying to talk, son, there's a reason why it hurts to speak, smile, or do any of the things you used to enjoy doing with your mouth.

You don't remember, huh? Well, piano boy over there was getting a bit of a pasting. You'd clotheslined his ass, and after a rather showy suplex, were on the cusp of dislocating his arm in a rather nice lock. Anyway, as mentioned previously, there are a lot of bottles around this here ring. He grabbed one, smashed it on the turnbuckle and proceeded to try and integrate it with your other facial features.

Shit, son, I've seen all kinds of nasty injuries, we used a nailgun once, and some dipshit loaded it up with the wrong nails. Poor Bob 'Tendon-Tugger' Pastorella caught one in the eye. Dumb bastard, acting on instinct I guess, tries to pull the darned thing out, failing to adequately think through his plan. Next thing you know, he's screaming louder than a banshee in season and doing laps of the ring, holding his eyeball on the end of that nail as if it was a candy apple. Only way we could get him to stop hollering was to administer a baseball bat to the back of his head. He still comes in from time to time, though he don't say too much to me. On account of the fact it was me holding that nailgun at the time.

Anyway, I digress, mainly because you look like seventy-four shades of fucked up. Piano boy rammed the broken bottle through the bottom of your mouth. Now? It's like you have two sets of teeth in that big ol' skull of yours. One lot are a lovely enamel white, the other set is made of glass, blood and bits of spongy tongue.

I'm gonna be honest with you, son, I think your karaoke days are over.

Ahh shit, my bad, I didn't mean to make you laugh, I'll be dead serious from now until the paramedics manage to extricate that Coors bottle from your face. Please, don't move your mouth or swallow too much. For one, the sound of that glass grinding against your teeth is making my balls shrink, and two, I don't want you swallowing nothing, and then shitting it out, when they might've been able to stitch it back on again.

You know what though, son? You did alright, there are grown men in the front row who have lost several pounds of weight through puking at the mere sight of your face, and what's left of piano boy over yonder. One of the strings wound around his ankle and, well, in the process of attempting to free himself, he degloved his foot. You want a skin sock? I could see about getting it for you? Wouldn't be no trouble? We could pickle it, and leave that jar on your own stoop when you get fixed up.

Hey, don't look like that, son, chin up, you should be proud, your momma might not be, but the woman who carried you around for nine months and squeezed you out of her holiest of holies, ain't never gonna be beaming with maternal pride at this particular life choice of yours, and its inevitable consequences.

You see, this is lesson five. Everyone takes a pasting, don't matter if you're Samson or Delilah, everyone gets their licks. Sure, looks like you've taken enough for eleven people about now, but that just means that you'll come back stronger.

Plus, and I mean this with the greatest respect, I've got your name all worked out. Now before I say it, some folk will think that it's derogatory, but that won't last long, only up until the time that they hear the story, and see the pictures. Think of this as an honor, most don't get their own fighting name till they're five or six fights in, but I'd say you've earned it...

Glassjaw.

What do you reckon, son?

It's time to...
EMBRACE YOUR FATE

See what could happen to you if you insist on fighting back? You could get horribly disfigured or maimed, forced to live the rest of your days in torturous agony.

Come on, no-one wants to endure all that horribleness do they? Course not. They would be very silly. But don't take my word for it, the next story on **Page 32** highlights what could happen to you if you decide to go against people that are just trying to do what's best for you.

DON'T YOU YEARN
FOR CHANGE?

Retracting up to his silken nest in the corner of the living room, Frank the Flashback Spider pulled his legs up to his carapace and closed his eyes. *These damn people, all they want from me is to hang from the ceiling and show them long gone memories.*

As his spindly legs hugged his bulbous body they scratched against a Polaroid picture. Frank's eyes flicked open, staring at the faded photograph. His daughter, Felicity.

"I'm just popping out to give the homeless pit ponies a reminder of happier days," were her last words as she squeezed through the hole in the kitchen window frame. "I'll be back by tea," she'd promised.

Frank eyed up the dragonfly he'd lovingly caught and imprisoned within his butt string netting. It had regained full consciousness by now, it had been three days, after all. It squirmed against its bindings, but the chance of escape was non-existent. "She would have loved to have bitten into you and slowly gorged on your innards," Frank confided in the bug, who struggled harder, determined to try and escape the mad arachnid.

The humans below were milling around, seemingly lost now they'd regained control of their actions. The new arrivals perched on the sofa, and discussed what kinds of cake and tea work best in the apocalypse. The man with the pot on his head looked upwards. Frank knew that look; it was one of reminiscence.

NO.

Ever since he had come inside last winter, trying not freeze to death or get dive bombed by hungry robins, Frank had done what he was born to do, provide flashbacks when needed. But what had he got in return? This lousy, dusty corner? Pfft, he'd had better. That summer spent in the corner of The Duke of Pie's shed in '13 was something he'd never forget. If he hadn't accidentally burnt it to the ground one night after a seventeen-day drink and drugs bender,

262

he'd still be there.

Then again, if he hadn't have given in to arson, he never would've met Fiona, and Felicity never would have been born.

"Definitely like her mum," Frank moaned, stroking the photograph with the scratchy nib of the larger of his front legs. "Always looking out for others. I'd rather just stay in my web, get pissed up on the weekend, and do Pilates during the week. That's what I call balance."

Frank looked across to the kitchen window. The hole she had pulled herself through was still there, a tiny tunnel to the world beyond. "Fine, let your old dad come and see what trouble you've got yourself into now." He scuttled across to the dragonfly and bit its face, paralysing it once more. "Don't get too lively, Flick will be back to tuck into you in no time."

The man with the pot was looking up at him now, relying on his rubbish two-dimensional memory to try and remind him of the time he got chased through a polystyrene prosthesis factory, inadvertently falling onto a number of the new lines. Whilst he had a smile, he longed to recall the tactile sensation and feel the breath of the supervisor on his cheek.

The human's face lit up as he saw Frank the Flashback Spider tumble effortlessly from the artexed ceiling, shimmering rope being spun from his behind. The smile faded as the spider carried on down, stopping only when he came into contact with the ratty carpet. Eager to not get stomped on, Frank scurried behind the chaise longue and worked his way to the kitchen, keeping parallel to the skirting board.

With the humans bamboozled as to his whereabouts, frantically moving furniture and lifting up cups and saucers, Frank shot out a length of silk, which stuck to the side of the doorframe. With a little leap and a push away from the floor, he swung diagonally upwards at speed. At the apex of his journey, he severed the link of body-to-web and soared through the air like the hilarious flying killer spiders of Bermondsey, famed for their skits on current affairs and their magic tricks involving top hats and hand grenades.

Frank landed on the worktop like an Olympic gymnast;

263

no sooner had his eight legs touched down than he was off again, scooting towards the sink, a plan forming in his mind. It had been some time since he had been outside, even longer since he had gone out for a purpose other than finding somewhere new to live, or cover the neighbouring post box in the thickest of his webbing after the postman had failed to deliver issue twenty of his three-hundred-part magazine which detailed how to build a one-sixth scale model of an actual dining table.

He knew that finding Felicity would be no easy matter. He'd have to shake up the local grubs, put the squeeze on some old contacts, perhaps even whack a bluebottle or two in order to earn enough cred to get the lowdown on the streets.

Frank dusted down his battered old fedora. "It's been a few years since we walked these mean old streets, but I gotta find her...make sure she's safe. It's a bug-eat-bug world out there; I just hope she ain't got herself into anything too heavy."

He twirled the chamber on his revolver, before cracking it open and loading it with shells. "Don't you worry, doll, daddy's coming for ya, no matter what you've done, or where you've been, I'll bring you home." He snapped the gun shut, before easing the hammer down. "And god help anyone who gets in my way."

Pulling his legs in, Frank squeezed through the woodworm's hole. Feeling the breeze on his face, he pulled the collar of his trench coat up and walked down the wall to the back garden.

THE CASE OF THE MISSING DAME AND THE DEADLY MONSTER

PART I: GOTTA START SOMEWHERE

The summer sky had turned to ruin, the last vestiges of colour bled out like a stuck pig. Frank lit up a Lucky Seven cigarette and took in the view as every last drop of colour was bleached out from the world, leaving everything greyscale. "About figures." He shook the match and flicked it into the hedgerow, which was draped in strands of reeking offal.

This world was a mystery, like waking up in bed next to a stranger; he had become somewhat accustomed to being voluntarily incarcerated. "Playing it too safe, old man," he whinged. As the first drop of rain hit the brim of his hat, Frank tied the belt of his trench coat tight and headed into the undergrowth.

At least beneath the overgrown lawn, now covered with a matting of festering skin and a net of veins dispensed from the visceral downpour, the rain didn't get in. Frank weaved between blades of grass, nodding a terse hello at a family of sheltering pillbugs, who pulled their young son in close. "Yep, some things never change." Frank tipped his hat at the lady pillbug, whose antennae quivered at the sight of the dishevelled spider.

His reputation seemed intact; perhaps the insect world had thought him consigned to nothing more than legendary status. That might help. Maybe some of the local barkeeps would dispense with information a bit easier. Less effort for his aching limbs to shake down and rough up. Though, truth be told, he never minded getting loose with his fists whenever the situation called for it. Many a night he'd ended up either standing over some poor mook in the gutter, or staring back up at a goon who'd got the better of him. No

265

matter, some nights you hit the bar...

Frank chuckled; he needed a drink, something to wet his ol' whistle. It had been long, too long. Not since Felicity had burst from her egg had he tasted the burn of a bourbon sour as it sizzled its way down into his guts. That night, he'd promised anyone who'd listen that he'd change, that his philandering days were over. They hadn't believed him then, who would? A no-good bum from the wrong part of town, who spent as much time breaking the law as running down those who were wanted for their own transgressions.

No one was a saint.

Not in this town.

He knew where he had to go, only one place would have all the players in there that he needed to put a move on. "Old Chester's," down by the sole ash tree in Victoria park. He needed answers, not tomorrow, not next week, today, tonight, hell, for all he knew, it might already be too late. Why had he let her disappearance go on so long?

He couldn't blame the booze. Heck, he couldn't even blame the floozies any more. Nope, this was all on him. His own goddamn apathy. She was always looking out for other folk. Always wanting to help, never asking for nothing in return. Altruism, that's what they called it. "Stupid," that's what Frank thought. "Sooner or later, someone is gonna take advantage of your good nature." Always a warning, but an empty one. He never thought it would actually happen, why would anyone want to hurt a dame as sweet as his fair Felicity?

Nope, something was up, and not just his dander. Something was wrong with this place, a dark cloak of evil draped over its fetid shoulders, holding in all the pus and sweat and squeezing the goodness out. It was the patient zero of the impending apocalypse, only thing you could do with it was put it out of its misery quick, or else it'd just go on and infect everything and everyone you give a damn about in this godforsaken cesspool.

His mood pulled on him like a hangman's noose. The smoking wasn't helping, either. Still, you can't stay quit forever. Sooner or later, everything catches up with you. Someone's always got to get paid. You just gotta keep that bill away from yours as long as you can.

266

Frank dropped the smouldering cigarette butt onto the floor, squishing it dead with his size tens. As soon as the last tendrils of phantasmal smoke left its body, he'd sparked up another. "Figure I may as well chain smoke my way through it."

He ducked under the rotten fence panel, the horizon coming into view from the unkempt hinterland to a greying plain which ran out as far as his eyes could see. Squat houses and derelict tower blocks sat on the sidelines, as if waiting to be brought onto an important ball game. Frank could make out the cathedral in the distance, nothing but a greasy silhouette on the pallid sky. A cancerous tumour clung to its spire, waving a fist of loathing to the heavens, cursing any god foolish enough to listen to its lamentations.

"I know what you're feeling, partner." He felt the weight of the pistol inside his jacket, making sure the grip was pointing the right way. If things went sideways —and like the rain, now pelting down around him, it usually did— it always paid to have a little helping hand close by. Some folk only understood one thing in this place. Sure, violence begets violence, but when it's all you've ever known, it can be like a milk maid. Give 'em a nuzzle and the back of your hand, no point in feeling bad, there ain't enough pity to go 'round no more. "Save it for the needy." Frank ducked his head into the wind and rain, his course set for a clump of trees a little way off.

It was only when they were looming over him like a husband who had come back from work early ready to leave you with a fresh shiner, that Frank looked up again. He'd spent so long walking, lost in his own thoughts, that he'd near forgotten what he was doing out on this stretch of monochrome tundra. He could hear the band playing before he could see the place. He knew he'd be as welcome as a whore at Thanksgiving dinner, but if speed was key, then his choices were limited.

"Frank Spannacetti, as I live and breathe," a voice lisped, so bad that you daren't ask it to spell *Mississippi* out loud.

An arm so thick and corded that it could be mistaken for a length of twine was jabbed into his ribs, a misplaced hand of welcome. Frank could feel it messing with his abdomen, tickling the barrel of his shooter; he needed that, especially

267

here, so he pulled in close to the beetle. "Jasper, they still got you out here? I'd have thought Old Chester would have you as top billing by now?"

The stag beetle bristled. Caught in the trap of indecision, he saw Frank's mouth pull upwards in a smile. "Can't play no mo', not after what Mickey Five-Legs did to me." Jasper pulled back his chitinous shell slightly, revealing an appendage as broken as Frank's empty promises.

"Now that's a damn shame, ain't seen anyone play the jazz kazoo like you, J-Man."

An awkward silence fell, the kind you get when your reasons for staying out late don't tally with the receipts in your pocket, now strewn over the dining table for all to see. Frank shook Jasper's hand and slipped a creased bill between shell and body, patting it safe so the bouncer knew where it was. "Damn shame," he repeated, hoping it would jolt some life back into proceedings.

"Ain't no thang, OC kept me on the payroll, put me out here. Can't complain none. Beats wallowing in my pit, that's fo' sure," Jasper looked Frank up and down. "Speaking of which, what brings you here? Way I remember it, OC barred your ass on account of what you did with his wife."

"*Ex*-wife, I seem to recall."

"Uh-huh," Jasper crossed what was left of his arms.

"He still sore about that? Or do I need to go and start grovelling?"

Jasper puffed his chest out, the doorway behind him receding like the sun during an eclipse. But not unlike the solar transition, the bouncer chuckled, stood to one side, and pushed the door open. "Only one way to find out fo' sure, Frankie boy."

Frank tipped his hat. "Much obliged to ya, I sure hope you find a way to get back playing, the band don't sound as good as I 'member."

"Don't thank me yet, OC is as liable to throw you back out them doors as I was letting you through 'em."

Frank peeked beyond the bouncer into the den of iniquity, shadowy shapes morphing within the inky murk. Dodgy deeds in progress, miscreants and vagabonds all. He blew a ring of smoke. "Yep...about figures."

PART 2:
BOOMSTICK ON THE ROCKS

The confines of Old Chester's was packed with every kind of insect imaginable. Millipedes did laps around the walls, numbers painted onto their hind quarters, as the patrons hooted and wailed, willing their ride on to victory. Daddy longlegs, aphids, slugs, even a pair of ladybirds, threw bundles of cash at Polly the bookie, struggling to keep up with the influx of bets. "That's all, ladies and gentlemen," she shouted over the din, causing a wave of cursing, and shaken, balled fists.

Frank ducked under the enthusiastic arms of a praying mantis, accepting the sincere apology with a scowl and the threat of a slap. The mantis had already turned back to the race, egging on its own choice; number three, a yellowy-golden millipede that banked round the penultimate turn so fast that its legs struggled to hold on.

As the P.I. reached the bar and slapped a leg on the surface, a blend of cheering and loud ruing of bad luck echoed around the hollowed-out tree trunk. Polly flitted between her punters, pressing crumpled notes into certain palms, and extricating debts from the crevices of others. All done with a smile on her face, an anecdote ready at the back of her throat, and a switchblade close at hand, just in case. The rounds complete, the millipedes having long retreated to the rotten branches in the loft, preparations for the next bout of entertainment began. Tables were pushed back to the walls, and a large circle was scratched onto the pitted floor with a nugget of chalk.

"Hey," Frank tapped the tip of his leg against an empty shot glass, trying to attract the barman's attention.

The clicking having shaken him from his reverie, Ted the earthworm pulsed his way towards Frank, his body segments undulating as he went. "You're back? Didn't Old Chester say he was going to carve his name into your mandibles if you ever returned?"

"An empty threat, I'm sure."

269

"Whatever, what you drinking? I got a feeling you're gonna need it."

Frank tapped the empty glass with his leg. "Give me two fingers of bourbon."

"Ice?"

"Don't insult me, Ted, it's been a long time since I cut you in half."

"And even longer since I stuck myself together again."

"Then enough of the small talk already," Frank turned his back on the worm, sparked another cigarette, and reclined against the bar.

Behind him, he could hear the clink of glass-on-glass; all around, he saw bugs look his way before turning back to their party and whispering campfire stories. It made no difference whether they were true or a little larger than life, the only thing worse than folk talking about you is when they say nothing at all. As his eyes jumped from table-to-table, he noticed that everyone had fallen to a hush. Like a stand-up comedian alone on stage, the spotlight burning down on him, Frank felt every single one of their bulbous, lidded eyeballs stare his way. He heard a glass, laden with oily liquor, slam down on the wooden bar top behind him. "It's about damn time."

Frank spun round, picked up the glass, and raised it to his lips. Ted was cowering in the corner by the leaf shoots and other assorted bar snacks; in his place stood a mean old moth, his wings pocked with holes like undarned socks, and ugly to boot. At the end of an arm, so withered and atrophied that it seemed incapable of holding anything, was a sawn-off shotgun, the business end of which was levelled at Frank's head. He stared blankly down two open barrels, a pair of hungry black pits. With the steel leaving an indent in his head, Frank pressed against it, pushing the bearer back a touch. Despite his heart hammering away inside his carapace like a bird weaselling out grubs, Frank picked up the glass and toasted his armed host. "Much obliged to you, OC."

To underscore his threat, the moth pulled back the hammer on the shooter. "I've got to admit, you've got some balls coming 'round these parts, especially after what you did."

270

Frank, with the stunted barrels still pressing into his forehead, clinked the glass against the wooden stock. "Here's to your health, OC." Retracting, Frank knocked the drink back in one, letting every last drop of fiery booze drip down the back of his throat. With one leg wiping his lips, Frank turned the glass upside down and slammed it on the counter. "See you've given up watering down the stock, some things *do* change."

The moth chuckled. "And some things don't." With the weapon beginning to shake, Old Chester lowered the gun and placed it next to the upturned glass. "You're lucky I don't core you like an apple, boy."

With his heart rate returning to normal, Frank nudged the glass forward. "I'm mighty grateful for that, OC, really, I am. Look, I know we've got beef, but all things considered? You know as well as I do that there's no way I wouldn't be here if I didn't have to be. It's important."

Old Chester, without looking, reached behind him, lifted the bottle of Old Kansas bourbon from the shelf, and rested it on the bar. Using the bottom of the bottle to flip the glass over, he kept his eyes on Frank as he poured another two fingers' worth of whisky, before getting another glass and filling it up. "That's as maybe, Frankie, but I thought I made it clear last time what would happen if you darkened my doorway again." The two bugs picked up their drinks and raised their glass to each other.

"Just hear me out, then you can do whatever you feel you need to, to ease your conscience. I won't stop you."

Sickly laughter bubbled from Old Chester's throat, as if he'd been gargling with spare phlegm. The rest of the bar joined in with the mocking.

Frank, feeling a little light-headed from the booze, turned around slowly, taking in the scene. If he were the comedian on the bill tonight, he'd be relieved that the crowd were laughing, at least. Though it hurt to know that they weren't laughing *with* him, so much as *at* him. He looked back at Old Chester, who cradled the glass in his spindly appendages. "Look, it's about-"

Old Chester pressed the tip of one arm against Frank's mouth. "Shh, don't say nothing to ruin this moment. I don't care what you're here for, not yet, anyways. You

271

disrespected me, hell, you've hardly ingratiated yourself with most of these fine folk in here tonight. You want something from Old Chester? Fine. First, you're gonna have to do something for *me*."

Here it comes. Like a punch-drunk prize-fighter, Frank picked up his glass and threw the contents down his throat. Slamming the glass down, he gripped hold of the edge of the counter. "And what might that be, OC? Way I see it, as much as you hate my guts, you know that killing me ain't real good for business."

"You're right, me killing you would not go down very well in these parts. The authorities might stick their proboscises in, my license is up for renewal soon, so blowing your adulterous head from your body would be mighty foolish."

"Excellent, I knew you'd see sense, so, if we could get to the matter at hand?"

Old Chester turned his head to one side and whistled a singular shrill note. The regulars in the bar stood up and began to head over to where the tables had been cleared, and a perfect circle had been scrawled onto the floor. "Shut the hell up, Frank. As I said, *me* killing you would be terrible, that's why I'm gonna let Earl over there do it, all legal like, in front of all these fine people too, to boot."

"Huh?"

The moth behind the counter stretched out an arm and pointed towards the braying crowd, who had kept a hole just big enough for a know-it-all spider to get through. In the gap stood the biggest earwig he had ever seen. "What the hell do you call this, OC?"

After another gurgling bout of chuckling, Old Chester spat on the floor. "Payback."

Frank was fixated on the earwig, who stood up on its front legs, pincers in the air, swinging back and forth, snapping the air. "What do you expect me to do here, OC? Take on *that*?"

Old Chester filled up Frank's glass. "Yep. I remember back in the day, seeing you in the battle circle was something to behold. Tell me...old man, you been keeping in shape?"

Breathing his fly gut in, Frank sucked in his cheeks. "You know how it is, OC, it's like riding a flying ant, once you learn, you never forget."

"Then you won't mind showing your skills off?"

"And if I win, you'll help?"

The moth cackled again, rubbing tears from its eyes. "Boy, if you win, which I very much doubt you will, but if you do? Then consider your slate clean, and whatever you want, I'll do."

Pulling one leg across his body and stretching it out, Frank knocked back his drink and staggered towards the hollering crowd. "Guess this was never gonna be easy, that dame is gonna be in mighty big trouble when I rescue her from whatever mess she's got herself into."

PART 3:
FEEL THE RHYTHM,
FEEL THE RHYME

As Frank crossed the white line, transitioning from the bar into the battle circle, the band began to play. Stubby Jake, a cricket, played the drums with precision, his legs kicking the double bass drums in perfect synchronicity, a cigarette perpetually wedged in the corner of his mouth. He took small drags on it as he rolled the drumsticks over the taut skins, allowing palls of smoke to tumble from his lips like a Bangkok sweat shop.

Fatty T, a bed bug from the Wilton Heights, dolefully plucked the strings of the double bass, each ponderous note shaking the thorax of everyone inside the bar. Twin sisters, mosquitoes Fran and Jan, took turns to build the beat with their saxophones. One on Alto, the other on Tenor, they layered a scene of melancholy and woe. "Like I need these negative vibes right now, man," Frank whinged.

The spider strutted to the opposite side of the ring, eyeing up the earwig, who was twisting his individual body segments one-by-one, his gaze never tearing away from Frank. "So what's your name, slim?"

Stopping in mid-correction, the earwig rippled from top to bottom, his shell popping in time with the wave. "My mom calls me Herbert, my friends, Herby, my enemies, they call me...Killer-E," the last syllable delivered like an alcoholic postman on their last round of the week, the DTs long since settled into their marrow.

Frank sparked another Lucky Seven; taking a drag, he pointed the cigarette at his opponent. "In that case, I guess I'll call you Junior."

Herby snaked his way across the ring, his tail snapping as he went. "What did you call me, fool?"

"Junior," Frank repeated, taking the opportunity to drown Herbert in a cheap cloud of smoke.

"You tripping, homie? Deaf too? Why yo calling me

274

Junior for?"

Leaning in, Frank tapped his ash to one side. "I'm about to school you, *son*. You can strut around this place, thinking you're this and that, but you don't have a damn clue who you're up against, do you?"

Herby moved in closer, his face a whisker away from Frank's. "Why don't you tell me, old man?"

Frank pointed to a lintel which ran above the makeshift arena, a series of deep grooves carved within the bark. "Every single one of those marks is a tombstone. Of someone, just like you, who stepped up in here, wearing the shoes you think fit you best, and who got what was coming. Sure, you may think you've got skills, but, boy? It might be best you go back to your *mom's* now, tell her Herbert is real sorry."

The earwig maintained his posture, although his cocksure smirk faltered for the faintest of moments before he regained his composure. "Nah, I'm fine where I am, let's get this on." Pretending to deliver a punch that never came, Herby flicked his head back and strutted back to his side of the ring, taking in the adulation of the inebriated crowd as he went.

Frank turned, hung his head, and closed his eyes. It was true, back in the day, when he would tread those boards every night, he was the real deal. Everyone who had crossed that line and gone toe-to-toe with him had crawled out of Old Chester's a broken bug, or been wrung out in a bucket. But how long ago was that, now?

Frank gazed up at the gouges, their lustre long since gone, the wood faded back to grey, nothing but dust and shadows remaining. They were like ghosts hanging out in a cemetery, full of tales of when they were alive, living off past glories, unwilling and unable to accept what was lost and move on.

"Perhaps I should've stayed in my corner, busting out the same for those humans?" Frank looked across to Herbert who was swaying in time with the music. "Fuck it, this ain't for me." He pulled a picture from his jacket pocket, the folded crease lines taking nothing away from his daughter. "This is for you, Flick. I just hope this old arachnid ain't forgotten what to do, or this case is gonna be your

275

papa's last."

Shoving the picture back inside his coat, Frank loosened his belt, pushed his fedora back so it opened up like the rising sun, and shouted across to Stubby Jake, "Hey, you fancy putting on something a bit more suitable?"

The cigarette bobbed in the cricket's mouth as he smiled momentarily, before he gave a quick reverie across the hi-hats, sinking back to the snare, mixing it in with looping volleys on the toms. "How's *that* riddim, Frankie?" Stubby Jake drawled.

"Now you're talking." Frank began to click his fingers in time with the syncopated beat, "Hey, OC, we getting started tonight? I got places to go, you know? Bugs to see."

Old Chester growled and marched to the centre of the circle as the music played on, fading out like paint in water, except for the rhythm section, which plodded on. The crotchety moth held his hands up. "Ladies and gentlemen, welcome to Old Chester's. Tonight, we've got a little treat for you..."

The crowd hooted and hollered, bottles clinked together, and drunken feet tried to stomp in time with the beat, many failing miserably. Old Chester pointed across to Herbert. "From the wrong side of the Buzzkill Zapper, he's got a style so fresh, you can butter your jacket potatoes with it. He's laying out his rivals like dominoes, the one and only rhyme-animal, here comes KILLER-E!"

The noise level rose, threatening to drown out the band who gamefully increased their ferocity to match, sinking down as the shouting abated. Old Chester turned to Frank. "One-time champion, and undefeated in seventy-five battles...he puts the flow into deflowered, the musical divider, the spider from the Large Hadron Collider, FRANKIE FURY!"

There was a round of polite applause, a smattering of encouragement, but otherwise the noise levels plummeted like Asian stocks after Pearl Harbour. "Bunch of ingrates..."

Old Chester held his hands up, and the band ceased mid-beat. "LET'S GET THIS SCAT BATTLE ON!"

On command, the band struck up once more, joined by the rest of the brass section. Jasper stuck his head through a gap in the door and watched, itching to get his kazoo out.

Old Chester melded back into the masses, before flitting back to the bar and pouring himself a healthy slug of Tanqueray gin.

Killer-E snatched the microphone from the stand and rapped his pincers across it, eliciting a crackling and popping from the speakers. Taking to the centre of the ring, he began. "Skip-bap-a-boo-bah, skip-bap-a-boo, your main man Killer-E gonna rock this place right here wit you. No matter if you have six legs, no matter if you have eight, my lyrics will carry you skywards, and drop your fine ass on my dinner plate. Fwip-wap-a-boo-boo, fwip-wap-a-foo, this old spider is wonky, this old man has no clue, if he steps up on me in the alley out back, I'm gonna bus him back to Cancun. Bee-bop-a-bring-bring-skippidy-a-dring-dring-a-ree, y'all need to have a drink, the next one is on me."

Frank had circled his opponent during the verse, chain smoking until the smouldering cherry had threatened to light his coat up. As the earwig finished, he let go of the mic, and Frank caught it in mid-flight. The crowd were offering high-fives and chest-bumps to Herbert; the music carried on, looping round, giving Frank some time to clear his head.

With the vibrant audience a mere backdrop, the realisation of what he was about to do hit him. He had sworn he was through with this life, the drinking, the wrassling, the scat, but here he was, back again. This life didn't let go easy, especially those it favoured. You can run, you can hide, you can climb into the farthest, darkest alcove in a stinking human's home (a stinking human who has a pot for a head) and show them the past, but all that'll happen is you'll be pulled back into this divine circus once again.

"Bee-bop-a-bah-bah, bee-bop-a-bee, send in the illest clown, and deliver them to me. While their fat fingers make me balloon animals, they'll dance a slappy shoe jig for free. I may not have their curly hair, all I got is this fat frown, but when you bother to come up for air, I'm gonna smack your stupid ass back down. Chim-charooga-a-krim-kree, all I heard from this crowd is Killer-Who? When I'm done scat-battling with you little bug, I'm gonna dedicate the next song to you. Pop-pop-a-plim-plam, skree-nip-rop-rop-a-too, I'm sure OC will still pimp you out to your mom's, though, when I'm done messing around with you."

277

There were loud oohs and ahhs from the crowd, many of whom had never been lucky enough to witness Frank in his prime. A few even made sizzling sounds, incurring the wrath of Herbert, who jabbed at them with his hind quarters. Frank body-popped across the ring and threw the mic up, happy he hadn't clattered his face against the floor and had actually pulled the move off successfully.

Killer-E passed the mic between his multiple legs before raising it to his mouth. "Say it after me, y'all, sing it loud and proud-a-ly, this old fart stepped up in our crib, thinking it was Inglewood, not Salisbury. I don't know where you've been all these years, but round here we like to rhyme. No good coming out swinging with your pencil dick, that shit is just so infantile. Skibbady-doo-wap, skibbady-dee-doo, I've got a special delivery just for you. Pippidy-pop-pop, a-pippidy-dee-doo, says return to sender, but we're not through. All the scat that you're hustling, don't even deserve dumping in a foolscap file. Out of the kindness of my heart, Imma gonna fold you up real tight and air freight you to the Nile. Bom-bom-skippity-skip-a-choo."

Frank allowed himself a contented smile; he was getting to this upstart. A band of sweat had bloomed on Herbert's do-rag, and saturated the cheap material. No-one in the history of scat battle had ever resorted to talking about postal deliveries. Frank knew there and then that the earwig was running scared. Grabbing the microphone from a member of the audience, who had taken possession of it as the earwig did Cossack dancing in the centre of the ring, Frank positioned his fedora at a jaunty angle. With a tip of his hat to the band, the tempo changed, its cadence adopting the appearance of a feral animal on the run. Booming bass kicked out, pushing the crowd back, and the high notes ran invisible fingers up and down antennae and vertebrae, tingling every nerve centre in their insectoid bodies.

As Herbert came to a standstill, his frame unable to keep up with the runaway melody, Frank placed an Egyptian cotton cloth over the mic before leaping into the air. Landing with his feet planted, face to the floor, he resumed, "Skippity-bippity-boppity-mope-mope, it's the time and place to recognise, that even if you think your rhymes are dope, you ain't gonna do nothing but fantasise. Some truths you know just ain't, some lies you believe are true, but when I get into this sick break, this whole crowd'll know you're through. If all you know are the words you scat today, then no wonder they'll be your last, you needed to show me some respect young blood, instead I'll consign you to the past. So peace out to you, Killer-E, I gotta destroy you now post haste, cos if I leave any of your legs standing, then my reputation will be outta place. Big apologies to those you love, this really isn't fair, if you're standing in a glasshouse right now, I'd suggest you get outta there. Skimmity-doo-boo-chikka-noice, this phat bassline is my weapon of choice, bammity-bam-tim-a-bammity-doom, my main man Guile says SONIC BOOM."

The music stopped, as if run off a rain-slicked road, save for the thumping bass, which continued to pulse like a heartbeat. Frank took a deep breath, while Old Chester crossed himself and ducked behind the bar. "Ooohhhh, shit," was all he could muster.

As Frank scatted, the tempo morphed so that it kept perfect time with the noise emanating from the spider. "Bibbly-bap-bap-a-skibbidy-bap-bap-a-bap-bap-" was all the audience could make out before the words went supersonic. A veritable buffet of impossibly constructed vowels and consonants, served together in a seemingly bottomless dish, were scatted into existence. A clap like a peal of thunder burst out from the speaker as a visible soundwave, beginning as a halo, pure white, speckled distortion on the outside, expanded outwards, knocking over anything it came in contact with. As the wave hit Killer-E, it lifted him from the floor and held him in place. The chords wrapped round the earwig's body, worming their way between every section of his carapace. As they made their way inside, they reverberated, bouncing around each and every atom as if it were a pinball machine with unlimited credit and inflated bumpers. The pub lights went out, tripping the fuse and delivering the entire tree trunk into darkness.

Yet in the gloom, Herbert was illuminated like a Chinese lantern stuck in an eddy on lift-off. His body shook, the drums and bass having long fallen silent, the sonic boom

279

having pushed the musicians to the floor like everyone else in the room, with the exception of the two vocalists. Frank continued to bark nonsensical words and sounds into the powered-down microphone, gradually slowing down, "-a-bibbidy-scap-a-pibbly-scap-a-pibbly...doooooooooooo."

As the note died on his breath, the earwig exploded, the musical notes having created fission with his own atoms and caused an internal meltdown, his body unable to regulate the incredible levels of freeform scat that had enveloped him. The lighting groaned back on as the fuse was flipped, Old Chester daring to look out from the fuse box cupboard, surveying the aftermath. Pieces of insect were sprayed everywhere; bugs were picking what was left of Herbert from their pints of fermented blueberry juice.

At the epicentre, Frank pulled his hat down and touched the brim respectfully, letting the microphone tumble to the floor where it disintegrated into a cloud of ash. Picking up one half of the earwig's pincer, the spider stood on his back legs, dusted down a space on the lintel, and gouged one more victory epithet into the surface. The crowd, slowly coming back to their senses, not quite believing what they had witnessed, began to break out in stunned applause.

Frank cast the crescent pincer to the floor, and staggered over to the bar, slumping against it, pulling up a stool to fully collapse onto. He raised a leg, and Old Chester scurried across. "That...that was incredible. I didn't think you still had it in you."

Waving him closer, Frank whispered in his ear. "Now, you're going to do two things, OC, or Doris will be mopping you off the ceiling too."

Old Chester gulped. "Anything, anything!"

"Two fingers of bourbon," Frank pulled the tatty photo from his jacket and slid it across the bar, "and you're gonna tell me everything you know about where my baby is."

PART 4:
BLOOD IS THICKER THAN BLOOD

The bartender had given him everything he needed. Why wouldn't he? When your only other option is to have every molecule in your body vibrate and explode, it's better to give up the little you have, than lose everything you got. Jasper had opened the door as Frank made his way out, still weary and throat sore. Even he couldn't believe that he still had the power, although he knew he would never again scat in anger.

Herbert didn't deserve what he had coming to him, but then, who truly does? "If you're gonna stand in my way, you better be prepared to pay the consequences." Frank pulled his collar up to try and stop the wind blowing down his back. The information he'd been given didn't make much sense. He put that down to the beating he'd just dished out, but even if it were true, then he'd need more than a fumble in the theatre from Lady Luck before this night was through.

"The cathedral...the beast on the spire. That's where you'll find her." Old Chester's words came back to haunt him like the ghost of a murdered lover. What did that devilspawn have to do with this? Why the hell had Flick gone there?

Questions. Damn questions and accusations, that's all he had. He thought he wanted answers, but the ones he'd been dealt so far seemed to have been all part of a rigged game. One the house was determined to win, no matter what the cost. Nope, he didn't have time to determine whether it was the truth or not, one thing the old moth said resonated more than most. "You don't have much time, by dawn, she'll be dead."

How Frank hadn't put the old bastard through the wall, he'd never know. Still, having often played the part of messenger, he knew it did no good to shoot 'em. Nope, fate would deal with Old Chester, that much was true. You can't treat folk like candles all the time, at some point, one'll burn your whole goddamn world down to cinder.

With the world still painted in shades of black-and-white, Frank saw that the humans had started to panic. They were coming out of their houses, some desperately trying to load their vehicles with as many of their possessions as possible. Others stood out in the streets just for a better glimpse of the creature that was the new addition to the skyline. The beast still clung to the cathedral spire like a barnacle to the bottom of a rowboat. A balled fist raised to the heavens, cursing in a long dead tongue, its vocally angular lamentations making the onlookers cover their ears.

Frank didn't care a jot; the beast could be reading out the shipping forecast for all he cared. The only thing the barrage of consonants was good for, was that as he scuttled across the streets, weaving in and out of congealing lumps of viscera, it acted like a homing beacon. As he made his way towards his destination, no one paid him any heed. Where normally he would stick to the corner of buildings, and the cracked concrete, lest he be squished to a gooey pulp, today he was free to amble wherever he pleased. Everyone's attention was on something far bigger, something which couldn't be dealt with in such an easily dismissible fashion.

The focus away from the floor allowed Frank to get to the cathedral gateway in record time. As he climbed on top of the stone wall, he could make out the fearsome beast in better detail.

Its flanks were covered in thick hide. Talons extending from each toe had pierced the roof tiles with ease, holding the monster in place. A small trunk swung from side-to-side as it admonished the gods on its unplanned delivery into this plain. Whilst it was grateful for the sweet release, its birthing was a painful and agonising one.

So he was here. "Now what?" He mumbled, tapping the bottom of the cigarette box, recoiling when he realised he was down to his final two smokes. "Save one for the victory party." Frank lit one and shoved the other back inside the box, before pushing that deep into an inside jacket pocket.

Old Chester had been unable, or unwilling, to provide any information on Felicity's exact location, saying nothing more than, "You'll know when you get there, trust me." But now he was at the building, he didn't have a clue. Sighing, he rappelled from the top of the archway, landing gently on the ground, his legs working as soon as the connection had been made. If he was a betting man —and he'd sworn off that around the same time as he'd sworn off most things— Flick would be near that monster, barely out of its sight.

Yep, there was only one place she would be. Right at the top of that damn spire, scratching the sickly sky's belly as the clouds hung low, swollen by water, ready to cry a river over not just this city but the entire world. As Frank made his way across the gravelled path, the first drop of rain tumbled down and hit the ground. The spider took one last drag and flicked the expended cigarette to one side. "Hang on now, girl, papa's coming to get ya."

Frank stuck to the south side of the spire. For one, the wind direction was from the opposite side, the growing storm making three sides of the spire slick in no time at all. Second? The beast hung from above, also seeking to shelter itself from the worsening weather. The dark grey clouds matched the feeling around the city. Whilst it began to scour the streets clean, creating rivers of thinned blood, it felt like a heart attack waiting to happen. A clawed hand clutched at its own breast, trying to alleviate the hacksawing pain which was searing through every street and alleyway.

A few feet above his head, where one of the monster's clawed feet had laid anchor, there was a gaping hole in the roof. Nothing much to the short-sighted, but to Frank, he saw a glistening web of silk within its rafters, and not just any kind, the sort that only his family could spin. It stuck out like a chorus girl in a soup line. Frank dug deep into his reserves of stamina and closed the distance.

The instant he stepped inside the smashed open abyss, the world went silent. The wind, which had become a harsh Drill Sergeant choosing not to spare the rod, had become impotent. The rain still slashed across the grey frigid sky, but didn't dare enter this sanctuary of dust and decay. There was a smell of rot in the air, of wood allowed to fester. Yet nothing stirred within this sundered cave. Frank tiptoed and examined the web; it was Felicity's, alright, a solitary greenfly was interred in the uppermost corner. "Always your favourite, darling." But there was no other sign of her. Frank ducked back out into the howling void, looking up at the beast, trying to see if there were any other nooks and crannies in which his daughter might be harboured.

Then it hit him. Why had she spun a web? If she was under duress...

"Father, you shouldn't have come." Her voice, dripping like syrup, came from behind him, back within the shadows which filled the roof space.

Frank turned around, scanning the inky blackness, trying to locate her. "What did you think I would do, Flick? You're my flesh and blood, I wouldn't leave you out here."

She materialised from the murk as if she had become one with it, wearing it like an expensive cloak to a ball. As she sauntered towards him, a leg resting on the join between abdomen and thorax, Frank gulped. It was her alright, make no mistake, but there was something about her that seemed off, like milk left out in the sun. "Come on now, let's get you back home, this is not our fight." He held out a leg.

"How would you know?"

The words smacked him in the face like a one-two jab combination; he reeled backwards from the barbs and it took him a few seconds to compose himself. "I beg your pardon, missy?"

Felicity came to a standstill, positioned like a model from those magazines she used to read. "I said...how would you know, *Papa*?"

He knew that tone, hell, he'd been on the receiving end of *that* tone most of his life. Every dame he'd let down, screwed over or bailed on, they'd pull this out, the final *Fuck You Frankie-Boy, this is what you're missing*. Frank pushed the brim of his hat up, giving her the stink eye in return. "Why you talking to your old man like that? Don't you know what I've been through to come find you?"

"You mean you finally realised I'd gone? What hit first, the guilt, or your sense of duty?"

It was delivered like a hammer punch to the kidneys. Frank winced; he knew then that he'd messed up. Not for the first time, sure, but this was different, this was something he wasn't sure he could talk his way out of. Hiding the hurt, he stood up tall, and clicked his legs together. "I said, come on. We're leaving. *Now.*"

"Whatever you say, my dear pa-pa." She folded her arms.

"Well now, that's better, we can have a little talk about that attitude of yours when we get back to our corner."

Felicity sighed, a bored noise like a cat with an expired kill, and stepped slowly across to him.

Her father stood on the edge and peeked down. The wall of shiny stone ran down to the ground, now covered in a thin gruel of mist. He heard the click-click-click of legs behind him, then the manicured tips came to a halt. He could feel her breath against the nape of his neck. "Stick close, we don't want to get separated in this pea souper."

"That would be terrible."

As Frank teetered over the lip, he felt spindly legs press into his back. "Steady on now, Flick, you nearly sent me over, then." The realisation hit him in the kisser like an uppercut as soon as the words had tumbled out of his mouth. His head spun round, looking into eyes familiar yet different, a smile stretched across his daughter's face; one born of malice, not gratitude.

"I can't let you, papa. We've come too far to stop now. She needs me."

Frank furrowed his spiderbrow. "Hold your horses, what are you talking about? Who's *she* exactly?"

Felicity gestured skywards, where the beast, even in its diatribe, kept an eye on proceedings. "She contacted me. She knows things, like the past, the future."

"We *know* the past, you forget that? And you know as well as I do that the past ain't nothing but a guidebook to a future that ain't even been wrote yet. *It* can change, *everything* can change, in the blink of an eye," Frank stood tall. "Come on, now, I don't have time for this, we're leaving."

"Nope. I'm not going anywhere, she needs me. With my gift, she can learn from the mistakes of the past, make sure that this time, nothing and no-one can stand in her way. It's her time...it's our time...it's *my* time."

"Felicity, so help me...you are coming home with me *now*. This ain't up for debate, I'm your father, you will do as

I say."

Felicity stepped forward, making Frank teeter above the abyss. "No."

"What did you just say?"

"I said, *no*. She needs me, she trusts me, values what I have to say, what have you ever done?"

"Are you serious? I've raised you since you crawled out of your egg. I've given up everything for you."

"No, papa, all you did was resent me for having to stop your lifestyle. I see the way you look at me. You haven't paid me any attention for years."

Frank wobbled. "Come on now, that ain't fair. I've always known that you were a better spider than me, you've always been the good one, way more than I could be."

"YOU DON'T KNOW ME!"

Frank held out his front legs. "Fine, okay, I get it. You're mad. Come on, let's get back home, we can talk, you can tell me everything. I'll listen. I get it, okay? I'm sorry."

For a moment, the pair stood there, half-looking at each other, their gazes lost in a miasma of uncertainty and doubt.

Felicity raised her head in defiance. "No. It's too late. I'm sorry, papa."

"What do you mean, you're sorry?" Frank looked behind him; his legs had gathered together, their grip on the ledge tenuous, as the realisation of what was about to happen hit him like a train. "No, don't you dare-"

"Everyone is going to die. Starting with you." Felicity leant in, and prodded her father in the middle of his chest. Frank tried to clutch her arm, but she slipped out of his desperate grasp. She was strong, so strong, more than he'd given her slight frame credit for. his legs scrabbled to try and maintain purchase, but the shock of the deed had caught him off guard. His legs skidded, and just like that...he felt disconnected from everything, a leaf tumbling from its branch. Frank looked up to the heavens as he fell. He saw the beast beyond, its twisted gargoyle face glaring balefully at him, its hide sheened by rain. But even more than that, he saw his little girl, his Felicity, looking down at him as he was pitched into thin air. Etched on her face was a smile carved from something primal, a leg raised, waving at his demise.

286

Frank closed his eyes, not wanting her treachery to be the last thing he would ever see. He thought back to happier times, when he had the entire world at the tip of his legs.

PART 5:
ALWAYS WITH THE COMPLAINING

Open your eyes.

Open your eyes, goddammit!

There, that wasn't too bad now, was it? Sure, everything is still in black-and-white, the rain is still being bailed out from the almighty's basement up above, but you're alive, ain't ya?

Well, ain't ya?

I think the amount of pain you're in right now suggests that you are. Always nice to work something out on your lonesome when your world has been thrown upside down and everything you thought you could count on turned out to be shit. Gives you a certain amount of satisfaction, huh?

Good. Now...get up.

Quit your complaining, pain ain't nothing but temporary, it's a reminder that you've still got piss and vinegar inside of ya. Besides, you ain't got time to lounge around on the floor.

I said, GET UP!

Everything hurts, none more so than my pride. Guess that's what a tumble from a fifteen-storey building will do to ya. Good job for me that I am equipped with a rope...of sorts. It sure as shit weren't made to arrest me as I approach terminal velocity, having been pushed from a not altogether insignificant height by someone I thought gave a hill of beans about me.

We'll get to the wheres and whatnots soon enough, but one thing for certain is that she owes me an explanation. That's the least she can do, considering she just tried to commit patricide. I might not have been the perfect father, but that don't give her the right to try and end me that way. Shit, that's gonna take some getting used to, but right here and now, those kind of thoughts ain't gonna do nothing to rectify the situation you find yourself in.

Baby steps, my man. Motherfucking baby steps. So now you've quit your whining, and the screaming has subsided, how's about you get your good-for-nothing butt up. That spire ain't gonna climb itself, you know?

A few of my legs are busted up pretty bad. The one at the front shouldn't be pointing that way neither, but lying here bitching about it ain't gonna fix it. So bite your lip, and get your good for nothing keister up off this floor.

There. That wasn't as terrible as you made it out to be. Sure, we'll miss that leg, but if it was its time to go, then who am I to stop it? Hold on, now, don't go trying to dash when you can barely stumble. This ain't no time for any macho bullshit, it's all about those baby steps. Now, first things first, apart from the leg, is anything else messed up?

Hmmm, it looks like my web-spinning days are numbered, for the time being at least, that's just dandy.

Fine, okay, okay, I'll dig deep to find that positive mental attitude bullshit. It's just peachy. So I'm a spider who can't spin no web right now, it ain't no thang, I'm sure if it comes to it, my coping mechanism will become a part of the arachnid genome for the rest of time. Evolution, that's all this is. A transition from one thing to another. No biggie.

So, let's summarise: my daughter, who I thought had been kidnapped, is seemingly in cahoots with this beast. I ain't sure why, and I ain't entirely sure how, but right now there's only one thing I can do. I gotta stop them. This beaten-up, good-for-nothing nobody, who spent all their life getting by sponging from the worst side of folk has now gotta find some sense of selflessness and stop them.

I need a drink.

Scratch that, I need a *lot* of drink.

And smokes, why the hell do I only have one smoke left?

Fine, all you're doing now is procrastinating, I get it, I can't blame ya. Shit, in some way, I'd like nothing more than to crawl back to Old Chester's, sit on my old stoop, and drink myself dry. But no-one —and I don't give a shit if you're gonna eat every goddamn thing in this city, or if you're my own flesh and blood— no-one tries to kill me and gets away with it.

As long as there's breath in this here body of mine, I'm gonna find a way to stop 'em both. All I've got to do is scale this tower once more, find a way to stop this putz, and then deal with my wayward kin.

Pfft, it's a cinch. I could do this with one leg tied behind my back.

Oh, right, or one being wrenched from my abdomen in a fall which should've killed me.

Well, it didn't. So suck it up.

Ow.

Don't breathe that hard, I think something's broken inside. I ain't sure exactly how long I've got, or if it's even going to be enough, but you are going to cut the yap and climb up this motherfucker.

No ifs, buts or maybes.

Besides, climbing ain't nothing but falling in reverse, and as demonstrated so ably just now, I've got the falling bit down real good.

PART 6:
DESPERATE TIMES

The beast's litany to long-forgotten deities complete, Qzxprycatj pulled back its head and let out an ungodly howl, scattering the rainclouds which had seemingly doomed the day to constant downpour. From its vantage point atop the spire, it surveyed its surroundings, seeking a place to begin its cull of humanity.

"Take me with you."

Qzxprycatj looked down at its shoulder and saw the minute spider squatting between the cracks in its skin. "What comes next will not be pleasant, you would be wise to wait here for my return." Its words were harsh and guttural.

"But I thought you wanted my help? What if you are bested once more? I'd be on my own again," Felicity sighed.

With a monstrous claw placed gently beneath her head, Qzxprycatj lifted the spider's gaze to its own. "Nothing can beat me this time, your visions of the past have shown me my failings. It cannot happen again. I will scourge this city first. For you. All I do now, I do for you."

Felicity wiped away a tear. "Then go, rend them limb-from-limb. Leave none alive."

Qzxprycatj let the spider climb aboard its claw before bending down to stow the insect back inside the hole in the roof. Felicity stepped off and dusted herself down. The rain had come to a stop, nothing more than a gauze of fine drizzle coating the monster's scaly body with fine droplets.

"Not so fast, sister."

The pair looked to the voice, seeing Frank limp from the bowels of the spire, revolver in hand. "What? Didn't expect to see me again?"

Sighing, Felicity whispered. "It would've been better if you had died, *Father*."

Pulling back the hammer, Frank asked, "And why would that be, *Daughter*?"

Her face lit up like a lake of phosphorus. "Because now,

291

she gets to kill you instead, and it will be far more painful than falling to your death, of that I can assure you."

The beast clambered down the spire so that its head was level with the hole, its clawed hands clinging to the lip. Secure, it reached for Frank with one of its hands, intent on grabbing up the irritation. Frank fell to his knees and laughed; a peal of chuckling that resonated down the spine of the ancient cathedral down to the nave below, and spilling out of the broken windows and doorway. Both beast and daughter stopped stock still, unsure what was so damned funny. "This is no joke, father, it is the end for you."

Still Frank laughed, continuing his unhinged cackling and demented chortling as he struggled to clear his eyes. Qzxprycatj grew tired of the interruption to its schedule and reached out faster, determined to squish the inconvenience and get on with its purpose. Before it could close its colossal hand around the spider, Frank ducked down, breaking off another useless limb in the process, his joviality turning to agony in the snapping of appendage. It didn't arrest his forward motion. A forward roll took him to within striking distance of Felicity, having ducked beneath the lazy swipe of the creature. With the back of the pistol grip, he clubbed his daughter round the head, delivering her into unconsciousness; she hit the floor with a whimper, falling still.

With a snort of annoyance, Qzxprycatj lashed out, seeking to smear the irritation against floor or wall, it mattered not, anything just to be rid of it. Frank let off a round at the beast's thumb, doing little but cause a minor irritation. Still, to Frank, it felt good, the memories of his previous encounters were coming back; impossible odds, seemingly insurmountable foes, all of them, without exception were dealt with. This...*thing* would be no exception. Sure, it may have the size, the reach, the track record of murder and mayhem, but that meant nothing. "You're on my patch now, sunshine."

Frank's butt twitched. Still no web, but it didn't matter, he just had to get close enough, he just needed one lucky break; one ace dealt by Lady Luck and the odds would be evened out. He rocked quickly to one side, landing on his bruised thorax as the beast tried to swat him, succeeding in nothing more than removing more roof tiles, allowing the grey skies to claim back some of the shade. On he went, scuttling across the roof beam, the injuries sustained in the fall forgotten about. Now was not the time to dwell on what he didn't have, it was time to focus on what he *did*. Frank knew he only had one advantage, and it wasn't his agility.

This became apparent as Qzxprycatj clipped Frank's back end, making him skid sideways into the corner where roof met slate. "Get up," he commanded his broken limbs. They obeyed, but the cost was going to be high, that much he knew. Now only a few feet from the monster's head, Frank trusted his fate to gravity, flinging himself through the air. Time slowed to a crawl, and another swipe of taloned hand displaced the air beneath, causing him to rotate in the air, but his course remained set. Spinning through the air, Frank pulled on every sinew, every ligament, and righted himself, managing to land atop the monster's snout as the air was pushed from his lungs.

An eye, deep grey with a black slit which ran from top to bottom, regarded him with pure hatred. From behind, Frank could hear something scraping. He dared to look, and saw the monster drag its razor-sharp claw up its own muzzle, intent on scraping him free, and disposing of him. "Just...a...few more steps."

Frank pushed himself up to a standing position, the noise from behind drowning everything out. The throbbing of his heart in his head, the pain, the voice telling him he could go on no longer, all of it was scratched out of existence until all that remained was Frank and two inches. Two mere inches to his goal, and not a lot of time to get there. He threw his head back and roared, spurred on, galloping as fast as his six remaining legs would go, feeling the lactic acid trying to leaden every single goddamn step. The eye was all he could see now, as if the hateful sun had been lassoed from its lofty arrogant perch and dragged down to witness the ken of mortals.

With the last ounce of effort, and the talon about to rub him from existence, Frank darted forward, his mandibles open, fangs long since considered useless, dripping with his special venom.

Just as the claw caught up with the tip of Frank's body,

293

the spider closed its fangs on the dewy eyeball of the monster. As the payload was delivered, the beast stopped, maintaining nothing but its hold on the spire, its body frozen. Within its mind, archived synapses, relegated to data retention, sparked into life. They burned fiercely, and a lightning bolt of recollection shot out before a storm of memories crackled up and down the cerebral cortex.

"Where am I?" Qzxprycatj asked. Its form was devoid of feeling, swimming in a tide of nothingness.

Here.

There.

Everywhere.

Nowhere.

Qzxprycatj roared, though it could feel the ripple down its throat, the sound came out shallow and unfulfilling.

Like so much of your life.

The creature barely had time to question the words, the speaker seeming so familiar, before a verdant landscape melted into view. Taking a look around, Qzxprycatj saw broken bodies beneath its feet. The blood, slowly drying in the high afternoon sun, pulled its skin taut. The coppery tang of fresh meat still clung to its lips.

There was familiarity about this, though. It wasn't the place of exile, that devilish plain had roiling surfaces which refused to settle. Tectonic plates constantly reformed the world. Where one day there would be a deep canyon, the next would see it turned into a mountain that gouged the distended belly of the sky. Molten magma would drip from the open sores, scalding the terrors which stalked the landscapes and called it home.

No, it had been to this place before, though only fleetingly. Like a blink in the passing of time. A footnote. A brief vacation which it had longed for but which had only brought disappointment. Qzxprycatj bent over and regarded one of the barely-alive humans. Their useless legs dragged behind them as they tried to claw their way to the edge of the forest to what they perceived to be safety.

The monster stabbed the man through his palsied limb,

impaling him to the ground, like an entomologist with a rare specimen. At first, the man didn't notice, his leg already disconnected from the nervous system. it was only its lack of movement that made him look up. Then the screaming started.

The noise offended Qzxprycatj, for it snatched the man up and flung him into its mouth, crunching down as it landed between its jaws. One gulp and the pulped mass slid down its gullet.

Your last morsel.

Qzxprycatj heard something other than the disembodied voice. A circlet of hollering and crying, coming from beneath the boughs of the trees. Its pupils dilated.

Now you remember.

Don't you?

Memories of another time, one it had thought long since cast into the pit of forgetfulness, came flooding back. From the undergrowth came more men. These men waved lengths of wood, encrusted with shiny stones, and arcane chants spilled from their tongues. Not one shred of fear or doubt. Qzxprycatj bucked skywards and landed thunderously. Despite the commotion and dust being thrown up, the men formed a loose circle around the monster. The noise grew and grew, twisting into an inverse cyclone of shouting, before it died down as quickly as it had started.

Then, one stepped free of the pack, and held his staff above his head. "I am Brother Noah, and your time of pillaging and murder is at an end. BEGONE!" His fellow priests cheered and shook their weapons at the beast.

Unsure of what to do, Qzxprycatj decided to retreat. It had fed well this day, it did not need this inconvenience. Emitting a final roar which sprayed the canopy with diluted blood and spittle, it turned tail and trotted to the section of forest it had entered through. Broken tree trunks and smashed vegetation led it back to its cave.

But in its way were more of the men, who raked its flank with their staffs. Qzxprycatj howled in pain, fear, a long-forgotten emotion, flared in its head. In its desperation, it sought out where the picket line was the thinnest, and ran.

It could feel the branches thwack and scrape against its

295

legs, and it could hear the wooting of men behind it, everything combining to propel it forward.

"No. Not that way, not this again," Qzxprycatj shouted, but its words had no bearing. It was as if it had been split in twain, one half's destiny set, the other a voyeur, unable to alter the inevitability of what was coming next.

Your death.

With its attention divided, Qzxprycatj failed to see the forest ahead terminating, giving way to the edge of a cliff. Too late it looked ahead, its feet dug into the ground, trying to arrest its forward motion, but it was not enough. Despite the divots carved into the fallow ground, it was launched into the air.

Momentum carried it forwards for a few seconds, before its weight played into the hands of gravity. Qzxprycatj began to plummet downwards. It could feel the wind rush past its body, and it could feel the sides of the canyon, carved through the valley by millennia of erosion, loom over it. An inevitability engulfed the monster. It ceased to scrabble in the air, resigned to its fate.

What once was, shall be again.

Static ran across its vision, and the scored sides of the cliffs returned to doleful grey from earthy brown. The cathedral spire a backdrop, it felt weightless until the ground rushed up to meet it. Where they were introduced to each other, the creature's body cracked and splintered. Shattered bone lanced through internal organ, bursting through tough skin, leaving the broken body of Qzxprycatj look like the upturned spine of a boat in a shipyard.

Above it, mists of shallow breath bloomed out. It could feel nothing below its neck, no signal sent or received. Breathing became painful, a hacking cough doing little except tear its lungs further apart across spears of splintered bone. Its chest raised once, before it let out a wet rasping sigh. Its sallow skin settled over its armature, and it fell still.

Frank's eyes fluttered open. Beneath him, he could feel a jellified cushion, being partially embedded into the monster's eye. One of his legs still moved; it scratched across his trench coat and into the interior pocket. Tipping the box upwards, he shook the last cigarette into his mouth before flinging the empty carton away and groping for his lighter.

The end of the Lucky Seven sizzled as the flame was applied and breath was pulled in. Frank let the lighter tumble away, and closed his eyes, taking in one big pull. "I knew you had it in you...old man..." Frank blew the smoke out, before placing the cigarette between his swollen lips. His leg slapped to the side; head tilted, the smoke rose like a crooked chimney up to the sky. Above, the clouds parted, just for a moment, a beam of sunlight grazing his cheek.

The cathedral bore down on him; its spire like a priest administering the last rites. He breathed in and out, letting the acrid smoke into his chest. From within the spire, a single bell tolled. Frank's body sagged, and the cigarette peeled free from his lips and tumbled to the ground. The spotlight from above flared, just for a moment, before it retracted. "Every time a church bell rings..."

It's time to...
DISCOVER YOUR FATE

Is someone cutting onions up in here? Just head on over to **Page 217.** I think I need a moment.

LOSERVILLE
POPULATION: ONE (YOU)

So here we are, we've barely even begun our little journey, and you've already quit like a great big quitter. Fair enough, each to their own, I'd love to say you're missing out on a huge life-changing experience, but if I'm being honest, this is only a medium-sized life-changing event. At best.

Guess you want an ending, then, yeah? I don't think you've earned it, not even close, but I'm a man of my word, so let me sling some words down just so you can finish the preview on Amazon, or dig the packaging out of the bin and get the instructions on how to return the book to sender. Okay, so here we go. The appropriate ending for anybody who is incapable of seeing anything through:

Noah comes to in the shower. He's cold, alone, covered in claggy shower gel which has formed a sticky outer coating to his human skin. It was that same weird daydream once more, when he was a member of something or other that threatened to change the world. But alas, he is nothing but a lowly clerk in a door knocker factory downtown. He picks up the scraper, usually reserved for getting rid of the fish that stick to walls of his flat, and gouges away at the minty second skin he's acquired since last he lapsed into a fugue state.

One day, perhaps, he'll quit his job and do something with his life, but what's more likely is that he'll bang his head on an open cupboard door, pass out, and get eaten by the family of ravenous gerbils that live in the cavity walls.

The end.

Now...*go*. Away with you. Begone, ye of little patience, I need to prepare the vat of thoughts for my next work, and your negative vibes are bringing me down.

CONGRATULATIONS!
THIS IS ENDING
#7

'BE A GOOD EGG,
AND PICK UP THE SOAP WOULD YOU?'

There's a word for people like you. Quitter. Or...you've been trying to nail all the endings, either way, I ain't fussed. This is your book, so you do your own thang. If you've realised that you made a terribly hasty decision, just return to **Page 6** and we'll pretend that this never happened.

If you're done, then good day to you!

ERIC THE HALF A CHAPTER

"YES!" Ian leapt up, nearly upper-cutting Monique into a completely different story, a period drama set during the First Scrumpy Insurrection of 1981. Oblivious to his wild swinging, he began to moonwalk, fist-bumping Frank the Flashback Spider on his way round the room.

"It's not like you've won the lottery," Pothead Pete complained.

Blowing a raspberry, Ian shrugged his shoulders. "Don't care, I never win anything, you gotta take all these small victories and celebrate them. Come on, you lot, we best get a move on."

Noah tapped the bottom of his staff against the floor. "I move...for no man."

Monique sided with the priest. "Yeah, why do we have to go? Can't we just stay here?"

Ian was already heading for the door. "Look, when you travel in time, you come out in the same place, but at the date you chose. If I were to go and nab some cool ass dinosaurs and bring them back, they'd materialise in the midst of Pete's flat. We need to be by the monster so we can trash it, instead of my mate's gaff."

Pothead Pete started putting his trainers on. "He's got a point, come on you lot —get a wriggle on."

"Fine, if we must, but I'm making a note of this," Noah protested.

Monique scowled. "How do you know all this? Have you used it, Ian?"

Shoving the betting slip further into his pocket, Ian dabbed at the perspiration blooming on his forehead. "No...of course not, I just...read the instructions."

Unconvinced, but impressed that a man had actually read up on how to do something without jumping in feet-first and ballsing it all up, Monique decided that discretion was the better part of valour.

"Is it jumper weather?" Pothead Pete asked.

TAKING THE PISS NOW

Huddling behind a thick stone column supporting one side of the archway, the group peeked out into the cathedral grounds. Among the rain gore from earlier, sundered limbs and discarded gristly bits were strewn over the once immaculate lawn. One poor wretch, torn in two, crawled along the floor towards them, his blood-streaked hand raised skywards. "Help me, please...help."

"Where are your legs?" Pothead Pete hissed, as if their location was of paramount importance.

The stricken man, blood pumping from severed veins and arteries, rolled onto his back and pointed towards a distant tree. Located in the upper boughs were a pair of legs and a groin, encased in blood-soaked skinny jeans. "Please...I'm quite badly wounded...I think if you can help stem the bleeding, I may pull through."

Ian shook his head. "Okay you lot, go and help No-Legs if you want, but I best go back...to the past."

"On your own?" Noah asked.

"Well yeah, don't want you lot around, spoiling the atmos, bringing me down. There are going to be kickass dinosaurs running about the place. I bloody love dinosaurs. The last thing I want is for one of you miserable bastards to ruin the moment with some pithy comment. Plus, it all seems to be getting a bit dialogue heavy, I think it'd be the perfect juncture for some flowery prose."

Noah, Monique, Pothead Pete and No-Legs shared knowing looks.

"Okay, fine, perhaps not *flowery*, we all know what kind of lowbrow-dickhead wrote this. But we could do with a break from it all, yeah? It's not me, it's you. Now fuck off and let me go bag some dinosaurs."

"How many are you going to get?" Monique asked.

"Oh, I dunno, as long as they're mean-looking, have big teeth and are all scary and shit, as many as I can round up. Now, if you don't mind."

With that, Ian fiddled with the controls on the watch, somehow making 70 million years BC appear on the

301

seemingly basic digital wristwatch. Laughing at the implausibility of it all, Ian dipped the plastic bubble ring into the liquid and blew. An oily bubble popped out the other side. Bidding them all adieu with a two-fingered salute, Ian bunny-hopped into the orb. The circle wrapped around him, before it *POPPED!* them out of time and space.

JURASSIC PLAY PARK

Unless you've not been paying attention, for which I'll forgive you, Ian is rather partial to dinosaurs. His love of the things stretched back to when he was a little nipper. Despite having loads of toys, the plastic dinosaurs were always his favourite.

He'd create huge imaginary jungles and plains on the floor of his bedroom, the garish green and brown carpet — more at home in a country pub— providing an excellent matting for his febrile mind. Whilst mighty Diplodocus roamed amongst the piles of socks which doubled up as bushy treetops, their mouths plucking juicy leaves from the tall branches, Stegosaurus roamed beneath the canopy. Out on the exposed plains, fierce Tyrannosaurus rex fought each other over slain animals.

One dinosaur though, stood out from all of them. Triceratops. Ian was fascinated with them, their horns, and how they managed to take on bigger creatures and hold their own. Whenever he did his play battles, they always won.

His toy dinosaur collection was a mishmash of different makes, some woefully disparate in scale, but Ian didn't care one bit. His toy cars were trampled underfoot, military action figures —despite putting up a brave fight— were always taken down by a horde of snarling dinosaurs. Sprawled out on his floor: his prize Triceratops goring the shit out of a hapless T-Rex who had gotten too big for his clawed feet. Even when he grew up and other things took over: girls, drinking, obtaining the minimum wage, he would often think back to those simpler times.

With a satisfying *POP!*, the kind you get when squeezing a virginal sheet of bubble wrap, Ian fell to his knees and sunk within knee-deep grass. The first thing to assault his senses was the smell of dung, and looking to his right, he counted his lucky stars that he hadn't ended up where Noah just was, else he would have been deposited armpit-deep in a pile of steaming yellow shit.

Flies the size of his fist buzzed around the crap heap,

303

their thick proboscises plunged into the spongy mass. Once gorged, they retracted with a wet slurp. Some fluttered around Ian, attempting to prod him with their poo-jabber. He swatted them with his open palm, hoping he wouldn't actually come into contact with any of them. The last thing he wanted was for one of them to burst open and shower him with fly guts and bum slurry, especially that of unknown origin. With the bumbling flies now choosing to ignore him, Ian picked himself up and had a bit of a look around.

Where the cathedral had stood in the future was now the beginning of a forest, possibly a copse, but without the advantage of a map, *forest* would do as a suitable description for now. Shrieks sounded from above, and he looked up to see the unmistakable profile of Pterodactyls. With the sun behind them, they were merely black shapes against the pale blue sky. As they traversed the skies in a V formation, not unlike geese from his own time, Ian noticed there was something odd about them, although he couldn't figure out what. Thinking it perhaps some kind of optical illusion, the stifling heat, or more likely the after-effects of time travel, he decided to head for some shade within the forest.

Taking a few furtive steps into the woodland, he noted how the canopy above him blanched out most of the light. Looking back out at the grasslands, making a mental note of where the pile of dung was for later, it looked like the two areas were in different time zones.

With the bright light behind him, Ian worked his way into the bowels of the forest. From around him came hoots and clicks, buzzes and thwacks. Not too dissimilar from the noises he used to make when he was a kid, come to think of it.

Onwards he trekked; on the horizon he could see a swatch of light pulling him to its terminus. Ahead was a pile of leaves apparently arranged on purpose, collected even, as if some woodland warden had been busy sweeping. The closer he got, the more he realised they weren't leaves at all.

He knelt down and picked up a handful, turning them over in his hands. *This couldn't be possible, no way.* He discarded all but one and then held it against the side of his foot. Way too small for him, but they were definitely socks. Rummaging through the pile, there were all sorts in there, woollen ones, cotton ones, some were threadbare, with patches of fine gauze dotted around on the balls of the foot and the heel.

It's not that odd, could be another time traveller, and they just...made a pile of socks here. For shits and giggles.

Deciding that it must be a form of travel sickness, Ian stood up and continued towards the band of light in the distance. Everything would be alright; he was probably just dehydrated or something. Nothing to see here. As you were.

Reaching the edge of the forest, Ian could see a stream snake its way through the plains ahead. Ignoring health and safety protocol, he dashed over to it and dunked his head under the surface. Though not a particularly efficient way of taking on water, it did at least cool him down a touch.

Feeling a lot better, Ian sat on his haunches, and with the vegetation around being much more under control, he was able to see further; nothing but verdant growth and rolling hills. If ever you needed a stock image of green hillocks, this was it. The sun was no longer directly overhead and was currently playing peek-a-boo behind a large cloud which looked like a deformed Labradoodle.

The only sound was a surging clicking sound, the kind you hear on tropical islands. It was hypnotic. Taking the opportunity for a bit of a rest, Ian kicked his shoes off and lay on the ground, seeing if he could pick out any other distinctive shapes in the clouds.

An iron.

A pair of grinning drunkards, one telling another a story about a plucky owl.

Is that...?

Yeah, a boxer lashing out at a giant lemon with a mean right hook.

Ian decided this cloud game was quite fun, and between that and the constant insect noise, he could feel his eyes get heavier. What would be the harm in a quick nap? He sure as hell hadn't seen or heard any dinosaurs, and aside from the massive flies, he wasn't entirely convinced he'd dialled into the right time period.

He turned over on his side and ran a hand across the

305

floor. His eyes flicked open. Looking down, he saw that he was lying down on an actual fabric carpet. Ian jumped up, looking around frantically for the end of the floor, for it must be a rug or something, surely? But no, nothing. Jogging along the river, he could feel the soft warm carpet beneath his feet.

Just as he exclaimed, internally, *how odd* this was, a noise began to grow louder and louder, overtaking the inescapable insect cacophony. Ian cocked his ear, which is an odd saying when you think about it. You don't fanny your eyes at anything, do you?

Listening more intently, he tried to ignore the insects and focus solely on the new sound. As it got louder, he gulped, no...*this is impossible*. I mean, the sock leaves were one thing, and the carpet floor another, but this?

How the hell could there be cars in the distant past?

Having determined where the sound was coming from, Ian turned towards it. Running parallel to the edge of the forest was a collection of three vehicles. One was an open-topped jeep, the kind you normally get with some gruff military action figure included. Another was a dune buggy, and although there was an internal canopy of some kind, some*thing* was riding on top of it, the springy antenna swishing as it bore down on him.

The third vehicle truly took his breath away. It was a black London cab. As it got closer, Ian could see a head sticking out of a window, and recognised it straight away. Of course he knew what it was, it was his *favouritest* thing in the entire world. It was a Triceratops.

DOYOUTHINKIKNOWWHATIAMDOINGASAURUS

Ian tried to will his legs to move. The vehicles, though looming down on him, were still a little way off; he looked back and saw that the skirt of the forest was close enough. If he could get there, there was no way they could follow him, not in those bulky cars.

The buggy got to him first; try as he might, his body stood rooted to the carpeted floor. Atop the vehicle were a pair of bickering Velociraptors, snapping at each other, fighting over the controller. Their bodies looked, wrong, not flesh and bone, that was certain. The jeep pulled up next to the river, and two Deinonychuses, different in size and colour, jumped out of the cockpit, and stalked towards Ian, their fiendish claws flicking out and slashing the air.

Finally, the cab screeched to a halt. After a number of attempts, the Triceratops managed to extricate itself from the vehicle, its body clearly too bulky to drive properly. That, and the fact it hadn't passed its driving test. As it slammed the door shut, Ian finally worked out what was up with their bodies.

They were all made of plastic. Of very different construction techniques and quality, that much was certain, but plastic they were. Ian chuckled at the notion that dinosaurs died, became oil, which made plastic, and had now been reformed into dinosaurs once more, tickled him. I mean, most people would be a bit more freaked that plastic animals were advancing towards them, with malicious intent, as he stood there on a carpet, unable to move.

But hey, I just write this stuff, ya know? I'm not Ian. *You're* not Ian, you just chose this bit to see what nonsense I would come up with next. What would you do, Huh? Would you have frolicked in the sock leaf pile? Perhaps explored the dung from earlier? Tried to punch one of the giant flies in the face?

This much is certain: I couldn't be bothered making branches for those piddling choices. No way.

With the beasts bearing down on him, Ian gulped. He cast a quick glance at his time travel watch, just to make sure that it wasn't on the fritz. Nope, 70 million BC, sure as eggs are eggs. Well this was a turn up for the books, although judging by the fixed snarls on the dinosaur's faces, any chance of him being able to bag some and head back to the present looked pretty slim.

Ian tried to think back to the week he'd spent learning how to deal with ornery animals. Now, he knew that you're supposed to sock a shark on the nose, and if you see a honey badger, then blowing on its left nipple is a sure-fire way of making that sucker back off pronto. If a hungry pelican is intent on munching on your steaming entrails, then singing any new wave song from the eighties is the only way to quell their bloodlust. But dinosaurs? What the fuck? He discarded the advice about smearing yourself in horseradish to throw off grizzly bears as churlish, and thought back to the biggest, baddest animal he'd ever had to face. The one which had claimed the lives of seventeen of his fellow course-goers, and cost the esteemed Henry Gurt his eyesight.

The sperm whale.

Ian clicked his fingers and rummaged around in his pockets, hoping to all that was unholy and evil that he had brought it (or a suitable substitute) with him. He smiled as his fingers wrapped around the hard plastic.

As the plastic animals snapped their razor-sharp teeth at him and scratched at the woven floor with their talons, Ian sunk into a meditative pose and pulled out the clothes peg. With thumb and forefinger working in perfect unison, he opened and closed the little jaws, allowing them to clack together.

For a few seconds, the dinosaurs ceased their advance and looked at each other, wondering what the fuck was going on with their lunch. Why did it have the petrified remains of a limbless *Peg*asus baby in its fingers?

No matter, it looked squishy enough to eat, and if the only thing it could kill was a defenceless calf, then fuck it. The Triceratops roared at the others to tell them to back off, it was owed first dibs. As the bag of meat sat nonplussed in front of the horde, the three-horned beast prepared to charge and impale it on its mighty horns.

Stamping the ground like a bull getting its kicks on the

308

Pamplona bull run, it kicked up huge tufts of carpet and began to charge the sitting intruder. As it got closer, its eyes opened wide, *no fucking way.*

Yes, that was the dinosaur's internal monologue. Cool, huh?

It skidded to a halt mere feet away from the immovable object, who had its eyes closed, still playing with the corpse of the *Peg*asus baby.

I do hope you got the whole Pegasus thing. A peg...and a Pegasus. Smart, huh? See, I may look like a complete and total gimboid, but I'm capable of the odd moment of genius.

The Triceratops, not wishing to puncture the person, gently nudged it with its secondary horns. Slowly, Ian opened his eyes, a huge grin cracking along his face. "Yes! I knew it, I told the others that it's all down to the way you use the peg. They didn't believe me, and that's why that sperm whale ripped them to pieces. Losers."

The horned plastic dinosaur nudged him. "Hey, dude, knock it off, will ya?" Ian whinged.

The Triceratops stopped, gasped and stood back; his mouth open. "It *is* you! It's the creator!" With that, it supplicated itself on the ground, which, when you're made from rigid plastic, is not the easiest thing to do. Taking care to not bend its legs to the point of breakage, it lay there, mumbling to itself.

Ian scratched his head with the peg. "Hey, what now?"

"No way, this is...just...just..." one of the Velociraptors stuttered, before it too, threw itself to the ground, its snout nuzzling into one of the divots created by the Triceratops' claw gouging. One-by-one, the remaining creatures joined their brethren on the floor.

"Okay, so this is weird, now. I thought I'd come back in time to go and bag me some fearsome dinosaurs, but I seem to have stumbled into some kind of messed-up acid trip. Which one of you spiked my pint? I bet it was you, Noah...or whatever the hell you are now," Ian warned.

Scratching against the coarse flooring, the Triceratops turned its head to the side, enabling the enunciation of words. "You're the creator, the great master from the tales of legend. You formed these lands in the days of yore and seeded it with our forebears. For years, we have roamed the

309

lands, daring to go as far as...the tiled lands."

Every creature gasped at the utterance of those words, before muttering. "Tiled lands," over and over in some form of lamentation.

"Okay...so where did you get the sweet rides from?"

Daring to look up, although it wasn't articulated that way, so it was nigh on impossible, to be honest, the Triceratops whimpered. "What are these sweet rides of which you speak?" It quickly averted its gaze.

Ian walked past the prone animals and ran his hand over the London cab's bonnet. Not believing it, he tapped it with his knuckles, and a dull thud came back. "Hmmm..." He pried his fingers into the gap above the radiator and lifted up the bonnet. Revealing a plastic engine block, a perfect replica of the real thing, he slammed it back down again. "How the hell do these things work? Don't you have to use petrol or something?"

"P...et...roll?" the Triceratops rolled the letters around its mouth. "What is this pee-t-roll of which you speak?"

"Doesn't matter, today has been decidedly odd, I didn't think when I woke up this morning that one of the sanest parts of the day would be attempting to explain the workings of the internal combustion engine to a plastic Triceratops."

"No, your masterfulness," the animals mumbled collectively.

"Okay, knock it off, just stand up, will you? It's disconcerting speaking to you as it is, let alone looking at you lot from this angle. You look like you're dry humping the floor."

After cursory glances at Ian and each other, to see if it was some kind of test, they began to get to their chunky feet. A number of them were having difficulties, so Ian lent a hand, which caused strange cooing sounds from the beasts. As he dusted off pubic hair and sock fluff from their shiny hides, he asked, "So what's your name, then?"

One of the Deinonychuses strutted forwards. "I...oh, wonderful creator of shoebox mountain, am-"

Ian held up his hand, cutting him off, "Steady on there, Mister, or *Mrs* Claws, there's a few of you, and let's face it, you're extras. If I get your names, then it's just pointless

310

information for someone more important than us to remember."

Crestfallen, the Deinonychus clacked the air with its sharp talons and headed back it its mate. "Hey, come on, don't be like that. I still think you're great, and let's face it, not many people will have heard of you. If you're lucky, they'll go and look you up on an internet search engine. HUH? WOULDN'T THAT BE JUST REWARDS?"

Ian winked at the Deinonychus, who let out a solitary liquid plastic tear. The human turned to the Triceratops. "You, you're the important character in this bit, there was a whole section of foreshadowing background information given about you being my favourite dinosaur, so go on...what's your name?"

With his little mouth agape, the Triceratops fought to regain motor function of what approximated to its vocal chords. Coughing up a wad of hair, it said. "My name? It's Pablo."

"Pablo?"

"Uh-huh."

"Pablo the Triceratops?"

"That's me."

"Right..."

Ian shook his head. "No matter, good to meet you, Pablo. Look, I came back in time...apparently to try and get some proper bad motherfucking dinosaurs to come with me to the future so they can help me destroy a terrible apocalyptic monster. Do you think that's something you lot can help me with?"

Pablo puffed his chest out. Okay, so that's impossible, he shimmied on the spot, giving the impression that he was swelling with pride. "You've come back to the right time period, oh wizened governor of the skidmarked underpants valley, for killing apocalyptic monsters is our specialty."

"Really, that's handy, and totally uncoincidental. I'm coming around to this notion of serendipity," Ian said.

311

REVELATIONS

The ride back to Dinosaurville was across the carpeted plains where he had been found. Seated in the back of the London cab, which was just right for his proportions, Ian looked ahead, as vast plastic towers loomed on the horizon. A host of vehicles were parked in a long narrow lot on the edge of the habitation; it seemed that no transportation actually managed to snake its way through the streets of this plastic metropolis.

As the dinosaurs got out of their respective rides, a Stegosaurus with chamois leather clothes stuck to the end of his spines began to work over the surface of each. This, of course, was after throwing itself to the ground when it saw their guest was none other than the imperious ruler of the stash of curled up jam sandwiches.

The Velociraptors and Deinonychuses bid their farewells, and headed off to a large cardboard box bearing the sign, 'Doyouwantadrinkus.' From within, boisterous caterwauling and singing could be heard. "Don't mind them," Pablo said as he took the lead. "They're just gonna have a few halves of some gin we found in a metal tank beneath the tower of stickle bricks."

Ian laughed. "So, you could say it's *tankery* gin?"

Pablo looked at him blankly.

"Oh...right...you weren't there in the other chapter, were you? So, where are we going then, do we have to speak to the ruler of these parts?"

The Triceratops stopped.

"What?"

Pablo tapped the human gently with his horn. "We have no ruler, oh Ian of the wet mattress, n-"

"Woah, steady on there, Pablo, that was only if I had nightmares, okay? Anyway, how do you know about that? This place looks familiar..."

"Come on, I'll show you...I think you'll like it. It should help make a bit more sense of things."

Weaving amongst buildings of multiple construction techniques, Ian marvelled at the use of same-coloured Lego in the making of a row of terraced houses. Scrunched up paper was used as nests by Pterodactyls, some of whom wore bowler hats and smoked pipes. They seemed less in awe of the humanoid, looking over the rim of their monocles before continuing to read the evening paper.

Finally, they came to a large square building. Ian craned his neck upwards and saw that the sides were perfectly smooth, each corner ending in a rounded tower. "This looks like the bucket I used to make sandcastles with as a kid," he mumbled to himself.

In the centre of the wall was a tall pea-coloured gate, and Pablo made a loud braying sound that sounded a little like the Shakin' Stevens song, 'Green Door.' There was a grinding sound from within before it opened like a drawbridge, bidding them inwards.

The interior was shrouded in murk, a solitary opening in the roof doing little to cast any meaningful amount of light on proceedings. Behind them, the gate creaked and clanked shut, leaving them in an awkward dim silence. "You're not going to do weird sex things to me, are you?"

Pablo stamped his foot once on the ground, which caused a ripple of fairy lights to turn on. They were hung in a winding pattern, and the effect was rather breathtaking, just like a shorn scrotum (I suggest you try it). The room, though sizable, was empty aside from the cool lighting (obviously), and a pair of items.

The first was a throne, made from multi-coloured wooden blocks. The seat and backrest were padded out with rectangular purple bean bags, the kind you might be handed at a carnival and tasked with knocking unconscious a goldfish so you might win a coconut. Behind that, against the far wall, was a large photograph contained within a golden, gilded frame. Ian's jaw fell open. "Wh...where...where did you get that from?"

Pablo trudged over to the picture and prostrated himself in front of it. "It was left here...by the creator, the one who made Dinosaurville and the surrounding area. It is said that his mother and father forged the lands beyond, but we wouldn't know about that, as we do not venture further than the opening in the Great Skirting Board of Hallway."

In a daze, Ian stumbled to the photo. "That's me, I think

I was about six," he said, pointing to a blonde, freckle-faced boy, who was plonked on a green-and-brown carpet, in the middle of his toy dinosaur collection. "I don't understand..."

Standing up, Pablo pointed to the boy with his tusk. "He...you...are the creator; back in the days of yore, you forsook all other false offerings and chose us...the humble dinosaurs, as the preferred dwellers of these lands. You created the lake of Cherryade in mere seconds, and our forefathers frolicked in it, and lo, it was good. If a little sticky."

"I remember that, got a right bollocking from mum, if I remember rightly. Look," he pointed to the photo, showing a red stain in the carpet. "There it is, right there."

"Not content with letting us fend off the others, you taught us how to use the cars and trucks to our advantage. Those skills, along with others, were passed from one dinosaur to the next."

"This is all smashing and all, but I grew up. I stuck you all in a box, and mum ditched you in a charity shop in town. How the hell did all *this* happen?"

"The legend speaks of the great collection, when the creator, who had grown taller and more spotty, grew angry with our lack of articulation and inability to par-tay. As we sat in the bag of judgement, a great storm fell upon my forebears. One toy, a stuffed armadillo named Felicity, managed to glimpse out of the bag; the last thing she saw before she fell blind was a giant rainbow-coloured orb floating towards the trapped dinosaurs. There came the almighty *POP!*, and lo, we were transported to this place, like before, but further of vision. The creator, shrouded in a black hooded sweatshirt, cast them unto this place, complete with all the buildings you have seen, and the transportation. His booming voice said, 'All of you are now born free. Make best your world, for one day I shall return, and will need you to kick the shit out of an apocalyptic beast. So you'd best get training and that.' Then he was gone."

Ian glared at the Triceratops, who was beginning to well up. "That is fucking lame, you seriously expect me to believe that?"

"What I told you is true, at least...from a certain point of view."

"Oh no you don't, Pablo Wan Kenobi, don't give me none of that vague shit."

"This is what has been passed down from one plastic dinosaur to another. Look at the picture, if you don't believe me."

Ian ummed. "Nah, this is crap, sorry."

"Fine, I didn't want to have to do this. Do you remember just before you cast us into the bag of judgement?"

"Kinda...I think so..."

"There are other tales that have been passed down, you know. Tales of a time when the great creator would shake the sweaty pants palm tree and send showers of white coconut mi-"

"WOAH, THERE! Okay, okay, I believe you. Jeez, you lot sure do remember a lot of stuff, huh? So...if I did say I was coming back, and you lot believed me, are you really ready to help me kick some end-of-the-world monster arse?"

"Oh yes, Ian, dabber of the tissue, you bet your hairy man sacks we are."

LET'S GET R-R-R-READY
TO R-R-R-RUMBLE

The convoy of various vehicles came to a halt as Ian, with Pablo's help, crawled out from the back of a big tipper truck. "Are you sure it's here?" he asked the Triceratops.

Pablo cantered over to the steaming pile of crap. "Look, here it is, right where it always is."

Ian cautiously followed his new plastic BFF, and worked his way through a posse of small Tyrannosaurs who barely came up to his shoulder. His nose wrinkling as he caught a waft of the whiff, Ian looked at the dinosaurs suspiciously. "How do you lot...you know...go for a poopy?"

Pablo smiled. "We don't, oh trainer of the eighties montage, this is Kevin's."

"Who's Kevin?"

"A complete arsehole giant who goes around shitting all over the plains. Honestly, we steer clear of him nowadays, he's a moron. That's why we leave these grassy areas to him, more than one of us has stepped in his doo-doo. When it seeps in between the joins...urgh...the smell!" Pablo looked across to a pair of Ankylosauruses, who stood a distance away from the others.

"Fine." Ian fiddled with the watch until the time and date was set. "We'll rock up a few seconds after I left, it'll make for a big entrance."

"Is this going to work, oh scatterer of the sacred seed?"

Ian tied the ends of a length of string together, stretching it out to a large loop. "Well, I saw this guy do it in town once, so yeah...why not? It's going to work like a dream. Remember, as soon as the bubble is made, we *all* need to get in there before it pops, okay?" Ian looked around at the ragtag band of plastic dinosaurs, and received a number of awkward nods and arm waving in return.

Dipping the string into the bubble bottle, Ian carefully replaced the cap, and took a step backwards. With a flick of the wrist, he cast the string into the air and swished it as if he were the finest giant bubble maker in the entire world, which, to be fair, he probably was. I mean, what's the likelihood of one of the dinosaurs being able to do that? Not very. They lack dexterity, and opposable thumbs. Evolution wins again, HUZZAH FOR US!

A large oily bubble floated lazily above the grass, and Ian closed off the circle, sealing it. The dinosaurs gasped and tried to cross themselves, but failed. Because tiny plastic hands. Or –y'know, *claws*. "You lot ready? Let's go save the world!" Ian ushered the plastic creations forward, and one-by-one, they stepped into the bubble.

READY PLAYER ONE

POP!

"AAAAAARRRRRRRRRRRRRGGGGGGGGGGGGGGGGGHHHH HHHHHHHHHHH!" the scream pierced Ian's ears. Materialising back in the cathedral grounds, he fell to the floor, clutching the side of his head.

"My god..." Monique said.

Ian stood up triumphantly. "Yes, I know, it's me, I'm back. You're impressed, aren't you?"

"It's not that, Ian, look!" Monique, who conveniently was standing in front of him, pointed to one side.

With an annoyed huff borne of irritation and the need for a wee, Ian followed the gesticulating digit. He clamped a hand over his mouth. As freshly time-travelled dinosaurs formed an orderly procession to ready themselves for the upcoming fight, one, a Giraffatitan called Mary, mewled gently. She had transpagified (*totally* a word, by the way — it means to transpagify somewhere, like through space and time and that) in the same space as Noah.

The priest's legs were splayed either side of one of Mary's back legs; his tracksuit-covered knees kicked out, pedalling the air. Noah's arm, still clutching his rather fetching staff, stuck out from her sagging belly. The rest of him was hidden from view, although his screams echoed through the hollow innards of the Giraffatitan.

"Ah...slight hickity-cup, huh? Didn't really think about what would happen if someone or some*thing* transpagified in the same space as someone or some*thing* else. Least we know now, though huh?"

"AAAAAAAARRRRRRRGGGGGGGGGHHHHHHH, my legs, my legs, my old kingdom...for my legs," Noah's muffled voice echoed through Mary's leg hole.

Mary seemed pretty nonplussed about having gained two new legs and an arm, the latter of which might be of some use. There was something definitely different inside, though; the sensation was an odd one, and not entirely pleasant. Mary let out an enormous belch, and Noah's plaintive crying became louder.

"Look, Noah, we'll get you out of there after the impending big boss fight, okay? I'm sure we'll be able to sort something out, you just hang on in there, okay?" Ian shouted at the priest's armpit.

Noah swung the staff around, trying to clunk the impudent little shit on his head. His feeble efforts missed woefully, and he struck the side of Mary, causing him to drop the staff onto the floor. "Yoink," Ian said helpfully, as he picked the weapon up. "Cheers, mate."

"No problem, you bastard," came the muffled reply, with a thumbs-up.

With the staff procured, Ian strode confidently to the head of the dinosaur host.

Qzxprycatj had been enjoying tucking into a busload of German tourists. Though as she forced the last family down her gullet, it struck her that of all the people she'd eaten, they tasted the würst.

Hey, come on, that's pretty funny.

Seriously? I've been bringing out my A-GAME for y'all so far, you should be grateful, this could have been nothing but a procession of knob jokes and fart gags. And as for you, Escobar, you can fuck off!

Throwing aside the bus, which had been torn asunder like a tube of squeezy cheese, Qzxprycatj leapt off the roof of the cathedral and prowled towards the assortment of plastic creatures. It sniffed the air, noting that most of the things in front of it weren't edible and would most likely cause a blockage in its airway. Being from the Infernal plains, and aware of the price of medical insurance, Qzxprycatj made a mental note to not chew on anything smaller than its own finger. Not counting the claw. That should stop any possible choking or unwanted medical expenses.

Ian looked up at the monster, which seemed to be a lot fucking bigger now that it was looming over him like a priest at choir rehearsal. "Pablo...not wishing to shit all over your feet, but you lot aren't exactly as intimidating as this bad boy."

Pablo chuckled a dinosaur laugh, which sounded like an axe thunking repeatedly into a tree stump, if you're interested. If you're *super*-interested, I'm talking about an

319

oak tree stump too, in case you're into that sort of thing. "Oh, Ian, bedecker of the Holy dungarees, we have yet to form into our Mega-Dinosaur-Bot, which in no way impinges on any copyright of any existing giant dinosaur robots or transforming stuff, okay? We clear? Good."

"SWEET! I'll ride you lot into battle like a proper motherfucking badass," Ian wooted.

"Though we are missing Mary," Pablo pointed out.

"Is she an important component?"

"She forms the butt of the plasma carbine discharger; the recoil will be amplified."

"Ha ha ha ha ha ha ha ha ha ha," Ian chuckled.

"What is so funny, oh stubber of the toe?"

"You said *butt*."

"Seriously?"

Shrugging, Ian pointed at the mighty form of Qzxprycatj, who was taking advantage of the added dialogue to stalk closer. "Come on, enough of the butt jokes, form up, you dinosaur dudes. It's time to take out the trash."

Pablo turned to one of the Kentrosauruses, who looked puzzled, but that could've just been its default facial expression. Resting 'huh?' face.

Ian tapped Pablo on the shoulder. "What?"

"I thought Friday was bin day?"

"Oh, for fuck's sake, look, this is being dragged out *way* longer than necessary. Just do your thing so we can kick this monster's arse, and we can see what the reporter has to say afterwards. People have other stuff to do, you know?"

The Triceratops stomped about, before raising his horned head skywards. "DINOSAURS, COMBINE!"

All the plastic dinosaurs were pulled together as if they were sucked into the event horizon of a black hole. Dull clunks and thwacks near deafened Ian and Monique as the coterie collided against one another. Then came the grinding of plastic; coarse hides ground together, forming a completely new genre of Metal music. Groundo-plastic-new wave-metal. Even the mighty Qzxprycatj, who was used to such horrific sounds, staggered backwards, recoiling from the hideous din.

Ian looked upon the mass, which looked like a giant ball of multi-coloured clay, and to be honest, he was pretty unimpressed. As he was about to go and pet Mary, the ball of plastic crap hurtled into the air. Stopping just within the Earth's atmosphere, it began to fall back to the ground. As gravity pulled it down, flames and sparks flew from a tail of superheated air. With a mighty smash, it...well, *smash*ed into the ground.

A giant blocky plastic man was kneeling in a small crater caused by the impact.

Where once were dinosaurs now stood a mottled plastic knight, meditating on the eve of battle. Ian clapped, as he noted that there were at least eight points of articulation on the limbs alone; this would definitely help when the fighting finally happened.

(It's soon, I promise.)

Qzxprycatj growled, its long sticky tongue shooting from its mouth, spearing towards the kneeling knight. Just as it was about to ensnare the warrior, its hand shot up from its side and caught the slimy tendril. The beast's eyes opened in surprise; it tried to pull its tongue back into its mouth, but the hold was firm.

Slowly, the knight lifted his helmeted head up and faced his foe. Slits where eyes should be, illuminated from within, bathing the previously blackened pits a nice soothing blue. "Not today, oh denizen of terror," it said, its voice deep and bassy.

Still Qzxprycatj pulled on its own tongue as the knight stood up, easily half the height again of the apocalyptic beast. He opened his hand and the tongue flew back, slapping the beast in the face. "Ha ha ha, right in the kisser!" Ian burst out in laughter before he shrugged and dispensed with the faux New York gangster accent he had affected.

The beast slurped its tongue back into its mouth, before running it over the array of sharp teeth on display and inching its way backwards in preparation for the cataclysmic fight.

Looking down at Ian, the knight extended a gauntleted hand. "Oh Ian, wouldst thou command this vassal and smite this despicable foe?"

"You bet your shiny plastic arse I wouldst."

The knight picked Ian up, and lifted off his helmet to reveal a circular room with no windows, a beanbag, and a

321

TV with a games console wired into it. Before Ian could even muster a confused *huh*, the knight plonked him down on the beanbag and replaced his headgear.

The room sealed with a hiss like a steaming iron, and Ian was plunged into darkness. From out of the murk, the television blinked into life. A white circle grew on the screen until it filled the rectangular edges with its light. With the space illuminated, Ian was a little dismayed to discover that there were no snacks. Plus, he was building a fart, and though he wished to release it, there were no scented candles to hand.

Studying the controller, he was relieved to see that it was for the EggsBox Seven-Twenty, a console with which he had been intimately acquainted before the whole lack of electricity thing and television sale brought his gaming days to an end.

The console loading screen blinked, and a swirl of colour and squawking of sounds made him feel all safe and secure. The screen faded to black before another load screen appeared, purporting to be:

APOCALYPSE FIGHTER 2: ULTRA MEGA NEON++++++ EDITION.

It was not one that he was familiar with. Ian squirmed on the beanbag, making an annoying rustling sound.

Once that screen faded, he clicked on the CAMPAIGN menu option, as it was the only one available, and was taken to the character select screen. With his opponent already chosen, a rather excellently-rendered version of Qzxprycatj, Ian chose, 'Sir Fido Claudius,' the digital avatar of the knight he was interred within.

As the characters squared off against each other on screen, the **STAGE SELECT** screen slid up from the bottom. There was but one selection on offer, '**Cathedral Carnage**.' Ian waited as the screen faded to black.

Salisbury Cathedral appeared in full 2D wonderment. In the background were torn-apart bodies, and a tourist bus resting against the base of the spire. The digital pugilists made their way in from either side. Qzxprycatj scratched the air and howled in Summerian —luckily, the in-game subtitles were on. Ian read them out: "Ha ha ha ha ha, I shall feast upon your bones."

Sir Fido Claudius knelt reverently on the ground, and as he prayed, a disembodied posh English voice boomed. "We fight now for valour, hope and glory. We fight for the unfightable."

Deciding that whoever wrote the text needed a lesson in scriptwriting, Ian wiped his sweaty hands on his trousers. With the introductions over, he waited to hear the three words that would signal the start...of the end...of the beginning...of the possible end...of the-

You know what? I think you get it.

FIGHT!
Round One

As soon as the words faded away, and control was put in his hands, Ian had charged Qzxprycatj, and with a childhoodful of learning behind him, executed some of the ol' faithfuls:

A gauntleted hand shot out in front, then the fist separated from the arm and flew across the screen, catching the still-crouching Qzxprycatj in the face. A digitised scream sounded and the beast went backwards.

A right and left-hook combo was quickly followed by three uppercuts, each successive blow taking man and beast higher into the screen. Ian looked at Qzxprycatj's health bar and saw that it was already halfway down. As the pair landed, he blocked a number of quick slashes from the beast's razor-sharp claws. Clangs of metal sounded out.

Ian jumped backwards and Qzxprycatj slashed away at thin air. "Your ass is grass, Cochise," he said, before hitting:

The game cried out, "HOLY FIRE," and Sir Fido Claudius leant forwards with flames spewing out of the slits in his helmet. Qzxprycatj was caught off guard and took it straight to the face. Its health went down another quarter before it leaped into the air, turned into a tornado of fur and arse cheeks, and smashed into the knight, sending him backwards.

Qzxprycatj followed up with a succession of kicks and

324

looping punches. Ian managed to block the initial flurry, but a 180-degree tail flick from the beast staggered him backwards; the beast cackled as the whip-crack tail snapped against the armour. With a quick look up from the screen, Ian saw that he'd lost a third of his health in the beating.

Jumping awkwardly backwards, he sought to buy himself some time, before allowing a sly smile to emerge. "Let's see if this works."

The knight dashed across the screen, pulling out a huge fucking sword as it did. Even the pixelated figure of Qzxprycatj gawped in awe. With a crash of thunder, and the screen flashing enough to nearly make Ian break dance, the sword cleaved the beast from head-to-toe. As the last block of health disappeared from Qzxprycatj, the screen slowed down to a crawl, allowing Ian to take in the wonder of the victory.

VICTORY!
SIR FIDO CLAUDIUS

Ian punched the air, shouting into the headset, "Piece of piss, this should be over soon, you cock-loving piece of shit. Your mum's so fat, she has to use an Army drone to take a selfie." A string of snarling and Summerian swear words formed the reply.

FIGHT!
Round Two

Ian cracked his knuckles and waited for the stage to swirl into life and the fighters to do their usual goading. Sensing an opportunity to end this quickly, save the planet and hopefully get the girl, he readied himself. His thumb was poised.

Straight away, Qzxprycatj leapt towards him with a weak kick.

"Pfft, pur-lease, is that the best you've got, dick-breath?"

As the beast landed in front of Ian, and a nanosecond before he was about to unleash a HOLY FIRE, it hit him with a puny punch. Then another. And another. Before Ian could say, "Oh shit," the creature's taloned hands had become a blur on the screen.

Punch after punch pummelled Sir Fido Claudius, the sound of grinding metal and fevered snarls drowning out the disharmony of Ian's swearing. With his health bar going down quicker than a two-quid gigolo at Mardi Gras, Ian managed to jump backwards before realising his mistake.

"NOOOOOOOOOOOOOOOOOOOOOO!" he screamed. Sir Fido Claudius hit the invisible barrier at the screen's edge and slid downwards. Sensing blood, Qzxprycatj carried out a jumping fang dive and sunk its jaws into the knight's head.

The last blobs of health dripped away, and as the screen flickered once more, the beast chomped down on the helpless knight. Ian squeezed the controller, making its plastic parts squeak against each other (he did consider launching it against the wall, but thought better of it).

VICTORY
QZXPRYCATJ

The headset was awash with unintelligible chants, laughing and clicks. "Laugh it up, trunkface, that was a cheap move, still one to go..."

FIGHT!
Round Three

The realisation that the fate of every man, woman and child on earth was in his sweaty palms ran across Ian's mind. He dried his hands on his trousers, cricked his neck once to the left, once to the right, then twice more to the left.

He knew Qzxprycatj would try to button-mash its way to victory once more, but there was one thing it didn't know. Ian knew that he would. Knowing that someone doesn't know what you know though, is only half of the battle, no? For if they knew, even for a fraction, that you knew what they knew, but not originally what you knew, would it be entirely new?

Perplexing, huh?

The figures relaxed into their fighting stances, Qzxprycatj sprung up into the air, but it was too slow; Ian was already bounding skywards.

As the frenzied apocalyptic monster plunged down, fangs and claws tearing and chewing the air, Sir Fido Claudius pulled his fine cloak around himself and turned into a whirling dervish, clattering into the airborne form of Qzxprycatj. The beast smacked into the floor, Ian followed up with a few low kicks, and when it stood up, a quick foot sweep sent it to the ground once more.

The screen shook, and Ian jumped backwards twice, creating the space he needed for his signature move:

Sir Fido Claudius' armour sprouted spikes from every conceivable join and orifice, turning him into a jagged blade of death and doom. Like a whirlwind, the blur of barbs and

327

fiendish points spun across the screen like a dragster. As it collided with Qzxprycatj, the screen struggled to keep up with the hits and damage being meted out. The monster's health emptied like a pisshead's stomach lining after seven bottles of vodka.

Sir Fido Claudius came to a halt. The points and edges retracted back into his armour as the character panted slightly. Recoiling from the assault, Qzxprycatj launched into a flurry of high and low kicks. Ian frantically tried to block as many as he could, although he could see that he was again being pushed back across the screen, back into the dreaded dead zone. The Dread Zone, if you will. Once there, victory for the beast was a surety —not to mention world domination.

Ian jumped backwards and forwards, managing to avoid the flurry of blows but landing inside his own range. Cursing his rotten luck, he quickly flicked out:

AIR + **AIR** + **L** + **HOLD**

The television shouted, KNIGHT-DRIVER, as Sir Fido Claudius rocketed into the air before plunging down, helmet-first, onto the beast. This stunned Qzxprycatj, and the creature staggered back to the centre of the screen.

The words every APOCALYPSE FIGHTER 2: ULTRA MEGA NEON++++++ EDITION player longed to see, appeared on the screen in blood:

END THIS ULTRA MEGA NEON ++++++ APOCALYPTIC FIGHT NOW!

Ian knew what he had to do; he had to execute the showiest, flashiest APOCALYPATALITY there was. His finger joints cried pitifully, anticipating the lasting damage. As Sir Claudius marched forwards, Ian busted out:

AIR + **MASH** + **MASH**

With finger cartilage and sinew stretched to breaking point,

Ian wiped the sweat from his brow. The screen, though, was still frozen. Sir Fido Claudius juddered on the spot, Qzxprycatj still stood there like a wrung towel, awaiting its fate. "What the hell?"

Ian leant forward and looked at the front of the EggsBox Seven-Twenty. His heart dropped into his spleen, and, sinking to his knees, his back arched and he threw his head to the heavens. "NOOOOOOOOOOOOOOO, WHY? WHY NOW?"

As the human screamed inside the head of the plastic knight, seventeen red lights surrounding the on/off button glowed balefully. The dreaded seventeen red lights of doom, this console wasn't going to be working again. Bloody typical, huh? I hope it's in warranty. I mean, yeah, they'll replace it for free, but you still have to speak to them on the phone, with their bloody scripted questions and answers.

Then you gotta box the damn thing up, take it into work, and wait for the courier to pick it up. Then four or five days later, you'll get a replacement. What do you do in the meantime, though? Converse with people? Fuck that noise. Get yourself down the pub.

Still, least that only happened once. Twice? Three times? Four? Yeah…four, you bastard. Go on, git. I'm sulking now.

It's time to...
DISCOVER YOUR FATE

What the fudge? Think you better rage-quit, or do a hard reset over to **Page 10** to see what happens now.

MUTANT BUILDING 101

The whitewall tyre came to a convenient halt touching a thick, painted white line underlining the word 'STOP'. As one bored soldier trudged towards the driver window, hurriedly scanning down a list of names on a clipboard, his fellow entrance guardian sauntered over to the passenger door and rapped his chapped knuckles on the window.

Accompanied by a squeaking, the glass barrier slowly inched down into the thick metal door, the soldier rested his arms on the sill, tipped his tin helmet back and drawled, "Say, you ain't one o' those Reds are ya boy?"

The child looked up into the fat ruddy face inches away, he recoiled from the stench of stale sweat and cigarettes. Breathing through his mouth he replied, "No sir, we're good honest Americans. My papa works here, helping build stuff to keep those pesky Ruskies away."

"Good on ya boy. Say, what cha got there?"

Small hands held up a see-through plastic box with a green lid, breathing holes had been bored through the top, plastic shavings stood up from the drilled edges like ornamental trees. "This here is Sidney sir, he's my pet snake," the kid answered matter of factly, holding the container deep into the personal space of the inquisitive guard.

A chubby hand plucked the helmet off his head, the other rubbed a sheet of sweat from his brow. A milk snake, wrapped in bands of red, yellow and black looked from its transparent cage and flicked its tongue out lazily at the new spectator, losing interest quickly, it coiled up into a multi coloured length of flex and went to sleep.

"Say, I'm not so sure you should be bringing pets into this here top secret military base. Hey Bert..."

Having finished checking the drivers credentials and ticking the name off the list, Bert looked over to his chum, "Can it, Randy, this here is Doctor Schmidt and his young 'un Timmy, they could have Castro and Krushchev getting to second base in the back and we'd have to smile and pass them a wet towel."

Randy replaced his helmet, spitefully flicked the plastic box invoking a dead eyed stare from the snake, and headed over to the thoroughly unimposing barrier of a metal pole clutching a circular 'STOP' sign, which he lifted by pushing down on one end.

As the soldiers saluted, the DeSoto Fireflite growled like an irked alsation and drove towards a large concrete hanger sitting like a squatting dwarf at the end of a blacktop road. "Gee dad, I sure love bring your child to work day," swooned Timmy.

Dr Schmidt nodded curtly and swung the car round to reverse into the parking bay emblazoned with his name, "Don't touch anything," he warned.

Timmy nodded with the enthusiasm of a puppy working as a tennis ball chewing tester. "You betcha papa, I won't touch a thing, isn't that right Sidney?" The snake sulked, thoroughly unimpressed within the Perspex box.

The thin door clicked back into the frame, and another nameless square jawed soldier saluted whilst simultaneously pulling his M14 tight in to his cliff face of a chest. "Doctor Schmidt, this way please," shouted a scrawny bespectacled man, his bleached white lab coat betrayed no sign of ever having entered the real world.

"Sanderson, what have you got for me?" Schmidt asked, leaving Timmy floundering in his wake. The boy watched on, as his father walked off with the funny man and looked around at the assorted items in the corridor. Cork noticeboards with bizarre messages pinned to them, announcing cash for 'a good time', hung over a table with overflowing ashtrays and discarded coffee cups, elliptical brown lip stains were stamped on the rims.

The soldier guarding the door resumed his duties and added another dredged coffee mug to the burgeoning collection. He cast Timmy a wary gaze, "Wotcha looking at kid?" he demanded, the question was answered with a French shrug and the guard got back to staring at a patch of missing paint on the wall, which bore a striking resemblance to Jayne Mansfield.

Timmy idly kicked the first in a line of metal barrels which ran down the opposing wall of the hallway, a dull clank told him that it was full. Noticing a strange symbol on

331

a sticker plastered to the side of the casks, he placed Sidney's home on top of the barrels, and began tracing a line around what looked like a black three bladed propeller, stamped onto a yellow background.

He made sure to make the appropriate plane sounds whilst doing so.

"So are you telling me that it's a complete failure Sanderson? But how can that be? We had enough Uranium from the last batch to make the whole east coast glow in the dark," Doctor Schmidt said angrily, his assistant shrunk from him like a scalded child, hugging himself with his bone-thin arms.

"I...I...I don't know what to say Doctor Sch-"

A hand shot up causing the intended words to dribble into nothingness, "It's okay Sanderson, I'm not blaming you. Just we promised the President we'd have a new lead on this by winter, and we're running out of time."

Sanderson relaxed a little and shoved his glasses back up the bridge of his nose, "Perhaps we got the mix wrong? We can't be far off, the last test we did showed us we were close. So close."

"Well we can't waste time standing here. Bring the data with you, we'll head over to the offices and go over it, it's got to be something simple. You men. Start disposing of the waste from the last test would you? Put it down in the cellar with the rest," Schmidt commanded, a shoal of soldiers with sack trucks burst into life and buzzed past the scientists and into the corridor whence they came.

Doctor Schmidt wrestled with bulky ring-binders and reams of printed wide carriage paper. Commanding the agility of an arthritic sumo wrestler, he barged his way back into the hallway where Timmy was learning the finer points of three card stud from Chad the hanger guard.

"Come on Timmy, follow me, hope you got your filing fingers on, cos plans have changed," Doctor Schmidt panted out, his words caused the kid to huff and do an air-kick in frustration.

As the Doctor reached the door, Timmy called out, "Papa, where's Sidney? I left him right there on those big metal barrels and they're all gone now."

His father sighed disapprovingly, "I told you to leave him at home didn't I? Come on. Hey Chad, would you mind going to waste storage and bringing my son's snake over to the offices? There's a good fellow."

The torchlight slashed through the deserted basement, Chad grumbled to himself about the absurdity of a highly trained killing machine being asked to locate and return a kid's pet snake, "Goddamn waste of taxpayer's dollars if you ask me," he whinged aloud.

The rod of light ran over the tops of barrels and came to rest on the rectangular plastic box, Sidney was staring off into space, lost in a daydream about hunting mice in the overgrown field where he had been snakenapped. He rued the day the snivelling child had grabbed hold of him and ran all the way home, clutching him tightly in his sweaty wart ridged hands.

His insides were still trying to settle back into their original shape.

Chad picked up the box and turned to leave, as he did so, he felt the hair stand up on the back of his hand, it was like a fair maiden stroking him suggestively. He brought his hand up to his face and squealed as his brain confirmed the unwanted diagnosis of an arachnid playmate.

The container incarcerating the snake crashed to the floor as Chad emitted notes usually reserved for a falsetto. He brushed the spider off and spun around, his mind convincing him that a multitude of arachno-babies were now burrowing into his flesh and setting up home in dank folds of his body. The butt of his rifle smacked into a barrel with a loud CLANG, followed by a trickling and slurping sound.

Looking down, Chad shone the torch onto the floor, a

333

pool of luminous green liquid was being discharged onto the ground, creating a slow, but steadily moving wave of sludge. In its wake was the snake box, mumbling to himself again, "I don't git paid nuff for this," he turned around and made his way back to the doorway.

As his hand wrapped around the cold metal door handle, he heard a tearing and shrieking sound from behind him, as if a labour of unclipped moles were burrowing out of an orang-utan's love sack. The sound died with a gurgling and slapping sound, accentuated by metal hitting concrete, annoyed that he would probably need a bigger mop and bucket, Chad turned around and looked into the gloom.

The pool of green goo was still visible on the floor, it looked like it had stopped moving, which was a relief, but there were areas which appeared to be obstructed. "For Pete's sake..." He clicked the torch back into life and scanned the darkness, beginning at the base of Lake Greencrap, which bubbled and protested at the light. As the beam rolled up, he froze and emitted another squeal which did not match his butch physique.

A beam of fat red light bathed him from head to toe, in the amount of time it took for Chad's wife to say "No," to his generous offer to see 'The Sound Of Music' on Broadway, he was reduced to a pile of fine carbon and bone. The light desisted and the room went back to a gentle green glow.

Timmy's paper clip sorting adventure came to an abrupt climax as the emergency klaxon wailed into life like a grizzly newborn baby. The metal poles which they were affixed to, shuddered with the reverberations, people walked out of their offices and hangers in a daze, as if woken from a pleasant dream.

Doctor Schmidt, Sanderson and Timmy stood on the path which ran from the main base to the offices, which lived on the perimeter, not cool enough to hang out with their far more foreboding building brethren. The child held his hands to his face, shielding his eyes like a visor and scanned the distance, a crackle of automatic gunfire broke up the moaning sound of the alarm. The trio shared nervous glances before jogging back to where they had just come from.

As they approached they saw a semi-circle of khaki smothered soldiers, rifles pulled into their shoulders, loosing off rounds into a darkened doorway. "Sergeant, what are you doing? There are explosives in there, one stray bullet and we'll all go up," Doctor Schmidt shouted over the barrage of noise.

The makeshift firing squad stopped, looked at the civilian and reloaded with barely checked contempt. A Sergeant, brandishing his Colt 45, held up a hand to his men. His teeth relented their bear trap grip on his cigar, rolling the end around in his fingers, the Sergeant grunted, "Sir, there's something in that there hanger, two of my men went in and aside from a bright red light, nothing has come out again, now if you don't mind, let us get back to our indiscriminate fire, it ain't hurting anyone."

The gruff Sergeant turned from Doctor Schmidt and allowed his teeth to resume cigar chomping duties, "Men, on the count of three, open fire into the building again. Ivansson, good shooting son, you've only got a few unbroken window panes to go. Ready, One..."

A series of metallic clanks and thuds rang out as the soldiers readied for another volley. From the guts of the hanger, a strange high pitched squeal worked its way down the labyrinthian corridors.

"...two..."

The squeal built up to a crescendo, the narrow hallways and side rooms added to the harmonics and created a wave of alien noise, Ivansson fell to his knees, clutching his ears with his hands, trying to keep the sound from boiling his brain.

"...thr-"

Before the Sergeant could finish his brief countdown, a large hairy leg crashed through the outer wall which had been perforated by the initial assault, masonry and shards of glass were ejected from the impact site.

Another leg burst through the wall, the soldiers, their get up and go, gone, staggered back from the strange sight, only the Sergeant defiantly stood his ground. As he raised the pistol and aimed at the middle point between both legs; a large reptilian head, wrapped in neat bands of red, yellow and black emerged from the gloom. Its long, smooth forked tongue flicked the air. A pair of large black orbs, passing themselves off as eyes, looked unblinkingly at the world beyond its birthing chamber.

"What in tarnation are you? Men, get ready to fire, this here thing is an illegal on our base, f-"

Before the Sergeant could complete what turned out to be his last order, the snake eyes shot out a beam of superhot red light, the one expended bullet was vapourised as it left the pistol muzzle, its elemental parts mixed with the skeletal and powdered remains of the man. The cigar, still aflame at one end, sat atop the ashen heap, acting as a budget entry eternal flame.

More masonry cracked and fell to the floor as the creature pulled its way into the warm morning air. The head was part of a long thick neck which formed the body of the beast, the tail waved behind it. It was transported on eight legs, each ending in a sort of thin, pointy finger nail, which made a clacking sound as they struck the ground and scuttled into the vast expanse of concrete which sat next to the hangar.

It stood around eight foot tall, the shadow of the building masked its bizarre form, one of the soldiers found a reserve of courage and attempted to rally the wavering men, "Come on fella's, there's nothing to him, we can take him."

The snake head swung this way and that, taking in the sights surrounding him, spindly legs carried the creature into the sunlight. As the first ray of sun stroked the beasts head, its mouth opened with a mix of pain and pleasure. The legs quickened and the monster stood in its entirety beneath the warm disc of light from above.

"Ha, look at him, he's scared, eight of us, one of him, let's get him boys," the soldier shouted again. Sufficiently geed up, they all formed a line and aimed at the abomination. A cracking and ticking sound rumbled through the ground. As the sun shone on the monster, it bowed its head, its body and legs started to shake as if electricity coursed through its corrupted veins.

With a massive screech, the snakes head arched backwards, the creature started to expand like a virulent strain in a petri dish. All the while, there was the sound of bones being stretched, cracked and then fused together. Skin ripped, tendons snapped and clicked, still the screeching rose highest of all.

The soldiers stood slack jawed and looked at the beast growing in size, it was as if it had knocked back a container or twelve of industrial strength Miracle-Gro, their trigger fingers forgot any sense of self-preservation.

At once the base fell silent, the klaxon stopped bleating, the potshots from sentries abated and the screeching ended. The giant snake head looked down from the sky onto the toy soldiers scattered around its feet, each leg was now half the size of the hangar it had scuttled out from, the body ran to around two thirds the length of the building too.

The giant forked tongue flapped in the air, tasting the dust and pheromones, it grew disinterested and discharged another burst of red light from its eyes, wiping out the canteen in one shot. A ripple of gunfire rang around the base as those not stupefied with fear sought to fight back. Each shot that hit the scaly hide bounced off, doing no harm. Even the bullets which connected with the creatures gangly legs fared no better, ricocheting off the steel like bone within.

"Sidney?" Timmy asked tamely, his pet which now formed one half of a giant mutated monster ambled lazily around the facility, spearing some, disintegrating many and flicking the odd human into the electric fence. It seemed to like hearing them snap, crackle and pop.

"What are we going to do Doctor? WHAT ARE WE GOING TO DO?" screamed Sanderson, clawing at his own face with stubby fingers, the nails long since chewed off and spat onto the ground. Behind him a woman screamed and fainted.

Doctor Schmidt struck the assistant across the face with a mighty slap, "Pull yourself together man, this is nothing more than science, you hear me? SCIENCE. All we have to do is go and see where this happened, I can then formulate a plan from there, come on, it must've been in the basement where Timmy's snake was taken, let's go."

337

Frank lay in his foxhole, making sure the *thing* hadn't seen him, he squeezed off a few more ineffectual rounds, "Hey Red," he bellowed.

Two foxholes down, Red was in the process of reloading, "What's that Frank?"

"What the hell do we call this thing Red? I mean, that monster we had down in New Mexico, half-scorpion and half-tornado, that was easy, Scornado. Man, that was one cool name, tough sonnavabitch, but you weren't going to forget him in a hurry, but this one?"

The pair ducked back in their crappy ditches as a chubby red beam took out the two foxholes in-between them, thin wisps of smoke rose from piles of freshly created ash. Red rolled onto his front and shot off a few rounds, "Dunno, half snake and half spider, so...Snider?"

Frank joined him in the mini salvo, the bullets pinged off the creature, who had turned his attention from them and was firing wild shots at fleeing Huey's, "Yeah, erm, a Spake? Spiderake? Snader?"

The mangled remains of a helicopter slammed into the ground, a survivor crawled from the burning wreckage only to be stabbed through the head by the unnamed creature's foreleg.

Red pushed another mag into his M14, "Well, I guess the best we have for now is we call him Spike, but can't say I'm too happy about it. Sounds more like a beatnik vampire than a terrifying monster, remember Sharkadillo? Heck, that was a good name. Look Frank, the tanks are finally here."

Within the dingy basement, muffled explosions and pained screeches were still audible, "Look papa, over there, all that green gunk, there's Sidney's box and all. Aww shucks." The kid deflated seeing his handiwork having gone to waste,

338

Doctor Schmidt patted him on the head roughly.

With a test tube in one hand and a spoon from a coffee mug, Sanderson knelt down by the vibrant liquid and scooped some into the glass tube, it fizzed and bubbled, "Strange..." he remarked.

Doctor Schmidt shone the torch through the vial, as the light hit the goo, it erupted like a baleful volcano, shooting lumps of coagulated green goo into the air, Sanderson dropped the test tube instinctively, "Interesting," the good Doctor concluded thoughtfully.

He spun and looked at the two of them, "The enemy of my enemy is my friend..." he mused rhetorically. Pulling out a folded IRS envelope from his jacket, he licked the end of a pencil he had retrieved from his breast pocket, making hasty scribbling sounds, he scrawled in a frenzy.

Mere seconds later he slipped the pencil back into his pocket, folded the envelope and passed it to his son, "Timmy, I want you and Sanderson here to go into town and bring me these items, okay?" He looked up at the assistant and passed him a Mervyn's keyring with two brass keys, "Take my car, don't be long, we need the Snakider up there to still be in the vicinity if this is to work."

The DeSoto Fireflite shot through the now unmanned checkpoint a half hour later, Timmy sat in the front seat, peering into the footwell behind him at the goods they had procured in town. Sanderson skidded around burnt out tank husks, one driver hung out of the turret, his upper body reduced to a smoking skeleton whilst his legs and midriff remained all fleshy and dewy.

Another chunky beam lanced through the last of the guard towers which up until that morning had stood proudly on each corner of the sprawling estate. One of the guards who had not been reduced to cremation output, screamed as he fell to the floor. His death curdle ceased as the structure fell on top of him and pushed the life, and his lungs, from his broken body.

339

The Snakider tip-tapped around the concrete ground, the metal things which had made a lot of noise and fired bigger things at him, had stopped working around ten minutes ago. He had made some sport of a couple of them, deciding to hold back on the lazer eyes and instead try and tip them onto their backs. Two tanks were in such a state, their tracks churned aimlessly in the air, the occupants lying in piles of bone and dust as they had fled from the upheaval.

Sanderson yanked the wheel violently, as a red beam lashed out at them, he careened into a stern looking officer who was hiding in the midst of a verdant prickly bush. The impact sent the cowardly man flying through the air, the Snakider flicked out its tongue like a whip and severed the man in two.

Parking abruptly, the assistant grabbed armfuls of stuff from the back of the car, Timmy did likewise and the duo dashed back into the hangar and made their way to the basement.

Doctor Schmidt stood in the doorway to the goo room, with a trolley and an expectant grin, "Did you get it all?" he asked excitedly.

Sanderson, flushed with exertion nodded limply, "Most of it Doctor, though I'm not sure what you intend to do with it all."

The words were met with a smile laden with self-importance, "Sanderson, I intend to use science to defeat this monster. It was created from this liquid, we shall use the same thing which spawned it to create something which will destroy it. Tell me Sanderson, what is the natural enemy of a snake?"

The assistant puffed his cheeks out at the sudden general knowledge quiz question, "Erm...I guess it would be a-"

Doctor Schmidt held up a cage with a miffed set of eyes looking out, "That's right Sanderson, a mongoose, and tell me Timmy, what likes to eat spiders?"

Timmy looked up into his father's eyes and chewed the inside of his mouth, "Well papa, Old Yeller back home eats those spiders we get on the porch."

He was met with a disappointing shake of the head, "Son, you know the answer, I gave you the list to get this all didn't I?" he walked across to a tall cage covered with a thick cloth, picked it up and held it out to Timmy, "son, an *eagle* eats spiders."

Sanderson coughed awkwardly, "Oh Doctor...I meant to say, the pet shop in town was all out of eagles sir."

"But, I was explicit in my list, mongoose, eagle, nine inch nails, a shotgun, duct tape and a Twinky," the Doctor replied forcefully, "so if you didn't get an eagle, what mighty bird of prey did you get me?"

The assistant sagged and refused to hold his boss' stare, "I'm sorry Doctor Schmidt, it was all they had."

"POLLY WANT A CRACKER," chirped out from the cage interior, Schmidt pulled the cloth off slowly, revealing a brightly coloured parrot. With a shake of the head, he looked at Sanderson with a stare that spoke of bottomless and crushing dismay.

"But...but...I wanted an eagle, y'know, symbol of America, what better animal could we splice with a mongoose than the majestic eagle. Something that would really look good on the résumé, the President would gladly sign our grant cheque for-"

"POLLY WANT A CRACKER"

Doctor Schmidt hit the cage, "Shut it," he shouted.

"SHUT IT," replied the parrot.

"This could go on a while, fine, a parrot will do. Now I must get all of this stuff just so..." Doctor Schmidt crouched down and rifled through the items.

Sanderson regained some of his poise, "Doctor, I get the mongoose and parrot, which is a sentence I never thought I'd utter until this morning, but the rest of the stuff? What's that for?"

The Doctor was a whirlwind of activity, "Of course Sanderson, I forget that you are not the intellectual titan that I am. Well, if you haven't noticed, the Snakider-"

"Is that the best name you could come up with Doctor? I was thinking Spike or-"

Doctor Schmidt threw a look at Sanderson that hinted what myriad of injuries would befall him if he interrupted again, "As I was saying, the *Snakider* has got lazer beams in his eyes, not too sure how that happened, so I figured I'd beef up our little creation a bit. These nails should mean that it has talons of pure iron, the shotgun a devastating ranged weapon infused with the radiation slurry."

Sanderson coughed nervously, "And the duct tape and Twinky Doctor?"

Schmidt ripped off the Twinky wrapper with his teeth, "I'm hungry, and my tail pipe is on the verge of falling off, so need to fix it later on."

The assistant looked at him blankly.

"What? You were going to town anyway, may as well get me a few things whilst you were there. Right, everything is loaded onto the trolley as needed, now comes the real work," Doctor Schmidt had put both cages on the bottom of the trolley, scattered a handful of nails through the wire bars and rested the gun on top of the lot. He coughed impatiently

Sanderson shrugged his shoulders, as if asked the answer to an obvious question.

"Sanderson, do you honestly think I'm going to go in there? We're like scientific implements, I am a Geiger counter, precise, exacting, you are more of a spatula, now push the trolley in there and rupture a radiation drum over it. There's a good fellow."

Sanderson sighed and began the short journey into the basement, "Oh, and Sanderson," Doctor Schmidt piped up, the assistant looked across in the hope that it was a big joke and all was forgiven.

"Yes Doctor?"

"Two things really. One, I wouldn't get any on you, you'll probably die. Two, I wouldn't be in there too long when it happens, as the creature will likely see you as a threat, and…well…see point one. Good luck," with the words of encouragement spoken, Doctor Schmidt pulled the doors to, and peered through one of the windows nervously.

The Snakider lanced another fleeing scientist with its pointy leg and flicked the still mewling body in the air, trying to catch him in its mouth. The bleeding man smacked against the giant snout and went into freefall, landing on the

concrete with a splat and a crunch.

Looking around at the wanton destruction, there were next to no buildings or vehicles left which hadn't felt the wrath of the mutated creature. Smoking ruins of A-4 Skyhawks were littered around the area, their strafing runs brought to an abrupt conclusion as the red lazer beam blasted them from the sky.

Deciding that the grass looked greener on the other side of the fence, the Snakider thought it was time to branch out, leave the nest and make something of itself in the real world. It skittered over to the entrance where a painted STOP sign tried to make it stay within the confines of the base.

As the first of its legs crossed the line, seemingly in uproar at the failure to heed the sign, a CAW-CAW made the Snakider look back. A brightly coloured ferret the size of a Cadillac scurried from the hangar entrance and stood still, letting the embrace of the sunlight wrap its feathered furry body in its warmth.

The beaked face reared towards the heavens, rows of razor sharp teeth glinted from within the maw, the beast, fused with the light grew like Sea Monkeys on amphetamine. As it reached its full size, it unfurled gigantic wings of such magnificent colour and hue. A showy flick of its wings resulted in rows of five feet long metal spikes flash out from the ridges of bone. It swished its tail round as if disgruntled by a swarm of flies.

The wings flapped, slowly at first, each swish displaced vast amounts of air, the beast rose effortlessly into the air, to celebrate its ascension to the sky, it opened its beak and let out an ear shattering "POLLY WANTS A CRACKER."

Frank dusted off the remains of the tank crew which had coated him in a fine film of ash, "Red. Hey Red," he shouted.

Red dragged the sheet of metal off the top of his foxhole, the panel had come loose as the last Huey had tried, unsuccessfully, to evacuate the top brass to the secret

343

bunker in the next county, "What do ya want Frank?" he hollered back.

"Have you seen this new one? What the heck do we call this? It ain't like nuthin' I've ever seen, is that a muskrat?"

Peering over the jagged charred piece of helicopter door, Red looked upon the creature that took to the air, "Jeepers, I think it's a mongoose. My god. They've done it. Those bastards have really done it."

Coughing out lungfuls of tank commander, Frank shouted back, "So, is it a Mongrot? A Paroose? I must say, these folk ain't helping us out are they?"

"And why use a parrot? Surely they shoulda used an eagle or even a kittyhawk. I dunno, just something a bit grander, it's like they're not even trying anymore," Red replied.

The Mongarrot flapped its way over to the two men hunkered in the ground, its tail swung between its legs, the wind from the wings blew the fur to one side, revealing a large chasm in the end. "Say, Red, that tail, does that look like the business end of a shotgun to you?"

A loud BOOM signalled the end of the pair as radioactive buck shot was discharged at them at high velocity. Strands of bright green goo laced over Frank's face, as he patted it, the viscous fluid ate through his skin, his screams marginally drowned out the sound of his skull fizzing away to nothing until his vocal chords melted and his entire body dissolved in on itself.

"SHUT IT," the Mongarrot cawed and turned languidly towards the Snakider who now had its full undivided attention.

"Doctor, did your creation just kill those men?" Sanderson asked sheepishly, the reply was a withering stare, and the three of them maintained their vigil from the hangar in an awkward silence.

The Snakider clip-clopped across the concrete towards the Mongarrot, as it closed the distance, it let off a beam which caught the flying creature on the shoulder. Letting out an agonised "CAW," the winged monster climbed into the air swiftly. At the apex of its ascent, the Mongarrot banked sharply, tucked its huge wings into its body and corkscrewed towards the Snakider.

As the blur of red and orange swooped in, the Snakider stood idle, trying to work out what the hell was going on. The answer came swiftly. As the winged beastie came in low, it flicked its wings out, metal lances caught the light and twinkled. The Snakider realised what was happening too late, and tried to duck. One of the wing tips raked down a side of the scaly body, rending flesh and sending broken sheets of scale whizzing through the air.

Doctor Schmidt, Sanderson and Timmy covered their ears as the wounded beast let out a shriek, a Frisbee of razor sharp scale thunked into the wall above them, they each swallowed down their fear and sunk back to their watching positions.

Green blood jetted from the wound, splashing against the bone dry ground, it hissed and popped as it sloshed against the concrete, chewing chunks from the surface. The Mongarrot pulled up from its attack run and landed on the top of the hangar roof, looking down like a harlequin gargoyle, "HA HA," it cawed down at the injured mutant.

The Snakider reeled from the strike, turned towards its mocking assailant and let fly another lazer beam which missed its nemesis but struck the supporting beam beneath the braying Mongarrot. A ball clenching squeal of bending metal was the opening bar to the next movement as the roof gave in to both the weight of the creature resting on top and the blast which has shorn it in two.

With a puff of dust and debris, the Mongarrot landed in amongst the wreckage of the hangar roof, the three humans had scurried from beneath its boughs moments before and were now cowering behind Doctor Schmidt's car.

With a shriek, the Snakider scuttled over to the ruined building, letting off frenzied bursts of deadly red lazer as it went. These slammed into the ground and the surrounding pile of destroyed building, one misplaced shot went on to shave Vostok 2, where Gherman Titov was having a snooze in low orbit.

345

As the Snakider arrived at the collapsed hangar, its front legs jabbed into the pile of rubble, amongst the sound of bone scraping stone, CAWs of pain rang out. The dust cloud settled and the Mongarrot was visible, laying on its back amongst the remnants of the building, its wings pinned down with huge chunks of roof.

Sensing victory, the Snakider ceased its stabbing and walked over the loose pile of hangar offal, the two mutant faces were a few feet apart. The Snakider's forked tongue rolled out slowly and licked the Mongarrot's face, a strange texture of fur and feathers.

Black pools of nothingness looked down onto the trapped creature, to heighten the effect and drag out the inevitable, the Snakider gradually ignited its eye lazer beams, so that they took on the same colour as two bowls of blood.

Before the Snakider had a chance to fire, the Mongarrot's tail silently wormed its way through a blown out doorframe. With one lightning quick jab, the tip slammed into the side of the Snakider's scaly head, as it realised its time was nigh, the radioactive shotgun tail fired at point blank range, sending huge gobbets of green blood, fused white bone and scales over the remains of the stricken hangar.

The Snakider slumped to one side, pumping out thick green goo over bent steel girders, its legs clicked against each other, trying to rebel against the notion that it was dead. With an almighty effort, the Mongarrot heaved itself free from its shallow grave.

Shaking the dust off with several mighty flaps of its wings, it took a moment and preened itself.

Satisfied, the mutant clamped its jaw around the body of the Snakider, which still shuddered in the embrace of death. Beating its wings like it was trying to drag the earth towards the moon, it took to the sky. With the wilting body of the monster flapping in its mouth, they ascended into the bright morning blue sky.

"Well done Doctor Schmidt, that was quite something," Sanderson said, extending a hand to his boss.

Schmidt took the proffered hand and shook it firmly, "That it was Sanderson. That it was. Mighty close too. By the way, I didn't mean to hold onto the door handle quite so tightly earlier, was just an autonomic response, sure you understand."

The building atmosphere was broken by the desecrated body of the Snakider landing onto the spiked belly of the hangar with a loud crunch and splat. From above, the trio looked on as the Mongarrot soared majestically in the sky, it looped this way and that, diving and then pulling up with a feat of jaw dropping aerial acrobatic skill.

"Good choice with the parrot too Sanderson, gives it the personal touch, the President will like that, especially if we can teach him some pithy remarks when he crushes the commies," Doctor Schmidt clapped a paternal hand on his assistants shoulder.

"He really is quite a wonder...what's that in his mouth?" Sanderson asked, pointing at the blob in the sky, looming larger with every passing second, "Is that?"

The Mongarrot flew in low over the base, as it did so, it released the crushed fuselage of a DC8 onto the boundary fence, it did an inverted loop and fired a blast from its radiation tail shotgun into the smouldering wreckage before peeling away into the air again.

Doctor Schmidt pounded his fist into his hand, "Dammit. Okay Timmy, Sanderson, I want you two to go back into town and get me the following; A jackal, an owl or similar winged predator, seriously Sanderson, you have to think *big* this time okay? I'll also need some TNT, a nailgun, some turtle wax and heck, go on and get us some Marlboro Red, I get the feeling it's going to be a long day."

It's time to...
EMBRACE YOUR FATE

Now they were a couple of excellent monsters! Imagine having lasers for eyes, how cool would that be?! Sadly, the noble Qzxprycatj does not have such things, but what she lacks in killer eyes, she makes up for with sharp claws and psychic powers that could (and will if you're lucky enough) drive you insane. What good fortune it would be, if she chose to bestow either upon your pathetic form?

347

I mean...

Sorry, I got a little caught up then, must be all that turmeric you put on yourself, I guess I'm allergic? As everything soaks in, I think we can enjoy one more story, over on **Page 225,** before you get smushed up in her regal mouth.

That turmeric sure is strong! I'm saying all kinds of crazy things.

CHOKE ON 'EM

Ladies and gentlemen, this is a truly remarkable day. As we hid in the vestibule of our majestic cathedral, wondering which member of the Belgian coach party we should offer to the monster first, we heard a thunderous clatter.

As we made our way outside, we saw three intrepid fighters, one, a skeleton of some kind, with eyes and a brain, the leader, at a guess.

Claire, can you focus in on the other one? It looks like a Halloween ghost, but by god, it smells of men's underpants. There's also what appears to be a knight, although according to this note I've just been handed, it's actually an armadillo.

Yeah, right. Anyway, it's on fire, and they're standing over the defeated creature.

Oh the things they are bound to tell us, such feats of wonder and daring. But right now, the skeleton and armadillo are standing *in* the dead monster's mouth. The ghost is using its long arms to tickle the thing's throat. Maybe they left their lucky sword in there? Folks, I thought I had seen everything today. People turning on people. Being nailed to walls. Eyes being plucked out of heads with little more than-

Hang on. I can hear something. It's like...a gurgling, reminds me of that time the council had to clear that blockage from the sewers outside my house following my failed attempt at setting up my own liposuction clinic in the basement.

WHOA!

What was that? Something just shot out of the beast's mouth. Claire, can you zoom in on the cathedral wall? Is that...? Yes, it's an armchair, but it looks like someone is stuck inside it. I repeat. Someone, a human being, no...a woman, is physically one with the chair. I've not seen anything as strange as this since a few seconds back when I told you about the other three weirdos.

As you can see, the three of them have gone over to armchair woman, they're checking for a pulse. I'm not sure

349

how that's even possible, but they're giving it a go. Is she? Is she? The fiery armadillo is trying to give CPR, but almost just set the chair on fire. Looks like the skeleton is giving it a go. But he has no lungs.

It's a wonder these things managed to win at all. The ghost is now giving it a go. Oh...they've stopped. Is she? Is she dead?

Yes. She's dead. She has to be. She's not moving. The other three look really forlorn, one of them has little willies coming out of his eyes and is leaking water all over the floor. I'm guessing that the armchair woman was their secret weapon, and I must say, it was a bold move, and it most certainly worked.

I have no doubt that they will build statues up and down the county to honour her sacrifice, that her death was not in vain. In the annals of history, we will-

Hang on, are they cheering? Ah, she's alive after all. Of course she is. Had to ruin my moment, eh? Are they...they are, they're looking to break open my hastily-erected barricade to get into the cathedral. Claire, we should...

This is Adam Smedley, going on the lam. Back to you in the studio, Mike.

CONGRATULATIONS!
THIS IS ENDING
#8

'LOOK UP SUPER IN A DICTIONARY, AND YOU'LL SEE YOUR PICTURE.'

If you could have a super power, but without it being anything too obvious, perhaps one inflicted upon you by a grumpy writer, what would it be? As you ponder, if you want to return to the last major choice you made, so you can see what else is out there, go to **Page 224**. Or, if you fancy a pint back in the Bustard, in those early days of the apocalypse, then go find **Page 150**.

FROZEN SECRETS

Ian pointed to ol' Clive. "You sir, I like the cut of your jib, you're right, we need to reach out to our neighbours and amass an army the likes this country hasn't seen since the Tea and Crumpet Wars in the late seventies."

Feeling pleased with himself, ol' Clive grabbed hold of his crotch, the jib-cut slacks he had found on that homeless person were paying off, this was *his* time, of that he was sure. Toby, on the other hand, was crestfallen. The decapitated skull fell slack in his hands, almost discarded onto the floor, then a sly smile crept across his face. "So...we're...erm...ya know, taking our time, are we?" He pulled the dripping head up to his eyeline. "Excellent...I'm going to just...nip to the toilet for a little bit."

As he made his way past the staring masses, Eddie, who was acquiring quite a reputation in the Wiltshire Skittles league, gave Toby a passing nudge and a wink. "We get ya. Say no more."

Embarrassed, Toby turned around slowly, his cheeks beetroot. "What do you mean?"

Still nudging and winking as if he was suffering from a severe case of tics Eddie pointed at the bodyless head, its tongue already blue, hanging out from the mouth at a jaunty angle. "You're off to do some weird sex stuff, huh?"

Wishing to hide the true nature of his lavatory vacation, which *was* some weird sex stuff with a wrenched-off head, Toby pointed towards the front windows. "Hey, is that Melissa Buxom, the one-time glamour model, ya know, with the big babylons?"

The predominantly male crowd swivelled on the spot and leered out of the window. A passing tourist, Max Spieluhr, stopped stock still, and wondered why the slack-jawed yokels of a public house were gawping at him. Running a hand through his hair, he withdrew it to see that it was still slick with the blood and guts he had been caught up in earlier. Realising he looked like a walking tampon, Max flicked his hair and strutted off.

With the locals bamboozled, Toby opened the dead

priest's mouth and forced it against Eddie's neck. Upon connection, he closed the jaw up with the palm of his hand and, holding the entire skull trap tightly, ripped out the man's jugular. As blood spurted against the noticeboard, rendering all manner of advertisements and wanted posters unreadable, Eddie patted the blood fountain that was his neck, before collapsing to the floor.

Following the revelation that it wasn't the busty Melissa Buxom, who was best-remembered for holding the Guinness Book of Records record for the highest number of empty wine bottles ensconced up her foo-foo, they looked agape at the new sign of brutal mutilation.

Toby shrugged and pointed to Noah's head, a scrap of neck skin hanging from his remarkably well-conditioned teeth. "The priest bastard wasn't quite dead, took a lump out of poor Eddie before I had a chance to stop him."

With a collective, "Ahhh," the crowd turned back to the bar. The excitement had left many gasping, and with many a drink sunk following the nefarious priest's antics, they were eager to restore their alcohol-to-blood ratio, which was sliding dangerously towards sobriety. With the alibi taken hook, line and sinker, Toby disappeared down the corridor and headed into the gents, his underpants elastic straining with thoughts of necrophiliac pleasurings.

Ted slapped the stopper back into the strange container and stashed it behind a row of Advocaat, which had last been requested around 1993.

"Come on, you lot, get your laughing gear around this, though don't be asking for a second, it's likely to cause permanent blindness." Ted raised his shot glass and waited patiently until his beloved customers had each snatched up a drink.

Ian held the glass, closed his eyes, and breathed in the heady aroma. He was transported to a mechanics bay, underneath an E-reg Ford Fiesta with a leaking oil filter. That was mixed with hints of lemongrass, newspaper clippings, and a slather of maternal disappointment. It wasn't totally unpleasant, but judging by Monique's face, which looked like her eyebrows hadn't been drawn on properly, he had gotten off easy. "To Salisbury," he shouted, receiving his words echoed back to him by twenty-three slurred voices.

"To Eddie," he called out; again, the pissheads sang it back.

Wondering how far he could go, Ian bellowed, "A sphincter says what?"

The pub patrons, arms tiring from holding the shot glass aloft in a stress position, of which an SAS recruiter was taking notes, slurred a "what" in reply.

Ian laughed, and yelled, "AHHHHHHHHHH," in their faces. "Got you all, you said *what*, which means you're a sphincter."

Roger the Dogger scratched his receding forehead. "Eh? I thought the sphinx was in Egypt?"

A round of mumbling and wild gesticulation took place before Ted stepped in to end the madness. "Ignore that little bum hair nugget, here's to ol' Clive and his cunning plan."

Finally, the crowd clinked their glasses and knocked back the gloopy brown liquid. Some placed their glasses back on the bar, and scraped their tongues with filth-encrusted fingernails, while others began to complete online forms with the Police to report cases of oral violation. Ian and Monique, who were complete lightweights by comparison, gagged and immediately asked Ted if they could have a water chaser.

A few though, the weirdos, those who'd helped collect the dregs which went in the mysterious brew, savoured every claggy drop. After licking the insides of their glasses out, they began to work their way through the others lest a single strand of its DNA be left behind. Mainly because they enjoyed the taste, but also because the remains of the Obese Badger proprietor were one of the ingredients, and, apocalypse or no, the last thing they needed was evidence left about the place.

Toby appeared from the toilets and placed the head onto the bar by the charity box for the local blind dogs, cunningly shaped like a sitting canine. This was to quell the confusion caused by the old duck that used to be in its place. They had been inundated with requests for blind ducks, only to disappoint people. The change to the collection box came swiftly afterwards, and the person who made the decision, who was actually a blind mallard, was fired and made homeless.

Noah's eyes were partially hanging out, a sure sign of a mighty pounding. Dribbles of what looked like gone off, lumpy yoghurt ran down the priest's chin, while Toby scratched dried spots of semen from the back of his hand and necked his shot.

With everyone accounted for, and the gasping alcoholics sated, briefly, ol' Clive tapped his false hand on the bar top. Having their attention, he pulled out a rather handy map of Southern England and a pack of felt-tip pens.

Circling the mighty county of Wiltshire with a green pen, he fought the urge to draw a picture of himself fisting the mascot of the Salisbury Cockerels, the premier basketball team in Southern England. "We, as some of you know, are here..." this elicited some sharp squeals; a few amongst the drunken masses had never ventured past the county boundaries, preferring to stick to what they knew.

Ol' Clive took his time to lick the end of the red pen, which had been somewhat overused when he completed his 'Tomato and Strawberry' colouring-book collection. They took pride of place above his mantelpiece, and many a visitor commented on their aesthetic beauty and whimsical nature. After a few squeaky scribbles, the pen bloomed into life, and ol' Clive drew rings around the neighbouring counties of Hampshire, Dorset, Gloucestershire, Somerset and Berkshire. With his penwork getting some good cooing and applause, he gestured towards Ted for a fresh pint of Moonraker.

"Now, communications with these counties has been difficult of late, especially following the naked invasion last Easter. Plus, with the mobile phone networks about to receive an influx of people trying to make sure that none of their loved ones have been gobbled up already, we need to invoke the old ways."

Ted gasped, his hands frozen, lager spewing over the top of the glass and running into the slop tray. Jodie slapped him from his reverie and he came to with an irritated growl at the spilt beer, and a rosy cheek. "You don't mean... ?"

Ol' Clive replaced his felt-tips back into their plastic case. "Yes, Ted...we need to go and wake up the message badgers."

Those not involved in the conversation looked at each

other, their faces a welt of bemusement and scurvy. Ian finally plucked up the courage to ask the succinct question whose answer they all yearned to discover. "What the fuck are message badgers? They're not indigenous to this country, this is all getting a little bit silly now."

Ted and Ol' Clive looked at each other before erupting in laughter. A few others in the bar joined in, not wishing to miss out on a good old laugh, although they had no idea what the fuck was going on. Ol' Clive slapped a suspiciously-smelling hand on Ian's shoulder. "Young man, these are not just normal badgers, they were bred from a herd that broke out of Longleat country park a hundred years ago. With above average intelligence, they set up a small community on the outskirts of town, that we call Laverstock today. There, they traded with humans and learnt our tongue. In time, we taught them of the rivalries between our noble counties and they were beside themselves with woe and misery.

"You see, these badgers promised each other —as they scaled the barbed wire fences which ran around the estate, and escaped being gunned down by machine gun nests and hunted by vicious puma in hot air balloons —that no animal should live in a state of war. They made us see that our petty differences were just that. They set up the inter-county conference where the peace treaty was signed. With their work done, they returned to their homes, only to discover they'd been turfed out. Because...well...they're filthy badger fuckers, aren't they?

"The owner of the Inglourious Bustard back then took them in, and cryogenically froze them in the cellar behind the casks of scrumpy. With the promise that if their services were required in the future, they would be revived and their quest charged to them once more." With a pint ready and waiting for him, Ol' Clive raised the glass in the air and took a big gulp.

Monique shook her head. "There is so much wrong with that entire statement, I don't know where to begin. I'm just going to take it on good faith that at least fifty percent of it is true."

"Much obliged to you, Jugs,"

"Did you just call me Jugs?" Monique bristled, lunging

at the barman, and if it wasn't for Ian managing to catch her in time, it's highly likely she would've scratched his face off.

"What's wrong with being called Jugs?"

"I'm not an object, you boor, I'm a person, with feelings and opinions, you have no right to objectify me in that way. Shall I call you *ballbags*?"

Ted unhitched his trousers from the braces which ran over his shoulders, and slapped his saggy sacks onto the bar. "Don't mind if you do, wanna give them a stroke while you're there?"

Monique grabbed hold of a dart which was embedded in the noticeboard, and slammed it into the fleshy bit between his hidden pickled onion testicles. Ted whistled the tune of Chumbawumba's surprise hit, 'Tubthumping', before picking the rusting point from his wrinkled bag. "Cheeky, I normally have to pay double for that."

As Ted replaced his junk back in his trousers, Ian shouted, "For fuck's sake, this is just getting stupid now. There's a seven-cheeked monster from the otherworld effing and jeffing in a dead language from the top of the cathedral, and a woman and two men have died, one of whom has since been used as a spunk spittoon. You've got some message badgers in the cellar? Great, will one of you go and fucking wake them up? In the meantime, pour us some more drinks, and stop pissing off the women clientele, okay?"

Letting the elastic braces ping and slap against his skin, Ted asked, "The women's what? We don't allow the use of the C word in this pub, you potty-mouthed sod." He pointed to a large bottle of Bells whiskey, which was a third full of change. "The C word is a quid fine."

Grudgingly, and in an attempt to get the story back on track, Ian rummaged around in his pocket for some shrapnel and threw it into the bottle. "Happy? Now can we please get on with it? There could be people literally wishing they'd bailed out than read this time-wasting tosh."

Not you, though, eh?

Mate?

Mate?

Fine...look, I'll make it up to you, the next chapter will be a real doozy, promise. Look what you've had so far. It's been pretty trouser level, though, eh? No worries, I'll up my game, I will add something in the next bit which will BLOW YOUR MIND.

No, it's not a bomb. I tried, but the print-on-demand people got a bit sniffy about it. I'm now on a watchlist. Which sounds far sexier than it actually is.

Trust me.

Onwards!

BASEMENT BADGERS

The descent into the cellar had been light-free and smelly. Damp dog in the darkness if you will. "Brace yourself," Ted warned. At once, there was a click, and the locale was bathed in the sickly yellow light of cheap lightbulbs. Ted, looking as smug as a politician completing his expense form, bid Ian and Monique welcome with his arms held out. "This is where the magic happens."

Ian, using a Bustard brand ballpoint pen, picked up a heavily soiled gimp mask from a dusty shelf. The mouth zipper had been broken, the little metal teeth buckled and worn. "Yeah...looks like it."

Embarrassed, Ted snatched the mask and stuffed it into his pocket. "That was my late wife's, brings back bad memories."

"Can we just get on with it, please? I'm beginning to realise why, in the three years I've lived around the corner from this place, not once have I never ventured inside. If this is all some trick you play on newcomers to lure them into your den of iniquity, well...it's a little on the elaborate side," Ian said.

Ted smelt his fingers and lost himself to days gone by. Coming back to the present, he pointed towards the back of the dank room. "Come on, they're over here—you still got that heater, missy?"

"Are you sure this is going to work? It seems a little on the small side."

Winking, Ted replied, "Size isn't everything, love."

The trio walked through the basement in blissful silence. One corner was the preserve of the metal casks used for the bar upstairs, plastic pipes snaking from the tops of the barrels, through the ceiling, and to the beer taps up top. Toby had been left in charge of the bar, with strict instructions not to fuck about and give anyone free drinks, on pain of a most horrendous death.

The rest of the space was taken up by huge wooden boxes. Ian took a closer look at one, and saw that it contained the lost ark of the covenant.

358

Which was nice.

Stacked neatly in a row were the mummified remains of Saturday night entertainers from the eighties, who originated from the local area. He chuckled when he saw that Lionel Lovert, the host of 'I Bet You Wouldn't,' was a resident. Ian had loved that show; two teams of five family members would make outlandish bets with each other, starting off small, but ending in death-defying acts of utter stupidity. It was the most watched show for two whole years, before the authorities finally decided that enough blood had been shed, and it was cancelled.

Unbeknownst to all, the show had actually been funded by the government to try and cull the population of stupid people in the UK. It was wholly successful, and eighty percent of all of those families identified in the 1982 census as clinically moronic were exterminated publicly. Each televised death would be a source of merriment around water coolers up and down the land on a Monday morning.

Lionel, though, when the show was cancelled, and realising that he was the light entertainment version of Pol Pot, couldn't live with the shame. He gorged himself to death on baked beans and was found naked in a bath of the things. To cover it up, the government reported that he had died of a heart attack whilst taking part in a charity activity of sitting in a bath of Heinz's finest. So, every time you hear of someone doing this very thing to raise money, think of poor Lionel Lovert.

Passing the worryingly large collection of bodies, they made their way to a wall of scrumpy barrels. "Just over 'ere," Ted drawled. Stopping before them, he hugged the tallest barrel, and groping behind, he found the lever and pulled it down. Like a Bond villain's hidden lair, but on a much dingier scale, the wall of mouldering casks creaked and separated, split in twain by huge hinges.

Beyond them, linked up to gleaming machines which made satisfying BING! noises and produced a kaleidoscope of colourful light patterns, sat five metal tubes, the front of which were made from glass that had frosted over. Monique, carefully making sure she didn't step on any of the pipes or wires, leaned over to the closest capsule.

She retracted her hand into her coat sleeve and wiped it

down the front of the viewing window. Inside was a badger, fast asleep, wearing a leopard-print loin cloth. As it snoozed, its lips moved, muttering in its dreamworld.

Really, it was telling the other badger to steer clear of its fresh fruit collection, for it had taken a while to build up such a vast amount, and the rest of them were lazy bastards unwilling to forage for their own.

Monique let out an involuntary, "Aww," and squished her face up the way women do when they see a kitten hold its little paw out, or an otter waddling around with its favourite rock tucked under its arm.

Ian looked over the impressive piece of technology before a pit of doubt started to grow in his guts. "Erm…Ted? All this stuff seems remarkably new, how long did you say these badgers have been down here?"

Shooting the whippersnapper a look, Ted replied, "Listen, a minute ago, *you* were the one who wanted to get the fuck on with the story and miss out some of the pertinent detail."

Ian looked shocked.

"What's that look for, city boy?"

"You know the word *pertinent*, I'm amazed."

"I also know the words *facetious prick*, so how's about we suspend disbelief and get on with it. I thought people were promised that shit would pick up? Not seeing much of that so far," Ted offered.

"Fine, I'm with you, just…I wish you'd made it look a bit less…you know…immaculate. Perhaps smear some mud over the metal. Look, someone has been down here recently and polished them," he said, holding up a tin of 'Spanko,' the best metal polish money could buy, specifically made for cryogenic freezing pods.

Monique clicked her fingers. "Can you two knock it off, and no, Ted, that doesn't mean we get to see Mister Pinky again. How do we wake them? Do we use the heater?"

Ted laughed. "Oh, little girl, you have much to learn. The heater is knackered, just wanted to bring it down here to get it out of the way, much obliged to you carrying it for me. No, in order to wake them, we just need to press the 'Wake Up' button over there. Do you wanna do the honours Ju…I mean, missy."

Placing the broken heater on a shelf with an array of other dead or malfunctioning electrical goods, which included amongst their number a possessed can opener that loved nothing more than taking off people's fingertips, Monique wiped her hands on her coat and walked across to the impressive-looking command console.

It lowered from the ceiling with a rather orchestral sound of steam hissing and electrical beeping; it would not have been out of place at a Jean-Michel Jarre concert, it was *that* good. A panel with a multitude of buttons, knobs and sliding things sat in front of her. Like a kid in a sweet shop, she refrained from just mashing them and seeing what happened. She pressed the handy 'Wake Up' button. Two dry ice machines rose from the floor and pumped out some suitably atmospheric gas, making them all go, "Ooooohhhhh."

From above, strobe lighting flickered and a woman's mechanical voice said in the obligatory staccato style, "Stasis interrupted. Fire in Cryogenic compartment. Repeat. Fire in Cryogenic compartment."

"What the fuck?" Ian screamed.

The mechanical voice burst into life again. "Ha ha ha, I totally got you. I've wanted to say that for years."

Ted burst into laughter. "This 'un loves watching sci-fi horror, got a bit of a soft spot for Aliens. Just be glad it didn't go all Event Horizon on you, still get hassle now from the brewery about their missing inspectors." He cast a nervous glance over to a large terracotta pot full of Azaleas, crossed himself for luck, and muttered something in Spanish.

Ignoring the obvious question of how the hell it watches films, Ian regained his composure and re-joined Monique by the panel. She was struggling to stop herself from laughing. The dry ice pumping ceased, having released enough —too much can be overkill—and the strobes slowed down to a more sedate blinking. There was a loud clunk and a hissing sound, as if a blow-up doll had received a terminal puncture.

Monique was unable to help herself and walked towards the capsule once more. The lid popped open and raised, revealing the stirring message badger. Its little eyes

361

struggled to open, so it rubbed away with little furry paws to get rid of the sleepy dust. Finally, it looked into Monique's eyes, its little mouth opened, and it said, "Good day sweet princess, for what reason have I been awoken from my slumber?"

Speechless, Ian barged her out of the way. "Look, message badger, there's a huge fuck-off blue monster spooning our most famous historic monument. We need you and your little truffle-snuffling buddies to go and rustle up some help, ya know, from the other counties."

"Boars snuffle for truffles," Monique added helpfully.

Loin cloth message badger groggily pulled himself up. "I see, these seem like dire times indeed. Before my kin and I can do your bidding, I believe something is owing to us...barkeep Ted?"

Looking around, Ian saw that Ted had prostrated himself on the floor, his face flush against the clammy stone. Wanting the story moved on a bit, Ian kicked him in the hip. "Oi, Ted, they're after something from you. Also, how the hell can this be? If they were frozen ages ago...actually, you know what, I'm not even going to ask."

Loin cloth message badger clambered uneasily from his metal pod, looking down at the man. Ted dared to look up. "Yes, of course, master, I have it here." Shaking fingers reached into his trouser pocket, and after taking out a set of keys, a half-eaten packet of Victory Mints and the violated gimp mask, he handed the message badger a folded-up scrap of paper.

Snatching it from the man, Loin cloth message badger looked at it, and then to his peers, who were climbing out of their stasis capsules and stretching their legs, each wearing a different item of clothing. There was a clown, a cowboy (cowbadger?), an astronaut and a traffic warden, each looking expectantly at the loin cloth message badger. "Well?" Clown message badger asked.

Carefully opening the scrap of paper, Loin Cloth's face lit up as he read the words. "Yes my brothers, our two-thousand-way accumulator came in, the money has been sent to the designated account in the Cayman Islands as discussed." This made all the message badgers cheer and give each other high fives. Even the mechanical voice stopped quoting films and pretending to be Stephen Hawking long enough to congratulate them.

Passing the betting slip to traffic warden message badger, he knelt down and ran his filthy little badger digits through the back of Ted's hair. Grabbing hold of the greasy mop, he pulled Ted's head upwards, inadvertently clicking his dodgy neck back into place. "Well done, pink monkey, you have done as we commanded. Now, we go to reclaim what is ours."

Ian stepped forward. "Woah there, little buddy, did you not hear me? Have you got ice in that little brain of yours? There is a fucking huge monster out there, intent on wiping out all of humanity, and possibly the world. We need your help."

Contemplating the human's words, Loin Cloth, with Ted's hair still in his paw, raised his middle digit and blew a raspberry. "I don't give a flying fuck —do you know how long we've been kept prisoner down here? This pink monkey bastard used to come down here and...*do things* to cowboy message badger whilst he slept. He thought we didn't know, but I saw...everything."

Cowboy's face lit up like a New Year's Eve fireworks celebration. Running his badger fingers through his matted fur, he realised now that there was no accidental cryogenic liquid leak, it was pink monkey man goo. Sinking to his knees, he raised his tiny balled fists to the heavens. "Nooooooo, why, oh wise message badger god? Why have you forsaken me?"

Loin Cloth sighed. "Okay, don't milk it. We had one condition for accepting our land being annexed and our rights stripped from us, a long and impossible accumulator being placed on our behalf. Now that we are awoken and the bet came in, we can get out of here. As for you..." he looked down at Ted's whimpering face. Little fingers clenched the hair tighter, and like bouncing a red rubber ball against the ground, loin cloth message badger began to pound Ted's face against the stone floor.

Chipped teeth and pieces of spongy, bitten-off tongue sprayed the floor. Cackling like a mad scientist having discovered the art of genetic splicing, Loin Cloth continued to pummel the barkeep's head against the floor until all that

363

remained was a bloodied section of skull and hair.

Satisfied, he let go of the head and wiped his paws down Ted's shirt, though gore was a real bitch to get out of thawing fur. No matter, he'd clean it up later. Monique stepped forward. "Please, message badgers, I know these people have done you a wrong, but do not damn us for their failings. We need you...more than ever...don't you see, if you do this, then we will be forever in your debt, and you'd be given anything your little furry faces would desire?"

Loin Cloth snapped his fingers at traffic warden message badger, who passed the betting slip to Monique, who passed it on to Ian, as sport wasn't really her thing. "Look at that big-chested pink monkey, we don't need you humans any more, we have enough money there to build a lovely little forest retreat, away from any psychotic end of the world monster. She just wants to eat and drive you mad, she'll leave us alone. So, good day." With that, the five message badgers turned and headed towards the exit.

Ian laughed and turned around to them as they made their way out. "Oi, fucknuts, you're not going anywhere."

The badgers stopped and turned around; each had some kind of sinister facial twitch or tic thing going on. Loin Cloth pulled a piece of glass from his namesake article of clothing, and flashed it at Ian. "Who's going to stop us? You? Leave it alone, pink monkey, else I'll cut ya."

"Fine...just one little detail you forgot to check, your clairvoyance let you down, oh dickwad." Ian waved the betting slip at him. An utterly pissed-off loin cloth message badger stormed towards Ian, tossing his shiv between his hands, mainly for effect.

He snatched the slip away and scanned the list of sporting events. "You lie, pink monkey man, we're rich, they all came in."

Ian pointed to one line. "All bar one...what *idiot* would bet on Everton winning the Premiership in the 2004/05 season? I think you'll find that the only tropical thing you'll be seeing will be the pictures from the travel agents down the road."

Loin Cloth bit his lip, before scowling at Cowboy. "I *told* you that wouldn't happen, you should've listened to me and the holy divining cornflakes."

364

With the fire of saving humanity stoked, Ian took the shard of broken glass from the badger's hand and threw it behind him, the shard landing in the remnants of Ted's destroyed head. "I think you'll find that's check *and* mate, you weird looking freak, now...let's talk business, and how you're going to help us."

Grudgingly, the five defeated badgers trudged over to the twitching corpse of Ted, and thrashed out the details of their mission. Monique couldn't help but give each of them a little squidge; well, they *were* dressed-up badgers! She loved all that stuff.

BEST LAID PLANS
OF PISSHEADS AND MEN

Bodies spilled from the top of the pile and freefell onto the ground below. In the fortnight since the summoning of the mighty Qzxprycatj, it had moved from shouting atop the cathedral spire to the more spacious surroundings around Stonehenge. Historians supposed now that the haphazard ring of stones was some ancient portal to the otherworld. Truth was, it served as a handy place to dump all the eviscerated bodies it was working through.

The stones themselves were still visible; crushed desiccated human forms acting as mortar, holding the mound of putrefying flesh together into one giant jelly. Inside the visitor's centre, the Wiltshire arm of the resistance movement cowered, waiting for a sighting of the beast.

"Where's it to?" Ol' Clive asked for the seventeenth time since breakfast.

Ignoring his weird West-Country-ism, Ian pressed a dirty finger to his lips and pointed to the body mound in the distance. "Not seen it yet, must still be out hunting."

"Out hunting" was a strange choice of words, as the creature had cleared entire cities of their population within mere minutes. Derby held the record of resisting the longest at one hour and twenty-one minutes. By contrast, the French town of Nice was bringing up the rear with a paltry fifteen minutes. Biscuiteers supposed that Qzxprycatj went there on account of the Nice biscuit, realising too late that it wasn't actually populated by biscuits but by crunchy French people. It was reckoned that the speed of its destruction was as a direct result of this fact having been discovered.

"There," Monique hissed, pointing to the summit of the carcass mountain.

With a puff of smoke and a hint of sparkles, Qzxprycatj appeared into the morning air. "Bloomin' priest could've told us about the teleportation thingymajig, eh? Good job we done him in."

Toby grinned and patted Noah's green-skinned head,

which was affixed to his belt by a length of twine that ran through the ears and around his belt loop. How the head had survived the last two weeks and Toby's depraved machinations was quite the mystery. Though, in his defence, he had made sure to apply adequate lotion to the necrotic skin lest it get the hose again.

Ian tutted. "There were a lot of things that bloody priest could've told us which would've helped. That it's as quick as a hummingbird on speed, has the appetite of a teenager and claws as sharp as a paper's edge." Despite it doing naught, he glowered at Noah's head, feeling no remorse whatsoever in the holy man's skull being sexually debased on a daily basis.

Ol' Clive bit off the last of his fingernails, chewing it slowly; despite searching high and low, he couldn't find any e-cigarette refills for the past week, and the lack of chemicals was setting him on edge. "I hope those bloody badgers have done what you asked them to."

"They'll be here," Ian promised.

Or this'll be the shortest offensive of all time.

Monique pointed to the horizon, her new role as event-pointer proving to her that there is life after a failed suicide bomber's non-death. "Look, a signal."

"But from who?" Ol' Clive muttered, looking around for something else to chew on.

"It's whom," Jodie added.

As the pair descended into bickering, Ian clunked their heads together. "Between Qzxprycatj with a silent J, and whom with a silent M, I think we have more important things to worry about, huh? You know, like trying to save the entire world. So knock it off, okay?" Grudgingly, the pair went back to their respective annoying habits. Jodie had discovered the art of cheek clucking, and made it her mission to cluck frequently. How she had not been bludgeoned to death in her sleep was a mystery to most.

"Regard! To the north-east," Monique pointed.

Making his hands into a pretend pair of binoculars, Ian gingerly rose his head and peered over to where Monique was pointing. "It's red...looks like Hampshire is with us." A pall of orange smoke rose. "Berkshire ride into hell with us as well, this is good. Monique, keep an eye out for the

367

others, will you? Thanks, sweet cheeks!" The pair embraced and tongue-jousted ferociously, giving them both the beginnings of yet another mouth ulcer.

With a slurp, Ian broke free from Monique's slathering mouth and wiped his sodden lips with the back of his hand, which tasted of corned beef and shame. "Can I have a look?" Ol' Clive asked. Eyeing him up to see if he was taking the piss, Ian passed him the make-believe pair of binoculars.

Ol' Clive took them reverently and peeked over the top of the gift shop counter, one hand twiddling an invisible wheel to help focus in on the view. "Looks like the others are there too, over yonder."

Ian patted him on the shoulder. Ol' Clive offered him the binoculars back, but Ian shook his head. "No, old man, you keep hold of them...you know...in case I don't make it."

"But what if *I* don't make it?"

"Then it won't matter, will it? I'll just get a new pair, thus." To demonstrate the point, Ian held aloft a new pair of imaginary binoculars. "See? I have an endless supply. Now, let's get on with the briefing."

The space on the floor in front of him had been swept clear, and a pretty good three-dimensional model of the area had been made. Dead insects formed the pile of bodies; mainly beetles, which had gotten in and eaten a lot of potatoes.

Ian pointed to the model visitor centre, which was, in actuality, one of the ridiculously handy replica models on sale in the visitor centre gift shop. It still had the price attached. "We are here, and the beast sits atop his grisly mound a few hundred metres away. It is highly likely it knows we are here."

Jodie raised a hand. "How is that even possible?"

"The smoke signals are a dead giveaway, probably should've suggested something else."

"Oh...yeah."

"Your incessant clucking doesn't help, either."

"Sorry."

cluck

"So, whilst we do not have the element of surprise, we have something which would not have been afforded to us if we had followed Toby and attacked straight away. Numbers and organisation. Sorry, Toby."

Toby shrugged. "No matter, If we'd gone down the other path, I don't think I would've found my true soulmate." He ran a hand down Noah's contorted face and popped the priest's thick leathery tongue back into his mouth. "What?"

"Look, here's the deal, folks, we get one shot at this. At this very moment, anyone armed with a firearm is crawling their way towards the beast. We have two sections, one team with shotguns are going to get in real close, whilst those with their fancy rifles will form two picket lines, either side, to catch it in a crossfire." Ian helpfully indicated the location of these groups with some plastic toy soldiers that he'd stolen from a child a few days earlier in the knowledge he would need them for this exact moment.

"They will fire the first shots...of freedom."

Sharon rubbed her hands together; the days of playing pool and darts to hone her body into a temple of pain were shaped for this moment. She yearned to hear an impassioned speech to send her into the realms of unbridled violence that would only stop when the monster lay dead before her. She let out a semi-orgasmic yelp.

Spurred on, Ian dared to stand. "And we shall sally forth from our trenches and...visitor centre, some even from the derelict vehicles left in the car park. Armed with the weapons of our forebears, and far sturdier than a pool cue, we shall fall upon this foul miscreant and show it that if we are to be extinguished from the universe like a flame from a scented candle, then it shall be by a method of our own choosing."

A murmur began to ripple around the group as Sharon moaned and writhed some more.

"With the remnants of the ash tree fashioned into staves like the priest dude said, we shall smite it like it's never been smited. Erm...smitted. Smiten? Ah – yes. Got it. *Smut*. Like it's never been smut. Years from now, when your children's children's children speak of this day and the stand we took, they will raise a drink of whatever alcoholic beverage is popular, hopefully not that stuff Ted made, and celebrate the sacrifice we made, upon the altar...of humanity."

People began to sit up and incite hope; Sharon clamped a hand over her mouth as the words began to bring her to climax.

"Not one more family shall we watch get eaten alive and their body parts sprayed over the side of buildings. Little Timmy...you shall sleep soundly in your bed tonight, within one of the resettlement camps, which seem to have made things rather too easy for the monster. For we are your salvation, we are hope...WE ARE-"

"BOLLOCKS!" Ol' Clive shouted.

Ian turned and slapped him. "Dude, you just ruined it."

Sharon squirmed in her moist pants and trousers, lit herself a cigarette, and made a nice glass of orange squash.

Holding his face, Ol' Clive shook off the assault and pointed out of the broken window. "No, look! The Gloucestershire idiots have gone off too soon!"

"Typical...always too eager." Ian shook his head. "Right, everyone, sod it, let's go and beat the shit out of the monster, death or glory awaits!"

THE MOTHER-IN-LAW
OF ALL BATTLES

Part of the pact between man and message badger was that they were purely tasked with getting the other counties' pissheads on board. Nowhere upon the treaty they had written —on Ted's pallid and liver-spotted back— did it stipulate that they were expected to take part in any of the fighting. As all the survivors from the six counties rose, their hands trembling with DTs, the five message badgers sat in a lofty tree, eating nachos and sinking bottles of beer. Having learned nothing from their accumulator loss, they already had a book going on the outcome of the fight; whoever won in real terms, some of them would at least have something to celebrate.

With the Gloucestershire contingent no longer able to contain their urge to pummel, punch and stab, they ran across the open ground shouting unintelligible words, perhaps something about a tractor? I dunno, it's impossible to make out from my position, here, in an alternate universe.

With the rubbish plan already in dismay, they had at least dispelled the notion that any plan, regardless of its worth, never survives past the first contact with the enemy. They all knew, deep down, that they were on a hiding to nothing. Whilst it wasn't a futile gesture, it was done more in the knowledge that they had at least tried, and not cowered in the pub, pulled the curtains shut and drunk themselves into a funk, the depths of which would only be solved by some big blue monster with five arse cheeks more than necessary pulling the roof off and chowing down on everyone.

That's just one of the possibilities, of course, who am I to say?

Qzxprycatj was sitting on her beingbag made out of human beings (see what I did there?), contemplating which part of the world she wanted to scour of humanity next. Vast tracts of America and Europe lay in metaphorical tatters. Entire cities, towns and villages had been reduced to avenues of blood, guts and void fluid. Whilst this painted a grim tableau for wandering groups of reporters, the smell was something else entirely.

As it licked its claws clean from the latest bloody purging of a town nestled in the Pyrenees, it heard the pathetic mewling of its prey all around. At first, it thought the mound it had lovingly created had come back to life. Having lived in the otherworld for so long, it had heard stories of zombies and the like. Though, in fairness, it did think they were all bullshit. Yet, the noise was definitely there. It rolled onto its front to work out if it really was the undead, only to see hordes of its dinner running towards it.

This bunch of running nibbles seemed different than the ones it had spent the last couple of weeks eating and slaughtering with wilful abandon. They held weapons, and sticks with flames on top, some even had those metal pointy things that shot out those little pellets which tickled it.

Ahhh, Qzxprycatj allowed herself a momentary flashback to those first few days. Row-after-row of people dressed in green, charging, firing little balls, how it tickled Qzxprycatj so. After smashing them to a bloody pulp, larger metal things scurried from the trees. They looked like beetles, but had larger metal pointy things. The things they fired stung a little, but they stopped shooting them after she had drop-kicked them into the sky

That made Qzxprycatj happy.

Well, this was a turn up for the books, but a nice surprise; how did they know it was Qzxprycatj's birthday today? Instead of having to go and look for its brunch, brunch was coming to *it*, so it truly was turning out to be a good day indeed. Not only were they running around to make a giant squishy pudding for her, they'd also remembered how old she was and brought the right number of birthday candles, too.

A solitary tear tracked down Qzxprycatj's cheek; if she wasn't built to destroy these puny humans, she might actually have loved them. Ah well, nom nom nom time.

Ian struggled to keep up with the vanguard as they streaked towards the hill of festering dead people. The beast seemed to be crying like a child who had just dropped their ice cream on the floor, before she somersaulted off the cadaver pile and landed on the ground with a mighty boom.

The advance slowed, mainly due to the distance they had to run. Seriously, Gloucestershire! Half the point in doing the whole *sneaking up to it* thing was so that people didn't have to run that far —think of their knees!

Idiots.

Luckily, as the Gloucestershire lot had ballsed-up the crappy plan, they were already out in front and met Qzxprycatj first. Rifles cracked, bullets pinged off the creature's thick hide, and as they reloaded, the vanguard joined the battle.

Tammy Williams was the first to sidle up to the beast's scaly flank, and with its attention elsewhere, she pulled the nail-covered rolling pin over her head and twatted the creature on its hip. The weapon connected with the blue hide and bounced off. Feeling a twinge, the monster turned and looked down at Tammy, who let out a nervous smile and a wave.

Seeing that the human had committed the heinous crime of waving at it, which in the otherworld was a grave insult, Qzxprycatj growled, raised her foot and flattened the offender, leaving nothing but a greasy smear against the ground. She was the first to fall in what became known as...The Big Dust Up.

Rubbish name, huh? I know, I know, I can't say I'm too wowed with it either, you know, but what can I do? I am but a mere writer, passing on the events which have...passed. If only there was something I could do to change it into something more...I dunno...*majestic? Amazing? Grand?*

Wait a minute...did you just have the same thought as me?

You did?

Jolly good, I'll go and pop my clothes on the back of the chair, and you go get the grapes, I wonder if we can fit them all inside...

Ahhh, sorry, it's the other thought, huh? Yeah, I'm going to bloody do it. They won't know if I change the name of their rubbish fight, will they? Most of them are dead.

Oops, sorry, I meant to add this:

*** SPOILER ALERT ***

Bit late now, eh? Yeah, I suppose I could redo that bit and move it about so it makes more sense, but what's the point? Sod it, I'm leaving it, although just for you, I will change the name of the battle.

She was the first to fall in what became known as...The Mega-Hyper-Fucking-Massive-Fight-Way-Better-Than-The-First-Fight-Which-I-Completely-Left-To-Your-Imagination-A-Tron.

Punchy, huh?

Qzxprycatj stomped this way and that, flattening swathes of the Gloucestershire contingent; sure, she would have loved to have added them to her giant stack of bodies, but she had learnt from her first incarnation.

Don't fuck about! Kill the bastards, cos you never know when you're going to fall onto a woolly mammoth's tusks, or some robed twats will kill you and bind you back to the otherworld in a frankly AMAZING fight.

Ian slowed down to a jog; sure, the plan had gone sideways, but it might actually help in the long run. The beast had at least come down from its corpse hillock, that was one of his biggest worries first off. Granted, it was killing a *lot* of people, but that was to be expected. You don't get your freedom by just turning up on the day and playing a few rounds of rock, paper, scissors. If you do, then it's got to be Russian rock, paper, scissors, where the loser gets shot in the face.

Now the beast was down on their level, goring people with its weird curved teeth and throwing them in the air like it was some kind of contest. Ian caught up with Monique and her band of fighters, managing to breathe in so that the spots disappeared from in front of his eyes. "Are you ready?" He panted.

Monique looked at her comrades. "Yeah, think it's our time to do some bashing."

Ian smiled, and gave her the wink and the gun. "Come on then, sweet lips, let's go kill this bastard." The group hunched down and trotted towards the carnage.

By now, the ash tree staff wielders had finally got to the scene; each county had a small number in their midst, and they now swung their weapons at the beast. Qzxprycatj felt an ancient pain strike her toe; howling in pain, she reared to the heavens, shouting, "YOU FUCKING BASTARDS, NOT ON MY BIRTHDAY, SURELY?" in Sumerian, which is, as I said before, a dead language, so I can't really translate it accurately for you.

Looking down, her eyes widened as she saw the deadly staves which had helped slay her millennia earlier. No, not today, bitches, she wasn't going to go out like that again. Thinking back to her monster training, Qzxprycatj took a deep breath. Her cheeks blew out like a giant hot air balloon as she frantically looked around, running low on oxygen, searching for one of the delicacies holding one of her birthday candles.

Ignoring more lances of searing pain and agony, she rolled onto her side, taking out the Melksham contingent of shotgun-toting farmers. The torchbearer looked into the baleful eyes of its destroyer as the flame danced precariously on top of the wood, guttering and growing. Conjuring up gases from her seventh bowel, Qzxprycatj turned around, relaxed her gargantuan bum cheeks and let forth a fart which matched her monstrous form.

As the gas hit the naked flame, it burst into a fireball and grew outwards. The torchbearer, now set ablaze, ran around in screaming pain and agony. Feeling a little bad, Qzxprycatj stood up and squished on it, not wishing to see it suffer; it had helped, after all. With her arsehole now a foul-smelling flamethrower, she wiggled her hips from side-to-side, seeking to light up the motherfuckers who had been causing her the first pain she had felt since finding out that H.P. Lovecraft had based all his stories on his bath time toys, and not her devilish acts.

The boot was well and truly on the other foot now. Which is an odd saying, really. Why would you put your left boot on your right foot? Even if you were curious, you know it isn't going to work very well, huh? I suppose if you had an elephant foot, say, or even a horse's hoof...but still. Odd.

The potential smiters were now being routed, keen to avoid being set on fire. Ian, Monique and the group used the chaos to their advantage in order to sneak up alongside the beast. Gesturing to each other that it was now time, they opened up their rucksacks and pulled out grappling hooks tethered to strong rope, fetched from Hampshire and Dorset docks. This was true working-togetherness.

Twirling them round to gain some momentum, they counted to five, for that was a good number to count to, before they flung them up and over the beast's back. On the other side of Qzxprycatj, members of the Andover Rotarian club ducked as the metal hooks dropped down on them from the air. Two of their number were struck; one died instantaneously. Hopefully, their epitaph had something cool on it though, rather than 'Death by Grappling hook,' which sounds a bit shite, eh?

"You there! Heave, damn your eyes, HEAVE! It's the only way we'll bring this monster to heel," Ian bellowed.

At first, the Rotarians looked across a bit puzzled, a few were annoyed. Well, look at it from their point of view, old Dennis Upton and Maud Bennett were laying in a pool of their own blood and teeth. Then they realised what was at stake and manned the fuck up.

"HEAVE!"

Working together, the Salisbury and Andover men and women put aside their historic squabbles and yanked with all their might. THE ROPE. Yanked *the rope*. Honestly, your mind is in the gutter.

Qzxprycatj was halfway through toasting one man who had tried to sneak up on her, before she felt a tug on her back. What started off as a slight annoyance turned into an 'oh shit' moment as she felt herself being pulled towards the ground. She burped, and the flow of ancient fetid gut gas ceased, killing the gas supply to the rather effective napalm thrower her mouth had become.

People stopped to see what had caused the monster to stop burning their mates alive. Feeling a tiny glimmer of hope, those who were about to shit themselves and run away turned back. Those who were actually shitting themselves finished, ignored the wiping protocol, and headed back to the fight, skid marks be damned!

More and more ropes were hurled over the creature's back. As people arrived in the first wave, they joined in and pulled on the rope, pinning the creature in place. Like a swarm of killer ants running over something impressive for their size, I dunno, let's say a komodo dragon, they took up the slack and heaved.

Qzxprycatj was gradually pulled to her knees, and then onto her belly, the sheer weight beginning to take its toll. Ash staff bearers, saved from being turned into molten flesh slag, lashed out at the creature and raked its body with their weapons. The beast let out keening screams as its skin was rent open. Those with shotguns ran up to the tears in the flesh and fired their weapons into the gashes, making the creature scream louder in pain.

Satisfied they weren't going to fuck it up, Ian pulled Monique in close and gave her a tongue sandwich, patting her bum affectionately. Then he started to climb up the creature's ribcage. The past few weeks had seen the pair fall in love, in a way that only the certainty of death can do. Sometimes, only the threat of being worm food can make you see that life is precious, that you should seize the day, give someone a go, see if they can love you how you always wanted to be loved.

Fucking hell, is someone cutting onions up in here?

Ian stood atop the beast's spine and looked down at the remnants of the six counties army as it held the world-humper down. Those who could, slashed and beat the creature, others took selfies, knowing that soon, once electricity was restored and mobile phone masts were working again, they could post them on Instagurn and Vainbook.

Walking down the beast's back, he stepped over lengths of taut rope; the last thing Ian needed now was to be unable to see where he was going and trip over. He'd look like a right knobber and would never hear the end of it.

Making his way to the beast's head, he stood on an eyelid and looked down. A giant red orb with a black slit in its centre regarded him impassively. Ian stood in between the eyes and held his hands aloft. "People of the six counties, we have fought this day, not as individuals, but together! Together we have won not only our freedom, but also that of the world. When this day is done, let us always work together, for we can truly achieve anything from this day on."

He reached into his backpack, and after an awkward few seconds, pulled out a spear, the end whittled to a ridiculously sharp point. For the briefest of moments, he thought he saw a flicker of humanity in the monster's eyes, a spark of regret. Ignoring it completely, he rammed the ash spear into the space between Qzxprycatj's eyes. It pierced the skin easily and sliced through the bone. Trying to rear its head to the sky to call for its mummy, Ian rested his hands on top of the spear handle. "You had your chance, you ancient creature of death. Know that when you go, I will bind you to the otherworld in such a way that you can never set foot on Earth again. Begone, vile creature, BEGONE."

Pulling his rucksack round to his chest to act as padding, Ian threw himself into the air and landed on top of the spear, driving it into the lobe of life within Qzxprycatj's brain. After twitching a number of times, it fell still, slain once more.

Ian clambered off the sullen head and landed on the floor to a wall of cheering and clapping. Monique fought her way through the throng and the pair embraced. Managing a quick feel of his wang, she patted him on the arse. "Ian, you did it! Now what do we do? We surely need to bind the beast?"

Winking, he grabbed her by the waist, his thumbs nuzzling the bottom of her boobs. "Don't worry, I have this," he said, pulling out an appropriate book with a convenient title, 'Binding Creatures Of The Otherworld In Fiendish Ways.'

The pair laughed as they embraced and rubbed each other inappropriately before they were borne aloft by the crowd just so everyone could get a good glimpse.

Plus, it makes for a kickass pan out.

It's time to...
DISCOVER YOUR FATE

I don't believe it! Did that really just happen? Help carry the victors over to **Page 116** and find out!

TIME FOR TEA

"Shall I be mother?" asked Shaun through a forced grin, the others around the table nodded, he picked up the tall china teapot and looked across the thick oak table to Mandy. Her tightly curled hair cascaded off her shoulders, she was looking down, nervously, at her invitation to the tea room opening.

Shaun coughed gently rousing Mandy from her study, she looked up like a startled panda, cast wary glances at her fellow patrons and then slid her cup and saucer across the expanse of the table, past the sugar bowl and small jugs of ice cold milk. It squeaked slightly as it cruised across the join of two planks, "Oops", she said timidly, instantly withdrawing back to the invitation in her thin bony hands.

Shaun's hand trembled gently, black-brown liquid poured from the spout and into Mandy's delicate bone china cup, it slopped around within, some splashing onto the table. "Careful mate", said an annoyed Tony, "you nearly got some on me there." Shaun looked across at Tony sat to his right, his short blonde hair, blue eyes and brusque manner gave him all the airs and graces of an SS officer.

Around the tea room there was a gentle undercurrent of murmuring, in total, three tables of four people were seated, engaged in hushed conversation, sipping tea or reading through the menu. Shaun slowly slid the cup and saucer back to Mandy, being careful not to spill anything. Tony held his cup and saucer out to Shaun, who took it off him and laid it on the table.

"Bit of an odd place to have this gaff, in a basement", Tony looked around, checking out the other customers, each seemingly lost in their own worlds. Shaun passed the filled cup and saucer back to Tony and asked, "Have you not read your invitation yet? Might be some useful information in there."

Tony shook his head, "Nope, not yet mate, will do in a bit, all very odd though huh? Cheers for the tea mate." A thick arm covered in near transparent blonde hair reached out for the milk, between his sausage like fingers, the jug seemed comedically small.

Shaun poured himself some tea and turned to Carl, "Pass me your cup", he asked politely. Carl looked at Shaun and put a hand over his cup, "No thanks, I'm good, can't stand tea, makes me gaseous, you know? More of a latte man, comprende?" he replied snidely.

Shaun and Mandy gulped as one, wide eyes looked at Carl, who regarded each of them in turn with disdain. "What?" he asked aloofly, Mandy started biting her lip, the grip on her invitation tightened, the card started to creak under the pressure, she started muttering under her breath.

Shaun rested the teapot on the table and looked at Carl, "Mate, seriously, have you read your invitation? I really think you should have some tea, please", he started to frantically look around for some person unseen. The gentle hubbub of the basement continued, someone at one of the other tables shot them a glance, before a kick under the table got their attention again back to the ongoing conversation.

"I said, I'm fine. Thank you", Carl enunciated, he placed his gloved hands on the table, resting on a closed envelope bearing his name.

Shaun shook his head and looked angrily at Carl, "Why did you accept an invitation to a tea room opening if you don't like tea?"

Carl lowered his red tinted sunglasses so they rested on the end of his nose, his slick back hair reflected the light from the ceiling. "I go to all of these pop-up places, it's what I do, just yesterday I was at a smashing little Tibetan restaurant in a caravan setup in Victoria Park. I turn up, be seen and then leave."

Tony laughed, "Ha ha, we've got ourselves a genuine, bona fide hipster, what a dick", he stirred his cup with a small silver spoon, the clinking tolling like a miniature bell. He tapped the spoon on the cups rim and placed it back on the saucer. "Right, let's see what this is" he said to himself, and picked up the envelope with his name on it, a chunky finger plunged into the join and tore it open, as he pulled the card out from within his face froze, the colour drained away in an instant, "No fucking way..." was all he could muster.

Carl pushed his glasses back up the bridge of his nose,

"Now, I better go, got some acquaintances to meet before dinner tonight at Il Maestoso Salmone in town, have to go and get a pick me up first though." He placed his hands on the table and began to push himself away, as he did so, the air conditioning vent above his head swung open with an ominous creak.

A rusting telescopic metal pipe descended from the yawning hole directly above Carl's head, "My, my, Health and Safety will have a field day with this place", he said with utter contempt, looking up into the murk of the pipe.

All eyes were now transfixed on their table, from above came the sound of a stubborn, creaking valve being turned followed by a gush of liquid. The pipe was around a foot from the top of Carl's head, still sat in his metal chair, shaded eyes looking into the abyss.

There came a hissing sound as a viscous green liquid poured from the tube and straight over Carl's head, Shaun and Mandy who were sat either side of him pushed themselves away instinctively.

Carl emitted a ball-shrinking screech and started to swat at his face with his gloved hands, as he did so, globules of skin and flesh came off in his frenzied swiping. His slicked hair began to slide off the top of his head, taking his creased forehead with it and exposing the skull underneath. By now his screams had subsided to nothing more than a wet gurgle, the acid eating through his throat.

The tea room patrons shrieked in horror, petrified in their seats. As his ears dissolved into flesh coloured slurry, Carl's sunglasses slipped off what was left of his face and onto his lap. From his eye sockets ran a reddish pink goo, tendrils of optic nerve slopped out before crackling and melting.

Carl now consisted of a skeleton, wrapped in a slowly disintegrating leather jacket, bubbling crimson liquid popped and burst the length of his body as he was slowly eaten away. With no muscles to support it, his skull plopped forwards, the bottom jaw hung from one side before falling onto his lap, clinking against his suglasses.

Underneath the screams of the patrons there was a gentle fizzing sound like cola bubbles tinkling in a bottle.

The pipe clumsily retracted back into the ceiling cavity,

381

the plastic air conditioning cover still swung gently. The smell of burnt flesh and tissue hung heavily in the air, Mandy coughed and wretched, trying to clear the taste from her throat.

Tony looked back to the card contained within the envelope and the simple note within; 'Follow the commands and enjoy afternoon tea or they die' was printed next to a grainy picture of his mother gardening outside her house, someone had drawn a crude knife sticking from her back. He looked over at Shaun, "You got the same thing I'm guessing?" he asked solemnly, showing the card.

Shaun nodded, "My brother, he's just started Uni, got a picture of him passed out in the toilets after a night out, how did they-" he was interrupted by the sound of piped music, an easy listening version of Way Out West's 'Melt' played through tinny speakers positioned within the walls.

A burst of static crushed through the music, silence descended upon the room. "Oh dear, looks one of the patrons didn't want to play along, how silly. I don't see any of you enjoying your tea", said a creepy, high pitched male voice.

From one of the other tables, a burly man shouted out, "This is bullshit! You can't keep us here, I'm gonna phone the filth and they'll be here to arrest your sick ass." Shaun, Mandy and Tony looked across at the man, who pulled a phone from his pocket and started to unlock it.

The voice warned, "Now, now, this is a respectable family establishment, we won't have potty mouths here, and we most certainly will not have mobile telephones being used. You all need to enjoy the ambience, the lovely, lovely ambience."

The man raised his middle finger, "Fuck you pal, I'm calling them now....has anyone got a signal in this craphole?" Silence fell over the remaining customers, the air grew thick with tension and wariness.

It was broken by a cackling from the speakers, "Oh my, you seem to have discovered that our little boutique is a haven from the modern world and quite unable to pick up mobile telephone signals-"

A slight lull was broken by the sinister voice again "-now, you have to pay for your insolence young man, all I asked was for you to enjoy your afternoon tea. Maybe even sample our crumpets later, they're simply divine."

The man grew in surliness, "Fuck you pal, why don't you get your sick ass out here and I'll shove your crumpets up your arse, see how you get on with that you fucking squeaky fuck." People shot glances at each other, perhaps sensing that this was just some kind of prank, an elaborate one admittedly, but that was possible, right?

"Thought so", yelled the man and he slumped back in his chair. The lights flickered momentarily, Mandy whimpered, the lights then gutted completely, leaving them all in darkness.

A loud clunk sounded which switched the desenter from incandescent rage to screaming and yelling unintelligable curses. Through the gloom four crackling, barbed tongues of lightning struck him at once, causing his arms to be flung stiffly out to his side, with his head arched back violently, a distorted pain-filled similie which was his voice was stuck on one half of a word "Fu...fu...fu...fu...fu...", like a broken record player.

The only light source in the dingy basement was eminating from the man, as the electricity coursed through him, bones wrapped in now translucent skin cast him like a ghastly Jack-O-Lantern. He thrashed around in his chair as if some miscreant had vile control over him, a pall of acrid smoke started to rise from his head. Without warning his hair caught on fire, disappearing in a fleeting woosh of flame, eyes bulged from their housing, wide with pain, glowing from within they projected a tributary of scarlet veins over his upper cheeks and forehead.

Through his pain wracked features, the basement dwellers could tell that the current had increased, the shaking became more vigourous, bones in his hands cracked as they contracted, skin crackled with coruscating waves of grotesque light. His eyes burst in an explosion of fetid fluid and fleshy pulp, the goo flying over his fellow table dwellers, a smouldering tuft of back hair caused a ripple of blue flame to wash over his body as if he had been dipped in kerosene.

As quickly as it started, the electricity stopped, the room fell dark again, in the gloom, Shaun could hear people

383

breathing heavily, crying, gagging with fear. The ceiling lights flickered back to life, showing a scorched corpse resting on the table, the face had been petrified like a giant block of charcoal, only kernels of yellow teeth offered any variance in colour.

The speakers sparked into life again, "My my, electricity really can be quite dangerous, especially in these old buildings, you go careful down there my pretties, we don't want any more accidents, do we?"

Shaun shook his head and looked over to Mandy who was now catatonic with fear. The speaker crackled again, "Your waiter Dirk will be with you presently, he has your Specials menus, please show him a degree of courtesy, good staff can be so troublesome to find", a muffled clunk signalled the end of the speech.

On cue, the door at the top of the stairs leading from the basement clicked as it was released from the frame, it whined open before slamming shut again. After a slight pause, they could all hear a thud-thud-thud from heavy boots stomping down the wooden stairs.

The stairs were contained behind a thin partition wall, the stomping grew louder, each step ratcheted up the anxiety in the room. The clomping stopped and the waiter was revealed, a hulk of a man, dressed in a grubby white shirt covered in all manners of unidentifiable stains. A pair of equally filthy, tight grey trousers clung to his tree trunk legs which ended in heavy army surplus boots, the ends scuffed and slightly grey.

Over his clothes he had a blood stained apron tied tightly around him. Shaun looked at the man's face, from where he was sat, it looked like it was hung on wrong, as if someone had tied weights to the skin under his chin.

Dirk clutched a wad of paper, his jaw hung slack, a steady stream of saliva ran from the corner of his mouth, he looked around the room dispassionately as if he was looking at a daytime television show. Tony kicked Shaun under the table, gave him a slight nod, and then another towards the teapot sat in the middle of the table. Shaun realised his intention and shook his head slightly, Tony squinted with frustration and looked down into his lap.

The giant of a man lumbered over to the first table, still

resplendent with their full complement of four people, he forced a piece of paper into the hand of every terrified occupant before moving on to the table with the still smoking corpse.

He again passed out a piece of paper to each person, seemingly unaware of the smouldering body, he squashed the paper into a blackened hand, which cracked and separated at the wrist, before moving towards Shaun's table. As he got closer, Shaun could see that the man's face swayed slightly with every step, he focused on the odd movement, then realisation kicked in.

The waiter's face was not his own, it was a cross-stitch pattern of human flesh, differing tones were cobbled together with thick black cotton, some patches had outcrops of hair, others still daubed with make up. He recoiled at the sight of it, forgetting entirely about Tony's intentions.

A piece of paper was given to Mandy and Shaun, the goliath again seemed unaware that Carl was nothing more than a pile of bones and a puddle of melted flesh and tissue. The paper fizzled as he dropped it into what was left of Carl's lap, it dissolved quickly inbetween Carl's pelvic bone.

Dirk's gormless gaze turned to Tony, who seemed enthralled and repulsed in equal measure by the sight of the ragtag assembly of the waiter's face, he wavered briefly before grabbing hold of the teapot and clocking Dirk around the head with it.

The fine china teapot smashed instantly, showering them all with lukewarm tea and pieces of pottery. The waiter though remained unmoved, one hand still held the specials menu out to Tony, the other hand reached round his back.

Tony stood and looked up into the dull eyes of the waiter, the impact had done nothing except embed some small pieces of china into the man's face mask. Tony gulped, his Adam's apple bulged out, as he did so the man slashed horizontally with a speed his ungainly height did not match. A jet of blood sprayed over Shaun's face who gulped in surprise.

Tony's eyes widened, he clamped both hands desperately to his throat, trying to stem the bleeding. His fingers were red and sticky as he tried to hold his neck together, they went through the slit and into his windpipe, he could feel his own fingers tickling his tonsils, the sensation a stark opposite to the one of excruciating pain he was experiencing.

Mandy still sat there shaking, a geyser of blood was being pumped over her, matting her hair. Tony collapsed like a taser victim, on his way down his forehead smacked into the thick table, as his head bounced it tore the last vestiges of skin and tendon which still connected his head to his neck. A sickening slurp and crack later, and his headless body finally met the floor, his head rolled around in a puddle made up of a mixture of his bodily fluids, eyes still open with shock.

The man placed the paper where Andy had sat, slid the dripping butchers knife back into his belt and lumbered back to the stairs and out of sight. Shaun wiped the sleeve of his jumper over his face, trying to remove Tony's blood.

The upstairs door slammed again, and the speaker clicked into life, "Oh dear, another customer unhappy with our service, I'll have to mark Dirk down as *Average* on the satisfaction survey. Never mind friends, you have your Specials to look forward to now, enjoy."

Shaun looked across to Mandy, her face and hair was drenched in blood, it dripped lazily from her hair and onto the table, he could hear her muttering to herself, though he couldn't make out what she was saying.

"Hey, hey Mandy" he said softly, moving his hands across the table towards her, she flinched involuntarily as they reached her personal bubble, she looked up at him, as if woken suddenly from a dream.

She looked back at him, the whites of her eyes a stark contrast to the drying blood over her face. "He....he.....he.....he's....." she tried to say, unable to form words into a coherent sentence.

Shaun nodded and looked at her, "It'll be okay Mandy, we'll get out of this." Over her shoulder he could see one of the other guests stand up from her table, dab a napkin gently across her lips and walk towards them.

The lady stood behind Mandy, she was short and squat, her midriff bulging from where her jeans were fastened tightly around her waist. "I'm sorry" she said softly, holding the napkin in each hand, reached over Mandys head and pulled it against her throat, Mandy started to wheeze, the lady pulled tighter.

At first Shaun was too shocked by what he saw, his brain unable to comprehend this latest act of violence, even beneath her blood soaked face, Shaun could make out a blue tinge, veins pulsed and rose to the surface, "What the hell are you doing?" he demanded angrily, the woman repeated her apology and pulled tighter.

Shaun stood up and moved around the table, the woman paid him no heed and continued to drain the air out of Mandy. "STOP!" he shouted, the woman looked at him sympathetically and again offered her apologies. Before he knew it, he had lashed out, his fist had connected with the woman's nose, blood was smeared on the top of her lip, her hold on Mandy relinquished.

He looked at the woman and her nose was now flat against her face, she raised the napkin to her own face, dabbed it, and saw the blood. She looked at it impassively, Mandy turned to face the woman, rubbing her throat, trying to get some feeling back. The woman looked down at her and closed her hands around Mandy's throat, desperately trying to throttle her.

"Get off her!" Shaun bellowed again, he smacked the palm of his hand into the woman's face again, meeting the base of her nose. Her eyes rolled back into her skull, as a thin river of blood trickled from one of her eye sockets, her grip fell slack and she dropped to the floor, dead.

Shaun knelt down by Mandy, gently shaking her, "Hey, Mandy, it's okay, I dunno what the hell she was doing but you're okay now." The peace was short-lived, a scream broke the air from the other table.

They both looked over, on the table of the electrocuted man there were two men locked in a struggle, a glint of metal could be seen in a hand, though it was impossible to see who held it. The men seemed to embrace, one then suddenly jerked upwards, the other fell back, hands clutching a savage wound in his chest. "I'm sorry, I'm really sorry" his assailant was telling his victim.

He knelt down by the stabbed man, who appeared to be whispering, trying to give his valediction. "What's that buddy, I can't hear you", said the knife wielder, and bent closer, as he did so, the man slammed a clenched fist into the others skull, before collapsing back onto the floor in an expanding pool of his own blood.

The man stood up, bloodied knife in one hand, the other clasped over his ear, he staggered uneasily, steadying himself on the table, "Oh god", Shaun said, his voice laden with disgust. As the man withdrew his hand from the side of his head, Shaun could see a long necked screwdriver had been driven through the ear and deep into the man's skull.

The knife clattered to the floor, quickly followed by the man, landing on his victim and attacker. Shaun reeled from the sight of the blood and gore, a whip like crack broke his introspection, he looked across to the other table and saw a woman trying to staunch a chest wound. He traced a path to the sole survivor from the burned man's table, holding a small smoking pistol, his forehead was sheened with sweat.

The man walked forwards purposefully, as he neared the person he had just shot, a woman in her early fifites lashed out at him with an old style wooden police truncheon. The man's head rocked to one side, a purple contusion already forming by the man's temple. He staggered like a drunkard on a Saturday night, the pistol fell from his hand and he slumped to the floor. He started to convulse, a thick white paste laden with flecks of blood vomited forth and he fell still.

Shaun looked at the other table, the woman who had been shot was leaning back in her chair, arms hung limply by her side. He ran his hands through his hair, his jagged nails scratched his skin, "No, no, no, NO", he wailed in anguish. He looked over to Mandy, she was still rubbing her bruised neck with one hand, the other idly held the piece of paper the slasher had dropped off moments before.

That was when the madness had started, he rubbed his head, trying to make things clear, trying to get some sense of what the hell was going on. His thinking was interrupted again by a banshee wail, he looked across to the table where the only other survivors were seated, the woman in her early fifties was crawling over the table, she had ditched the truncheon and now held a meat cleaver, the steel caught the ceiling light and seemed imbued with an inner glow.

The man was studying the piece of paper he had been given when he heard the cry. He tried to dodge to one side, but the cleaver bit deep into his shoulder, he screamed in pain. The older woman had fire in her eyes, her grey fringe rubbing across her eyebrows. She fought to heave the blade from his collarbone.

As she pulled, he screamed louder, like a semi-stunned animal at an abatoir, the weight of the woman toppled them both over onto the floor, the blade dug deeper into his chest, fully embedded within, he screamed again.

The grey haired woman now straddled him, still trying to yank out the cleaver buried in the man's body. The man's one free hand scrabbled desperately around for something, anything, to try and get this mad woman off him, to try and buy himself some time, his hand fell on the small pistol.

Gritting his teeth through the pain, he pulled the pistol up to bear, holding the gun to the woman's temple, he squeezed the trigger. The force of the point blank shot caused the woman to fall to one side, as she did so, she maintained her grip on the cleaver's handle, the pressure on it caused the man's collarbone and neck to be opened up like a bear trap.

The man screamed in agony as his arm was practically severed from the rest of his body, his heart continued to pump blood around his arteries, chugging his life force onto the concrete floor. He let out a pained growl and fell silent.

Shaun looked around the basement, bodies lay in various states of dismemberment and agony, he looked over to Mandy, who read the piece of paper and folded it in half.

He crouched on the floor, panting, his mind still awash with images of complete and utter horror. He reconciled something internally and brought himself to his feet, a wave of determination surged through him anew, this place and madness would not claim them, he was going to make sure of it.

"Mandy, hey Mandy, it's okay, I don't know what the hell they were doing, but we are not like that, okay, we've got each other, we're going to be okay", Shaun picked up a napkin and started to try and rub some of the congealing blood from her face.

Mandy put one hand on the folded piece of paper in front of her and slid it across to Shaun, he looked at her quizzically and dropped the blood smeared napkin onto the table. He picked the note up cautiously, "What's this Mandy? What does it say?"

He unfolded the paper and saw on one side was a picture of himself, it was a few days ago when he was shopping for some furniture, "Huh, that's odd", he remarked, he looked at the words on the other side;

YOU MUST KILL THIS MAN.

THE LAST ONE LEFT ALIVE WILL LIVE.

THERE IS A CHISEL TAPED
TO THE UNDER-SIDE OF THE TABLE.

GET IT

KILL

Mandy's hand wrapped around the hilt of the woodworking tool, Shaun looked down at her in surprise, "What? But you won't....", before he could finish, Mandy thrust the dull, thick blade into his stomach and twisted it sharply. Shaun put out a weak hand, trying to fend her away, but his strength had deserted him, he patted her feebly. Mandy looked into his eyes, struggling to hold back the tears which were welling inside.

"I'm s...s...s...sorry Shaun", was all she could muster, he fell to the floor still clutching the chisel which was interred firmly in his intestinal tract, the bottom half of his body felt warm and tingly. His head rolled to the side and he looked into the death stare of the cleavered man, he coughed up a thick wad of spit and blood and fell slack.

Mandy stood up from the table, looking around at the carnage which had unfolded so quickly, the speaker popped and played a chorus of Queen's 'We Are The Champions', before the eerie voice came back on.

"Well done my dear, well done indeed, we hope you

enjoyed your time here with us today. Please don't forget to leave feedback for our staff, and remember your complimentary shortbread as you leave."

The speaker crackled off, the door at the top of the stairs clicked open. Mandy, awash with adrenaline ran up the stairs, to freedom.

It's time to...
EMBRACE YOUR FATE

Wasn't that a rousing tale? Epitomising the true spirit of humanity. That even in the face of such adversity, we can find a way to do what needs to be done and accept our inevitable demise. Actually...this story has a sequel, isn't that quaint!

For those of you that think a cup of tea isn't quite strong enough for dealing with the fact that you're probably going to get nibbled on soon, this next story, over on **Page 91** is set in a pub, so you can enjoy a nice beer, a glass of wine, or maybe even a shot of something. Don't worry, the alcohol will make you more receptive to accepting whatever horrible imminent death awaits you in this book.

WHAT *DO* YOU GET MONSTERS
FOR A WEDDING PRESENT?

Thanks Mike, here we are, outside Salisbury cathedral once more. The last time Claire and I were here, we were dodging lumps of smashed-up bodies as they rained down on us, as a giant apocalyptic monster was birthed, right over there.

Today though, we're here under better circumstances. It's been three weeks since those terrible moments, when we all thought we were witnessing the end of days. I, like many of you, did many things on that fateful day, thinking it was to be my last. Whilst it's not time to fully atone for all those things, some of which I'll carry to my early grave, I would at least like to take this opportunity now to apologise to the residents of the Green Grass residential home.

My actions were foolhardy in the extreme, and to any who felt my sexual advances were unwarranted, please, accept my apologies.

Now, with that said and done, at the behest of the channel, and my therapist, I can get back to it. We are here today to celebrate a most wondrous occasion. The spire, though damaged, has been hosed down, and the last remnants of monster foo-foo juice have been scrubbed from the ancient stone. Today, we are here to gaze upon a most odd couple, as they are married in front of the people who were going to be its food.

We've had assurances from both of them that no one will be eaten during the ceremony, and if you've been following the news over the past few weeks, you'll already know that they seem a lot more preoccupied with some*thing* other than murder.

If you know what I mean.

So, as we look out at the pair of lovestruck monsters, on this glorious summer's afternoon —definitely t-shirt weather— we can all reflect on how the most important thing to us all, including ghastly creatures, is love.

This is Adam Smedley, for New Wiltshire Today, in Salisbury.

CONGRATULATIONS!
THIS IS ENDING
#9

'CONFETTI AND A WEE DROP OF PIXELLATED MAN MILK FOR SUPPER.'

I must apologise to Justin's parents for killing them in that story, they were bloody decent to me for a period in my late teens, and I'll forever be grateful. Putting them in this book is a weird way of saying thanks, I guess.

Anyway...if you want to find out what other scrapes you can get into, or if I kill off any more of my friends' parents, use this shortcut and head back to the pub on **Page 150**.

WHAT'S IN A NAME?

Winding their way through the back streets and deserted thoroughfares of noble Salisbury, the trio spoke only when pointing to gross clumps of sinew and organ, which had come down in the gore shower a few hours earlier. Noah had taken to tying a carrier bag around each foot to protect the integrity of his white tracksuit. Given the way the day had panned out so far, he wished he'd had the foresight to have worn something a little more colour-coordinated with an abattoir.

Curtains to houses and flats were closed; flickering light burst around the cloth as televisions inside showed the beast from every angle. Some were highly flattering, and, with it still telling the world what it was planning on doing, it looked rather dashing. If mummy apocalypse beast was watching, she would've cried tears of joy in amongst mauling her way through another tower block.

Finally, after what seemed like a good twenty minutes or so, they arrived outside a nondescript three-floored building, halfway up a hill. Ian's pointing finger hovered over the doorbell for the ground floor flat. "Well, come on, then, we don't have all day, do we?" Monique said, pointing to the fist-waving beast that was visible through a passageway between the neighbouring buildings.

Ian turned to the pair. "Right, before we go in, a few things. Pete can be a little...*interesting* at times."

Peeling off a length of skin from the back of his calf, Noah said, "Interesting how? Does he have the largest collection of diaphragms outside of the Klinkerhoffen Diaphragm Museum in Köln?"

"No."

"Is he the proud owner of the complete set of Encyclopaedia Britannica?"

"No."

"Could he-"

"Oh, for heaven's sake," Monique grunted, and kicked the front door in.

Ian realised his mouth was agape, and wanting it

ungaped, closed it, before opening it again to admonish her. "You've been around *him* too long, you have. It's not the done thing, I know you're a born-again suicide bomber but you can't go around kicking in people's front doors. We're not barbarians, you know."

Shrugging, Monique stepped into the hallway and scraped her boots on the welcome mat, which had worn away to say 'COM', which confused the hell out of most visitors. Inside, there was a closed white door, with the number one helpfully nailed to it, and a set of stairs which ended in a T-junction. From beyond the door came the sound of a dog barking.

"You didn't mention that he is the keeper of a hellhound," Noah said.

"That's not even the interesting th-"

Then, as the three of them stood like complete dicks in the hallway, the door opened up. "Who the fuck do you think you are?"

Ian waved sheepishly. "Hiya, Pete...surprise?" Whilst Noah and Monique took in a deep breath. Deliberately.

"Ian, long time no see," said Pete, opening the door. "Are these your friends?" Cerberus, his bull mastiff-chihuahua mix, growled and strained as he was held back by a worn leather collar.

"Not really...this one tried to blow me up earlier, while matey in the tracksuit and holding the pebble-encrusted staff, kicked in *my* front door. Claims to be working for some ostrich deity."

"Odd...pleased to meet you both anyway." Pete held out his free hand. Getting nothing from the tracksuited man, he extended it to the woman, who remained rooted to the spot, pointing at him. "What?" he asked.

"Yo...yo...your *face*..." Monique finally managed to blurt out.

Pete shoved Cerberus back into the confines of the flat, where he continued to bark and scratch at the door.

"What? Have I got sputum on me?" he said, running his hands over his face.

"No...you've got a pot where your head should be!"

"Oh, *that*! Well, yeah, that's why everyone calls me Pothead Pete. Ha, most people think I'm some kind of marry-jew-wana dealer, or something. I've had more policemen root around my cavity than you've had hot baths, it's a perennial problem. Unless it's WPC Nagle of course, in which case, she can dispense with the gloves and go in dry..." Pete looked upwards to the corner of the hallway, where Frank the Flashback Spider squirmed in his web.

As Frank hurriedly formed the scene to be replayed from the shiny silk in his butt, Monique and Noah looked at Ian conspiratorially. "Why didn't you tell us?" she hissed.

"I did try, but between numbnuts here asking stupid questions and you being a boorish brute and kicking his door in, you didn't give me much chance. Anyway...I did tell you that his name was Pothead Pete, it was your own fault for leaping to the wrong conclusion."

NOT SURE THIS
IS EVEN A CHAPTER

With the dog stashed inside the bedroom, much to its door clawing chagrin, the humanoids sat in awkward silence on the two mismatched sofas. Whilst Ian and Noah shared nervous glances, Monique was staring intently at Pete's head. "Do you mind if I touch it?"

"Of course not, be my guest. Though you're not going to kick it in, are you? It's just that after the front door incident..."

Giggling like an anime girl, Monique reached for Pete's potted head. First off, it just felt so wrong that she pulled back immediately as if she had received a mild electric shock. Which would be impossible as the material was unable to conduct electricity.

Plucking up courage, she plonked her hand where an ear should be, and held it there. After a few brief seconds, she ran it slowly down the bulbous body, to where it opened up to the atypical, fleshy neck. "Wow, it feels like real clay."

"That it is," Pete replied proudly, "a few dings here and there, but otherwise, it's in good working order." As he stared at her, his eyes peered out from two oval holes in the baked earthenware. They were flush with the pot, and had no join whatsoever. The mouth was similarly designed; an elliptical slit opened up exactly where you'd expect. Though what would probably be his lips, didn't move, Monique could see a tongue flapping about inside. His nose was a stunted, flared, stumpy handle, with two holes made underneath. Given the construction of his head, it was no surprise that every breath out made a faint whistling sound, that, over enough time in his company, would inevitably become really fucking annoying.

Pete giggled, and Monique pulled her hand away. "Sorry, am I being annoying?"

"No, no, it just tickled, is all."

She resumed her pot-stroking. "So, have you always been like this, or was it some kind of pottery accident?"

The high-pitched giggling stopped as Pete looked into

middle distance, where Frank the Flashback Spider abseiled down from the ceiling where he had been loitering for the inevitable. "No, my dear…something much worse…"

Ian coughed, and leant in. "Do we really have time for this? I mean, there's a huge fucking monster shrieking from the top of the cathedral, with seven arse cheeks and an opening act that consists of pelting blood and guts from the sky. I really th-"

Monique whipped her neck at him, taking her head with it, as that's part of the whole design, you see. Try it yourself, gently at first, I don't want to cause you a mischief. *Gently* whip your neck to the right, and see what happens.

Yeah, cool huh? Nice little design feature, I think, comes in handy for when you watch tennis matches, or when you're keeping an eye out for the bus.

"Ian, don't be so rude."

"Me? You were the one who kicked the shit out of his front door."

"I'm quite intrigued, to be honest," Noah ventured.

Frank the Flashback Spider didn't give a shit about any of this conjecture. He, like me, knew you would want to hear the story, so as the others continued to bicker, he spun his little web. He even managed to snag a couple of little greenfly, too, which he wound in memory silk and tied to the corner, ready to have a nibble on later. Making flashback webs was a tiring business, you know.

"Okay, fine! Let's go and listen to the story, I've heard it anyway, so if you don't mind, I'm going to play Gratuitous Violence 7 on my phone until you're done," Ian sulked.

With the tinny sounds of grunting and automatic weapons fire coming out from his phone speakers, Monique and Noah edged forwards and peered into the midst of the flashback web.

Pete scratched his face, which made everyone's skin itch, as the sound is bloody horrible. Think of nails down a chalkboard, or nails over a clay pot, that'll do it. "Sorry, my bad. Okay then…" He too looked into the sparkling web Frank had woven. "It all began one hot summer's day…"

RUBBISH FLASHBACK

...I was playing with my chums down at the dump. Ahhh, those halcyon days, where summer holidays seemed to go on forever and ice cream vans sang in the streets, beckoning you to feast from their frozen creamy teats.

There were three of us, Benny, Sam and me, we were playing our favourite game: Who Can Hide in the Chest Freezer the Longest Before Fear of Suffocation Made You Pound on the Side of the Door. You'd pray that you had enough strength to make a loud enough sound, or you'd join the dead bodies of Heidi and Jason who didn't make it past the qualifiers.

I remember the headlines in the local paper, 'MISSING KIDS – POLICE HUNT FOR PAEDO.' Unbeknownst to them, their decomposing little bodies were the lumpy carpet in an old LEC Chest Freezer at the local landfill site. I don't think they ever found the remains, none of us ever grassed, that's for sure. We had a simple rule, 'what happens at the dump, stays at the dump.' Okay, so it made it difficult in later life when I had to go through a fuckton of psychiatric tests after the whole...ya know...*tunnelling to the centre of the earth* incident.

Anyway, I had managed to make it into three-minute territory when the combination of rancid meat and the lack of air forced me to quit. As the pair slid off the lid —just in case anyone tried to break the rules and smuggle in some oxygen— I gulped for air in the muggy afternoon, uttering those five damn words that have haunted me to this day. "Let's go do something else."

They both shrugged their shoulders, and just as they were about to put me back in the freezer for my second heat, I convinced them that we should play a new game. I could see on their faces that although they wanted to carry on, the prospect of a new way of making the most of the bounty we had on our doorsteps was too much for them.

"Like what?" Benny asked.

I hadn't really thought it through, and whether it was the mix of Heidi's mulched skin under my fingernails, or the smell of Jason's skull cavity; now home to a family of fourteen hundred maggots, I blurted out. "Let's play diving for buried treasure."

Now, with them both interested, and my own brain deciding that it liked the sound of it, I had to come up with some rules, quick sharp. "Simple, we all start down by the pentagram of dead seagulls and head in different directions. We have fifteen minutes to find three objects."

"Like what?" Sam asked. He was a right knob if I'm being honest, always with the questions:

"What did you have for tea last night?"

"How many pencil sharpeners can you fit up your nose?"

"Why is my poo sand-coloured?"

"Does your mum take her clothes off in front of you, too?"

After a while, it got a little tedious. With the flashing spots having gone from in front of my eyes, and the feeling returning to my legs, I added in some pertinent details. "One object has to be metal, one something you can wear, and the third item has to be really cool— I'm talking *MC Hammer versus Vanilla Ice in a rap battle* cool. We'll all meet up after, and decide who's got the best things, okay?"

You could tell they weren't hugely excited, but as there were still loads of places we hadn't crawled through or thrown up on in the tip, they both said yes.

I remember...as I stood in the middle of the dead gull pentagram, their lifeless skeletal wings lifting in the breeze, that it would be nice to do something different with our time. We always stuck to the same things, playing football with the blow-up sex-doll's head, or flicking the elastic snake skins at each other, which had weird tasting liquid in, we never just said, "You know what, let's go do something different today."

Sometimes, nowadays, when I'm lying in bed at night, struggling to get comfortable on my pillow, with my pot for a head, I think back to that day, and wonder how life would've turned out if I'd just said, "Let's go find some packing materials, shove it down our shorts, and kick each other in the happy sack until there's only one left standing," instead.

Alas, for me, fate held something different in store.

As I ran off towards the sun, I galloped over an old bath and raced past a rusting climbing frame. Pah, I knew of these things, they held nothing I was after. Reaching the wrecked paddling pool, which the tramps used as a circle of death in their bare-knuckle fighting competitions, I knew I was now in unknown territory.

I saw a microwave sticking up from an old fireplace, and dashed to it. Prying open the door with a metal spatula, my little eyes lit up. Not from a faulty magnetron, but from what I saw inside. Nestled within was a partially melted toy car. Not much, you would think, but it had been melted around a hedgehog.

Its little face...I don't know how long it had been inside, but it was sure glad to see me. Its tiny little nose wrinkled and snuffled against the palm of my hand. Using the spatula, I managed to pry it out of the microwave, and found a smooth piece of ground.

Where its legs used to be, were the wheels, and after a little bit of getting used to 'em, it was scooting around like a pro. The red, white, and blue plastic box that surrounded it was all stretched and skewed, with just its face sticking out —and a few long spines.

Recognising this would easily fulfil my *something cool* quota, I began to look around for the other two items. Turns out I should've just stuck with that little fella, perhaps race him round the model buggy track they had. But no...

I climbed up a mound of used nappies and sanitary towels, which had been baked into a large triangle by the summer sun. Taking advantage of my...erm...vantage point, I scoured nearby for something which might hold a bit more treasure. There it was, glinting below, just to the side of an old go-kart which was rusting away.

Sliding down the north slope with the hedgehog tucked under my arm, I scampered over to the place I had seen the gleaming. After putting Wheely on his roof so he couldn't scurry away to freedom, I brushed aside the rubbish and gazed at my prize: a red metal potty. The paint was chipped in places, and the inside was still stained with skid marks and stomach lining. In places, the enamel surface had been eaten through by the vomit that hadn't been cleaned off.

It stank to high heaven, but if there was anything

401

guaranteed to help me win, it was a metal pan that smelt of farts. Sitting down, I saw that the sides were covered in muck from the dump, so I grabbed hold of my t-shirt and started to buff the scratched red surface.

There was a reason it had been discarded.

As I rubbed, I heard a sound from within the bowl, like someone blowing a raspberry. I stopped and turned it over; as I did so, there was a loud POP!, and this plume of smoke shot up into the air. I dropped the potty onto the floor, and was about to grab Wheely and leg it, when this ghostly figure appeared out of the fog. "Don't be afraid," it said.

I should've screamed, shouted, bellowed at the top of my lungs, that some potty genie had just manifested in front of me out of the filth and muck. But I didn't. "Okay, I won't be, Mister Smokeman."

I know, what a bellend, huh? In my defence, I hadn't seen Aladdin; I was out rooting through discarded furniture and collecting animal skulls in my spare time, not addicted to television.

It dusted itself down. "Thank you for freeing me, oh little one. I shall grant you three wishes. Here's the small print though, you can't ask me for more wishes as one of your wishes, okay? Seriously, that really gets on my tits, it's like, 'Hello! Three wishes are more than enough, you greedy bastard.' Aside from that, though, anything goes. Come on then kid, hit me with your best shot."

My mind was a blur, racing with near endless possibility, what would an eight-year old kid *really* desire?

"I want a puppy," I said, without any thought as to how I'd look after it, or if it would hurt Wheely's feelings.

The genie clapped his hands together, and WHOOSH!, another puff of smoke appeared in front of me. I could hear a slapping sound, similar to the noises that'd come from my mum and dad's room when they were having their wrestling matches. Dad used to wear this really tight spandex suit and a Donald Duck mask, kinda made him look a bit funny. Anyway, I waved the grey smog away, and there was a fish floundering against a sheet of lino. After doing about a squillion press ups its mouth stopped moving and it gave up on its intense exercise routine. Crestfallen, I looked up at the genie, who, I must say, seemed really fucking pleased

402

with himself. "I said I wanted a puppy." I had to fight to hold the tears back.

The genie leant in closer, and cocked his ear towards me. "HUH?"

With my bottom lip wobbling, I burbled back. "I wanted a puppy."

"Oh..."

"Yeah...you know with a little wet nose, and a wagging tail."

"...ah..."

"This isn't a puppy, though, it's a fish."

"...yeah, sorry, I thought you said you wanted a *guppy*."

We both looked at each other for a while before the genie finally piped up. "A guppy is a type of fish." It pointed to the dead water dweller. "Thought it was a bit of an odd request, to be honest, but in all the excitement of being free, I didn't think to ask."

I wiped the tears away. "That's okay, I've got two wishes left, yeah?"

The genie looked puzzled, before clapping his hands together and WHOOSH!, another puff of smoke. I coughed a bit, as the smoke was a bit much and really got down the back of my throat. There was yet more slapping, so I blew the fog away, and found there were two more fish, thrashing around either side of their dead mate. Once again, they went mad, first off, and then did loads of sit ups and press ups, before just stopping, and dying.

"What are they?"

"You said you wanted two new fishes."

"No, I asked if I had *two wishes* left."

"Huh?" The genie was leaning in even more now.

The penny finally dropped. "You're a little deaf, aren't you?"

"Yeah, sorry, it's what you get from a lifetime of people crapping on your home, that stuff gets everywhere." As if to illustrate the point, it wrung its spectral clothing, and nuggets of shit were rinsed out with the liquid.

I jumped backwards, nearly knocking Wheely over. "Steady on! You nearly got that lot on my head!"

"Pot-for-a-head, I hear you loud and clear, buddy."

Clap.

403

WHOOSH!
One pot for a head.

MORE EXPOSITION

Monique dabbed a tissue against the pits of her eyes. "That's *so* sad..."

A bout of slow clapping from the other sofa interrupted the moment. "That is the longest, most convoluted piece of exposition from a bit-part character I have ever had the misfortune to sit through. This dude is in this shindig purely as a vehicle to set up an entire section, and we've had to sit through it for *what* reason?"

"I quite liked the bit about the hedgehog in the melted car," Noah offered.

Pothead Pete stood up. "I'm sorry, Ian, why are you round here, exactly?"

Ian strode over to the window, peeled the net curtains from the glass and pointed to the distance where Qzxprycatj had finally drawn its long-winded diatribe to a conclusion and was now engaged in throwing people into the air and trying to catch them in its maw. "Do you see that? Yeah? It is here to kill every single person on the planet. We were in the pub and had a number of choices. This one person — who is bloody amazing, I would like to add— chose this path. Completely fucking over my dream of becoming a super-hero, by the way. Regretting that much? Anyway, the selection was made on the promise of a motherfucking time machine. Now look, we are on the fourth chapter of this story arc, and we're about as close to getting our hands on the time machine as Noah is to losing his 'psychotic monk' moniker."

"He does make a good point," Noah agreed.

"Well, you could've just said when you came round, you know? I didn't have to pour my heart out to you," Pothead protested.

Monique patted his terracotta bonce. "Well, *I* enjoyed your backstory."

"Pete, me ol' buddy, can we please borrow your time machine so we can rock on down to another little fork on Decision Road and get on with it?"

"Yeah, though there is a slight problem..."

"Of course there fucking is...what is it this time? Wheely the melted porcupine has nicked it, and as we speak, is on a time cruise through the Dark Ages?"

"No, nothing like that, just I let my upstairs neighbours borrow it."

"And?"

"They're probably using it for weird sex stuff."

"Naturally...okay, so, before I go bursting in on them, what exactly does this time machine look like? Guessing loads of flashing lights, twiddly knobs, dials with loads of unintelligible readings on them, that kind of thing?"

"Not exactly, you're looking for a vintage Vaggio digital wristwatch, which is linked to a bottle of bubbles by a length of curly red wire." Pete waved his hands wildly, trying desperately to impart some sense of gigantic scale.

"How are we friends?" Ian asked.

"I didn't think we were that close, aside from that summer we went busking round southern Europe and got ourselves into some crazy escapades..." Frank the Flashback Spider stirred from his fitful sleep, tutted, and began to rappel down his dulled web once more.

"No, no, no, I am not wasting *any* more time watching some crappy moments in history."

"Ohh, please, Ian, I really liked the last one," Monique pleaded, digging out her saddest puppy dog eyes. Which for a vegan, animal rights activist, to carry around orbs plucked from a miserable hound, is quite beyond me to be honest, but hey, I just work here.

"Fine, you lot stay here, least if I go on my own, I know it'll get done properly." He looked across to the group, who were already drooling and cooing at the latest flashback lovingly prepared by Frank.

EVERYBODY NEEDS
GOOD NEIGHBOURS

Standing at the bottom of the stairs, Ian took a deep breath and contemplated everything you've read so far. *Sod the lot of 'em*, he thought; if they were happy to let some giant multi-arse-cheeked monster eat them, so be it. He, on the other hand, had plans. Simple things like wanting to go and see the latest 'Gore Pincher' film, 'Part Eight –The Gore Pinches Back.' Despite his apparent lack of career direction, he wasn't going to work at Margaret Thatcher Burger forever anyway. He figured if he could save up enough cash, he could become one of those entrepreneurs he often read about. All he needed was a lucky break, something which could help change his fortunes.

As a lightbulb came on in his head, he snapped his fingers together.

Of course!

He had hatched upon a plan so cunning that all it needed was a reedy, twirled moustache, a monocle and a trilby, and it would be a right sneaky bastard of a plan. Best thing was, no one would ever know. All he had to do was get his mitts on the time machine, and make a little contingency plan or twelve.

With a new-found lust for life, and the lyrics to said song going 'round his head, Ian bounded up the stairs two at a time, hamstrings be damned!

At the T-junction, there was a door to his immediate left, and a small corridor that led to another door on his right. Figuring the time-traveller's flat was that way, he crept down the corridor. With the light being on a timer, it DINK!ed into blackness, and he was left ruing his decision not to bring some kind of candle or flaming torch. Still, as the door was right in front of him, he raised his hand to knock before another rogue thought crept into his skull like a burglar returning their bounty.

Taking a step back, he kicked the door in and ran into the flat screaming at the top of his lungs. *If they can do it, so can I.*

407

A corridor painted in red ended with a large window and a fire escape. There were two doors on the right-hand wall. The closest one was ajar, and, girding his loins for whatever scenes of depravity lay in wait, Ian leapt into the room.

Within, a cloud of thick smoke hung in the air; seemingly, this place had its own finely balanced ecosystem. "What the fuck, man?" came a voice from within the haze.

Breathing in lungsful of the acrid air, Ian was starting to feel a little lightheaded. Cravings for potato-based snacks and a nice cup of tea was growing like discontent at a rally for the poor, hosted by the Queen, pointing out how everyone could make do and mend by using white vinegar to clean their jewelled goods.

Ian wafted his hands around trying to clear the marijuana mist. All he could discern so far was that the walls were a smashing lime green, and the ceiling was a lurid purple. He took a step forwards and smacked his knee on the edge of a coffee table. "Motherfucker," he screamed.

"Nice one, knobber, you made me spill it," another voice called out.

Amongst the tutting, he could hear rusting springs groaning and squeaking. As their burden was lifted, a man's gaunt little face appeared out of the mist. Although he was a skinhead, his emaciated form presented about as much threat as a fart in an ocean, and it looked like he was surviving purely on narcotics, custard doughnuts and copious amounts of tea. "What are you doing in here, dude? Not really the done thing to kick in someone's front door, lad. We're all set for the apocalypse, and you burst in like you're the filth."

"Sorry..."

"That's cool. I mean...it's not, but at least you apologised."

"It's only popped out of the housing; the hinges are still intact."

"Well, that's something. Look, mate, we're kinda doing our own thing here, what do you want, exactly?"

408

"First off, I'm glad you're not doing weird sex shit with the time machine...which I kinda need to borrow. If that's alright?"

"Time machine? Ohh, right, Pothead Pete from downstairs, yeah? We only use it when we need a top-up, you're after Paul and Sarah on the top floor. They're into the weird shit."

"Ahh, bollocks. Sorry mate, didn't mean to barge in here and ruin your evening."

"That's cool, do you want a quick toke?"

"Best not, I think I'm already pretty fucked just from standing here."

There was a cackling from within the haze. "That's what my brother said, he popped round for a few days. He's been in the toilet for nine hours now, I think we broke him..."

"Shouldn't you go and...I dunno, check on him?" Ian asked.

"Nah, he'll be fine, won't you, Chris?"

The three of them held their breaths and waited for a sign of life.

"Chris?"

The ticking of a clock was the only sound, other than a spliff being drained, and held in.

"Yeah...I'm fine. Be out in a minute."

The skinhead disappeared from view, the springs straining as he sat down. "See, he's fine, but it's gonna feel weird asking him for that ounce of gear back..."

"If *he* ain't gonna use it..." the woman said.

Ian turned around slowly, seeking the solace of the corridor; at least *there*, he didn't feel as though everything was a bit pointless. Back there he had a desire to do something about the impending doom of mankind rather than endlessly debate it over a packet of caramel digestives and the nuances of professional baseball on Channel Five. "Okay, cheers guys, and again, sorry about the door."

As he stepped back into the smoke-free corridor, the woman's voice was borne aloft on an internal eddy. "No worries, just close it the best you can, yeah?"

Teasing the door into a position where it at least looked like it was okay, Ian trudged across to the other door. Part of him wanted to kick it in, too, but decided it would be

409

better to knock. He pulled the knocker out, and in doing so, the door creaked open, invitingly.

Ian tiptoed up the steps, finally arriving at the top. Down a small hallway, he saw that the living room was empty. *That was quicker than I hoped for, saved a few words.* After a quick check in the bathroom, which also ended in zero people with a time-machine-watch being found, he pushed the bedroom door open with his toe and braced himself for untold depravity within.

Nothing.

The curtains were partially closed, and through the chink, he could see that the beast was slamming bodies onto the top of the cathedral spire, forming them into a great big shish kebab.

The room itself was in a right state, bed sheets were pulled back, exposing creases and all manner of stains. Pillows were scattered across the mattress and duvet, like a comfort levy having broken its banks. Sighing, Ian was about to suggest that the gang needed to head back to an earlier decision, when something on the dressing table caught his eye.

Whilst he wasn't a hundred percent sure, it looked like a bubble bottle, like the kind he'd had as a kid. Sensing that his luck had changed, and happy that at least he had been spared some scenes of gratuitous sexual wanton desire which might push the book into the R-rated territory, he shuffled along the floor to it.

It was nestled in between a book about butt plugs and a box of quadruple-ply tissues, handy for industrial spillages. He picked the bottle up and pressed the lid closed, not wanting to spill anything. Attached, a red wire - used solely in the construction of DIY time machines - snaked off under a pair of homemade crotchless boxer shorts and towards the wardrobe.

Ian pulled open the wardrobe doors and recoiled as he saw two corpses hanging from the rail amongst summer dresses and smart un-ironed shirts.

Both bodies were near naked, except for the lipstick scrawled over Paul's chest. Ian tried to read it, and though he could make out a shaky 'HELP,' he assumed it had been made more out of desperation than intent. Each unfortunate had eight-ball eyes, where the blood vessels had burst and filled the normally milky white orbs with blood, now congealed.

Their fat, swollen tongues hung out of their mouths as if they were about to start their shift in the stamp-licking factory. Around their necks were leather belts, securing them to the metal rail. Given their weight and the undoubted thrashing of first: masturbation, then: dread at being asphyxiated for real, and not in a kinky way, Ian deduced that it must've been sturdily built. None of this flat pack malarkey at all, nope, this was proper workmanship. Averting his eyes from Sarah's dead boobies, he pulled on the wire and ended up lifting Paul's wrist, where his watch was attached.

A spit-filled squawk interrupted his train of thought, and he looked down to see a hogtied Dodo, presenting its feathered behind to the groin of Paul. With a roll of his eyes, and keen to avoid touching the deceased, Ian leant into the muggy wardrobe, removed the ball gag from the stricken animal, and set it free. For his troubles, he was given a firm peck from the chubby beak before the animal defied convention and took off. No sooner had it attained flight than it headed for the window.

Unfortunately, though it was a testament to the cleaning prowess of 'Pane and Gain,' window cleaner extraordinaire, it failed to detect that the single pane window was in the default closed position, and went straight through the glass. With thick shards now embedded in its body, it corkscrewed downwards until it landed on the concrete with a solid-sounding SPLAT.

Putting the re-extinct animal out of his mind, Ian stood up and grabbed hold of the Vaggio watch. As he tugged upwards, Paul's hand, stuck fast to his now flaccid knob with crusted-on smegma and shame, pulled on his plonker one last time. Seeing that it was all going a bit weird, Ian yanked it quickly upwards to break the bond, before removing the watch from the greying wrist.

He stepped back and took one last look at the danger wank aftermath before doing the decent thing, closing both doors and locking them shut. It would be a nice little surprise for the next person who rented the flat. Assuming,

411

of course, that they lived through all of this troublesome apocalypse business.

Going through to the living room after a quick pit stop in the bathroom to rinse the watch clean, Ian moved the sofa out of the way and looked at the time machine. The watch display, though blinking in acknowledgement that it was working, didn't change time at all.

After fumbling with the buttons, he set it for 1 August 2015. A solid-sounding *beep* beeped, going some way to assuring him that this preposterous thing might actually work. Ian took the stick out of the bubble bottle, which had a disturbing vulvic ending to it, and, in the closest act to sex he had experienced in some time, he blew on the end.

A rainbow-sheened bubble no bigger than a satsuma grew into life and floated listlessly around the living room. He looked at the bottle, hoping for some semblance of instruction, only to find a picture of a rather sinister Punch and Judy man on the front, with the headline, 'PUNCH.'

Then, another idea hit him. This was freaky, it was like the third in a few pages, he was definitely on to something; perhaps he was the true protagonist in this shitty story, after all. Ian picked up a balled tissue, not wanting to know what it had been used for, and threw it into the bubble.

As soon as it made contact with the undulating orb, it expanded to take in the extra girth before popping, and disappearing.

In for a penny.

He blew another bubble, which again, hovered about the place, as these things are wont to do. Unless little kids are around of course; those little tinkers should be put in front of a special commission at The Hague for crimes against bubbles. Murderous little bastards.

Ian pressed his finger against the wobbly ball. As it made contact with the oily surface, the bubble ballooned and encompassed him whole. With a loud POP!, it burst, and he disappeared along with it.

BACK FROM THE PRESENT

"...and that's how we escaped the clutches of the evil Baron von Schnitzelwürfer and his pet," Pothead Pete said, a tear blooming in the corner of this eye.

Monique was beside herself. "That's probably the best story I've ever heard in my entire life, so many twists and turns...so much emotion, and the *tentacles*!"

"Cor, yeah, the tentacles, they came out of nowhere," Noah agreed.

Frank the Flashback spider panted in his web. Using his last ounce of strength, he crawled up the silky rope to his main ceiling web to feast on the remnants of ill-gotten curses. His bum was hurting by now, he shouldn't have to spin so many flashbacks at this point in his life. It was about time his daughter, Felicity, pulled her eight legs out and stepped up to the plate. If only he knew where she was...

As the trio came out of their trance, the flat reappeared in all its drab glory. The first thing Monique saw was Ian waving at her. "Wow, you two sure had some adventures, huh? The time you were both forced into a round of deadly Russian Wrestling Roulette in that casino in Monaco...I've seen a completely different side to you now."

Ian went a bright red, pulling his collar out in a cartoon attempt to cool himself down. Monique stood up and sidled across to him, barely-contained lust in her eyes. Grabbing hold of his arse, she pulled him in close, her fingers slipping into his back pocket and her lips locking onto his. Their tongues slapped around like a pair of fearless kendo warriors. They separated, and Monique pulled a strip of paper from the arse of his jeans. "What's this?"

Lost in a world free of apocalyptic monsters summoned from board games and dead bodies swinging from the insides of wardrobes, Ian mumbled a "Huh?"

Opening the paper up, she looked at it for a few moments before kicking Ian square in the happy sack. He collapsed to the floor like a sack of skin and bone, managing only a mewling sound, like a puzzled kitten. Noah got up and walked across to the fallen man. "Hey, now, you can't go around kicking men in the squidgy lumps without any form of provocation, that's not on."

Monique held up the paper. "*Someone* has been to the bookies and placed a number of bets on a plethora of sporting outcomes with ridiculous odds, and an eight-fold accumulator on the rash of celebrity deaths we've had recently."

Noah snatched the betting slip from Monique's fingers and read through the list, "You little bastard," he growled, before kicking Ian in the love spuds himself.

"I was going to share," Ian whimpered.

Scrunching up the paper, Monique threw it at Ian, who was in the foetal position of pain. "And to think I was going to stick my finger up your bum."

"It doesn't matter," Ian said, in an octave that was not his own. He grabbed hold of the sheet of paper, and shoved it whence it came. Fiddling around with the watch display, he pulled the bottle of bubbles out of his pocket.

"What do you think you're doing?" Monique asked.

"I'm gonna just nip back a little further than when I came back before, and this time, make sure I stash the betting slip somewhere safe. I'll cash it in later on, and shower you with gifts. Like buying a star named after you." With that, he blew a bubble in front of him, and just before Monique could squash his spunk marshmallows again, he crawled into it, and *POPPED!* out of the time stream once more.

PARALLEL UNIVERSE:
GAMMA DELTA ZELPHON 12

"...tugging firmly, yet fairly, at the tufts which sprouted from the head of Diablo del Snuffles, fierce monster of Catalonia, I managed to tuck Ian into a soft basket formed from the downy hair. He was flitting in and out of consciousness. Not surprising, really, considering the incredible series of trials the beast had set him. With the creature distracted by the poodle balloon animal, I sprung from the cover of its furry hide and plunged the dagger deep into its blackened heart. It staggered theatrically back and forth before collapsing, and that's how we escaped the clutches of the evil Baron von Schnitzelwürfer and his pet," Pothead Pete said, a tear blooming in the corner of this eye.

Monique was beside herself. "That's probably the best story I've ever heard in my entire life, so many twists and turns...so much emotion, and the tentacles!"

"Cor, yeah, the tentacles, they came out of nowhere," Noah agreed.

Frank the Flashback spider panted in his web. Using his last ounce of strength, he crawled up his silky rope to his main ceiling web, to feast on the remnants of ill-gotten curses. His bum was hurting by now, he shouldn't have to spin so many flashbacks at this point in his life. It was about time his daughter, Felicity, pulled her eight legs out and stepped up to the plate. If only Frank knew where she was...

As the trio came out of their trance, the flat reappeared in all its drab glory. The first thing Monique saw was Ian looming over her. "Wow, you two sure had some adventures, huh? The time you were both-"

"Yep, yep, rare ol' times indeed, now we need to get a wriggle on," Ian interrupted.

"Oh..." Monique sighed, "... I was hoping me and you could get a little better-acquainted."

Ian strutted over to the window, ripped the net curtain from its feeble rail, and pointed to the giant monster who was ripping people open as if they were mini Christmas crackers. "I'm all for it, I just think we need to focus on one ickle problem first."

"Did you get it?" Pothead Pete asked.

Carefully, Ian took the bubble bottle out of his pocket, and waved it. "Da-dah! You were right, they *were* doing weird sex stuff."

"I knew it! Gonna have to go and have a word later on, they were banging against the floor earlier on, sounded like they were auditioning for Riverdance."

"You might want to leave it...they're tired...dead tired..." Ian said, in his best Arnie accent.

Monique coughed. "Excellent, we can do as I suggested now, can't we? If we stop the Scrabble tiles being put down, or get rid of the Q's, then the ol' monster of doom won't be summoned in the first place."

Ian sunk to the floor and began to sob; Monique walked across to him and ran her fingers through her hair. "Aww, what's the matter? You worried that if we do that, we won't have a chance to...you know?"

Bursting a snot bubble and wiping the gunk on his sleeve, Ian shook his head. "It's not that..."

"What is it then, silly? You can tell me."

Ian looked up into her eyes, his own red and puffy. "... I want dinosaurs!"

Noah chopped a coffee table in half with his staff. "Or robots."

"Dinosaurs."

"Robots."

"Play it safe and just change a little bit of time," Monique added.

Ian sighed. "You two just don't get it, huh? Fine...I personally think dinosaurs would be the best bet, but I'm not going to decide what we should do."

It's time to...
DICTATE YOUR FATE

If you reckon the only thing that can save humanity (and Ian's sleeve from being drenched in snot) are kickass dinosaurs, you'd better head on over to **Page 300.**

However, if you think that you should embrace technology and deadly killer robots from the future are the way forward - hopefully with spindly blade things on their arms that come out and go thwip thwip thwip thwip thwip and cut people's heads off - you should hover on over to **Page 164.**

Steady on, there! The simplest route between two points is a straight frickin' line! Just go back in time a little bit before the game of Scrabble and stop it before it ever happens in the first place. Simples. Go to **Page 12** and do it.

What the bloody hell? You're going to let fictional characters suggest what YOU should do? Bollocks to that, how about we take a little detour and follow the true star of this little section? Go to **Page 262** and let's see what this book really can be. EPIC. That's what.

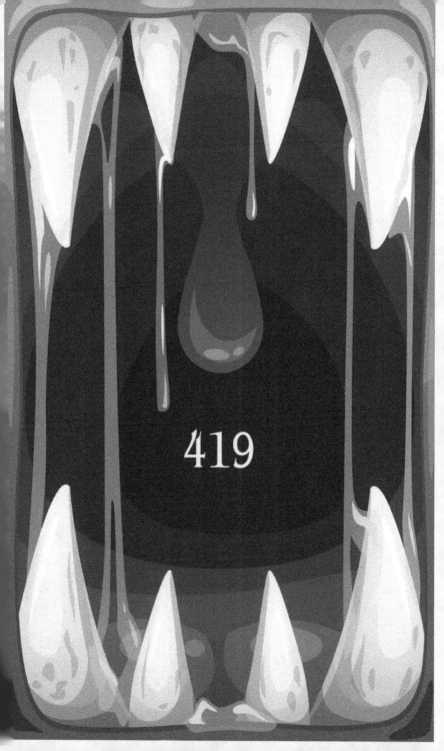

419

CONGRATULATIONS!
THIS IS ENDING
#10

'IF THIS WAS A RESIDENT EVIL GAME, YOU'D GET AN 'S+' RANK.'

I'm not allowed to have children, an agreement made with the human race on account of my...specialness. But...for you to get here, and not cheat (I hope), then I am filled with a weird paternal pride.

I've been considering putting a short story collection together for a while, but wanted a different way of getting it out there. What better way then, than to weave it through a book with so many weird and wonderful stories already?

For those super fans of mine out there, and I'm hoping I have at least one, you'd have noticed that one of the stories you've just read was a previously unreleased one. A little thank you from me, to you.

Now, bask in this magnificent glow you've created, and if you want to see the other stories in the book, then continue your victory parade over to where you decoded my fiendish puzzle on **Page 144**. You can then get stuck into the normal stories (that people who aren't as awesome as you got to read).

Good work!

ENDING CHECKLIST

To help those of you who simply HAVE to find every single one of the different endings, I've listed them all below. Can you read them all?

1. Jurassic knights in a BIFF POW fight.

2. Do androids dream of Megalomania?

3. Historical monument vandalism, and the National Trust. Discuss.

4. A paradoxical way of doing things.

5. A genuine first in literature, and no-one can take that from me. Not even you, Rusty Beauchamp!

6. No plan? No hope for you then, El Stinky.

7. Be a good egg, and pick up the soap would you?

8. Look up super in a dictionary, and you'll see your picture.

9. Confetti and a wee drop of pixelated man milk for supper.

10. If this was a Resident Evil game, you'd get an 'S+' rank.

Hello!

How was that for you? I hope you enjoyed it, this book took nearly four years to finish up (for a variety of reasons), and it spans both my old and new styles of writing.

If this is the first taste of my brain and you want to pick up any of my other books, then here is the definitive list of them, along with a few words as to what you can expect:

CLASS THREE – Zom-com novel about two brothers trying to get to safety on day one of the zombie apocalypse.

CLASS FOUR: THOSE WHO SURVIVE – Follow-up to CLASS THREE, as people now struggle to survive in the new world.

CELEBRITY CULTURE – Bizarro novella about celebrity virologists, awards ceremonies and assorted weirdness.

PRIME DIRECTIVE – Sci-fi/horror novella which follows the first crewed mission to Mars. What secrets will they uncover?

HEXAGRAM – Six stories set across five hundred years, charting how knowledge can be twisted and changed to different ends.

CHUMP – Collection of zombie stories, everything from the wild-west to undead fish, clean-up crews to the truth around why the Eastern-Bloc boycotted the 1984 Olympics.

MR SUCKY – My homage to slasher films, when a serial-killer is killed by his intended victim, his spirit is interred inside of a vacuum cleaner. Hellbent on revenge, his biggest fight might be the one in his own head.

CANNIBAL NUNS FROM OUTER SPACE! – The titular aliens land for their annual feast on another idyllic British village, who can stop them?

DON'T SMELL THE FLOWERS! THEY WANT TO STEAL YOUR BONES! – I do my best to warn humanity about the floral menace, and am bloody silly and ridiculous in the process.

Thanks for taking the time to read **CONGRATULATIONS! YOU'VE ACCIDENTALLY SUMMONED A WORLD-ENDING MONSTER. WHAT NOW?** I hope you managed to find most, if not all of the endings, including the super-secret section that weaved its way through the entire book. If you missed it and want a hint on how to find it, give me a shout! You can hit me up any of the below and I'll get back to you as quickly as I can:

Website: http://duncanpbradshaw.co.uk/
Facebook: https://www.facebook.com/duncanpbradshaw/
Twitter: https://twitter.com/DuncanPBradshaw

Unless I'm dead of course, in which case, I take the secret with me to the grave! Toodle-pip.

Duncan P(uzzle). Bradshaw

The Sinister Horror Company is an independent UK publisher of genre fiction. Their mission a simple one – to write, publish and launch innovative and exciting genre fiction.

For further information on the Sinister Horror Company visit:

SinisterHorrorCompany.com

Facebook.com/sinisterhorrorcompany

Twitter @SinisterHC

SINISTERHORRORCOMPANY.COM

CPSIA information can be obtained
at www.ICGtesting.com
Printed in the USA
LVHW091758030921
696898LV00002B/104

9 781999 751258